Bonelines

Bonelines

Tony Whitehead & Phil Smith

tp

Published in this first edition in 2020 by:

Triarchy Press
Axminster, UK

www.triarchypress.net

A catalogue record for this book is available from the British Library.

ISBNs:
Print: 978-1-913743-06-2
ePub: 978-1-913743-07-9
pdf: 978-1-913743-08-6

Printed and bound by TJ International Ltd

tp

Preface

In *Bonelines* we wrote and we were written.

The angels and monsters of the novel were not our inventions. They stepped forward to us from places that then reappeared, anonymously, in the writing; from the rood screen in the church at Torbryan, the nearby medieval ruins of a cave-chapel, and the haunts of the ancient Dumnonii people up on Denbury Hill. We had set out with no particular outcome in mind; our starting point was to see if we could find any resonance of the works of US author of weird fiction H. P. Lovecraft in the villages of his ancestors in south Devon (UK). We began by walking a 'Lovecraft Triangle' as if his stories were maps of these places. Very soon we felt a prefiguration of the fictions there.

Our project quickly changed, however. We had found physical evidence of the Lovecrafts, for sure; from an ancestor's oddly geometrical grave to a church where a great uncle had been choirmaster (before some now obscure controversy saw his removal) and an inn where another great uncle was publican. Far more powerful, though, was the way our quest triggered a more ambiguous and less literary mythos. Unplanned, we found ourselves conducting some kind of ambulant conjuring of story, ecology and ambience that entwined local technologists with lay archaeologists and their folkloric theories with the culture of the local iron age Dumnonii people and the qualities of the local geology. What we found was partly there and partly our imagining. We shored up our intuitions with desk-based research and we consulted local historians, archaeologists and museum keepers, but the myths came firstly from their places; for a few months it was as if we could walk the stories out of the lanes and hills as a stylus plays the music in the grooves of a record.

Dialogue was another of our ways in; unfolding themes together as we walked. Of course, some of what emerged we brought with us, or borrowed as we went along, and certainly the shape of the land and the activity of flora and fauna responding to the changes of the season finessed our ideas, but mostly it was the places that spoke up above the low rumble of the Lovecraft fictions. Cthulhu and the Shoggoths were minor and indistinct agents in the 'Triangle'; the patterns that uncovered themselves were more local, unpredictable and less consistent than a literary 'world'; the stinging, brushing, blowing, seething and tripping terrain directed us to what it desired.

There is space here for one example: West Ogwell.

We approached this scattered community through green fields and herds of Devon reds, the yellowish tower of its deconsecrated church appearing between canopies of giant oaks. It all felt just a little too aesthetically bucolic, and later we discovered that these were the repurposed landscaped grounds of a former manor house, now 'Gaia House' (a meditational retreat) with a 'Hermit's Tower' and a 'Walking Room' presided over by a cross-legged skeleton.

The scatter of dwellings and church, with neither village green nor cross-shaped Fore Street, was indicative of its pre-Saxon iron age origins. The church was sat on top of a knob of metamorphic rock. On our first visit, we found behind the altar a fetish of feather, rag, flowers, twine and stick; on our second a large hornbeam bough covered in green lichen placed before the altar where it caught the sunlight falling through the windows. Outside in the churchyard we were regaled with tales of apparitions by 'The Whistler', the self-appointed guardian of the graves.

It turned out that a rather good found-footage horror movie ('The Borderlands', 2014), which we had each both seen and enjoyed, had been shot in the church and in the nearby lanes; its climax is the awakening of a Lovecraftian serpent sleeping curled up inside the hill beneath the church.

Everywhere we went there were similar out of kilter tales, hidden layers and quirky details or perverse artefacts; yet none of this ever felt alien, arbitrary or disconnected. Instead, these oddities joined with us in dialogue, they reappeared and then reappeared again, weaving in and out of an ever-thickening spread of quilted narratives we were accruing.

We had walked troubled. Our walking and writing together coincided with personal upheavals for both of us, and this almost certainly played some part in opening us quite so intensely to what came through in the lanes. At the same time – and these processes were never wholly discrete – we were self-consciously formulating, through walking and talking, responses to wider upsets than our own; climate catastrophe, political malaise, and a crisis within discourses with which we had some sympathy: left politics, green activism, wyrd practices and thinking.

We were frustrated with the dullness of green politics and their fixation on threat, apocalypse and moralistic reparations; with the trajectory of much esoteric practice towards respectability and a place on a continuum with Christianity or into questionable systems that leant themselves to control and submission. We were unnerved by a moulding of public discourse that included a shift within accelerationism to 'dark enlightenment' and the dalliance of some deep ecologists with nationalism, coincident with a new waywardness in neo-liberal opinion that was being manipulated across digital and conventional media to ingest eugenicist, transhumanist and hypermodern ideas.

We never had any planned intention, nor the means to do anything about any of our speculative rambling, but over the months that we walked and talked what seemed to us to be obscure obsessions began to appear high up the news agenda on social media and on news websites: extreme weather, Cambridge Analytica, Elon Musk, far right infiltration of ecological activism, Extinction Rebellion...

When the novel *Bonelines* was written, it was more of a spillage into fiction of what seemed impossible to contemplate (let alone implement) in reality, written in strokes of frustration. In opposition to the takeover of both establishment and its oppositions by malign 'alternatives' that hid opportunism within authoritarianism and authoritarianism within libertarianism and anti-flesh digitised transhumanism deep within the sleeves of the moment's Matryoshka doll. In fiction we were able to imagine an alternative to all of this that was self-organising, DIY, multiplicitous and non-functionalist, a way to realigning conviviality with amoral forces in the ground. The writing of *Bonelines* performed a reverse version of our playing the stories from the ground with our walking bodies; this time we dragged the discourse of the terrain across the grooves of computer keyboards to engrave it in the writing.

The 'ground' from which *Bonelines* rose lies mostly between Newton Abbot, Totnes and Ashburton in the southern part of the county of Devon (UK). There is an anonymity there, the area has no encompassing name; it consists of gently rolling hills, scattered communities punctuated by an occasional Saxon cruciform village, and a complex of often deserted Devon lanes, footpaths and pedestrian hollow ways. The density of habitation is low and there are few local jobs to be had these days. Unlike neighbouring Dartmoor and the South Hams, it is not a destination for tourists, and visitors are rare even from neighbouring towns; if we met anyone on the lanes they were almost always locals. There are some very remarkable places in the 'Lovecraft Triangle', but they are generally hidden from sight, on private land, or outwardly unappealing.

As stories emerged from this landscape, and as in our long pedestrian conversations we began to flesh out the skeleton of an exemplary fable with elements of a roman à clef, we widened our geographical scope and walked the land between Dawlish and Exminster, around Bovey Tracey and the lower Teign Valley, and the backstreets of Torquay; guided by the unfolding narrative demands of the novel. At the same time we were subjected to an intensity of coincidence and connection that would have been frightening if it had not been quite so exciting.

On one occasion we stood on the footpath of the coastal road between Torquay and Paignton with the poet Sam Kemp, discussing the fantasy of subterranean aliens conjured in the novel 'Vril: The Power of the Coming Race' by Torquay novelist and imperialist politician Edward Bulwer-Lytton; a few days later the pavement at this spot collapsed into a huge sink hole.

In our earliest drafts of the novel, we fictionalised a particular local country house and its Italian gardens (remerging from decades of vegetation growth) as the location for a modern sex cult with a leader loosely modelled on the ceremonial magician Kenneth Grant (who we unimaginatively named Grant Kentish). On obtaining an invitation to visit the property, we discovered that it had been a publishing house, its co-owner an author of dream dictionaries and tantric sex manuals.

In a graveyard we found a tomb decorated with three striking sculptures of female angels; a little research turned up a remarkable story – the drowning of three sisters in the Nile – which became more remarkable as bit by bit we turned up the details of a conspiracy organised from beyond the grave by the dead sisters' brother to father a messiah with the physical aid of a female medium and the brother of the prime minister. The resulting child was not informed of his vocation until already a member of the British secret service...

This oddness and super-connectivity happened ALL the time; the more we walked and looked and touched the more the veils wore thin. The density of the myth-like stories we found woven into the terrain chimes with the later findings that Phil has made with Helen Billinghurst in their book 'The Pattern'' (Triarchy Press, 2020) of a similarly intense physical marking in the landscape. Hypersensitized walking opens up such marks and stories at every turn. The German poet and thinker Johann Wolfgang von Goethe talks of observation not only as an attending to minute details, but also as an active deployment of imagination that allows 'the other' agency in the affect upon the observer. Most of such affect may be a result of our own internal dialogue replayed or looped, reaching down to our unconscious. But some of the remaining cause is external; it comes from elsewhere, outside. When the synchronicities build upon one another and the inhibitions fall away, then that balance changes and the little zones of anomaly grow within those who are receptive. That is the visionary part of all this.

In the old legends – 'The Matter of Britain', 'The Mabinogion' or the early medieval Irish myths – there is always an otherworld, sitting everywhere just below the surface of the everyday. This is the land of the Fae and at various times it has been an unquestioned given for those who lived, worked and wandered in the zone we were treading. In nineteenth century reflections that we found during our researches, this otherworld was described in detail by locals; indeed, even now, there are signs that such a sensibility has survived and we may at times have touched its edge in our ambulant conjuring. Certainly, one of the skills we had honed on our walks was that of discernment; differentiating between the 'to and fro' of an active mind and the voice of this other that comes in the form of chance happenings, in repose, or in a hypnogogic state when falling asleep or just before rising before a day of walking. Sometimes it comes simply by being present and paying attention; cultivating a 360-degree vision that rejects nothing, allows everything in and allows things freedom to make their own discernments and connections.

All of this we deployed to differing degrees in making *Bonelines*. But the text could not have been written without the direct force of the land. While the temptation was there to try to work out a frame in advance, we always had to wait, and our waiting was walking; being 'out there' was our method and our very ordinary and de-functionalised 'magical practice'. Part of that practice was allowing ourselves to say "this is OK"; dropping a discretion borne of excess scepticism. For sure, discernment requires scepticism – or we are quickly lost down the rabbit hole – but in the current cultural climate we needed to take a risk and not allow cynicism to kill the mythical beasts that had begun to lay golden eggs for us.

Once completed, our fictional text took us in a quite different direction to the one we had expected. In response to the novel, our publisher at Triarchy invited us to write a second book; a guide to the areas we had walked. This became the *Guidebook for an Armchair Pilgrimage*, richly illustrated with US photographer John Schott's images and published in 2019. 'Bonelines' the novel then became a hidden guiding text for us, a resource for other works and thoughts, but not something to be revealed in itself.

Then in 2020, the Covid pandemic swept across the world and a lockdown in the UK and elsewhere changed things. We decided, with the support of Triarchy Press, to publish *Bonelines* in a serialised form, making it available and without charge on the Triarchy website. Partly, and in common with other authors and artists, we wanted to make material available to people who otherwise might find their options limited. Partly, however, we were responding to what felt like an alignment between elements in the novel and what was happening in the streets and fields; the cars disappeared, the skies were blue and contrails entirely absent, in the quiet the sounds of the birds were louder and the air smelt different. Another world rose as the human one shrank back.

Now, as we write this, the world-with-virus has reached a different stage; a far more ambiguous one. There are multiple attempts to 'return to normal', but the virus is not so sure about that; infections fall in one place and rise in another, what briefly unified now shines a light on division. A surge to return to a normality that was already making us ill and vulnerable is just the kind of horror that *Bonelines* invokes and challenges.

This book is neither a literary masterpiece nor a genre classic; neither of us have the ability to write either. *Bonelines* is – like *Vril: The Power of the Coming Race*, though with a very different politics and philosophy – an attempt to use fiction to propose ideas and praxis; actions informed by ideas, ideas becoming actions. Much to our delight, you now hold this hard copy of *Bonelines* in your hands. This we doubt is any kind of end. For you, there is the challenge of disentangling the praxis from the fiction and determining what you want to do with it. For us, there is much new research still to do, and, once Tony's recently broken leg is mended, many miles still to walk. May it forever be.

Chagford & Plymouth, Devon
July 2020

Chapter 1

The heat stank of panic. The Everglades spoke no longer of England; they had flipped. The bony bodies of summer kids, wracked with an energy they had no use for, pumped sheens of perspiration down their bare chests. Young enough to get up to stuff and not worry their patriarchs, they had assembled; siblings had been sharply brushed off, mothers told they did not want the beach today, uncles and aunties promised long games of dominoes and re-viewings of tapes of 'Only Fools and Horses' stewing in their creaky VHS boxes. The whole resort reeked of overheating motherboards.

In tins marked KESTREL, sat upon antique formica tables that were cracked like the floors of empty lakes, lager was warming and flattening. In the Everglades, however, there was a painful kind of cool. Whatever it was it had settled its clammy hand on the unreal paleness of the children's torsos, patted their feverish brows, and kept the salted sweat from out their eyes. The seven kids were unworldly calm, pin-prick aware, self-possessed, and attentive to the words and actions they had been rehearsing on and off over three summers now. Every year, sneaking away and gathering for stolen time in the Everglades; a strip of surplus land on the edge of the camp, bordered by the industrial estate, separated from the sun-cream and dodgems world by a dank grey stream; linked by a greasy overflow pipe which only the initiated knew how to try. Here they could talk up a place of their own.

Under a relentless sun that day, adults got lazy, more lax than usual, let things go that at other times they forbade. The stale beer befuddled their afternoons. Minds were winding down from their industrial routines, further than usual, never looking forward. They had no idea what was coming, no idea what it might be, no idea how to respond, no idea at all. Never would.

The boy had been the first to arrive. He carried more flesh than the others; he had a kind of fixedness to him, even then. He collected things, amassed himself; dutifully he prepared the space, clearing some crisps packets that had blown across from the caravans, pocketing a crumpled Top Trump and sweeping a few dried leaves aside. His father would have been amazed to see him take charge of a space like this; he would never understand or value this son who thought so hard and sounded so dumb. When the boy looked over at what he had done, he did not breathe for a while. He knew he was no spark, yet he assiduously cultivated a dim and unquenchable slow glow of thought and care that recently had become a fire under the hot sun. He could perpetrate a humour that others rarely caught before it was too late; leaving them guessing. Everyone had assumed the worst about him, but he was coming through; more sophisticated than either they or he yet knew. Though he had found no ways to protect, nurture or sell himself. People laughed at his accent; even those who had the same one. He was the flesh he stood in and the things he felt. No one had ever given him the means to express any of that; but now he was making a means of his own. Ever since he started following the owners' girl.

She was strung like an electric fence; she didn't look that much but she could sting you, sheep or stallion. Her long black hair rocked about her face, and when she spoke it was in little bursts of smoke and chunks of glowing ember. She scared the adults. Not just because her Mum and Dad owned the camp, but there was something unnatural about her sureness of foot and mind. She thought like a mountain goat, springing from speculation to speculation.

He had spied her making furtive little dashes between the trailers. He knew she had the run of the place, yet she moved like someone who was prohibited. The boy had no way to express that, to himself or anyone else, but he felt it generously; that sense of being at odds with the things you should have been in harmony with. In music class he opened and shut his mouth; he dare not sing. But when the impulse came to follow the girl with the black hair, he had no way of denying it. Something drew him; and when it came to singing the refrains he could not help himself. Or curses, or spells, or whatever it was people said they were.

She was lither than him, of course, and for a while he did not know where her runs ended. Something told him he should wander forever aimlessly and somehow find her that way; but after a few days 'goin' round the Wrekin' he was rewarded with a glimpse of her, the owners' girl, skittering over the overflow bridge. He knew he would fall in, so he waded. He had expected her to laugh at him, or run from him, tell on him to his parents or hers. Instead, she indicated a lump of wood for him to sit on, threw him a blanket to dry himself on, and then she had started straight in on him, as if she had known all along that he was coming to the Everglades. She taught him three of her songs and one of the most important 'stories' before she told him her name.

They were not the usual stories.

And now they were coming true.

On the particular day in question, the day when the shadows broke loose from the things, the gang numbered seven; old hands by now, they knew by heart the stories and the rhymes. Some had been coming for three years, others for two. The Sett was well known for being a holiday resort to which families returned year after year. Something had been established here, between the place and the English Midlands, by the railway company; that was long ago, maybe a century and a half, but not long enough for it to run its course. Though it was unlikely that what those engineers and whiskery shareholders had in mind was a weird feathery thing with soft tendril-like nether regions.

The girl, the boy and the five pals barely and yet deeply knew what they were invoking; yelling and gesticulating to it to break the surface from a sclerotic past that had rarely given up anything. They didn't seem to mind either way; just to speak the words was bostin'.

"Muddy Mary!"

And they began to dance on the spongy undergrowth. Even on a day when white flesh was seared pink around the edges of bra straps and shoulders scraped raw by a raking sun, there was a looseness in the Everglades. There was a space for things to get in, there were pores opening in the tree trunks and moss carpets loose enough for an oily moisture to squeeze through.

"Muddy Mary!"

And the trees began to dance with them. Not that familiar dancing in soft winds, not the gentle swaying from side to side, but this was the jerky dance when the whole Everglades would all shift a caravan's length one way and then, bending, the other. It pulled a brain out of shape.

"Muddy Mary, mother of God,

Killed the Old Boy in his bath,

God went to Hell

And started to smell,

And now all the bad things are back!"

The girl bade them with open arms, her thin forearms cutting upwards like a flash of blades, her big hands paddling the air, and they scrambled to their feet and threw themselves as high as they could. Pogoing on the mush and bouncing their heads at the patchy canopy of summer leaves. They chorused silent gulps as they tried to catch their breaths between leaps. Somewhere over the railway tracks a ride was creaking; music no one had paid royalties for was blaring, mixing with the throb of a generator and the swish of a sprinkler. Someone cursed at a football commentary. Sausages and burgers sizzled flatly, cobs were sliced. So much filled the air around their grove, acrid blueness was crowding it in.

It was the tiny boy who first registered that something else had entered their magic circle. He had not felt this thing before, and at first he was unsure that he felt anything at all. Indeed, he was at that age when he was feeling so many things for the first time that he tended to treat novelty as part of the routine. It was only when the softness beneath his feet became an ultra-violent seething and shaking, when the gentlest of breezes ripped the green canopy wide apart and brought it careening down towards him, and, finally, when the ooze at the bottom of the stream rose in squirming intestines of mud, that he felt the familiar cold tingle of stinky fear.

The large boy caught the young one out of the corner of his eye; unsure if the snaking chords of grey shitty matter were rising out of the stream and into his throat, or vice versa. The leader swung her diamond-blue eyes from one boy to the other; what she saw was a sheet of light, tight and bloodless fingers shaking it for all it was worth. Glistening sprays of energy floated from the smeared sheet and revolved around the heads of the other six junior disciples. They all began to jerk violently in time with the thicker trees. One of the other girls bent over and the green-brown ground came up to meet her in curdling cord-like forms; strings of mud and moss rose up only to be battered down by the sudden expulsion of brown vomit from her nose. Beside her the fourth boy was rigid, his mouth drawn back in a terrified smirk. A tiny worm of blood was crawling down his leg and into a flip flop.

Space folded like a screwed up ball of bad drawing. The rest of the camp that had seemed so far away now concertinaed in on the Everglades. A red top newspaper was lowered, a can laid carefully on a concrete slab, a piece of kebab spat on a plate. One by one, men began to howl and bark. Practical mothers wiped their hands and set their legs in motion; a bottle of pop was upended and it sputtered across a porch. Inside the swampy corridor of the Everglades the discipleship of the fleshy boy grew thicker and more earnest; his eyes darted about his sockets looking for meaning, his frantic mind stitched together all the fragments and then cut them apart: the gushes of fluid, the swaying of the ground, the feathery chaos of a darting wren and an escaping egret flashing its orangey-yellow warning-signal feet as it scampered out of the water and over the path. And in their places, deep things made themselves plain; hidden things came out of their dens and showed themselves.

He didn't know if he spoke to invoke, or whether he was simply describing and worshipping, whatever that was:

"Muddy Mary, mother of God,
Killed the Old Boy in his bath,
God went to Hell
And started to smell,
And now all the bad things are back!"

"Jesus Christ, did you hear that!"

There was something strange coming across the Everglades. The owners' girl raised an arm against the approaching smear. Billows of barbecue smoke rose behind the rushing colours.

"Muddy Mary!" she cried out.

In answer a great tide of dark light, as if from inside a cave, swept into the trees, and then rushed out again; the way that waves would come in and out on the beach. This tide did not come in again; it had fled the stumbling, sprinting, gibbering and hairy-toed mob-thing that was crossing the fringes of the holiday camp, shedding pool sliders and baseball caps, stubbing toes and pressing dead skin on pebbles and twigs.

"She's raising the devil!"

It was confusing. The voices of the jumbling thing were adult. They never came here, and yet now they did. Just at the moment the deep seemed to be rising up, just as the deep seemed to be possessing them from down in their stomachs and up to the top of their faces, only now – when they were frothing at the mouth – were their mums and dads interested.

One of the younger girls went down in a heap. The little boy tried to cry for help, but his words were drowned by a snake of yellow and brown strings. It was the strangest magic. They were part of the tale; stranger than anything they had told each other. True oddness, it seemed, had to come from somewhere else, from afar, from beyond the gates of Lost Horizon, from some other thing and some other place.

"Get an ambulance, someone. Get the owner!"

She felt her insides melting. She felt the ground flooding up towards her. She felt the running together of their minds. She felt the fear of the young ones and the faith and angry fortitude of the big sweaty boy. She felt exhilarated; she was taking them all on a journey, in her mind she was leading them into a dark cave, dragging them through layers of the wet universe, and they were following. They were like a shoal of grey-brown stingy things, spewing themselves into the earth, striking out for the approaching darkness... all of them saw the same thing, and knew they did. And just before the last of them lost consciousness, there they were, all seven of them, swimming in the warm Devonian sea, while around them alien cephalopods and odd indescribable marine insects, gods in sea hare form and angel creatures that spasmed elegantly through the minty blue, floated in perfect harmony; each stroke in time with the others. The seven swam toward a ledge, then stood fluidly on the horizon of fruitcake rock, below which lay the deeply dark. To which, with a shared look, they took their first step.

Rough arms reached for them, muscled fingers grabbed at their ankles holding them back. Scooping embraces lifted them high and into towels in football colours, ufo and unicorn designs, engulfing them and they were swept away. They flew across the stream and path and, in formation, they zoomed and swerved through the camp; they saw all this, if they saw anything at all, through emptying eyelids. They, maybe, felt themselves laid on the ground; while all around them in barking and chanting choruses, frantic priests and priestesses were exorcising and cursing.

"That little Jezebel has been trained!"

"Groomed!"

"They've all been groomed! It's satanic abuse, I thought so! Satanic abuse!"

"Where the fuck are those owners? They are going to do time, somewhere where they know how to deal with nonces!"

"Calm down... look at my poor bab! Her donnies are all covered in shit..."

"The ambulances are going to be here in ten to fifteen minutes..."

"Jesus!"

"Can you all shut the fuck up, and quietly.... these children are seriously sick..."

"Seriously sick? Seriously sick? There's one little witch here's seriously sick! Sick in the head! Where are the frigging owners? Someone hold me back before I..."

"I heard what they were saying, it was... what do you call it.... heresy..."

"What?"

"No, blasphemy!"

"I heard that too."

"Against the Blessed Virgin, I heard her, she said Our Lady was mucky!"

"Mucky the little tart!"

"They're Satanists, they as good as admitted it to me the other day... New Age..."

"Whatever the difference, they're going down!"

"Call the police. This is a fucking crime scene."

"Can you gawbies cool down, our babs are poorly here..."

"This is some weird thing she's called down... it's some sick magic..."

"O shuttup, Frank, you don't believe that..."

Even those who were wiping sweat from the feverish brows on the limp bodies, and wiping drool from the edges of lips, held their breaths. The 'witch' opened her eyes, but they did not focus.

"What did she see in there?"

He coughed; it was Frank. The stage was his.

"There was a black thing around that little witch, I saw a black thing like a... like a parachute billowing but black, and the strings were moving ... like... like they knew..."

"What do mean, 'billowing'?"

"Can we stop listening to this yampy.... our babs are properly ill here..."

Though the eyes did not focus, still they took in the panorama, the whole wide dome of the camp, the giant heads and jowly necks bent, drawn faces, sunken eyes, giant-bellied men on their knees bending over the gang, tall piles of soiled wipes, and in the corner the flames that were beginning lick around her home...

"Those half-soaked..."

"No, let them. No one believes in the Devil."

"Not their house..."

"Couldn't care less if they're jedded..."

At the rim of her vision, beyond vomit-covered pietas, two men in floral shorts, bellies and cropped heads, massive babies, were piling dreamcatchers and gothic pottery, poems, crystals and wooden spoons onto a blazing pyre. Through the flames the blue lamps of a queue of ambulances were rolling into the camp, rising up and down in the potholes. The 'witch' could not hear the sirens, but she saw them: streaming flags of torn rags and screams with ruined mouths. On top of the bonfire the men had put the billboard; scorching heat was already searing off the words LOST HORIZON and a hand-made painting of a distant and better land and a simple, ancient people waiting by the sea; for a moment they blackened and then they pulled away in a dismissive gesture of smoke.

Chapter 2

No one kills an angel. Mandi Lyon changed that. Though it was never her intention to upset the balance of so many worlds on the morning she arrived back in the county of her birth. Raised by adoptive parents, from whom she had drifted away after college when work took her far and wide, eventually to the profitable reaches of the US media world, she was returning now to the camp site on which she had first grown up.

In the States she had had to grow up all over again. So, this would be her third advance on adulthood.

Anne and Bryan Widger had been killed instantly on a single carriageway stretch of the A308. It was a head-on collision with a Porsche driver anxious to get out of the West Country. The end had come suddenly, brutally, and without fanfare or premonition. Curled up against the window of the Paddington train, Mandi was trying to focus on the passing folds of Wiltshire hills, but the heads of her adoptive parents resolutely smashed through the glass of the windscreen again and again, the pieces of broken shield tearing the soft flesh from the bones of their faces and popping eyes from their sockets, until their leering death's heads zoomed around above the neat fields and clanged against the side of the train. Mandi closed her eyes and they came for her in the burgundy darkness.

It was no great surprise then, when she saw the bleeding angel.

The last thing she had seen, before closing her eyes against the cruelty, was a white horse carved into the chalk of the hills and racing piles of white limestone heaped onto a freight train sat in its siding. In the inner cinema of her fitful state, the wagons were full of teeth. A rolling ossuary, crossing the country, displaying its relics. Mandi could feel her own pearly whites working themselves loose; like she should add them to the inter-city reliquary. She was getting older, her skin was drying out, dark patches had appeared beneath her eyes; it had come the time to give something back to the country... she snapped into sharp wakefulness. Maudlin dreaming was more painful than loss.

This time, when she looked out of the muggy carriage, the flashbacks to the phone call and the instantaneous image of the crash had receded, replaced by an ache of foreboding as Mandi pictured her parents' camp rushing towards her across the fields, the formerly mobile homes torn from their fibrous umbilical cords, the shower block lumbering on its shallow foundations. Among the architectural spectres was a medieval looking figure in an icy costume, geometrical hair and blood streaming down her chin. It smiled; then she saw its mouth full of shattered, violated teeth, vandalised ruins of a Jewish graveyard. Somehow, though the blood streamed from between the remains of broken catafalques of dentistry and fell in dark gobbets from the angel's chin, the cold and perfect surfaces of her shift were left untouched, stainless. Her wings slowly spread up, glittering, into the clouds.

Mandi threw her head back into the seat. A wave of nausea rose through her throat and into the back of her nose. She was torn between snorting out the pressure and swallowing it as best she could, struggling to keep another violent movement from again stirring in her brains with the wire brush of her hangover. She began to gag on rising acid. Behind her eyes, the blood was white and hot, her throat lined with sand. She tried to distract herself by thinking through the one and a half bottles of Prosecco, and the something else there was before and the something else there had been after, and what might have happened around these stimulants to leave a bruise on her wrist and a tear in one of her barely justifiable shoes.

She strained to remember a conversation, more of an oration, she had delivered to the poor sucker; forget him, what was the idea? It had been brilliant, usable... it was at the after show party, or it may have been a PV, some sort of conceptual... anyway, there was a buffet of sorts with a band and... something to do with reliance and then something darker, spicier... she had been going on about snowflake companies, trying to pass off their responsibilities to individuals, that wasn't freedom, packaging manufacturers who are less than keen to pay a share of recycling costs, her idea was green but brutal, holding a knife to company information campaigns about individual responsibilities... she was going to turn that around on them. In the US, company law designates business institutions... yes, that was it, it was coming back, the genius hinge in her idea! In the US, companies are legally regarded as individuals, but unlike human individuals they are incapable of dying, until externally wound up... so, like sea urchins... for some reason she knew this, about sea urchins, of all things, that they are immortal if left to their own devices... sea urchins had nothing to do with it! Demons, that was it! Companies are demons, individuals that are immortal, but have no human soul. She would advocate ecologically-sound demon-slaughter, exorcism of the accountants, staking the heart of state capitalism, the disciplining of the executives... a wild hunt... she smiled in her daydream. Outside the golden carriage, flames somehow bright with darkness licked by at speed. In the centre of the furnace was a figure slashing at all around her with a laptop... her hair was alight, smoke billowed from under her skirts and... her teeth, her teeth... uuuuu... mmmmm...

She abruptly opened her eyes; an hour or more had passed and the countryside beyond the window was kinder and dimmer. The queasily rolling green of the giant fields had given way to a more stable patchwork. The train whooshed past a village, a canal with a pub perched on its bank, some narrow boats, and lines of old cottages flanked by something like recent suburbs, an anonymous factory on the village boundary, brick and corrugated iron farm buildings, some ruined walls in a field. All this skewered and held together by the plain symmetrical gothic of the church, built in mottled stone and sitting squat like an aged toad, content among the stone fungi of the cemetery. The wide West Door was generously open to all comers, and among its shadows, stood the angel with the smashed mouth.

Mandi looked away; struggling to find her iPod, then remembered she had picked up the wrong one in her rush. Irritated that she would have to get back in touch with the disposable crutch from last night to recover her own music. The Last Thing she wanted to be thinking about right now. She tried Shuffle and gave in to a dire hauntological melange of Kemper Norton, English Heretic, The Advisory Circle and some other dreary Anglo-centric droning 60s nostalgia merchant pretending to be bitter and difficult. Fortuitously, it seemed about right for the soundtrack to planning a funeral for people you were only ever semi-connected with. Over the years she had paid flying visits to the camp. Mostly though, the three of them had met at gastropubs halfway between their homes; her adoptive parents refusing to let her pay the bills. She had never let them come to London; keeping them, guiltily, at arm's length from her work at the Childquake charity where she had recently been promoted to CEO. Maybe she was reinventing the memory now, but she had some idea that when the phone rang she had been thinking of inviting Anne and Bryan... to what?

The chance had gone. Mandi argued with herself about getting some alcohol from the trolley. Decided against, then gave in. The first sip reminded her why there was an argument. The thin red wine lifted up the doubleness of her memories of Anne and Bryan; her angry dissatisfaction at their pseudo-parenting, their on-off, intimate and distracted nurturing. The nights of loneliness when they let her have 'her own space'. She knew that these were balances that no one gets right, balances she had never wished to have the chance to get wrong, and yet all that had never made her love them any less. Or love them very much. But she had never told them one way or the other; too busy raging at their carefulness, at their refusal to be clumsily intrusive, and, now, their disappearance just when she might have been willing and able to be clumsy herself. No, she was deluded. Clever people, they had brought up a child too clever for her own good; others, less loving than them, had read her flawed intelligence and she had been played again and again. She had learned how to turn her vulnerability into a facade, a baited hook, drawing in the powerful and playing them for all they were (considerably) worth. Well that was going to stop, she thought, a moment before the Merlot drained her resolve and the headache snake ate again into the top of her neck.

She enjoyed a sliver of relief just from the thought that London was receding behind her; she could entertain for a while the fantasy that she was leaving the place forever on her way to total disappearance. That she could throw off the double ankle manacles she wore; always the deadline, and always the faint marinating fear that someone would finally have worked her out, caught on to her imposter trick, dug up the dead bodies and found they were made up of bragging, uncovered the e-mail trail that contained nothing of interest to anyone, flicked through ancient social media posts and cross-checked with CCTV and found no one there.

The train entered a tunnel. Mandi felt the air push in through her ears, and a broken windscreen swallow her mind. In the jump cut from bright natural light to the dull bluey lamps of the First Great Western, the other passengers, positioned in the tableau of seating, were transformed into bit-part players in a haunting. With a sigh the sliding door at the end of the carriage drew back. The iconic wedge of train drove through the darkness. Behind a returning service trolley, decked with Quavers, Yorkie bars and shortbread fingers, the steward barked offers of hot drinks and alcohol. Responding to a request, she bent over a diaphanous elderly woman at a table, and when she smiled her teeth were smashed and blood ran down her chin into the waxed cardboard cup she was holding. Flash. Out of the tunnel and light drove all this nonsense away. Mandi gazed out of the window, where London was just a bad memory; a footprint the express escaped every day into soft hills and odd figurations in the fields: the great planes of solar panels, concrete pinball machines, orange dinosaurs, and weather-blanked adverts propped against wheelless trucks. Passing through slow comforts; the solid handle that held the cutting edge to the meat. Ahead of this stolid country, lay utopia and change, she hoped. Mandi tipped her cup and three small bottles of red wine into the flapping plastic bag of the passing cleaner; the bottles clinking on something at the bottom of the translucence. Hope hit her like a hammer and she wanted to turn back.

Chapter 3

Mandi changed at Exeter St Davids, and caught the local stopper. First, though, she bought herself a flat white and drank it beneath adverts for obscure touring theatre shows; ageing TV stars cranking up their smiles against crumpled velveteen backgrounds, like prizes in the dusty window of an arcade of one armed bandits.

By the time she dragged her lumpy, hastily packed suitcase onto the platform at Devil's Sett it was dark. The amusements had closed for the year; their modest structures barely visible against the obscure sky. Skeletal and dog-eared pirates swung above the crazy golf and a fuzzy line of industrial-style units stretched off towards the sea. Mandi crept through the gap under the railway tracks, past the silenced forms of the novelty shop and the sooty shell of the burned-out amusement centre. She could raise neither contempt nor delight at the sign for 'FLAMING HOT BURGERS' pinned to the temporary metal fencing around the smoke-besmirched ruin.

As the sun had sunk somewhere into Somerset, Mandi had rehearsed a few conversations. She had imagined soaking up commiserations, politely but firmly rejecting offers of help, welcoming in a controlled way a few memories of her suddenly absent fake-parents and even tried out a eulogy or two in her head. So, when she spotted a figure in the shadows of the camp's arch-like gateposts, she had a set of alternative responses already to hand.

"Mandi Lyon?"

Anne and Bryan's holiday camp stood out from the others. Instead of a 'BRIGHT SANDS' or a 'SUNNY HAVEN', the cranky letters on the billboard outside their camp spelled out 'LOST HORIZON' as if the inhabitants might have become disorientated and ended up there by chance. The place had long ago given up the pretence that it was a simple holiday camp, though Mandi was uncertain about the legal significance of that; many of the residents were permanent and though they still rented their properties, these were now their only homes. Some had been there since before Mandy was born. There were lights burning in the windows of the lines of immovable mobile homes; their approximate sameness dull in the thick moonless autumn evening. Inside, there would be great anxiety and insecurity, and Mandi knew that she had come to assume responsibility for calming those vivid fears. A wisp of steam rose from a trailer and then floated away. The camp seemed to be settling in on itself, like an animal sinking into the shelter of long grass, making itself small, as if a predator had come close.

Stepping into the sodium glow of the street lamps, the shaggy white-haired man held out his hand. Mandi took it and it was cold. She looked into his face and the eyes were warm and watery. She swallowed; suddenly fearful that they would leap from their sockets.

"My name's Crabbe. I have recently been working here as caretaker, for your parents. Please accept my condolences."

'Condolences'; Mandi had not prepared for 'condolences'. Why would an unexpected word matter? 'Condolences' were no different from 'commiserations'. Or 'sympathy'. Ready to feel misery, she was surprised by the word's dolefulness; it was ridiculous. She had no such words. She could not reply. She opened her mouth and it might as well have been a cave for all it could speak for itself. She felt the cold air on her teeth.

The caretaker was unnaturally still and comfortable. As if he was expertly putting Mandi at her ease. Yet the silence grew and grew. Expanding out across the dull blue-brown grid of the camp. Mandi followed the tiny darting movements of the caretaker's eyes. She had no idea what to say or how to respond. Her mind was a blank and getting blanker. Everything around was tightly focused, in high definition. The knobbly white-painted stones to mark the verge, the dimples on the kiosk shaped like a giant golf ball that sold candyfloss in the summer months, the leaves of palm trees snapped in recent high winds, the expanse of road, wide for the coach parties, dull orange and its surface shiny with the dampness brought on by evening. Nothing would ever come here again, no child would ever bang a bucket with a spade, no mother ever clutch swimming costumes rolled in a towel unless Mandi could speak and make it so.

"Perhaps you would like to put your things away, before..."

"Yes! Thank you."

"Shall I?"

"No, I'm fine..."

Tears rolled out of her eyes like balls around a pinball machine; they felt silvery and heavy on her cheeks.

"Take your time", said the caretaker, and swung about. His weatherproof trousers crackled and the anorak tied around his waist swished like a skirt. Even under the sodium lights, it was clear that he was dressed entirely in black, but for the smears of mud around his knees. His hand, although cold, had been soft, soft for someone who worked with their hands.

"You don't need to see anyone this evening."

"No, I want to get it done with."

"Done with?"

"Get it over with."

The caretaker stopped and looked at a pothole in the camp driveway, he kicked some gravel into its puddle.

"I think I should tell you, straight off, Ms Lyon..."

"Mandi."

"...Mandi... I'm not sure that it will be possible to get it done with tonight."

"O, I understand that. But I thought that I should at least reassure the residents."

"That you are taking on the community?"

"That I will do whatever is best, within my...."

What was the word? What was any word? What word might do? Or was a replacement for words? The cave of silence opened up again like black wings. The world on pause. Mandi felt her muscles seizing mid-stride. The crunch of gravel seemed to retreat deep inside the cave; if the caretaker was trying to help her out, his words were far too muffled for Mandi to mind. It probably only lasted a moment, a few seconds at most, but it was already clear to Mandi that there were large gaps opening up in her sense of things; there were important subject matters missing from the big picture.

"This is it. But, of course, you remember..."

Her fake parents had done their best to turn the little bungalow into an alien temple. Dreamcatchers hung in lines. The house name was in Arabic. Above an enamelled representation of the 'Mallard' steam train, twin giant antlers poked, long and branched and sharp, from what looked like an unfeasibly small skull; reaching into the night, as if feeling for the lost souls of Anne and Bryan. Mandi could only see the first flash again and again and their heads striking the reinforced screens and the skin peeled from their skulls. There was no button to press for a doorbell, but a chime and a hammer. Several walking sticks, all mostly shaped by nature, stood in the feet of two old boots, painted white. Beyond the frosted glass, Mandi could just about make out a red hanging and its golden sigil. Over the years of meeting on neutral ground, in tasteful refurbishments of old pubs, chewing seared scallops and sipping dry white wines, Mandi had forgotten just how weird her parents were. Out of their natural habitat, they must have become expert in adopting the trappings of normal; Mandi had put out of her mind all the mystical tat, as though she had never had any part in it.

"Do you have a key?"

"No...."

"I have their spare."

The caretaker inserted the key in the lock and then stood back to allow Mandi to turn it. She released the lock, pushed the thick door ajar and removed the key.

"You keep it."

She pocketed the key and felt inside for a light switch. It was only as she touched the angle of the switch itself, and ran her finger along its edge, did it occur to her that she had come home. The light clicked on and everything snapped back into place; as if in the darkness it had been in chaos, but now, illuminated, it had presented itself to her in a familiar mask.

She gasped.

For a moment she felt the caretaker's hand lightly supporting her, between her shoulder blades, and then it was gone.

"I'll leave you."

"No. Yes... but... come back..."

"I don't normally work in the... but, obviously... in half an hour?"

"An hour."

"Fine", and he was gone, blackness into blackness.

Mandi ran through the tiny hall, along the dog-leg of corridor and threw herself into what had been her room. Flicking the light switch as she fell through the frame of the door, she had expected to feel her horror rising at a room preserved exactly as she had left it twelve years before. Instead, she froze, half-folded at the knees. There was no trace of her here at all. Anne and Bryan had wiped her away. For a moment she thought she might have chosen the wrong door, forgetful after such a long absence, but there was no mistaking the oddly sloping ceiling and the walls painted in chipped black, tiny stars of orange and pink emerging from the next layers down. Other than the walls, everything else was storage. Boxes and boxes of banal cardboard. Ribbed cardboard, hard cardboard, flat-pack and bubble-wrapped. The boxes, cases and other receptacles reached right up to the ceiling in places. There was no bed, no set of drawers, no wardrobe, no den, no silk hanging, no posters, no shrines to this and that god. No VHS collection. No tank-like recorder. No telly. The whole anomalous, anachronistic world in which she had spent so much, too much, of her childhood was no more, nuked, vaporised, and repurposed as storage space. Falling to her knees, Mandi sprang straight back up, pushing off a tower of cases, she rushed down the dog leg and around the house. A few glances and she quickly knew that if anything of hers was still there, it was modest and well hidden.

She lay down on the Persian carpet in the living room and felt herself falling in between its weft and warp – why had they erased her like that? – down into a deep basin of white, white, empty light.

Chapter 4

A few miles further down the coast, at the fingertip of the northern arm of The Bay, four white figures moved in sinister harmony. The headland had long ago been levelled by quarrying and a grey platform now stretched out a hundred yards into the sea. The ghost-like figures moved across the limestone shelf. For things so bright they moved so darkly.

The four figures rushed to the edge of the water, fell to their knees in unison, then onto their bellies; swinging high-powered rifles off their shoulders and onto their retractable supports. Four eyes trained through four scopes upon a single shadow on the water. Only to those educated eyes was anything present there; to any casual onlooker – an early morning dog walker, a wild camper emerging from a hidden tent – there was only a dark sea under a grey sky.

Phutt, phutt, phutt... phutt. Each of the white snipers got off a single round and for a moment half a mile offshore the ocean was cut white like chalk on a blackboard. Then it darkened again. All four firers wrestled lightweight binoculars up to their eyes; but if there was blood it was as black as the sea and invisible to them. Whatever shadow they might have thought they saw before, there was none there now. As swiftly as they arrived, they departed, sweeping up their weapons and running bent-kneed back across the silvery platform to the leafy-roofed paths that ran around the sides of the sheer quarry face. Just before disappearing into the green, they checked one last time for any unfortunate witness who might have caught more than the flutter of gulls or a last gasp of sea mist. Nothing. They conveyed satisfaction to each other in glances, then, before turning into the tunnels, rolled down their white masks over four sets of lips coloured in different shades of red, and under four powdered chins.

Their nigh-silent shapes were swallowed by the black greens of the moonless wooded cliff. Nothing moved on the limestone platform. Then, with a crackle of Puffa jacket, a man with a face like a wide dish, rose from his knees from beyond a pile of discarded quarry workings. Shielding the screen with his hand, he checked what his video camera had caught, made a note in a small red Silvine notebook, then clasped his chest and shook violently.

Chapter 5

The ocean gulped as the red shape hit it, falling. Warm and shallow waters rose up around the sail-like shape; giant pillars of spume that wrapped the dark thing in whiteness. For a few seconds a shining lily of bubbles stood out above the waves, while beneath them the gradually sinking flotilla of tiny corpses, the remnants of miniscule ocean creatures that had worked as much of their passage as they mortally could, blew up in clouds of muddiness. A shoal of Arctolepis fled, their arrowhead bodies slicing through the blue, soft heads swivelling to and fro; a giant Dunkleosteus, nine metres in length, soaked up the vibrations, its jointed neck armour pushed back upon itself and the invisible underwater wave striking between its stony teeth. On the ocean floor a rainbow forest of stalked crinoids turned their flowery umbrella-heads to the commotion on the surface.

The dark red shape spread itself for a moment, like a massive carpet, a Liopleurodon-sized parasol of tissue, the writhing spokes of which emitted vicious spines, jabbing blindly at the foam. With a hiccup, it seemed to spread further, increasing its girth, then the whole thing flipped over. With a thump the waters folded in on themselves, handlebar eyes and a white beak rose up from its insides and with a beat the parasol spasmed and sent the creature heading for the darker waters, for the unusual caves, for the resting places of the strange things that even the deep-swimming Cladoselaches rarely saw.

High up – or was it deep within? – an exhausted God, slumped across His creation, broken and seduced, wondering what it was that He had allowed, capable of reaching even His cold and ageless Perfection, bringing His worst fears – fears that He did not even know He had until that moment – to such a stained fruition in a passion of mucus, suckers, froth, sinew, blood and desire. Before long the light blue Devonian seas had returned to their soft continuity, a gentle blanket running up to the edges of the limestone mountains already emerging from its ossuary-floor; a benign corridor to Gondwana. Glittering as the scales of lobe-fins reflected the bright sun from below, that empty God tried to look upon the face of the waters, tried to tell Himself and any creature that would listen that it was good; but He knew that there was now a red darkness down there, where light and darkness were still unseparated, locked to each other in a furious lust, and that He did not know what it was, though He knew it was there, down there, known only to the Trilobites and sinking detritus of gelatinous zooplanktons, the Salps and Medusae Jellies upon which She snacked; waiting and preparing Herself, for another assault upon His Perfection.

Chapter 6

Mandi opened her eyes. The early morning gloom revealed dim shapes of musty furniture. Unable to bring herself to sleep in her foster parent's bed, Mandi had arranged a few cushions from the sofa on the living room floor and covered herself with a thin duvet. The scent of old incense had grown increasingly nauseating. No sooner had she lain down, than she was up again, fetching herself a glass of water, into which she slipped a couple of co-codamol, before sinking back onto the cushions, watching them dissolve.

The co-codamol soon took its effect, bringing some relief to Mandi's pounding head, but sleep had taken longer to come. Mandi had got to her feet, flicked on the kettle by the sink, and then stiffly bent over the lounge fire, muscles still cramped by the confines of the seats on the trains. Turning the numbered dial until it clicked; lighted gas hissed across the radiants. She liked the way that everything was in easy reach, one of the simple pleasures of mobile homes.

To the right of the fireplace was her parents' bookshelf. Flicking on a lamp, Mandi scanned the titles, looking for something to read. Each volume was dedicated to a different aspect of paganism, witchcraft or the occult. She sighed in frustration at their narrow concerns. All the books had been arranged by theme or author. Three titles on Santeria next to a handful on Chaos magic. Then a generous section on modern witchcraft and, inevitably, a few Crowleys, Valientes and a couple of beautifully bound Scarlet Imprints. Mandi hated them all.

Mandi had flicked on her mobile. No 4G, so no chance of socialising. Just a text from the disposable guy asking if he could have his iPod back. Mandi smiled at three desperate xxxs that ended the message. Men's hopes, she thought, so frequently outweigh their sense of reality. She texted back, asking him for a postal address, promising to send it back in return for hers and suggesting he leave it at the front desk at her office. She pondered the use of a smiley, but that might be misconstrued, and she plumped for nothing. Casual cruelty calmed her nerves and she laid back down into the cushions, drifted far from incense into darkness, and the next thing she knew, was waking, dreamless, grey lumps of heavy furniture towering above her.

The caretaker opened the door slowly and modestly. Eased himself through a gap no wider than necessary and closed the door deftly behind him, turning a key rapidly in the Yale lock of his home.

"No one locks their doors in Lost Horizon," she said.

"You saw the penny arcade. There's someone around."

Yet none of the doors they called at that morning were locked. The residents were more anxious about Mandi's arrival than warding off fire-raisers.

Most of the camp was locked up for the winter. Bryan and Anne's home was stationed close to the gates, a sentinel to it all. Once past their home, there were rows of identical trailer-chalets; empty now, they made for an odd walk: part film location, part salesroom. Why did working class people from industrial counties choose to stay in such mass-manufactured hutches? And why did middle-class folk, as homogenous as could be, feel they had a licence to sneer at these comfy little homes from home? Anonymous containers filled for a week or two with summer meanings, squeezing families into foreign shapes. Bryan had been working his way through this part of the site; the boundary where the crash had interrupted his work was quite distinct; rather than the neat hollows with the mattresses tipped on their end, the cabins were a riot of sheets and minor holiday detritus. At this border, Bryan had made neat piles of cheap buckets with busted handles, cracked mirrors and damaged St George's flags. Mandi swept up an armful of Christmas bunting that had blown in from somewhere else on the resort and threw it on top of the mess of red crosses.

There was something disturbingly systematic about the caretaker's introductions. Rather than go trailer to trailer, he wove around and through the rows, before doubling back to a home they had passed much earlier; as if there were a proper order at odds with the cartographical logic of the camp. Mandi supposed she must have known some of these people quite well in her teens, but they were no more familiar to her than distant relatives on the edges of a wedding photo, people that no one spoke of anymore. As they entered each of the cabins, she got the same feeling each time, of an eccentricity that was trying to impress itself upon her, but always in the same way. There were different styles, however, and the caretaker had arranged their visit in an ordering of these.

First came the followers of the Light with their airy properties, windows that let in the day, mirrors that expanded the boundaries of their homes, First Nations images, fairies and angelology. Here were people who followed to the letter the Wiccan rede "An it harm none, do what ye will"; folk who had repurposed the Christian image of the witch as Satan's bride to their own version of gentle earth healer. Then the Darker side with their sigils, tattoos, pentacles and chalices, Gothery and completist collections of Psychic TV recordings. These darker folk, with an uneasy relationship to Crowley, preferring the unbridled "Do what thou wilt shall be the whole of the law" to the Wiccans' innocuous version. Their witch was Lilith.

Mandi could not help the feeling, when she was not lapsing into drowsiness, that these people hardly knew her adoptive parents at all. She had imagined that this would be a tight community, bound together by shared ideas and a cosy over-knowing, the kind of complacent set up that she despised. Yet there was nothing of that; instead she felt that the camp was in the grip of a helpless paranoia. The kind of thing you would feel in a company before a round of compulsory redundancies; she had seen such faces when she worked in HR and it had been her job, as the junior, to deliver the bad news. It would be wrong to say she enjoyed the cruelty of it, but she relished any necessity for cutting herself off from sympathy in the interests of a greater thing. That greater thing was her secret lover; on the outside she slinked around the feeding frenzies of individualism, keeping the zealots to their word, but in her dreams there was always something else, some principle, behind it all, within it all, deep down. There was a pattern guiding those thrashing bodies and virtuously greedy splashes. The nights she enjoyed the most were in the arms of that pattern, wasting time with a bottle of crude Merlot and Netflix, then curling up in fresh cotton sheets and feeling that spiritual thing, that pulsing disembodied landscape just below the mattress, the demesne where she was queen. That was why she was a cut above the others, she reassured herself, because she didn't just believe in any of this stuff; she was in love with it, and her love was blessed by...

"What? Sorry..."

She was suddenly aware that the fairy princess and her dreadlocked knight were staring across at her from their threadbare sofa expecting some kind of response.

"I'm sorry... lost in... with the deaths and all that... could you run me through that again?"

And under the gaze of the caretaker, Mandi dutifully attended to the plans and fears of the piskie pair.

"Hijacking, that's what we're saying! If you don't do something the funeral will be hijacked!"

The knight swept some biscuit crumbs from his beard and the princess brushed them onto the carpet and rearranged her shawl.

"We wouldn't want the... Goths, we call them... you know who I mean?"

The caretaker sharpened his stare. Mandi nodded and shot a warning glance at the caretaker.

"Then you know what they're like." She didn't, but she could make a good guess. "They want to make out that your Mum and Dad were one of them..."

"Two of them", the knight corrected, and grinned, pleased with himself, folded his arms and knocked his coffee mug from the arm of the sofa. Brown liquid fell thinly over a box of fantasy figures.

"O!"

The princess sprang lightly to her feet and was then swiftly on her knees mopping up with a J Cloth, soaking up the greasy coffee, and dabbing the laminated surface before anything could sink in. For some reason, and she did not like to imagine that there was any real reason, Mandi was minded of the grey-brown stream that sneaked around the edges of the camp, a stickiness underfoot and a fetid smell. She felt the hairs on her arm rising and a clammy bead or two hanging on her forehead. She needed some fresh air, but that would have to wait.

"We're concerned for their memory, Amanda. That is important to people like us."

As though it was not to her.

"Let me do this", said the princess, returning to the sofa having tossed the J cloth into the cluttered sink. "Amanda. Your Mum and Dad were lovely people, and they deserve to be remembered that way. There wasn't an ounce of nastiness in either of them. Nothing was ever too much for them; a repair here and there, keeping the place clean, running smooth, letting people have their own space, they didn't poke their nose into other people's business like you can get in some pagan communities, know what I mean?"

Why would Mandi know? Why would she think she knew? How much had she forgotten?

"We'd like everyone to remember the best side of your Mum and Dad. They were generous, they had big souls, they had bright spirits. There was no side to them. That's who they were. Plain good. That's why... I'm sorry I have to say this, Amanda, but that's why you have to stop the others from using the funeral as a... pulpit!"

She spat the word out, like spoiled milk.

"They will!" announced the knight, shaking his hair into a twirling skirt. A paper lampshade on the table behind the sofa was caught in the draught and very, very slowly keeled onto its side. The knight turned in surprise but could not make out what had happened.

"Please help us, Amanda. We are fighting for your Mum and Dad."

"What do you want me to do?"

The fairy princess smoothed down her long skirt and then folded her hands into a woven sigil in her lap.

"We wish you to hand over the officiating at the ceremony to a neutral figure; there are many respected wise folk in the area, not the immediate area, but Totnes maybe? Your parents deserve a neutral ceremony."

"I see", said Mandi, standing. The handmade chair creaking in relief. The caretaker stood, as if her own shadow were following her. "Send me some names."

And they were swiftly out of there, Mandi striding down the lane between the cabins before it struck her that she had no idea where to go to next and turned to the caretaker.

"This way," and he turned them around and led the way to the door of the darker forces.

The darker forces had their headquarters in a large flat caravan-like structure at the far reaches of the permanent section of the camp. Those parts which had once made it mobile were now melted into a concrete base which in turn was now covered by a carpet of green moss. Even in the grey winter light, the moss shone with a sparkling gem-like aura. Guarding the steps up to the cabin were cairns made variously of stones and animal bones. Many of the bones had succumbed to the green invasion, the white had all but disappeared beneath the wash of algae. The effect was of a damp but glowing kingdom; but inside was very different. It was more of a warehouse. Multiple copies of the same volumes sat about in fierce pillars, some bound with fibrous straps. The walls were lined with gaudy shelves of red and black volumes, multiple copies of the same editions. The two managers of this odd little entrepôt had managed to combine into their dress a certain bookishness with Dungeons and Dragons camp. Crescent-shaped reading glasses obscured thick mascara, a warrior's skirt over woolly tights, fingerless black gloves and curved fingers flattened at the end by endless thumping on keyboards. Screens winked at their work stations.

"Come in!"

Cassandra (not her real name the caretaker explained later, in case Mandi was concerned about the "Tracy" on the rental agreement) waved a handful of jiffy bags as if she were about to skim fleets of ninja throwing stars at her guests. Tossing the paper shuriken aside, she slid an office chair across the room. Mimir (same arrangement as Cassandra, the caretaker later assured her) produced another chair from behind one of the bibliopiles and steered it, at Cassandra's bidding. Mandi was asked to choose one or the other. She hated these slippery things.

"First, please accept our congratulations on the transition. Time is artificial. Be assured that your Mother and Father..."

"My adoptive parents to be ... precise..."

"O... that they..."

"There is no death", offered Mimir. "Only a change of worlds."

Mandi wondered about thanking them, but the idea of 'precision' had suddenly struck her as intensely absurd, particularly here in their paper keep.

"Do you mind if I had a moment? To look at your books?"

They probably thought that Mandi needed a moment to collect her thoughts and feelings, but those had been assembled, logged, salted and stored behind the absurdly thick door of her vault a while ago. No, she was laughing and she wanted to enjoy the respite it gave her. Checking the spines, she turned her back on the room; pulling down a random volume here and there to scan the blurbs; she built up a rapid snapshot of the couple's publishing predilections. They were remarkably eclectic: staring out at Mandi were unicorns with dopey eyes, angels flashing gossamer wings, mailed fists and magicians in monkish outfits, chalices swilling with suspiciously viscous stuff, random bare-breasted dryads and all the watery sensualism a charlatan publishers might wish for without a hint of genuine transcendence. How did they get away with it?

"So, you are....what?"

"O", said Mimir. "That's not... us! We serve as a kind of shell company for vanity writers; angels, fairies, stuff that nobody reads, the writer's family and immediate circle, perhaps, and when I say 'read' I mean 'buy'. No one reads much past the first few pages. But it creates the..."

"Illusion?"

"The magic! Of publication. It's a service. And it pays for the real stuff."

Cassandra pulled aside some ferocious packages of goth fantasy, crying out. In preciously carved shelves, sat tiny chapbooks. Eased from their positions, Cassandra presented a few on her open palms.

"Look, don't touch; you'll draw the energy."

There was almost nothing there. Just the suggestion of power. Cassandra prised open the covers of one. Hand printed, expensive heavily grained paper, watermark, simple sigils. That was it.

"Not to be messed with."

Cassandra placed them back in the shelves and Mimir pushed the piles of bound fantasies back into place. The kings were in their castles, all was well for the time being.

A long silence descended over the trailer.

"I've come to find out if there is anything .... for my Mum and Dad's funeral, we're making the arrangements. I imagine you would want to come."

Mimir and Cassandra did not react and Mandi was unsure if, in their minds, the question needed no reply, or they were still deciding.

"We want to be inclusive..."

Why was she playing this stupid game?

"I don't know if you know this, Amanda..."

Cassandra handed the baton to Mimir.

"Let's talk straight."

Mimir folded his arms, but Cassandra took the baton straight back.

"Truth is this, Amanda. We knew your Mum and Dad better than anyone here, and they would not appreciate having their transition marred by the love and light and 'harm none' brigade. That was not their magic. They were into something stronger. They were... mild people, but I got the impression they liked to get results. Do you get my meaning?"

"I don't remember them ever mentioning you..."

"We weren't close, but it was obvious... they weren't fairy and crystal people..."

"Thank you. We have a lot to do."

Mandi rose from her chair and the caretaker was already holding open the front door. The fresh air felt sharp and good on Mandi's cheeks. She breathed in gulps as if someone had had their thumbs on her throat. Mimir and Cassandra stood, baffled, at their door.

"I know exactly what you want", called Mandi and strode down the lane between the dwellings of housesitting hobbits, bookkeeping princesses, entrepreneurial fairies and desktop chieftains. "Leave it to me!" Weak strings of smoke and steam rose from the caravans and shacks. Ducks clanked through the distant mist.

When she and the caretaker arrived back at Bryan and Anne's home, Cassandra was already waiting for them.

"I hope you don't mind, I let myself in. It's better if we talk without the Viking, woman to woman."

Mandi glanced sideways at the caretaker.

"He's fine", said Cassandra. "He's different. He takes care. Do you mind if I smoke?"

As Cassandra rolled a joint, filling it with some rough and ragged weed, home grown by the rancid smell of it, she laid out her fears as if she were rolling out a map. Mandi had not noticed her stick or the old-fashioned callipers that supported the lower part of her right leg. Someone had yarn-bombed it. As she spoke, Cassandra gazed about the room in wonder.

"Have you been here before?"

"No one has. This was the holy of holies. I've never seen any of this, but I can read it like a book. That's not what I've come to talk about. Amanda, you were involved in a terrible thing. Your parents, your adoptive parents weren't they? I can't exaggerate what it must have been like for them, and for you, I'm sure. The papers, the media, they indulged in this... spasm of collective amnesia... like the dogshit, the moment the authorities said it was the fault of the dogshit, who was interested? Who remembers three kiddies killed by dogshit? Who wants to read about that over their cornflakes?"

"Other cereals are available."

Cassandra didn't understand and ploughed on.

"That was a time when the media didn't even use the term 'shit'! Dogshit was something that only really, really boring people bothered about; and even they didn't use the word. There was no celebrity dogshit, no A list dogshit, no VIP dogshit room, no executive dogshit..."

"Yeah, I get it."

"See, even you don't want to hear! It was a smart move on their part! Because, what was the alternative for them? Yeh, they could have put your Mom and Dad, adoptive, inside, put them on trial, they could have had you taken away, secure facility, say you were.... what? Evil? Deranged? A case of psychological whatever. They can do those things, you know? I know for a fact, because I was told by one of their best friends, that they fought – your Mom and Dad, adoptive – they fought tooth and nail to keep you out of the clutches of the psychologists. And, fair play, the authorities didn't really want to go there. Dogshit was their stroke of genius. Bingo – it was all a problem with the drains. How many poltergeist incidents are down to faulty wiring and bad pipes? Houses on geological faults! Get my drift? Your Mom and Dad got away with it, because the authorities knew that if they did put them on the stand..."

'On the stand'? What was this, a John Grisham thing?

"...they had to accept the possibility that the child abuse thing would fall apart, where was the evidence? Your Mom and Dad were good people! They adopted, for Chrissake! And then what were they left with? Magic."

"Cassandra, please don't take this the wrong way..."

The caretaker shifted, so barely noticeable that Mandi turned to him. He was frozen.

"...but I have no fucking idea what you are talking about."

"No, no, no, no... no reason why you would. It's a long, long time ago... sounds like a fairy story. But it wasn't. The media may have forgotten, the sheeple may have gone back to their dreams, but the pagan community has never forgotten. That's why your Mom and Dad, adoptive or not...."

"No, they were... no question about it... they were not my actual parents..."

"They had a very special place in our community. When your community has had its witches burned for hundreds of years... they were our living martyrs. They were almost gods, Amanda, gods. Aristocracy, at the very least...'

Mandi realised that she was talking about Anne and Bryan, not Morgan le Fay and the Pendle Witches.

"Most of us, if we are really honest with ourselves, don't see much real magic. Don't get me wrong, the magic is real; we can... the best of, we can make an enemy fall ill and heal a friend, we can get you the lover you want, bingo, even if only for you to find out you don't really, we can get you a good deal on a second hand car and conjure you a minor demon if you're willing to put up with a lifetime of hassle, but what has any of that really changed? We know the spells, we celebrate the coincidences, the miracles, the way the world seems to respond to us, the arrival of unexpected animals, the schadenfreude when an enemy trips over the kerb, the magic of falling in love and of dying. But not so many of us get to stand at the door of the Otherworld and look right down. Your Mom and Dad were right there next to you..."

"I just told you. I don't remember anything. I know there was a fuss, and that at some time they had to stop certain people coming here, I wasn't allowed the... freedom I wanted at one time... because of something that had happened... but all kids are like that... setting fires, stealing from the shops..."

"No, Amanda, excuse me. Not all kids are like that. Not all kids are like you. Nobody's like you, baby. I've said too much."

Leaning on her stick, her young yet bony hands running over its shaft carved with interwoven plant forms, she levered herself out of the sofa, took a last long look around the room; reading it like an Egyptologist might a recently excavated room of hieroglyphics, hoovering it up with her thick mascara eyes. She tapped the stick three times on the carpet, followed its pattern to the front door, then turned so her shawl spread like a crow's wing.

"I've said too much. Forgive me. Dead dogs. Dead dogs. I saw you in our home, scared to fall asleep, don't be afraid of sleep. It's daily consciousness that is The Fall, the unconscious is the path to redemption."

"I'm sorry, I was just..."

And she was gone, the door blanking out her black swoop against the grey sky.

"I need to be getting on with..."

Her words trailed off, as if she had left a fading presence. Mandi stared accusingly at the caretaker.

"When, excuse me, is anyone going to tell me what the fuck this mystery is all about? Do you want some coffee?"

The caretaker refused blankly. Mandi had no energy left to argue with him. She was shocked. Never before had she owned up to anyone that she was tired. She was never tired. She was always tired. But she had a perpetual generator of energy, churning out anger and hard work, and she fed it with her exhaustion. Where did this tiredness come from?

She thanked the caretaker, conjuring a politeness that was physically painful for her. Crabbe repeated that there were "things to do", and Mandi watched him as he marched slowly off in the direction of the park office. Why did so many of them dress in black?

Back inside, Mandi put the kettle on the stove and slumped on the sofa. Instinctively she looked at her mobile, hoping that there might be some 4G, perhaps a temporary gust of signal brought in by the northerly breeze that she had felt picking up throughout the morning. But nothing. Not even a text.

A few years ago, one summer's day, Mandi had shared lunch with Anne and Bryan at the Barge Inn at Alton Barnes in Wiltshire. A couple of hours out from London, Mandi had endured the drive out of the city and across the chalk downs. The script of these lunches had been written not long after Mandi returned from the States and started meeting her adoptive parents again. Bryan would start by asking how Mandi was "getting along", a question so big and bland that Mandi always struggled to respond; she made things up, constructed huge falsehoods so absurd that Anne and Bryan were challenged to call her a liar. They never did. Then Anne would enquire about her relationships, asking in a faux tongue-in-cheek manner. Mandi hated the passive aggression in the questioning and called it out every time. She knew that Anne hated it too, she spoke it in quotation marks – thank god she spared them that awful four fingers thing – but could not help herself. Playing something she was not, something far worse than she was; but those games were starting to make more – and worse – sense now. She often wondered if she might have called a halt to the meetings, were it not for the energy they released into her next opinion piece; they gave her all the ammunition and pain she would need to lay waste to the fake displays of caring and self-absorbed noseying into the business of others that had skewed the moral compass of the baby-boomers. No, though, she was beginning to suspect that she had misread them completely; that they had been playing a much longer game. And Mandi hadn't even been on the pitch.

Although she had always kept in touch after leaving home, Mandi felt no particular closeness to her parents. Contact was more of a familial duty than anything borne out of fondness. For certain, she held a sort of love for them, but she was not interested enough in their lives to invest much effort in getting to know them – why had she not thought how strange that was at the time? How come she suddenly felt that twinge of guilt just before they died? Although she had bathed the wound in cocaine and dry white wine she remembered wishing that things were otherwise; but what could be more inauthentic than changing the past? The past was not a set of car keys you could mislay and find again. Once it was fucked, it was fucked for all eternity, it would not be coming back. And she was wasting her time fretting about it. Get it down and on the blog and forget about it. Forgetting. She was good at that, queen bitch at that, a goddess of that. She would get a lot of sympathy likes and retweets and a less than usually cantankerous comments thread from her male followers.

She had not been a goddess to her parents. Those occasional lunches were just fine as far as she was concerned. The drive was a welcome interruption to London driving. The food was never bad. Anne and Bryan had good taste in culinary matters, out of key with the rest of their 'alternative' dispositions; although they never mentioned the names of chefs or owners, they seemed to know people and people seemed to know them wherever they met.

Eventually, at these events, Anne and Bryan would both run out of questions and a pall would fall over the meal. Un ange passe. They were surprisingly uncomfortable in these long 'angelic' silences; almost as though they had expected that this 'nothing' was where all their questions would lead. Or that there was something they ought to be talking about, but never did. Mandi didn't mind the pauses; she could concentrate on the food, sip the wine and taste the parts of it; it was only a politeness that she hated that would bring her to responding to an imagined cue to ask how they were "getting along", a question never too huge or bland for Anne and Bryan. Each of these Wiltshire lunch dates were arranged to coincide with one of a number of investigations her adoptive parents were conducting into one earth mystery or another. Despite her distant feelings, this project-making always irritated the hell out of Mandi.

On one particular trip to Wiltshire, Bryan had talked about links between that summer's slew of crop circles and a geographical relationship to ancient burial mounds. She remembered that, but not the details. He had talked excitedly about geometric patterns, paraphrasing some new books he had speed-read. Mandi picked at her parmigiana and gulped, displacedly, at a third glass of wine; waiting for her chance to get in the factoid about random patterns like these being just as observable in the case of former branches of Woolworths. They took her scepticism in good heart, as she took their credulity. They thought the two things equivalent, she did not, and, infuriatingly and brilliantly, they regarded this contradiction with the same equanimity. She had taken another sip, ordered another glass, surrendered any idea of getting back to London that evening, and found it difficult not to agree with their agreeability.

When they met for the final time, Anne had been attempting to contact aliens, again. She had been visiting Warminster ever since the famous UFO flaps of the 1960s; in the early days digging Bryan out of bed on a whim for early morning dashes to the East. Now she had designed a new ritual to revive the meetings on the hilltops, the spontaneous gatherings of similar longing souls that never quite did enough to draw the serious attention of intergalactic messengers who, Anne still believed, had important information for humankind.

"In these end times" said Anne, "we need to try to understand what these aliens are trying to communicate to us. The Earth is in such upheaval, dear."

"Have you thought about what the future holds for the Earth, Mandi?" asked Bryan.

Mandi wondered what it would be like to talk to her parents about how she should decorate her flat. Her parents were obsessed with big ideas, the way some people are obsessed with football management. They got a giant kick out of it, win or lose, revelation or debunking, they were always loyal; but Mandi wanted to win, to be the Right Woman, she did not enjoy the gnashing of teeth. She wanted cymbals and glitter and reliable drugs.

Once, when yet another ange had passé, Mandi had explained that, no, she had not thought much about the future of the Earth, but she recycled and all that shit even though she knew much of it had been proved to be a con; that the only way things would change would be when big state did something about big things and let individuals consume whatever they wanted, learn to be resilient, stick up for themselves, instead of living like weeping snowflakes bewailing the state of the planet.

"Talking of our future" said Anne "there's a couple of things we need to let you know about."

Bryan took the baton.

"Your Mum and me wanted to let you know that we've written our wills and you, of course in the event of our deaths, are the sole beneficiary."

What to say? "Thank-you" did not really cut it. She knew that she should suggest that "they were too young to think about such things", not least because they were not young. But actually, she was wondering why they had waited until now.

"Well, I hope that's not needed for a while."

"Oh, so do we, dear, but we needed to prepare for these things, right now" replied Anne, kindly.

"I don't really need..."

"It's not for your need, dear", her fake mum responded sharply. Bryan silenced her with a sideways glance, and then over-smiled at Mandi. Mandi felt, suddenly, a little emotional. The "sort of love" she had for the two ageing hippies formed a lump in her throat; to see them struggling and just as uncomfortable as her. To see them getting it all wrong; for all their thinking about the future and their talk of harmony. She felt guilty and enjoyed it. And surprised at herself. She was puzzled, though, that they were not talking about passing separately. Surely that was the most likely; one of them would be beamed up into the passing alien craft before the other – she was pretty sure that they were immune to any kind of Heaven's Gate nonsense – in which case Anne would inherit from Bryan or vice-versa; why were they so keen to involve her right now? They presumably meant that after they both had gone she would get what was left. While she was pondering this, Anne and Bryan described repeatedly exactly where the paperwork that one day "would be important" could be found. Mandi helped herself to another large gulp of wine from her fourth glass. Right now, those memories were coming back in unhelpful detail.

The kettle started to whistle. Mandi started, suddenly back with herself, on the sofa. Anne and Bryan dead. Where did they say she would find the paperwork? Shit.

Anne and Bryan's bedroom felt utterly taboo. Placing her coffee on the small bedside table, already a desecration, Mandi sat cautiously on the duvet. She felt the tension between the aliveness of the intimacies she imagined her parents sharing there (while carefully avoiding any visualisations) and their now complete deadness. She knew she would have to go and see them soon. Sort out the release of the bodies. She imagined their bodies being drawn from mortuary cabinets, suspicious that that only happened in movies.

Mandi caught her reflection in the body length mirror on the wall. She saw a five-year-old girl who would bounce into her foster parents' room far too early in the morning and snuggle up between them. Whatever happened to her? She could smell them, she could smell that girl... sense her warmth. The feeling took her by surprise and she allowed herself to revel in it. She stretched out her arm to hug her mum. She expected a warm hand to cover hers. She expected movement. She did not expect a cold, lifeless skull caked in dried blood to roll towards her.

Mandi leapt back and off the bed. She had thought she left those nasty flashes on the train. She threw back her hair and sighed. She had an idea that the paperwork was in the built-in wardrobe. There was a small grey single filing drawer in there, she remembered; its brutal utility contrasted markedly with the decorative excesses of their other possessions. She had once hidden in that wardrobe, crouched beneath the rack of clothes, giddily excited when Anne or Bryan had entered the room looking for her. Once they had both come into the room, unaware of her presence; in hushed tones discussing "Steve" and "gone too far last night" and "it wasn't natural". She did not remember a Steve.

The drawer was precisely where she had remembered it. The paperwork was surprisingly orderly for a couple she knew only by their inefficiency and indifference to most things that did not involve the camp, particularly their own affairs. They never got their teeth fixed, never paid their TV licence on time. She first found the will; it was as per the discussion in The Barge Inn or Middlecote Arms or wherever it was. They had left contact details for a financial advisor and a bottom line figure for various savings accounts. She found it odd that Anne and Bryan would have a financial advisor. "Love of money is the root of all evil," Anne would often lecture Mandi. How blissfully unaware her parents had been, pagans quoting the Bible at her. What was their long game? Mandi had never corrected them; amused at how many of their beliefs were steeped in Christianity's Greatest Hits; was that where they were guiding her? At the time it served only to fuel her cynicism.

So, this was it. The papers they had described. No personal note. And a suspension file, slightly crumpled, crammed at the back of the drawer. She eased the file out from its niche; inside was a single manila foolscap envelope. She ran her fingers around the inside of the cardboard file but there was nothing else; no silver charm, Dartmoor pisky or childhood memento intended especially for her? The manila envelope was unmarked. Inside were a number of typed sheets of yellowing paper, dry and fragile like flies' wings. The heading on the first sheet read:

MS. Torquay Museum. May 1926

Why keep this obscure document with their bank statements? She read on.

That traces of an antediluvian civilisation with its attendant fauna and flora can be so readily found in the obscure lanes, fields and woodlands of this part of Devonshire has long been known to the coarse laborers that dwell in this lugubrious place. That this foetid and extinct civilization should, through blasphemous dreams, still cast its influence has been the ruin of my family and the reason we are soon to leave these shores for ever.

An opening paragraph that was mildly intriguing. Mandi was about to read on, when there was a sharp triple knock at the door of the trailer. Mandi remembered that, prior to their visits to the camp residents, she had persuaded Crabbe to take her on a walk around the boundary of Lost Horizon. "A bit of fresh air to clear my head." But mostly just to prove that she could manipulate the miserable old git; and check out the physical state of what was now her property. She dropped the various bank statements and legal forms back into the drawer, folded the manuscript into its envelope and tossed it in after the others. Before she closed the drawer and skipped to the door, keen not to let the caretaker slip away, she noticed something she had missed on first inspection. She retrieved the manila envelope; in the bottom right hand corner of the back of the envelope, in pencilled capitals, were the words: LOVECRAFT ORIGINAL.

Chapter 7

The sun rose from behind the sea. The gold disc rested on the flat roof of the ocean. All along the blood and orange cliffs stood yawning families. The exhausted elders had gathered on the red arches above the receding waters; word had reached them in the East through the heavy Yew and they had come, picking their way urgently for days along the faint traces of the ridge and portal ways, until they were ready to drop down through the valleys to the shore; strangers made welcome with acorn liqueur and oily fish in water. Weather cracked lips worked in the cold air as the elders chewed; spitting the bones onto the muddy rocks below. All their eyes, like those of the families, some still arriving, others almost broken by their vigils, were upon the giant and shadowy shape the last lappings of the outgoing tide were stranding on the red sand.

It had first been sighted nine sunrises ago, a dark nick on the skin of the deep.

Since then, drawing ever more witnesses from the woods of the Moor, from the safety of the enclosed tombs on the Great Hill, from the stone villages and rounded homesteads, the shape had grown like a stain; an uninterpretable language gibbering and shouting from the horizon, growing ever louder. At times it was as black as old beasts' blood in a bowl, at others like the shine of beetles, a blinding ruddiness, turning over and over, like a giant river hunter turning in the air to flash its golden chest; a flashing beacon alternately shielded and fired.

The elders had been called in unfamiliar desperation. The people had long ago given up on unreliable signs and rituals; the cyclopean architecture of the old ways fallen in the grass. Each blade of which told more truth than the old ceremonial archways and slabs of divination. Truth, the elders knew, stood in the trunks of trees, in the juice of fruit, in the way that water came up from a spring clear and full, the way that light fell through a gathering of young oaks; the truth was as transparent to a staggering child as any wobbling elder. The truth knew no dispensation for foolishness or ancestry, ancientness or decoration; when the time came all lay down upon the same bed of stones and rotted back to the loamy, red or brown certainty.

But now the thing out in the sea was driving them all inland, against the cold north wind at their backs. The whole people were walking in reverse. The green woodpeckers laughed, their insistent yaffles mocking the retreating tribe. The sheep complained of the unreasonableness of their desertion and imprisonment in hill forts. Even the Old Man had been called from his disgraced walking of the avenues in the high oak woods. But he was truly Old and no use to anyone but himself, and he was coming in his own unpunctual time.

No one yet had ventured upon the sands; except for The Thing.

Abandoned by the waters, it was revealing itself fully. The thick body of a monstrous fish, its face full of gums, its nether parts a sheaf of fins and legs and crawling things. The elders, summoned to make some comparison, stood helpless and speechless above the unfolding darkness on the strandline. They knew of no pattern like this, nothing from the old ways, nothing from the things they knew now – the veins of leaves, the twists of roots, the segments of flowers; none matched the dynamism and slitheriness of this pile of odorous life, boiling and writhing in the gilded sand.

As the north wind pressed against the backs of the retreating tribe, three women remained, standing alone under the cliffs. They had arrived together. Later, their families would jostle for priority and pre-eminence. Nothing would ever persuade the three families to distinguish between the moments of their arrival or the importance of their daughters' connection; two on the heights, one in the deep. The deeps are the heights and the heights are the deeps and the tunnels, caves and springs connect them.

The young women were from the middling sort of families; not known for preservation of the old places, nor for warrior deeds when occasional plunderers met their fates. They did their part when strangers were to be welcomed, they shared and traded and built and maintained their small round houses like their neighbours. They neither wore nor claimed any distinction from them. Nothing had set them apart, until this moment when the Dark Stranger called its daughters, none yet bonded with any other family, and they stepped forward, fearless. Had they recognised the invitation from their dreams? Had they fallen in a faint and fore-seen its dreadful beak and crowd of fingers wrestling up their shore? Two would answer the questions, later, and when their descriptions were completed no one would wish, let alone dare, to ask again.

For the moment, their three names rang from the cliffs. These people had no alphabet, no libraries or registries, but their names were no less precious to them than to those peoples that did. First the mothers spoke their names, then the sisters and brothers. The fathers were already moving silently and furiously back down the cliffs, crestfallen.

The great Thing rolled and its million fins flopped queasily up the incline of the beach, spilling strands that fought and re-engaged in contests for firmer holds. Along their surfaces suckers opened up by the nestful, like the beaks of hungry chicks, and each sucker writhed inside with spiders' traps, mucus webs and barbed saliva, strings of sticky tongue-like beads dangling and beckoning. The local people had welcomed many strange visitors, drinking up the smooth cloths and scarves, the hopeless invocatory symbols on shiny broaches; always hospitable, but never seduced. This stranger, however, was far more foreign, bile-raising and heart-exciting than anything that had come to trade before. Across the cliffs, the blood beat inside the people like the waves on the shore.

The three young ambassadors took three steps towards the Thing, only the woman in the centre took a fourth, into the mesh of dancing arms. The Thing threw out two long and padded ambassadors of its own, seizing on the child-woman and lifting her up and back. She hovered above the Thing, the wind began to whistle gently, her hair spread around her like a fantail, the low sun burnishing her blank face, her eyes turned inwards to her untranslatable feelings. The two remaining women stood their ground; the thick forearms of the Thing abased themselves around their toes and then rose up to their faces; falling backwards with a twist into the shallow waters, beginning the roll of the whole Thing, its globular torso raised itself up on hidden stilts, taller than the sandstone archways, a single eye staring deep into the soulwells of the elders, fixing their faces in masks of fear.

The eye sank down inside itself and the body shuddered like a burning homestead, suddenly losing its supports and sinking, trembling and swelling; the young woman still brandished above its quivering mass. Then it exploded without warning and birthed heaps of wriggling things in a rush of broken water; tiny fishes flapped, crab-like skeletons struggled to roll over on their hard burdens, and tiny versions of the Thing Itself unfolded around each other, hooking onto the ankles and toes of the two young women standing at the base of the Beast from the Deep. The pads at the ends of the two long proboscises lifted the arms of the chosen woman-child in gestures of beckoning and acceptance. Her two fellow initiates responded; peeling the tiny octopi from their toes they laid them gently in the shallows, lifting crustaceans from their flesh they shepherded them down the sands with guiding pushes, the fish they cupped in their palms and lowered them onto the outgoing waves.

Once in the waters, the Thing collected her babies to her sides and into her folds and pockets, sweeping the waters with long fins. Sensing that their Great Mother was about to depart, that whatever commerce had taken place was over, the remaining hundreds of slimy squids, desperate fish and soft lobster-things wormed and crawled and dragged themselves waterwards. The men had sensed it too and balanced the long spears with flint heads on their palms, running across the beach. Some aimed for the Thing itself, others threatened the tiny creeping things on the strandline. But the two young women still on the sand turned from the crowd of hurrying homunculi longing for their baptism and faced their own fathers, placing their bodies between the flint edges and the slimy Thing and its kind. The father of its captive and elevated princess wept with fury; the daughter of another father, one of the two ambassadors, pushed herself onto his flint head until her blood began to spurt from the flesh at her neck. The father of the Squid-Princess withdrew his spear and the other men did likewise; their flint blades dropped to the sand.

In triumph the Thing thrust its captive even higher into the blue of the morning; around her head bright stars sparkled for a moment, then the Thing rolled again and was suddenly beyond the gentle shelf of sand and into deeper waters, dragging her under. A curtain of spray rose and a cold mist marched over the two young women and down upon the faces of the fathers. A gasp was wrung from the families lined along the red cliff. Softened by the recent storms, parts of the cliff began to tumble down its steep incline; a spill of sand first, and then boulders.

The Thing was surrounded by a churning crowd of little things, boiling the water around her and driving her farther and farther from the shore, until, her thick spindles of flesh having trapped all her children in fasts and holds, she rolled for what seemed a final move and pulled the whole tribe beneath the waves. The cliffs let out a collective howl, a piece of land as big as the Thing itself dislodged, hurling a family into a meaningless heap of limbs on the hard sand below. From where it had fallen, a miserable trickle of tears dribbled down the frozen iron desert, exposed to the sun for the first time in 300 million years.

The sea spat and the Thing lifted its seal-like shoulders from the brine; then, its two giant fingers were raised, as if to thread twine through the eye of a bone needle, the proboscises of the Thing raised up the Squid Princess, her eyes as blue as the ocean, waters streaming, spring-like, from her ears, nose and mouth. Three times the Thing rolled over dragging her Princess down and three times lifted her up again to hang upon the sky; then with a finality and a deep woomph of sound it crashed back and turned over and was lost to the deep. Only the stain of its shadow was seen again; as it first spread beneath the surface and then shrank again as it sought the sharp cut of the horizon.

The bereaved father raced into the surf, a second time lifting his arm to hurl his spear harpoon-like through the water. But his arm was caught as he brought it back into alignment with his shoulder by the strong thin fingers of another's daughter, the second unwounded ambassador. Instinctively, he turned the spear and caught her across the face with the centre of the shaft. Her expression did not change; still the look of supreme bliss, that had covered it for a while now, prevailed. The father stood back and the daughter of another opened her lips; a spring of blood fell from her lower lip, flecked with fragments of teeth. When she smiled, she smiled the smile of a conger eel. He had made her of the Deep. He turned and fled, dropping his spear, in horror at what he did and flung himself at the feet of the girl's mother, begging her to end his life there and then.

The elders halted such nonsense. They had stepped down from their useless exaltation on the archways and stumbled across the sand to where the two young women defended the deep and its shrinking shadow. But the elders had nothing to say; nothing at the heavy Yew had prepared them for this, nothing they had witnessed at their wells, not even the speaking heads had spoken of this, nothing in their meetings with the trees in their groves, joining the gatherings, had pre-empted a monstrous mother from the wet. They had arrived at the shore with a floundering dignity; but there was no liturgy to continue the ritual. They stood useless and gilded, the salt stinging in their wrinkled visages. The girls faced them, almost black against the thin blue of the sea, flashing red with splashes of their own blood. Then he came.

The Old Man, called for, many days before, had finally made it from the woods up on the heights, dragged from his trawling up and down the stone rows dragging up memories of things he had been told as a child about rituals that even his grandparents had never seen. Hoping that one day some magical emissary might appear from a distant god who had simply forgotten for so long to call and yet had suddenly been reminded of His people. He tottered across the sand, between the crowds of people stepping back to let him pass. He searched their eyes and faces for clues as to how he should begin his interpretation. They were as enigmatic and unhelpful as the dumb stone rows!

At a glance he took in the two bleeding women standing between him and the sea; this was not right, all gateways should have two different pillars, one flat and one pointed, one male and one female. He saw from their exalted faces that all righteousness and fear of the Great People had fled from them and they were running with their own madness like worms in a new cadaver. He would get no old truths from them!

Striding between the two pubescent guardians, the Old Man attempted to push his way past them, but they were stood too far apart and holding his palms to the faces of each of them, he made contact with neither, but instead tripped upon a piece of afterbirth and toppled into a heap of placenta.

The bereaved assembly roared until they wept; the outrageousness of it all emerging as a chorus of wolf howls, that fine line between fearful snarl and laughter. The Old Man lay as if dead, pretending dead, until he could stand their laughing no longer and grasping at a large rounded stone pushed himself to his feet with the last portions of his faith, swinging the giant pebble at the nearest young female head. The guardian ducked, her wildcat headpiece rolling down the sand's incline, the assembly expecting to see some part of her skull still in it. But her head seemed to regenerate and popped up from her long smock and back onto her shoulders. The Old Man formed an egg shape of surprise with his lips, which is how he died; the same expression frozen as the girl-guardian grabbed his ankle and tipped him helplessly back into a rockpool, his body writing and struggling against the inevitable airless death amongst the indifferent shrimp and blennies that now played between the final bubbles of his precious air. And so the last of the old priesthood died by a symbolism that even he had forgotten.

The trickle from the red cliff had become a spout, silver and glutinous in the rising light.

A kind of half-hearted nostalgic anger rippled through the men and one or two stepped forwards to discipline the girls. A flock of oystercatchers resting on the sand behind the chosen girls took fright at the movement of the men, and took precautionary wing, flapping and hovering, flashing their blankets of black and white; only for moments were the birds airborne, but for those moments it seemed as if something like huge feathered chequerboard wings had begun to grow from the shoulders of the two girls.

One by one the families approached the girls and made some display of honour and respect; but when the family of the sea-princess approached them, it was the girls that knelt and bowed and made many improvised signs and gestures. Beckoning them to lead, the girls guided the bereaved family from the beach, and the families processed inland, carrying the limbs of the broken family, back to the more familiar spaces of their everyday; leaving the elders to bury the old man's body in the sand for the crabs and lugworms to feast upon; denying him the final bed of stones, an anonymous grave out of sight of the sky was the mark of his shame.

Chapter 8

The cluster of birds curled, unfolded, splayed and puckered. Nothing unusual in that. The 'desert island' at the ends of the dunes always attracted heaving flocks of birds; mostly brief tourists on their way to or from an African wintering or a northern mating. The whole cluster abruptly sagged, squared off at its corners and then, unnaturally, shifted wholesale to the right.

"Didn't know birds c...", Mandi mumbled to herself.

They were not her quarry. That was making its way on a parallel path through the marram grass, about thirty yards ahead of her and clearly stalking its own prey. Dressed in green and grey camouflage trousers and hooded jacket, it stood out from any of the casual strollers who might have ventured out onto the dunes of The Sett that morning; partly by its dress, but partly by the pace it kept up through the thin and slippery sand. Like some persistence hunter, it rushed along, low to the ground and almost silent. Any racket or rustle was lost in the blustery gale blowing up from the sea.

Mandi's intention had been to locate the caretaker. He was nowhere to be found on the site; but one of the residents had assured her that he was known for taking a mid-morning or mid-afternoon walk to the end of the dunes, dependent on the tides, before resuming his duties. Just as Mandi was contemplating – as best she could at pace, though easier on the more solid lower path she had chosen – that if the camouflaged figure was stalking Crabbe then her attentions might be convenient, even fortuitous, when it threw itself to the ground, almost out of sight beneath the yellowing grass. Mandi clambered up the side of the dune, aware that this was not recommended by the wardens' notices that she would one day like to collect together in one place and burn. Or maybe plant them all in the same place; collect all the warning signs and nannie state noticeboards and assemble them in one huge forest of No and Don't and Beware.

BE AWARE! JELLYFISH ARE BEING WASHED UP ON THIS BEACH. KEEP CHILDREN & DOGS AWAY.

Whoever the tracker was, they knew nothing about covering their back. In the soft sand, Mandi was able to creep within a few inches of their splayed boot-shod feet. She could see their gloved hands manipulating a phone; they appeared to be videoing something up ahead on the 'desert island'. A rolled-up magazine poked from the back pocket of their liverish fatigues. Mandi knelt on one knee and looked beyond the stalker. High above the churning waters, where the estuary met the turning tide, a second manuscript of birds was unfurling, exploding into single characters and joining up in spiralling columns. The stalker's focus was lower; Mandi eased her body onto the sand, almost side by side with the recumbent stalker.

Through a gap between two dunes she could see that something odd was going on around the 'desert island'. Figures in white hazard suits were moving about, four or five of them, almost in a dance, swinging past each other, but making ground from the seaward to the landward side of the dunes. She could see the screen of the stalker's phone. On there the figures in white, only their upper bodies and hooded faces in view, were blurred and sinister, looking not unlike nuclear plant workers from someone's reactionary 1950s' imagination. Reflected in the screen, Mandi saw the moon-like face of the stalker; a man about her own age, soft features, fair eyebrows, milky blue eyes wide with terror and a slit for a mouth tense against the world. But if she could see him, he...

The moony stalker abruptly but silently rolled onto his back away from Mandi. She leapt to her feet and for one moment considered placing a foot square upon his chest.

"What the fuck do you think you're up to?"

"Aliens..." mumbled the stalker, straining to catch his balance as he careened to his feet, holding up his phone. He pointed in the general direction of the white figures, who Mandi could see quite clearly now were manipulating long nozzled sprays, carrying cream knapsacks of weedkiller or similar strapped to their backs.

"Aliens..."

And off he took, as fast as his camouflaged legs could carry him, back towards the entertainments and holiday camps of The Sett, kicking up fans of sand as he went.

"Nutter," Mandi decided.

The black figure of the caretaker had appeared among the white-suited wardens and a heated discussion was in progress. Above the argument a smaller flock of oystercatchers, recognisable to Mandi by their orange beaks and angular black and white plumage, banked gently and then swerved, almost tumbling upwards. Whatever the caretaker had said to the white weedkiller operatives, it was either controversial or exciting, because they all began to wave their arms, as if in time with the swinging chequerboard above them. Mandi had no wish to interrupt them; she only wanted to speak with the caretaker, so she took a seat in the grass.

The moon-faced man had dropped his magazine in the sand. Mandi rescued it and shook it free of crystal grains. It was some sort of conspiracy 'zine; not one she recognised, though she had read a whole load once for an article on the Huffington Post site. Mostly these nerds and nutters communicated digitally, but there were still a few traditionalists who refused to leave any electronic trace. The 'zine was titled 'Conspiracy Now!' Mandi flicked through a few pages; none of the usual round ups of anomalous news, but a collection of longish essays. Something on numerology and the Futures markets, the involvement of the Illuminati in the production of microbeads (hardly a necessary participation?), a historical feature about something called Operation Northwoods, nothing on aliens or ufos, but there was an entertaining article about birdwatchers that Mandi read as she waited for the caretaker and the sprayers to be finished with each other, glancing over occasionally to check how the argument was progressing.

'Who runs the country?' Sir John Betjeman, gentleman poet and judicious conservationist, once asked rhetorically. 'The RSPB. Their members are behind every hedge.'

Mandi almost roared. She loved bitchy Tories.

In a recent publication of his research, well-respected author Jason Jenkinson, PhD, suggests it is not the RSPB birdwatchers but the birds themselves that we should be wary of.

Mandi licked her lips and tasted the salt.

In 1998 a small group of physicists and avian biologists gathered at the Swiss Institute of Ornithology, Lausanne, to review the current literature on possible methods by which birds might make use of the earth's magnetic field to orientate themselves and to undertake their long migratory journeys. What the group suspected was that photons entering a bird's eye were causing chemical reactions in the bird's retina giving the bird a visual readout of their direction. Flying in one relation to the Earth's magnetic poles coloured their vision one way, flying in another relation coloured it differently; in short, through the complexities of a process known as 'quantum entanglement' it was proposed that birds could quite literally 'see' the poles. As there was no human equivalent to this sense, it was impossible to provide an analogy in human terms – the notion of their vision being coloured, for example, might be perceived quite differently by the bird – so the phenomenon is described in the literature as 'quantum vision'. The group agreed to pursue its theoretical work, and called itself Erithacus, after the scientific name for the European robin, on which the early work into this sensory phenomenon had been carried out."

This was vaguely interesting. Mandi had heard of something similar. Wasn't that Iraqi-British guy who was always on the BBC involved?

Parallel to the heavyweight theoretical work on quantum vision, the Oxford Laboratory of Ornithology was working hard on the neural basis for song learning in birds. This research had taken an interesting direction around the Millennium when for the first time ultra-sensitive neural probes were developed that were able to map the higher vocal centres of a range of avian subjects. Initially this was done in the hope of learning something by inference about language development in humans, but took an unexpected turn when Dr Amelia Harp, a brilliant young avian biologist, developed a tiny subcutaneous implant that could be inserted in the bird's skull that could send information about neural activity remotely to a field researcher. For the first time, it was possible to study the brain activity of a large population of a particular species in the field.

Harp's device quickly became the standard tool of ornithological research. At the thirteenth International Ornithological Congress at Dartington Hall in Devon in May 2013...

Hold on. Dartington was up the road. Ten miles away, a little more?

...a chance meeting between Harp and members of the Erithacus group in the bar of the White Heart....

Yes, she had had a drink there, long time back, the only time she had met up with Anne and Bryan close to the camp, but it was the 'White Hart' not 'Heart'. How were you supposed to take these things seriously if they couldn't even get the simple facts right? Like most journalism. Sloppy. A crow landed nearby, staring at her askance.

... led to discussions about the theoretical possibilities of testing quantum vision in the field. Professor Bert Marley suggested an experiment with robins in the grounds of the estate. Might it be possible, he speculated, to use the implant to gain an understanding of the lived experience of robin's vision. 'To see through a robin's eyes', as he crudely put it.

Mandi wondered what it would be like to see herself through the crow's eyes, but when she looked up, it had gone.

What happened that spring day, when the first implant was injected into a robin's skull, became known as the now infamous 'Dartington Experiment'. Its actual results are unclear as subsequent documentation was almost instantly classified and those involved have refused to discuss its findings (some even deny that any such experiment ever took place), but fragments are known from a handful of courageous freelance and non-tenured researchers disturbed by what they believe may be the consequences of this work and who have subsequently and energetically, but with little success, sought to gain the attention of both the orthodox scientific world and then the online conspiracy communities.

What is known is that the original work produced considerably more information than was expected; the acres of redacted text on those few documents extracted by Freedom of Information requests have proved that beyond doubt. Jason Jenkinson, one of the leading conspiracy theorists of the 'Dartington Experiment', even claims that an analysis of the initial and now redacted data, and its subsequent visualisation in the informal research group's computer models, clearly demonstrated that the 23X156 (the ring number of the robin provided with the implant) was observing her observers. The irony of this was not lost on the theoretical physicists (at least those of the Copenhagen persuasion) in the group. What's more, the information visualised was not about surface matters such as shape and form, but rather 23X156 appeared to be sensitive to her observers' feelings and even thoughts. According to one unattributed source: 'we felt that very quickly we became caught up in a loop of the subject's own devising, of the bird's own devising'. According to Jenkinson, the small bird could sense potential aggression in a predator (human in this case); and while the data was less than unequivocal, before the experiments were halted the investigators believed that they could distinguish in the bird's responses descriptions of human nervousness, sexual desire, attention, covetousness, elation and jealousy. More than this, the tiny robin could transmit this information to others of their flock, and, when a second receiver/broadcaster was implanted, this information was understood... a useful adaptive advantage, no doubt, and not wholly unsurprising. Once this had occurred, the research subjects, according to gossip around colleagues of members of the Erithacus group, were almost uncontainable and prone to strategies that resisted data gathering. Jenkinson quotes one anonymous source: 'what all the fuss tells you is that the experiment failed, the data was useless and whatever the birds experienced... is for the birds'. However, what remains a mystery and seems to have turned upside down the worlds of those involved, was the key (apparent) finding that 23X156 could 'see' and transmit her observers' innermost desires.

Jenkinson claims the project then 'went dark' and has remained on ice ever since.

Mandi's concentration – though the article was nonsensical, there was metaphorical material there, she could see the potential pitch – was broken by the shadows of a group of herring gulls that had seemingly stationed themselves above her; riding the thermals so that they remained stationary in relation to the ground while barely moving their wings. Mandi wondered how they did that; but one avian mystery was enough...

The official accounts state that the Erithacus group disbanded in September 2013 having, according to the press release, 'reached the conclusion of its theoretical work'. Professor Marley, following a minor stroke, retired to a quiet life to follow his love of birdwatching, moving to Kingsbridge and becoming an active bird ringer and council member of the Devon Bird Preservation Society. Amelia Harp, tragically, died in 2015 in a cycling accident while in the Pyrenees, a promising career brutally cut short, according to police reports, by the driver of a vintage Citroen DS temporarily blinded by the sun on a sharp mountain bend.

Here we go.

Jenkinson, in his book 'The Dartington Experiment Revealed', which draws together arguments published on various websites with much greater biographical detail, accepts none of this. He claims that Marley, far from being retired, is through his work as a ringer still actively progressing the fieldwork for the Erithacus group; recruiting many unsuspecting bird enthusiasts to gather data for the project. And he claims that Harp was deliberately killed at the point when she was about to blow the whistle on the whole project at a conference in Nice.

Well, if Professor Marley is still active, he is active not far away in Kingsbridge, halfway between the Bay and Plymouth...

Readers get to the nub of 'The Dartington Experiment Revealed' in chapter seven of the book. Entitled 'Open Your Eyes', the account claims to reveal the true nature of the Erithacus group's work. Simply put, states Jenkinson, 'the Group discovered it was possible to use birds to spy on people's desires. And the information that could be collected had vast commercial value'. Birds, by chance, are the perfect vehicle for such mass observation; sophisticated communicators, expert navigators and mental cartographers, musical artists and having the imagination and empathy of poets. They are one of the most widespread taxonomical groups in the world, common on every continent. And they are humans' constant companion. 'Look out of your window' writes Jenkinson, ominously 'the chances are you will see a bird. And that bird, we now know, is seeing you and your desires, and relaying what it sees to The Company'."

O for...

Jenkinson is cautious in what he says about The Company. Sometimes the term is capitalised sometimes not; sometimes he seems to be describing a crypto-organisation, sometimes a general movement of opinion in public society. Critics on conspiracy theory discussion groups are cynical, with many suggesting that Jenkinson has no idea what the 'Company' or 'company' is, except that it might be good for his book sales; some suspect that the Erithacus group is 'The Company' and that Jenkinson has created ambiguity around its existence in order to sensationalise his story. Whatever, the questions of what remains of the experiment, who it was for and what it was for are left hanging.

The final, most wayward and – for the casual reader – most entertaining chapter of Jenkinson's book, 'Resistance is fertile', advocates a fight back against the bird watchers in our parks and gardens; a popular witch hunt against ornithological enthusiasts, obsessive twitchers and even those unsuspecting citizens who have a bird table in their garden or leave a few nuts on their windowsill in the winter. Just before Harp died, Jenkinson claims, she discovered that one group of birds, the seagulls, are both immune to the implants and act as 'jamming devices' for the transmission of data. In fact, these seagulls (predominantly herring gulls, but other gulls may be involved) actively fight with other birds to prevent such data being transmitted, generating a confusion that may, in evolutionary terms, give the gulls an advantage that allows them to thrive. Initially, comforted by this observation, Harp's complacency was rattled when she discovered that the robins' initial resistance to sharing their data *was not some instinctive or 'natural' protective reaction, but a 'bargaining' delay during which they were communicating with much larger data gathering groups and technologies and were now effectively operating as the eyes, ears and wings of the giant information tech companies. In desperation, Harp theorised that by encouraging the further spread of seagulls it might be possible for an effective resistance against this avian mass data gathering to emerge. She was intelligent enough to offer this to her employers much in the way that hackers offer their knowledge to security companies, but a friendly robin on Harp's bird table gave the game away and secured her fate!*

In his conclusion to 'The Dartington Experiment Revealed' Jenkinson pleads that we should all support the herring gulls in their war in the skies above us against all the other birds (although he gives no evidence to support his belief that this has spread beyond the robins). He points out that this is no easy task given the 'bad rap' that seagulls get generally, both in the media and among the public...

The gulls were gone. So lost in the storytelling had she become – and this was perhaps the point of this kind of pseudo-journalism (there was something to be made from this, the way it triggered some innate desire to join things up) – that she had failed to notice the departure of the very birds that it was, supposedly, all about. It was not just the gulls; lying back and taking in the giant blue dome of the morning she could see no birds at all. Up on her knees, no cormorants were evident diving among the waves, and the oystercatchers that had moved off towards the tip of the 'desert island' were now out of view. Not even a stray crow or a post-Christmas robin.

"'Why' he asks tantalizingly 'are there constant calls by local councils to cull seagulls? Why all those 'don't feed the gulls' signs? Why are the tabloids full of anti-gull rhetoric?' His answer: 'the company'..."

No caretaker and no sprayers either. How long had she been reading this rubbish? Long enough for the whole ecology of the dunes to change. Mandi tossed the magazine back onto the sands and sprinted off towards the end of the spit. The sprayers must have passed her on the beach or down on the other side close to the golf links. She found the caretaker circling what looked like a pile of flotsam and jetsam on the strandline, picked out against the holiday resort just the other side of the waters of the estuary. The wind was unburdened here and blew straight and cold; its thin squeal was the only sound. The grass, if there ever had been much, was gone from the 'desert island', an oyster shape of lightish, almost white, sand. The whole space was bleached by the unlimited sun. Mandi had to pick her way around the dried carcass of an Angler Fish, tins with faint Cyrillic text, and serpentine lengths of synthetic rope.

"What was the argument with the weedkiller people?"

He did not seem to understand. Mandi opened her mouth to ask him something else but forgot what it was. She looked around. The wind dropped. The cars moved about on the front across the water behind a concrete wall, like machines in a silent movie. No birds. Nothing. The world stood still. Waiting. She dare not open her mouth for fear that a great dark emptiness would be released. It was the most peculiar feeling she had ever felt.

"What are you trying to say?" she finally managed to force out. Staring at the pattern of chewed rubber ball, breezeblock, furniture legs, blue and orange ropes, tree stump, plastic tops and tampon applicator; she felt it would be an insult to poke at it with the toe of her trainer. But he had no more idea what she was talking about than before.

As if they could communicate better with silences, they both paused, jittery, and then they simultaneously turned and walked side by side up the dune path; silently they made their way over the bleached tree roots, the fenced paths, the exposed gabions, and then up through the unsettled dunes, until they found the route towards the entertainments and rides, the industrial estate-like shops and pub; passing the remnants of a long gone border of vegetables and flowers, surviving beneath the thin arms of an anomalous hawthorn bush. All without a word passing between the two of them; Mandi felt that although they did not speak, there was some element of understanding between the two of them, at least in the way that they harmoniously negotiated the slipping sands. Without referring to it or breaking stride, the caretaker shooed away a crow that had settled by the side of the discarded issue of Conspiracy Now! and elegantly scooped up its pages into his long-fingered fork-like hands, hurling it into the first waste bin on the concrete sea defences. Jammed in on top of a full complement of chip papers and Styrofoam punnets, the pages fell open at the avian conspiracy piece.

"That birds may be being used as information gathering devices in the service of a shadowy company, or maybe for the marketing departments of multinational companies, or as some data magnet for society in general, is, even in the work of conspiracy theories, ingenious and far-fetched. It is the outrageousness of the claim (and the general excitement and hilarity with which *The Dartington Experiment Revealed* has been greeted on all sides) that, Jenkinson states, is all that has saved him from the same fate as Harp. 'Like Cassandra' he writes in the closing paragraph to *The Dartington Experiment Revealed*, 'I am no doubt doomed to tell the truth that no-one will believe. And this is why I am allowed to live. A harmless nut, a crank, worse than Icke and his like. But all I ask is that you are wary of those apparently friendly feathered creatures that crowd your bird tables and twitter above your streets for they are traders in the currency of your innermost desires'."

Far back, at the end of the dunes, the choppy waters were making their way up towards the strandline, nibbling at the oddly arranged pattern of plastic detritus and driftwood that Mandi was sure the caretaker had been arranging into some meaningful shape when she surprised him. Although he had not responded to her question, and she had fallen into one of her blanknesses for want of a follow up, she had thought she could make some sense of the combination of natural and synthetic objects, the arrangement of organic curls with metallic joints. Now, the encroaching tide was eradicating any hint of meaning that might have been there. At the other end of the long spit, Mandi and the caretaker walked side by side, unspeaking, passing the occasional dog walker, and a young couple hanging on each other's arms. High above them, a little back and to their right, a monstrous flock of something was murmurating, swinging, somersaulting, flapping like a sheet of frost-bitten skin, then bunching and exploding, pausing, rounding off at the corners, and the whole thing, impossibly, shifting instantly sideways a quarter of a mile.

That night, embedded among images of black triangular and disc-like craft, a short video of fuzzy white aliens was uploaded to the website of Tony 'The Summoner' Sumner-Crabbe.

Chapter 9

The next few of Mandi's days were taken up with chores and paperwork of a kind that twisted her unhappily tight. She had hoped the caretaker might ferry her about, but he claimed to always be busy, which meant she had to rely on lifts from the folk in the camp. She was conveyed in vehicles of varying eccentricity and only a tangential complicity with Newtonian mechanics; in company that meandered across a continuum of infuriating incoherence. These voyages of madness were punctuated by refrigerated conversations in staid back offices about lilies, coffins, death certificates, death taxes, deeds, tenancy agreements, sewerage systems, maintenance protocols, seating arrangements and per head catering options.

On the end of the third day Mandi retired to her adoptive parents' home with cans of Polish beer (incredibly cheap at the grocery store), a box set of Fellini films she had found in a charity shop and a box of pizza. Mourning was a physical disaster, but a cultural boon; like jilting for songwriters. Sadly, shortly after gobbling a first slice of Margherita, popping the ring pull and sinking into the opening credits of 'La Dolce Vita', Mandi was fast asleep and missed Christ flying over Rome, suspended from a helicopter, and Anita Ekberg cavorting in the fountain in that dress. By then Mandi was drinking at a darker fountain, her teeth cracking against its stern tap, cold water burning her throat. Reeling from the fountain, it was like every other public drinking facility she ever came across; dry and jammed with marbled cigarette ends.

When the miserable light of morning finally penetrated her eyelids, Mandi dragged herself out of the waste of sleep and got to work on herself. She scrubbed the night away. Put on new clothes. For no reason she marched out of the camp, under the Creep and headed for the dunes. She wanted to stand on the waste land at the edge of the estuary; surely there was a purity there that could freeze out this ritual of adaptation and boredom she had been shovelled into? Snap the whole thing.

It was a thin day. An apologetic sun dribbled through the haze. Marram grass swung unengaged. The day was off its hinges, there was no way of getting leverage on anything. Each of the slippery grains of sand under Mandi's feet was in a world of its own; one moment she was slipping backwards, pitching forwards the next. The Sett was out of true; the only thing standing in for its centre was the caretaker. His figure, all in black again, picked out like an inverted exclamation mark against the horizon. He seemed to be watching for something; somewhere off the end of the sand spit there was a playing in the water. Multiple splashes too far apart to be a single animal. Wasn't it too cold for a pod of dolphins?

Mandi had asked around about the caretaker. Most of the camp residents assumed he was an ordinary handyman, moving from job to job, but others had talked to him at more length. The details varied slightly, but Mandi had built up a picture of a retired academic who had severed family ties and set off on a pilgrimage of self-discovery only to founder in the first few miles with the discovery of a medical condition; he was a biological time bomb and had chosen to give up the grand voyage and instead spend his last weeks or months doing simple tasks around Lost Horizon. The general impression was that he had got to know Anne and Bryan rather better than anyone else; though, generally, the residents were disturbingly vague about anything to do with her parents. Mandi could not work out the balance between how much her parents had kept themselves apart from the community and how much they were effectively leaders of it. After Cassandra's sudden visit, she had gone back to the soothsayer's book-swamped home, but the magic had gone out of her; she did not want to talk and Mimir had hovered threateningly, as though he thought Cassandra had already gone too far. When Mandi broached the issue with other residents, even the older ones, they either feigned incomprehension or deafness, claiming not to have lived here at the time or put it all down to pagan infighting, without specifying what 'it all' had been.

The caretaker bent his monochrome figure down to the dog-eared sands, the gusty wind blowing up a stinging cloak around his stooping. Moving between frozen stances, as if playing a game of statues. With who? Mandi crept through the grass. The sun tinged the grey clouds a half-hearted yellow. Reaching the brim of the highest dunes, Mandi could see how the caretaker was bent over something in the sands; he shifted slightly as if viewing it from a different angle, an artist in a studio at work on a painting. Mandi had seen this kind of behaviour at private views; piss poor painters disguising their paucity of product behind the smokescreen of performance. The caretaker was clearly satisfied with his efforts, for he clapped his hands and turned abruptly back towards the camp, though not before making an odd bowing motion to the sea.

Mandi waited until the caretaker was out of sight and then slithered down to the beach. She followed the caretaker's footprints; that was hardly necessary. On the strandline was another large circular assemblage of objects: chewed rubber ball, breezeblock covered with barnacles, furniture legs, orange and blue ropes, tree stump, plastic bottle tops and tampon applicator, woven into various rubbery seaweeds. The construction looked similar to the one she had seen previously on the beach; not exactly so but approximately the same materials. The tide had been in and out numerous times since then, it could not have left these same things undisturbed. There was a hand in this and

Mandi thought it must be the caretaker's. But what did he mean by it? The first construction she had seen had 'spoken to her', but in the irritatingly and conveniently vague way that mystical things did; suggestive of snake oil and publishing opportunities, coffee table books and crop circle calendars. This latest aureole was far more discreet.

Mandi was about to kick the thing apart and chase after the caretaker, when she became aware of two things. Firstly, that whatever it was that was playing out there beyond the spit, white horses on sandbanks or whatever, was having a paroxysm; secondly, and less explainable, that the caretaker was standing directly behind her. Without turning she tried to picture him there; she knew he was. All that would come to her was his black silhouette, faceless, his features hidden inside his hood, his hands gloved, his coat zipped up to the bottom of his invisible chin. Yes, even a slight glint around the eyes, as if he were wearing goggles. The impulse to kick away the assemblage in the sands shrivelled in her thigh. The waves around the spit raved. She clenched her fists and turned.

Mandi tried to speak, but when she opened her lips she felt darkness on her tongue and an emptiness in her throat out of which nothing could come. A huge and winged something passed over the waters behind her. Though she knew the wind was seething, she could hear nothing of it. Time was a pocket watch wrapped in cotton wool, space put away in a lead-lined box. Nothing radiated, light stood still. Her mouth aged aeons; cities were raised and fell in the ruins of her gums. It was ridiculous; that she, Mandi, presented with any situation, no matter how trivial or absurd, would have, could have, nothing to say. Opinion was a dried angler fish skin.

In place of words, Mandi and the caretaker held each other's gazes, in the soft hands of professional controversialists. Professors of their own grounds, the theoretical carpets pulled from beneath their feet. The sands making new dunes around their boots. The caretaker was not a pillar of darkness, sat up on the rim of the dunes, his hood was back and the wind mussed his bristling white curls, the watery sunlight bouncing in his sad blue eyes. Pain played around his lips; he seemed more hunched than before, as if the strings that held him together were tightening inside. Mandi wanted to speak words of reproach, but they would not come; then words of sympathy, but she had none of those either. Instead, they both looked, in blinding comprehension, at each other; one at the other's troubled waiting, the other at an impatient wanting to know.

The caretaker was the first to move; turning back towards the camp end of the dunes. Mandi chased after him and caught up. Her stumbling run released words; the angel passed and they came tumbling, embarrassingly, out of her.

"You, you, you, I thought you, what were you, what is that? It was here before? That can't be. They told me, the people in the end trailer, you were professor of... why did you leave? Is something going to happen? To you? Why do I care this much, is it because you knew Anne and Bryan better than any of their.... what are they? Why are you here?"

In answer, the caretaker stopped and looked out across the flattening sea. She followed his gaze.

"What am I supposed to be seeing?"

"My purpose. Did they tell you that I am ill?"

"They... implied as much. They dropped their eyes."

"Cowards... you would call them... what?"

"Snowflakes."

"You know that's a racist term? But that would make me a 'snowflake'?"

"Correct. Or not necessarily. Go on."

He laughed. "Can I be honest with you?"

"No, probably not, but you are going to try anyway."

"I want to carry on here. I have something to finish, until it finishes me. I don't think you'll find a more conscientious caretaker than me. I never forgot the skills I learned when I was younger; I was an electrician's apprentice before I got caught in the jaws of the thinking establishment. Fixing dull things has always been my way of staying sane at weekends. That and a good wife; when she died I lost interest in thinking, I just wanted to use my hands, listen to what was inside, under all the chattering ideas. You think that's laughable?"

"How would I know? I'm not you."

"No, you're not me, but you can ruin my last few... months, by getting rid of me. I need the physical structure this job gives me."

"I don't see any structure. You seem to be on the dunes most of the time."

"Do you see anything in the camp not up to standard, not working, not fixed or up to speed?"

"That pile of flags and crap by the holiday trailers."

"Ah, that was Bryan. But I can clear it away if you want me to."

"Yeh. Do it."

"Bryan didn't want anyone going in there..."

"Look, Mister Crabbe. Professor Crabbe..."

"Ha! Yes, attack the enemy where it thinks it is strongest!"

"Was something going on with my Mum and Dad? Something that happened in the past that came back to haunt them? Did anyone tell you anything? Because they sure as hell won't tell me."

"I'll tell you what I know. Which is almost nothing. Yes, something happened, twenty years ago, around then. Everyone in Lost Horizon knows about it, but they don't really know what it was, or what it is. Some of them like to come on as if they know, but if you ask them, they don't. I've tested them; they know nothing."

"Do you?"

"No. I only know how much they don't know. I feel that gap, Amanda, and it's big. I've a sense of the shape of what they're not able to explain. That's all."

"Which is?"

"Something that threatens them all. Something that's still... live. At least for them. But what it is exactly, I have no idea. There's nothing online about it. I know that they don't like it, and they don't like not liking it, and they don't like... it not liking them."

"It?"

"I can't tell you that."

"Can't or won't."

"Even if I could, maybe I shouldn't, maybe if there is anything to it you should find it out for yourself, in your own way. Or leave it alone. From the way the residents react to you, I think you're the one who could find it out."

"Are you flattering me into minding my own business?"

"You would have made a difficult student!"

He gestured to the mess of objects in the sand.

"Those things are not mine. But I would ask you to respect them, and not disturb them. If you find one, let me know."

"Is there someone else on the Sett who is making them?"

"Not in the way you mean."

"They're from the sea?"

"That's all that's left, then. If it's not me, not someone else. It's from the sea."

The waters had calmed. The froth of a thrashing shoal, or whatever it was, gone. Only the lapping of gentle waves on the shore to suggest how high the winds had been. Though Mandi well knew that not so far away were Channel Islands and then the coast of France, the long unpunctured horizon might just as well have been the edge of the world.

"Not the birds, then?" she chirped brightly.

"Not the birds", he replied darkly.

Mandi glanced up. A group of curlews were buffeted back and forward by competing winds, like the scatter of a handful of leaves. When she looked down, the curlews resumed a gird formation; the back and forth of conversation between Mandi and the caretaker echoed in subtle ripples through their holding pattern.

The two unlikely companions passed under the Creep. The slides and rides, dodgems and crazy golf were frozen under winter tarps. Sparks from welding torches jumped, over-bright, across the roofs of the redundant railway carriages, stopped forever in their amputated sidings; holiday homes for the only just connected grandchildren of railway workers and a few train spotters who relished the discomfort. The entrance board at Lost Horizon showed a cloud-wreathed hill with a dark cave halfway up its green slope. That was not how Mandi had seen it on her first night back.

"Do you think my Mum and Dad were really pagans?"

The caretaker stopped and kicked at the water in a pothole.

"I think most of the folk around here are at playing at it. To them it's a lifestyle or a business. That's not how they regard themselves, of course, but that's how they look to my untutored but professionally analytical eye. If a person were truly a magician, would they make a fuss about it? Or would they keep their secrets secret?"

Mandi looked along the line of empty holiday trailers. If their magic were real, where was it hidden?

"You are a professor?"

"I was."

"Ever heard of Lovecraft?"

"On the camp?"

"No. Not unless... no, no, someone in history, someone who would have written something. Old writing."

"How old."

"Flowery. Victorian, maybe."

"Only ever heard of one Lovecraft like that... the only Lovecraft who was a writer, as far as I know, this is not my specialism, was H. P. Lovecraft."

"Who was?"

"Like I said, I'm not a specialist. He was a pulp horror writer, but with a very odd, constipated, rather eerie style..."

"Yeh, that's the one I thought of. But he's like... he's famous, isn't he? I've never read him, but I've hear people talking about him. Celeb intellectuals, gloomy geophilosophy types, they seem to rate him. Do you know his writing?"

"No, it's just one of those things one knows, without having any reason to."

"That's right. But he's really famous, right? An original manuscript of one of his... whatever..."

"Stories?"

"Maybe. That would be worth... maybe a lot?"

"Mandi, I don't know what you've found, but if you're worried about putting money into the camp, stop. If this place is storm insured then you're going to be fine..."

He shrugged and turned away, limping along the uneven track back towards the permanent camp. Becoming a black silhouette.

"What did they tell you?" she shouted after him.

Without turning again, he threw up his arms in a gross gesture of despair; a diamond of crows broke above him and scattered to the trees.

Chapter 10

A lot of things happened in quick succession. Like a bowling strike when one careening skittle takes down the rest one by one. The caretaker spoke to Cassandra and she was sceptical, so Cassandra passed him over to Mimir and Mimir was credulous and excited and got straight on his mobile to The Old Mortality Club who were presently squatting (they preferred 'house-sitting') the Italian Gardens outside one of the small villages in the flatlands close to the Great Hill.

"You're crazy", Cassandra told Mimir, "hooking up a young girl with that thing?"

"She's not a girl, you're thinking of her as when... she obviously knows how to take care of herself now."

"She'll need to. She may need some help."

And Cassandra began to gather together the instruments: a rattle, rhythm stick and bell. She crumbled flakes of a material she had collected long ago. Put a flame to them. The rising wave of nausea told Cassandra that she was in the fug of effectiveness. Mimir went for a walk. The caretaker had long before made his excuses and gone. The smoky trailer shook to the fury of the stricken sorceress, slamming her reinforced boot into the floor to the beat of a cloud inside her head, for she knew that her husband had sprinkled water at the foot of the vine, that sap would be pulsing through the gardens, buds opening and vines suddenly tugging harder to the mortar of the rockeries, baths and altars. Leafy priests would already be shuffling on their petal-robes and processing from their branches, fountains gushing and sluices releasing hot water across yellowy Cotswold stone, adding to the frothing of the crude plunge pools. Steam would gather and then, as if finding its self-confidence, march out across the vats and terraces of the encroached structure; as though a low budget horror movie were being shot in a cloth-eared neoclassical garden. Eras and sensibilities would wrap themselves around each other and it would be far from clear who was fertiliser and who was perpetrator and who would be present to care.

A taxi rolled up at the gates. Mandi paid the fare, stepped out, and the private hire shifted hurriedly away. She felt strangely nervous and clutched the manila envelope to her belly.

She looked about her. Though she had been hemmed in by high Devon hedges, she had sensed the expanse of fields and hills beyond, a single giant button of green rising and predominating. It must still be there, all around her; but the house was different. There was no certainty there, despite its size and refined splendour. An old handpainted sign had been screwed to the front porch: THE OLD MORTALITY CLUB. The sign seemed out of place to Mandi; there was something about its gothy retro-crudeness that clashed with the Italianate elegance of the portico. She rang the bell and nothing sounded. She rang again; again, nothing. She pushed at the door and it resisted. She hammered on the door and no one came. Mimir had been very insistent that they were "the real deal", but maybe the real deal had moved on to more suitable premises. From what she gathered from Mimir, it was unclear if the Club were squatting crusties or a nomadic version of The Groucho Club. When it came to issues of clarity around space and time, Mimir seemed to move according to the multi-dimensional timetable of a personal Valhalla.

Mandi began to skirt the high wall that encased the property, looking for a gate or gap. The dull beige wall seemed to pulse very slightly. From beyond the wall came the sounds of many voices raised in chaotic togetherness; not a chant but a cacophony, identifiably individual and yet somehow collectively excited. It sounded less than authentic; more like a tape recording of a 1950s cocktail party than directly from voices and bodies. Something giant splashed in water. No wonder no one could hear her knocking. The jouissant cries, more in extreme pleasure than pain, were accompanied by strange music; as if a trio of penny whistle, washing machine and synthesiser had been booked for the gig by mistake. Something thumped out a bass line; a reedy high-pitched line worked its way around harmonies with a mechanical whirr. Mandi preferred R&B.

"Come in! You are expected!"

Long silvered blonde locks fell from the cranium of a head and shoulders leaning out of the plane of the wall. Its face was wrinkled in smiles, eyes twinkling with mischief and excitement, its broad nose volcanic with pimples.

"Grant Kentish?"

"No!" and the figure leaned further out exposing a long, wrinkled neck and the generous cups of a cage bra. "I am one of his playthings! Hahahaha!"

Mandi was not playing along with this. She knew the signs of an ambush better than anyone.

"I have an appointment to meet with Dr. Kentish. He is expecting me. I have come about a manuscript."

"O, my dear, come on in! Of course he is, of course he is."

And she stepped out from the Romanesque-shaped wooden doorframe; a sarong in exploding turquoise knotted above a thin and tightly contoured thigh exposed by the lift of the material. Mandi was trying to fight off images of what this elder got up to keeping in this kind of trim. Her body seemed to amplify the sound as squeals and splashes mixed with the odd accompaniment of mechanical music surged through the doorway. The woman held out a freckled arm in a gesture of melodramatic welcome.

"I'd expected..."

"Don't expect, my dear, allow. You will get the answers you have come for. Everyone does." And she stepped back to allow Mandi to pass through the wall. Well, Mandi said to herself, you are for sure not in Kansas anymore; as the steam enveloped her and a fluted glass filled with a sticky-looking greenish liqueur was pressed into her hand. It smelt sweet. The steam was rising from a set of crude pools and plunge baths, their stone pillars draped with tarpaulin roofs, fed with hot water from long, thick plastic tubes; a generator throbbed nearby and in the haze Mandi could make out a small music group on a platform, its caped and long-haired Eno-clones playing, respectively, pan pipes, a laundry dryer, which its operator intermittently turned on and off, and synth keyboards. All around the stone lips of the pools, along low walls and across a stone pavilion, were draped ageing and barely clad bodies, mostly entwined in the limbs and words of others. There was something unnaturally generous in the way that the semi-naked figures, clustered beneath painfully orange heaters, paid attention to each other; as if joined in some ritual of mutual hypnotism. No one looked at another person like that in London, not even a forbidden lover.

"I'd expected..."

But the Romanesque door was shut and the woman in the sarong gone. Mandi was tempted to leave immediately. The whole thing was a put up, a test of her determination and interest; Kentish was an operator, clearly. He knew how to deal, how to unsettle a client, how to rattle the pupil before enforcing his scholarship; she wanted something from him, but he wanted a cut from her. She had checked him out online. Other than some jealous grumbling, he was extremely well regarded by academics in the field; a rare fruit, an autodidact who could hold his own with professional academics. The only voice Mandi found raised against him was that of a Tony 'The Summoner', a filmmaker and 'researcher' who had got it into his head that there was a black flying saucer, back engineered by Nazis, buried beneath the church at West Ogwell, a few miles South-East of the Old Mortality Club's HQ. Kentish's scepticism about The Summoner's theory and The Summoner's fury back both recommended Kentish to Mandi. A familiar figure at both Mind Body and Spirit fairs and university literature seminars, his specialism – American horror literature – had gathered him an doctorate by publication from a non-Ivy League but respected American university. He had not needed to buy his qualifications. So, why this charade?

Mandi found a stone jar, decorated with an impish face, into which to tip her poisonous liqueur. She looked around to check that she had not been noticed; the middle-aged revellers were too absorbed in the examination of each other's wrinkled tans to be concerned with her embarrassment. However, on a small granite pillar, a tiny wren stood at attention, regarding her in the range of its embracing gaze. The fluted glass was snatched from her hand by a passing young woman; the wren flew off and Mandi lost sight of bird and woman in the fresh billows of steam, while the plastic piping roared out even thicker streams of hot water.

The woman in the sarong reappeared from the steamy haze and beckoned to Mandi to follow her through the reclining middle-aged horde, toward a set of steps that rose alongside a miniaturised castle structure; there was a feeling of very old faked antiquity about the place. A lingering atmosphere of former figment and pretence that had become historic; and these pensioners were playing out some nostalgic, half-baked Roman version of it. Bargain-basement Pasolini. Mandi felt a little queasy; pleased that she could barely make out what it was that was being served on platters, or what it was of the bodies that entered and what it was that was entered. The pornographic muchness blurred into itself, swallowed in its own pools and miasmas. At the top of the steps, leaning on the yellowing concrete of the diminutive fake fortification, a silhouetted figure was sharpening into focus, colours emerging from the background of bright winter sunlight, a large thick weave coat hung about considerable shoulders, a mane of black hair under a jaunty grey top hat, a tweed waistcoat and high black boots. The figure turned on its heels and walked out of sight.

As she climbed the stone staircase, Mandi was aware for the first time of the ruin of the architecture; where there should be a door was a gash, where would once have been vines plunging, now masses of ivy hung shaggily. Every surface was covered with velveteen mosses or promiscuous lichens; orange, yellow and red.

The woman in the sarong abruptly, but gently took Mandi by the elbow and steered her through an archway, pierced by the trunk, thick as a fist, of a silvery-barked sapling, skeletal for winter, the masonry pieces gaping. Beyond the leaning arch the grounds flattened out and in the distance, framed by giant beeches, was the main house, stood upon its arches, its design hung somewhere between mansion and working mill. Its bow windows and elegant Georgian gables could not disguise the industrial crudeness of its massing. Mandi knew nothing about architecture or history, but she could smell nouveau-riche a mile off, even in fossil form. The flat plain of the lawn ran out and a path beneath a pergola, some trailing shrivelled plant cringing to it in the wind, was overshadowed by the beeches that stood protectively about the main building. A door at the back of the house was open and the woman in the sarong, shivering now, her arms visibly raised in goosebumps, left Mandi and ran wildly back to the party. Mandi was surprised to see the little muscles at the bottom of the hairs on the backs of both her own hands were standing up; she did not feel cold, and yet something ran through her, a chill inside rather than outside. The wrongness of the house, the unfriendly welcome, the sensual aggression of the party; Mandi did not like admitting it to herself, but she was a little scared and that pissed her off. In London this sort of crap was two a penny.

"If someone doesn't come and get me, I am going home!" she shouted through the open back door.

A broad, worried face, swathed in the black mane Mandi had seen on the steps, appeared at a window on the first floor and mouthed some words which might have been "stay there" or "go away". The face disappeared and Mandi stood, shifting from one foot to other, uncertain where she stood in relation to fear and fury.

"I am so sorry, you must be... what are you doing down there? Did Saraswati leave you there? I do apologise! Come around to the front of the house and I will let you in!"

The head withdrew and the sash window lowered. Mandi, reluctantly, followed his instructions. The house was a Janus. There was none of the industrial crudeness evident in the splendour of the main facade, its parts in symmetrical proportion with each other, its ornaments restrained; the pretence was wildly effective. Mandi felt as though she had arrived somewhere deeply perverse; the balance and adherence to rules out of place between the saturnalian gardens and the darkness of the sentinel trees. The scarlet door, beneath the curve of a Romanesque ornament, fell back and Grant Kentish stepped out, his left hand jutted forward in greeting, his right swathed in bandages.

"Pardon the acid burns of dissolution; the artist must suffer for his craft!"

He waved his bandages.

"Come in."

The house was a shell. As they climbed the staircase, Mandi's and Kentish's footsteps echoed down empty corridors, peeped around the corners of doors into bare rooms and echoed again there. The wallpaper had been stripped, ready for redecoration; flecks of sixties orange sat proud of dull welfare state designs and the arsenic greens of what might have been William Morris. Paint hung down in sheets from the high ceiling. Two flights up, Kentish veered off along an equally tattered corridor and waved Mandi into a small room; it was from here, she assumed, that Kentish had shouted to her. It was a stage set; like one of those ever-so-fashionable immersive theatre experiences she had been to, where they made your wear a mask, where no one knows what is going on nor where to go, and every now and then you fall upon an insanely detailed room filled with junk shop bric-a-brac gathered by underpaid designers and interns. Such was Kentish's study, or the stage set of Kentish's study. She was impressed, as she ran her eyes over the spines of a shelf of volumes, that they were all alien to her. She had expected something similar to the products on display at Mimir and Cassandra's 'publishing house', but these were something else; leather bound, smelling of vellum and rosin, their arcane titles, silvery or golden at the tops of their spines, and the exotic names that the authors, she presumed, had mostly chosen for themselves, signified the occupants and creeds of a monstrous fake city, a spectral cyclopean metropolis of half-baked fears and ignorances, poetic stupidities and endless liturgies, where no one had raised a family, but millions had lost their senses at some time or another. Here was a pathological culture as empty as the house. Sat before her, in a generously upholstered armchair, a Bakelite operation equipped with whisky glass, note pad and pencil strapped to one of its arms, was this fake city's expert. Tour guide to its mind.

Mandi ran her palms along the arms of her chair; trying to stop herself sinking too deeply into its soft interior.

"I hope you were not offended by our little party? We have been studying hard these past weeks; every now and then the workers of the soul deserve to lose their minds and give something back to their bodies."

"What is the nature of your Club, then?"

"Ah, the Club! Yes. I'm glad you asked. One has a bad habit of assuming everyone knows. No reason why you should, my dear, no reason at all!"

And he levered himself up from the armchair and, dapper and lizard like, skipped to a small flower-shaped table crowded with decanters.

"Brandy, whisky, whatever you like?"

"I'm fine."

"Fine is not enough here, Amanda. I know who you are and to know you better, it will help if you could show me a little more. I like a whisky at this time in the afternoon. I'd be flattered, but you would be educated, if you joined me?"

He patted his right knee in a gesture that Mandi did not recognise; though it might have been done in pain.

"Very well. But just a little water, just enough to taste."

"To taste. Good." He poured two fingers of Black Label into a tumbler and added a quarter inch of water from a goat-shaped glass jug. "Moderation in all things." He laughed as he handed her the glass.

"But YOU..." he almost yelled as he lowered himself back into the armchair, his whisky glass now filled as high as Mandi's – when did he do that? Stupid tricks, she thought – "are not moderate; you have ambitions and that manuscript that is burning in your hands, you imagine is what? A passport to riches? A cash cow?"

"I have an obligation to my parents' estate..."

"O, yes, your parents. Interesting people, Bryan and Anne. I wish I had known them better. Everybody does... wish that. What a mystery they were; of course, miserable people like to say that they kept themselves that way to make it appear as though they were interesting. But what if they really were? What if they were playing a game of double bluff? Why would they do that?"

It took Mandi a moment to realise that his question was not rhetorical; that Kentish was fishing for an answer.

"I'd like you to understand, Mister Kentish..."

"Grant, please."

"Grant... that my parents were important to me, but not close. I was adopted."

Kentish did not react; Mandi could not tell if he already knew or not.

"Nevertheless, I want to do as they would have wished me to. I don't understand why, but they..."

"Bequeathed?"

"I suppose so... they must have had a reason to leave this particular manuscript with all their other papers, somewhere they had told me specifically to look if they ever died."

"They told you that? Where to look if they ever died?"

"Yes."

Kentish raised his tumbler in a toasting gesture and then swilled down the contents. As he did so his long black locks fell back and Mandi thought she saw hints of grey at the roots. His top hat hung on a tall stand behind his chair, as though there were two Kentishes in the room; the one overseeing the behaviour of the other. The bareheaded one tapped at the Bakelite tray with his glass.

"And you think you have something written by H. P. Lovecraft? The American weird fiction writer, right? Don't you think that's a little unlikely? Here in Devon?"

"Mimir told me you were less surprised than he expected; that you were anxious to meet with me. He said "anxious"; I'm sure that was the word he used."

"Simple explanation, Amanda," and a young expression lit up his weathered face. His knotted hands unwound themselves and he straightened. "This is Lovecraft country. Prior to their emigration to the United States in the first half of the nineteenth century, HPL's great grandparents, and their ancestors before them, lived in a few villages within ten miles of this spot. Rarely moved beyond them, I imagine. But that was a long time before HPL was publishing; his Devon family died out long before he wrote a word, there's no evidence that he ever came to England, so whatever you have would have travelled if it's a genuine Lovecraft story. Have you read it? What do you make of it?"

"I skimmed it."

"You can't skim Lovecraft; his prose doesn't allow it. You might as well chug Château Montrose."

"Quite. Why don't you read it?"

She held the envelope towards him, but he stiffened in his chair and his arms fell down by his sides, hidden in the recesses of the upholstery, a flap of bandage trailed over a knee.

"Let's make a bargain. Why don't you read the story to me and I will give you my opinion? Could you do that?"

"Sure, it's a bit, flowery... but it's not complicated..."

"Then it's unlikely to be Lovecraft, but we won't know until we hear it."

"You'll be able to tell just by listening?"

"If it's an existing story of his then I will know instantly. If you have found an original and previously unknown manuscript of probably the most distinctive horror writer of all time, then it will be hard, let's say, not to have my suspicions. But let me warn you; over the years HPL has had many imitators and multiple homage-tales have been written in his style. Having said that, there is always something lacking in them, unpossessed of themselves; I think we will know one way or the other. Let's hear it."

Satisfied, he leaned back in his chair; his tumbler filled once more. Mandi took a quick sip from hers and opened the manila envelope, carefully revealing the pages inside.

"Hold them up!"

She held them up, the first page of words turned to Kentish. He did not strain forward, but seemed to cringe.

"Typed, hmmm? That's not any typewriter that was around when HPL was writing. I can tell that immediately. However, proceed; who knows by what route an original story might have reached us?"

He seemed relieved when Mandi rested the pages on her knees; a confused smile spreading across his lips as she cleared her throat. She sipped again and began to read.

That traces of an antediluvian civilisation with its attendant flora and fauna can be so readily found in the obscure lanes, fields and woodlands of this part of Devonshire has long been known to the coarse laborers that dwell in this lugubrious place. That this foetid and extinct civilization should, through blasphemous dreams, still cast its influence, however, has been the ruin of my family and the reason we are soon to leave these shores for ever with neither prospect nor hope of return....

"That's not unlike the voice of HPL. More interestingly, for you perhaps, I can you tell right now, that this is not from any of the existing known writings of Howard Phillips Lovecraft. Proceed."

> *I am a master carpenter, worsted spinner and chapman. I was born in 1775. I am married to Mary Full and the good lord has blessed us with six middling and honest children....*

"HPL writes in other voices, he's not fond of neutral narration."

> *We are currently staying in B--------, a small but adequate hamlet a few miles to the north of A-------. As I write this, there is much unrest in the countryside hereabouts, with pressing talk of riots in Newton Abbot.*

"Ten miles away? If that?"

> *The spirit of progress as represented in the threshing machines which have done much to improve agricultural production and profit is causing much anger amongst the more brute and uneducated of the rustic workers. In their pisky-led idleness they claim hardship, and demand of their honest landlords food, money and beer. However, this is of little import to my current situation and the bankruptcy proceedings of which I now must give honest and truthful account...*

"How often are money troubles a portal to the supernatural? The same with poetry. Carry on. I won't interrupt you again. Except to say... no, carry on!"

> *... 'truthful'... ...er...*

> *It is my hope that those that read these words will not judge my failings harshly, for they are the failings of an honest man defeated by circumstance and misfortune, but by those unspeakable things that are neither good nor real. What has befallen myself and my family started two winters ago. I was surveying land near T-------, (a mile or so from our then residence at P------) for fallen oaks from which I might, for a few shillings, obtain timber for the making of barrels, a hard but satisfying line of work for which I always have customers. A local landowner told me that recent winds had caused two large oaks to fall across a woodland track. These were causing him much nuisance and he said he would gladly donate the timber in return for their removal. He described them as being near 'The Old Grotto' and pointed the way along a wooded slope towards the distant church at T-----.*

Kentish shifted violently in his seat. "Carry on!"

"I picked my way carefully through the woods, following the track bordered on one side by a crude stone wall and on the other by a low limestone ridge. A cold north wind shook the trees, at times I would swear on any book good enough for a church that I heard a choir singing and some wooden instruments for accompaniment, and I saw rain approaching from the direction of the imposing mound of the Hill feared by the foolish. Above me, a little way up the slope, was a shallow cliff face with a gentle but decent overhang. This I imagined fondly would provide relief. After picking my way through a few troublesome brambles and over a beam or two some cautious soul had placed there some years before across an entrance, I crouched below the rocks as the rain arrived, safe in the natural bowl that I believed providence had provided. Somewhat exhausted by both the walk and some recent sleepless nights on account of baby Mary's puzzling restlessness, I closed my eyes, allowing myself, wrapped as I was in warm clothing, the hard-earned extravagance of a little sleep as the rain set in.

Kentish whispered something under his breath. To Mandi it sounded like "Don't, man!", but whether he was talking to the character in the story or to himself, she could not tell.

I know not how long I was there, maybe it were half an hour, maybe it were longer, but when I opened my eyes the rain had passed leaving the trees dripping and rivulets of water running down the limestone. Steadying myself on the rock I pulled myself up. As I did, something scuttled along the ground away from me. The speed at which it moved momentarily shocked me, as one might be surprised by the sudden and unnatural acceleration of a wolf spider. What possessed me I do not know, and Lord I now wish I had not, but something pressed on me to follow this obscure thing.

Its direction took me along the base of the cliff towards a pile of stones leading upwards to a small and nigh-perfectly round hole in the arching limestone through which I could see the trees beyond. The hole was just about large enough to walk through while crouching. On the other side, my eyes were drawn in fascination and honest enquiry to a second rocky outcrop. And, propitiously and appropriately given my days' task, I drew close to two large fallen oaks lying over a track beneath. Perhaps, I remember thinking in good faith, the scuttling creature was pointing me in the right direction.

A second movement. This time more distant, but no less distinct than afore. First a rustling on the ground through the leaves then, to my great horror, a shape moving across the sheer face of the outcrop. It was there for no more than a moment, disappearing rapidly into a crevice. Its form, I immediately thought, suggested a firebrat or silverfish, but it was in a scale and of a dimension the like of which I never saw. I shivered and my hair stood up tall from my skin. My curiosity, unsavoury and appetitious, outweighed my growing sense of ingenuous unease and I made my way to the abyss wherein the creature had disappeared.

A sharp slap of rain burst upon the window pane. Mandi jumped, but Kentish seemed not to hear it. The room had darkened, but she had not noticed until now; the sounds of the party, squeals and musical entertainment, had all but been replaced by the dull thuds of heavy rain. Mandi hardly dared to glance up from the page, so fiercely did Kentish seemed rapt by the tale, but she chanced a glance and was shocked by the wall of furious purple cumulus that was boiling above the beeches. She jerked back to the page.

Stepping carefully over the two fallen trees, I made my way along the cliff face wherein the creature had, I imagined, concealed itself. Dropping a little, and rounding a promontory I was greeted by the prospect far below me of a short channel cut into the floor of the forest, some fifteen or so yards long and six yards wide, preamble to the mouth of a cavern. The channel was supported on both sides by a crude stone wall and at its entrance I noted some obscure arrangements of stones laid, I thought deliberately to form a foundation or floor. It was, however, the dark mouth of the cavern that drew most powerfully both my eye and my attention. This was the nest to which the creature was retreating on catching a sight of me.

I lowered myself down the slope and stood on the clumsy stone mosaic. The channel, from my new position, suggested the remains now of an ancient building. This must be 'The Old Grotto' I thought, remembering the farmer's words, and played for a moment with an intellectual reconstruction of the building, here a door, above a simple roof and to the back the entrance to the cavern. An old hermitage perhaps, I had heard tales of these eremitic lives and they held some appeal, as befitting any man in a household of six children.

The storm outside had turned fierce; whatever music had played around the plunge pools, only the winds howled there now; the tops of the beeches raced and shook rabidly. Mandi glanced up at Kentish, but he was lost in the tale; his eyes shone out of the darkness of his face. Behind him the hat stand guarded dimly in the murk; the shelves of books, the peculiar collected items, the distended ornaments and rumpled engravings were all fluid now. The room, which had been so distinct and detailed was become marshy, shadowy, enigmatic.

My play with this fancy was cut violently short by the sight of movement in the cave. A shape, that of a person. I felt the need to shake my head to check my senses. Instinctively, and somewhat nervously, I shouted "Hello". Stepping towards the cavern entrance, I shouted "Hello" a second time. Now just inside the cavern, the vault of which arched some twelve feet above me, I stood, transfixed, my senses straining, trying to glean detail from the Cimmerian shade.

Then I heard it. Indistinct at first, but then more definite. Gentle approaching footsteps; a kind of rapid padding as a goat might cause upon a tiled floor.

"A goat?" thought Mandi. "I better end this shit." But when she looked up to speak Kentish had been completely lost in the darkness, his eyes were as black as his frown, and what she had thought was the room, was now distinctly like a cave. She saw Kentish twitch and she flinched back to the safety of the words, the words were containing the tale; if she could get to the end, they would be spared whatever it was that lurked inside and underneath and around them.

By now my heart was pounding. I called out again, but where there should be full voice there was little more than a quiet yelp. I thought of turning and running, but I was now held by the force of some unaccountable condition that fixed me to the spot. What emerged from the gloom no mortal man should have need to witness. That through education we can better our positions and have done with the follies of the aberrant supernatural and hobgoblin's gossip, but this figure, now in front of me, did shake my rationality to its foundations.

The figure, although I hesitate to call it human in any sense we know of the word, was that of a woman; at least let us call her female for want of some more precise equivalent. Visible now fully in the light of a lavish setting sun that had emerged histrionically from the clouds and illuminated the cavern, I saw she was clothed in a long green dress and wore a scarlet cloak around her shoulders. Her hair was a lustful red and fell untidily about her. In her left hand she held what looked like blacksmiths' tongs, but none of this compared to the horror of that face.

Mandi strained against the back of the armchair. With the fingers of her free hand, she dug the nails deep into the palm.

What intention the good Lord has for such horror I am at a loss to explain. How I am to describe what I saw? As I write my hand shakes and the candle flame that lights this parchment fizzes as if it wishes to extinguish the memory of such a thing, suggesting extinction, annihilation, doom. But I must light another candle and continue this account, for fear that I will give it the power it needs to further its task and gnaw at the souls of other men, until nothing remains.

Her face was not one face. Those features which in our loved ones change only imperceptibly with the passage of time, in this creature changed momentarily and multitudinously. Now the soulful eyes of a young woman in her prime, next the sunken wells of an aged and regretful spinster in her final hours. Now the smooth and conceited skin of a child, next the creased and anxious flesh of a mother worn by childbirth and the labours of the tub.

But it was the mouth that did pierce me. What unutterable blasphemy. Black lips as tight as sloe berries and cold blood. Sanguine fluid poured dark crimson from that hideous hole, staining her neck and chin and the intricately patterned frontispiece of her green vestment, running down to the hem and dripping between her legs to the cave floor.

Slowly, and deliberately, as if a performance, she smiled and as she did she raised the blacksmiths' tongs. Grabbing her left front tooth, she worked the denture loose and with a grinding tug removed it. I wanted to look away, but was unable. The creature then held out the tooth in the iron tongs and with a simple gesture, a smile, and a fulsome rush of blood, offered me the soiled thing. I felt the walls of the cave close in around me like a furious mob and I had a ringing in my ears. My legs gave way as I swooned, overtaken by emotion and weakness.

Mandi dared one glance. She could feel the pages between her fingers; Jesus, she was barely halfway through and Kentish seemed to have folded in two in his seat. No light shone from him, while the walls around him closed in even more, no longer the rounded spines of his library but dull and globular stalactite-like things, masses of something both soft and hard. Worse, much worse, was whatever was beginning to form within the soggy rock of the walls that now stood out from the limits of the room. Mandi remembered the train, and the figure in the cave-like recess of the church porch. It was coming again. She dare not look up any more, but she must race to the end. The words, spoken, although they were now muffled, as if swallowed by the recesses of the cave, were holding back something within the story, something for which words were a barrier, chains, a cage. She felt as if she were reading for her life.

> W... w...when I awoke I found myself sitting in what I quickly realised was a deeper chamber of the cavern. It was lit by a central fire, the light from which illuminated a damp almost spherical chamber whose walls were hung in a mass of flowstone, petrified rivulets that had formed into long ribbons of varying thickness. Where some of the ribbons merged, the calcite had formed into rounded shapes, simulacra that, in my still dazed state, suggested a hideous fauna of writhing many-armed cuttlefish and Hindoo mermaids that the darkness was kind to somewhat conceal.

> I tried to lift myself off the ground. As I placed my hand on the cave floor I felt a sudden stab to my palm. I found myself holding the incisor of some huge beast. And where it had found my hand, I found others. Teeth of varying sizes and categories, and with them, shining bones. The closer I looked, the more apparent it became that the cave floor was composed in generous portion of such osseous matter, perhaps many feet deep, the origins of which at that moment I shuddered to speculate upon, when all speculation was curtailed by the light touch of a hand on my right shoulder.

> I screamed instinctively and, in my crouched position, turned awkwardly, falling backwards onto the bone floor. Above me stood what I initially thought to be the creature from the cave entrance, though now the countenance of it had settled into that of a pretty female in its later youthful years. And there was no hint of blood now around her gently smiling lips. In a moment of relief, I realised that she might be my rescuer. The farmer's daughter perhaps, familiar with these caves and perhaps having spied me from a distance entering the caves whilst walking her father's fields.

'Thank the Lord' I said to the girl. 'Might you be able to help me out of this place?' hoping for some gesture of deliverance.

The girl, this Daughter of Aphony, in silence knelt in front of me. No, she was not my rescuer, and the fullness of her hideous intentions was now to be revealed.

Mandi paused. The more she read the worse the tale became; the deeper and deeper it seemed to drag them both into its cavernous labyrinth. Mandi wanted to look up, to see if the hallucinations of the story had materialised in the room, to see if Kentish was OK, was an ally against whatever it was that she had spoken into coming close. Or possessed by it? But she dared not; she read on. Almost showing the words, chanting them like spells to keep the imps, hobgoblins and black dogs from the door.

From her side, as if she made manufacture from thin air, the creature drew a scythe, the type of which I was familiar with in the calloused and insensible hands of the field labourers whose cursing and drinking despoiled the otherwise gentle landscape. Despite her youth and evident beauty I sensed the same crudity and sensuousness here before me as the girl began to loosen her dress at the neck, picking slowly and deliberately at the emerald green buttons. Such wantonness I thought an outrage, causing tension between my reason and the loud urgings of that sinful flesh which is a common burden to all men. I imagined M___ at home with our children and in my confusion began to speak the 23rd psalm aloud; but in the confusion of the chamber's air my words sounded more like the obscene shantees of the labourers than the choir's canticles.

The creature, insensible to my confusion, revealed her throat and chest to the level of her heart. Smiling sweetly she bade me look upon her, which in guilty truth I did, and she did slowly raise the tip of the scythe to the base of her throat and without an instant of hesitation drew the blade down her porcelain white skin, its translucence parting to allow pearls of blood to form along the incision. On completion of the mark she ran her ring finger along the wound and in one graceful movement offered me what I took to be its salty taste. I refused.

Undeterred by what I thought a moment's confusion in her eyes, she placed the blade's unforgiving edge now on her left index finger. 'Please stop' I called, the words lost in the depths of cavern's tunnels as she drew the scythe quickly and forcibly through skin and bone, cleanly and without a sound or a hint of pain in her still smiling face. The finger fell to the floor. I felt myself go faint and loose in the limbs as blood flowed from the revealed finger stump. Carefully, with her left hand she lifted the finger from amongst the teeth and white dry bones and offered it with an action so appealing that were it not for the horror of the object I would have taken it as from M____ I might receive a slice of lamb from the dinner table.

Mandi felt something cold and wet run down one of her wrists. Careful not to raise her eyes, careful to continue reading, she gently eased her fingernails out of the wounds she had made in her palm.

... 'I will not take the demon's gift', I repeated to myself.

I search privately in vain for reason or meaning to it all. I am at a loss, though throughout my internment in this official cavern of the local authorities, behind the shock and revulsion, there was a feeling, that these creatures meant me no harm at all. And indeed that they might be inviting me to partake in something innocent. That through accepting what I was offered I might become subjected to some necessary gnosis. However, as a rationalist, and a God-fearing subject of this kingdom, I could not, and will, with all my strength bear what seems the terrible and unjust consequences of my refusal.

This refusal was sealed and impiously confirmed by the witness of the creature's third offering. Even now, I hesitate before committing this part to paper; for it exceeded by a different quality of degradation what had gone before. But speak it I must, with the light of The Lord's Bright Truth, and in all humility these are the simple facts of what I was made to witness.

The creature replaced, with some care, her dismembered finger on the bone strewn floor, arranging three of the dog's teeth around it, one by the nail and two at the base, forming a triangle, the lower longer tip of which, along with the finger, pointed towards me. She closed her eyes for a few moments. Still paralysed by uncertainty, my voice was now lost; I felt as empty as the earth. After her prayer or whatever it was, she opened her eyes and once again smiled kindly. As she did I noticed a slight movement on the walls behind her...

Involuntarily, in a spasm electrified by the words, Mandi looked up. Kentish's folded body had begun to glow, and eerie light that matched none of the colours Mandi could give a name to had begun to leak into the space; Grant Kentish's eyes, eyes that shone in the darkness, were now the blackest parts of him. And behind, a thing shifted, gave a shimmy that was pretty. Mandi knew what was coming and thrust her face down through the gloom and back to the pages, scrambling to find the next word and finish the thing!

... one of the r... r... ribbon like formations moved. The cord of stone was gently pulsating, as if being filled by some noxious effluvium. Others, similar knobs and trails of limestone rock, began to breath in the same manner, as if the cliff were come into unnatural life and the cave walls one grey mass of heaving tentacles gesturing and inviting me in the same way as had the demoness in her form of a pretty girl.

I looked back in horror at the maiden, who had now once again picked up her scythe.

'Please God' I cried. And my words rippled through the bowl of wormish, serpentine, intestinal things that shook and trembled from the innards of the cavern, like unfortunate amphibious things turned inside out.

Holding the scythe at her throat, just below her left ear the girl glanced down at the triangular arrangement of teeth and, as she did, a dozen tendrils slipped down from the cave walls and inched towards her, reverently entwining first her legs and then her waist until it appeared she had herself become half serpent. A swarm of many legged creatures, giant invertebrates, silverfish, centipedes, cockroaches emerged impossibly from fissures between the tentacles; such was the absurdity of this stampede of unlikely beings that I laughed for joy at the likelihood that this was all a dream or vision. I was not comforted; the writhing mass appeared to give the she-devil great joy. She threw her head back in a kind of adoration, and as she did, drew the blade strongly across her throat. The wound gushed blood. How much more of this could I bear as I watched her carefully and deliberately with numerous cuts sever her head completely!

The skull, still smiling, its lips open in its preposterous kind of passion, rolled and was caught by two of the tentacles. The remaining tentacles now flowed all about her, as waters in a gully, some entering the gushing wound at her neck. Drawn with horror to the bloodied head I watched helpless as the tendrils offered me up the terrible thing. The third invitation. Its eyes were still open and still it made that smile;

"come in" it seemed to say "come in". And then a gentle sound, a slight movement of lips; my Good God, it was actually speaking, not in my head, but from its mouth! Whispered, that single word to this day I know not the meaning of, but that I cannot shut it out of my mind.

'Dumno.'

And with that single word my world collapsed...

But Mandi had not spoken the word. The word had sounded in the room, for Mandi, she was sure, had not moved her lips. She was still taking a breath when it sounded in the space; and the voice that spoke it was not like hers. She did not recognise it as a voice at all; but more like an escape of gas, a fart, or the sound a house might make when going cold at night. It was not a human sound. Mandi shivered. Kentish was still, his eyes risen up inside his skull following the shadows on the walls of his imagination.

Every rational thing that gave the ground solidity beneath my feet, that caused the sun to rise and set, the seasons to follow each other, the books to balance and the contracts fulfilled, word kept and promises honoured. Every single design the Good Lord had built into his perfect world, lay as waste around me. And as certainty retreated, the floor of the cave gave way and I felt myself falling into darkness.

I do not know what happened next, and in all honesty I am grateful for God's grace to have been spared the details of that fall and any sense of what lay beneath the floor of that hideous cave. Somehow, by what tentacular, visceral or magical means I shudder to think, I had been transported from the cave up into the forest above, and to the shallow cliff face where I had first sought shelter from the rain. The fall through the floor of the cave had clearly caused me to lose consciousness and drop into a sleep, the moon was high in the branches above me and the trees resounded to the insistent calls of two owls. It must have been some hours that I was lost.

Grateful for my release but now burdened with images of my captivity I stumbled back to P____. The following days were difficult. I fell first into melancholy, unable to talk to M___ about my encounter, or why I was so troubled. I could not work, the site of the sharp-edged tools of my profession filled me with revulsion. I feared that if I were to pick them up I might do some similar mischief to myself or to the children. And worst of all, in my dreams I kept repeating my time in the cave, struggling from the sight of blood and swarming tentacles, striking out aimlessly in the darkness and swinging the counterpane about the room. The children, hearing my confusion, began to dream their own dreams; G____ now wakes every night crying out against 'the many arms!', 'teeth in the arms!', 'the beak, the beak!' What awful inheritance have I passed on?

But what was very worst was a thing that I dare not even dream of, nor confess to anyone since; my hand is still and firm as I write this, but, within, my so 'l trembles and has no anchor. For I know there was a kind of insubstantial matter beneath the mosaic of teeth...

The room was brightening. The storm was passing. The shelves of books, the antique furniture, the cases of fossilised molluscs and posed taxidermies acting out scenes of predation and hometown humour. But none of that was any comfort to Mandi, as she garbled chains of prose, rushing the words together into streams of stringy gloop, the story distending like a single tentacle, covered in rough hooks and phrases, bioluminescent with metaphors from unreal zoologies.

...do not ask how I know this, but I do. There was a kind of being without existence, a kind of shadow without a primary object, a darkness that was never lit, a many-armed Nothing that is real and unreal and defies human thinking; for though I KNOW this thing, I cannot KNOW it! I feel and believe in it, I have faith in it every bit as much as I have faith in God, I could not withstand the lure and accusation of this blackness, blankness, toothless maw feeding on my hope, night cast upon my day, hood of absence tied around my mind, falling down inside; like a house built on a cliff falling slowly into an abyss.

The sun burst through the fleeing clouds; Kentish's frozen face glowed like an antique bronze unearthed by greedy tomb robbers.

I sought solace in the drink, to quieten the riot and decline of my mind. Those callous sons of the earth I had previously reviled became my confidents as we shared flagons of cider. The beer house became my church. In my stupefaction I would tell my story to eager ears, and by return was told ridiculous myths of particular hobgoblins in this or that part of the lane, of giant worms coiled beneath the chapels and hills full of fairy folk, malignant influences, the upturned hull of Noah's Ark beneath a field, unseen things and fancies that would trap and mesmerise the unwary traveller. 'Ah, they loves your teeth them little winged demons, always turn your pockets out when walking these lanes at night. Ha ha ha!'

Of course, it was all nonsense, yet when it came to walking home back down the lane or across the fields, I saw them, looking oft and again over their shoulders, eyes bright with fear, but my logic like theirs had so abandoned me that I became obsessed by seeking out these tales. One aged farmer, well-schooled and erudite, but ravaged by gout, after gladly accepting a few pennies for more Bordeaux liberally poured from the pub's dusty bottles, told me that my story was 'the story of the ancients' from the 'bible days before the flood'. That there was a kind of theology to the chaos in this land, an opposite gospel in these fields and deep lanes, that had been brought here by a fallen star and its crew, a race from the darkness of the skies, a race of fallen and unspeakable beings. Reaching for his battered copy of the good book he read me this passage from the Book of Revelation:

And the fifth angel sounded, and I saw a star fall from heaven unto the earth: and to him was given the key of the bottomless pit. And he opened the bottomless pit; and there arose a smoke out of the pit, as the smoke of a great furnace; and the sun and the air were darkened by reason of the smoke of the pit. And there came out of the smoke locusts upon the earth: and unto them was given power, as the scorpions of the earth have power.

He said that in the days before the word of God arrived, the people were rotten and worshiped strange idols and the hills ran wild with huge dogs. But God judged them and banished them beneath the earth where they became all white and thin and withered away and a different people came to live in these parts; hard working builders of churches and farms.

In my growing desperation I took my story and these tales to the Reverend J___ at T___. Sitting in the church nave he was quick to remind me that my return to the flock would be most welcome and the weekly collection had been much denuded by my contributions to the beer house...

Mandi could feel a single page now between her fingers. The ordeal was almost at an end. The hat stand had resumed its post; the darkness was entirely gone. The lines of the engravings stood sharply in their frames.

Mandi heard the page rustle between her fingertips, things felt real again. Birds outside were singing in protest at the storm. The roar of the leaves had wholly gone. All was held, all was safe. Kentish was reviving, movement returning to replace the mask his face had become.

> With some nervousness I started my tale. To spare the tender ears of the good Reverend, I was charitably economical with some details, and interspersed the story with the legends I had been told.

> However, I could not finish my tale for a sudden and unexpected sight of something so ghastly that I had to beg my pardon and flee that place. For behind the Reverend, in the tracery glass above the altar, high up towards the vaulted ceiling I noticed a collection of brightly coloured images of the hosts of saints. There, in all plainness on the left was the scythe-bearing demoness of the cave. And on the right a woman holding a tooth bearing a striking resemblance to one of the juicy faces I had endured in that terrible place. I fled the church and its startled priest, and ran, dodging hobgoblins, down the path.

> I wandered for days in the lanes and fields, alone and without company, feasting on blackberries and centipedes. My world was empty; my stomach felt cavernous and distraught. When I finally returned to my workshop and my customers brought me plans for new furniture, fittings or machinery, I could make no sense of the straight lines in the drawings. And M___'s spinning of wool was impossible for me to bear; each strand brought to mind those heinous tendrils that bore the head of a temptress. And all the while, that word...

Mandi could not speak it. But she must. Or it would be spoken. Kentish, as if fully recovered of his faculties, stirred and looked anxiously at Mandi, as if he understood the extent of the challenge and the value of the stake. She ground out the words between clenched teeth:

Dumno. Dumno. Dumno.

And the moment she had, she knew she had let them out, she knew she had made a terrible mistake, she had fallen for the trap, fell into the pit, though quite what it was she had done, she had no clear idea, except that some very bad things were celebrating deep in the darkness to which they had nearly been taken. But now, Mandi had left the door ajar. Left the key in the lock, left the lock on the latch. And that thing down in the deep darkness, it knew now, it knew how to get back to them, how to find its way.

By now my business was failing. Debts accrued and my wife pleaded with me to find a way back to my former self. How I wished I had never strayed into that terrible place; nor ever felt the Presence, greater and lesser than God Himself, that sat in its lair beneath the enamel floor.

And so it is that as I write this we are now packed to flee this place and start afresh in the New World, for I feel that only distance will rid us of this curse and bring us back to sanity; the doctors have granted me freedom on condition I write this missive to them, but I insist they are not to read it until we sail. We shall depart before the bankruptcy hearing at C___, slipping away quietly and leaving this madness behind. Taking nothing of this with us in our luggage. This place has been abandoned by God and I beseech anyone who should read this account to seek refuge away from here and leave these folded hills to the thorny briars on Satan's cloak and whatever else it is that languishes beneath the county.

Mandi put down the pages and looked up at Kentish, who was grinning manically; as if the thing had fixed his teeth in a grimace. She stared into his eyes for a glimmer of creepy malevolence; anything human. The tape had stuck in the machine, the programme was loading, the screen had frozen. Then the cosmos hiccupped and Grant Kentish was already halfway into a sarcastic rant that took in failure to restore power to the house, the sinuous dishonesty of book dealers and a deep exegesis of the metaphorical taxonomy of the 'LOVECRAFT ORIGINAL'. Finally, his verdict, brightly: a compelling tale, no doubt, but not HPL, more like an early draft of, no... some rough notes... and then he paused, unable to explain himself.

"... if someone who came before a writer could write a bad copy... a pastiche of their style, but before they came to write anything, a primitive model, a crude and primal ur-text, as Geoffrey of Monmouth stood for Shakespeare or Ovid before Arthur Golding transfigured him... as Homer for Chapman if Keats is right, I've never read either... this might be the raw material for an HPL tale, but nothing is realised and everything is too explicit, too obvious, it doesn't conjure anything except its description of itself."

"So, it's worthless?"

"I didn't say that, my dear, but what you need is an antiquarian, not a literary critic."

He glanced down at his belly and from its folds withdrew a large timepiece.

"Hell's bells. We're going to miss the fire wheels and we haven't had dinner. You can't go to the fire wheels on an empty stomach, Amanda!"

Mandi wasn't aware that she was going anywhere on any kind of stomach.

"Yes, you're coming! Where better to meet an antiquarian than a wholly fabricated re-enactment of a non-existent history! They can't keep themselves away! Where's the gong?"

He held up his finger. From deep in the bowels of the house, a tinny dinner gong was clanging repeatedly.

"Alright, alright, we're coming", and he swept Mandi from the room, as though she were a flock of angry geese. At the threshold, Mandi paused and looked back; she knew that Kentish would know too, but she had to. She had to know.

Chapter 11

January 1876

It was all blurry, always had been blurry, always would be blurry, this day like any other. Most blurry were the three dresses; the cream dresses; some light material for the hot day, and wraps against the cold that was coming with the night, the wide brimmed hats to keep away the burning sun exchanged for cream headscarves. It was always blurry to the boy; although he knew the deep reason for things, he could never see distinctly the things themselves. All was a kind of oneness to him. There were many causes, great causes, indeed, he overheard the whispers every day as the white gentlemen came and went, and then the shifting Egyptians gliding through the palaces of the whites, on home ground, a word here and a word there, but what were they causing? He noticed how these adults understood everything about what was happening, that they were the captains of happening, yet seemed to have so little idea of why the things that happened by their own agencies did occur and occur in such a manner. The captains were always surprised, like the dragoman pilot was always caught out by the gusts and breezes from the defiles. But he, just a donkey boy they sneered at, he understood the origins and conspiracies, motives and machinery, but never the results thereof. What a strange boy he was, he had thought to himself, as the party had passed through the moon-shadow of the giant triangles in the desert and the camels that had been drawn instinctively towards the river.

He knew his own motive as fear, the constant and faithful companion of his life. It had always been so, and he could not comprehend now how so little had happened to hurt him. But he knew the why of it; he saw every day the power and the authority in relaxation and guessed from the stories he had heard in the streets how quickly that might change. He had grown too big to be unrecognisable around the exits and entrances of Shepheard's, the recruiting officers had pointed their sticks at him, and he had known precisely why and how he must run from the environs of the hotel, though not to where and not for how long. That had been decided elsewhere; in the deep dark, that was clear. While all on land had become blurry again; but the white family had allowed him aboard, as if in a dream, drowsing in the bitter and merciless sun, the afternoon had sought to spite itself, defying the dragoman who had thrown a sheet to the deck in his fury and kicked him in the stomach when the ladies had turned their backs, retiring to their cabins. Cringing under a bulwark, the donkey boy had felt all these things, but he did not have words like these; the words he heard were different, and although there were many signs and strokes about his day, no one had ever explained them to him; instead the things that others called words or writing were like wisps of smoke, flocks of sparks that were quickly extinguished. For what he understood was something quite different; a rushing cold fire that was coming to cover the land, and he knew why it was. He had read its motives in the shapes of the gutters, the cracks in the bones, in the gaps between the triangles outside of the city, in the arrangements of the grains of sand in the desert and in the breakers of the dunes, the distance between their crests and the caprices hiding in their vales. There was nothing in this place that would be good for a while.

The Nile was deep and its reason was drowning. What it did was to fertilise the plane, he had overheard the sisters' tutor say one day, but he knew from the sands that the why was to drown them and bring forth from nothingness the green shoots by drowning; only by drowning did new life come and so the same catastrophes would happen every year. Like a real and true mother drowned her son with love, a river drowned all that stood in its embrace, from the women washing clothes on its banks to the glittery expanses of the dunes. Even from insipid yellowish nothingness great lawns suddenly sprang and made a garden of the arid expanses.

So he understood fully the why of the sisters. Why there were three, and must be three; why so many and why one or two would not do, though all that would happen would happen all the same and whatever the number, and why the why could only be this way. He knew the importance of the three to the why of the crisis, this he knew the moment he threw himself at their feet and saw in the hems of their skirts and the whispers they made with the sand the reason for their trip upon the Nile. He felt every moment of their preparation; the summoning of the servants, the payments to the bickering pilots, the girding of the picnics, the combing of hair and the tightening of their dresses. He felt their nakedness and vulnerability. Though he saw only the final parts of their preparations, he felt the tremors that had begun them. He eavesdropped the conversations of the suppliers and drivers as they conveyed, interpreted, finessed and commented on their milky orders, uninhibited by the presence of the donkey, and he knew what they intended with every one of their inflections; how impressions were conveyed and received, amplified and adapted to each other's motives; how these separate acts were forming up towards an inevitable catastrophe that would suck him down with it, just as much as the coming defeat in Abyssinia and the raging torrents in the ravine at Gundet would swirl about the routed fellahin in currents of blood and abandoned ordnance. He had as well drown in water as in blood; he would not fight for the Khedive.

Fleeing the fury of the dragoman captain, the donkey boy had crouched in the bows and felt the waters parting ahead of him, sliding away behind him, as if he were falling down the defile of a liquid mountain at the head of the wind. Though he could only tentatively grasp the great why in the river beneath the many whys of her currents, he knew her limbs, her thin stretching arms, the relentless teeth fringing her hundred lamprey mouths. He knew what both the lowliest servant and the greatest of the white fathers had intended, but they could not know the river's intention. They knew nothing of its grander scheme, nor read from its currents and greasy surface its immediate or complex aims. And so certain was he where they, his betters and equals (for no one was below him, hence his unfettered connection to the deep things), were uncertain, that he had placed his foot upon the boat and levered his body from the safety of the square stones of the quay; his intention was never to let down the honour of serving the genius of a place, whether it be the greatest of pharaonic tombs or the humblest of hotel kitchens, never to ignore the almost imperceptible whisper of all that had been denied him, for he knew that that was the reason-to-be of every living and unliving thing.

The swan-like dababeeah was sixteen miles off Minioh, the squalls ripping at its big lateen sail, twice the length of the vessel, towering over its hull, just as Gebel el Tayr, the Mountain of the Bird, towered over the sail and just as the great dome of the stars towered over the mountain below. The dragoman shouted and cursed about sandbanks and shallows and the treacherous curviness of the Nile, but the sisters would not let him moor. They waited in their cabins; and at the rounding of a point, the walls of the mountain rising sheer from the river's edge, the donkey boy felt the first gust of will among the squalls. The dragoman screamed, the crew reacted, but before they could let go the field-sized sail, a fist of wind flying down the defile and ploughing up the surface of the Nile was in its cotton and was turning the boat about to face its full force, upending it into darkness. The coconut wood mast speared at the bottom of Iteru and Aspidogaster parasites tightened their septa within the soft sponge of their hosts, Cleopatra bulimoides, slithering down the blade-like stems of hydrophytes. The wheel of life turned snail like, the tiller circling its shaft, the rudder unhinged and flapped wildly like the tail of a crocodile slapping down the river.

The world turned upside down, the donkey boy floated with the three sisters down into the deep darkness; the blurry passage to his death no more nor less distinct than all the other misunderstandings that had marked out his short life. The long tresses of the sisters spread like fans and as they all fell they left the mad rush of the surface behind, the cotton slips of the sisters swirling elegantly about their tumbling limbs like the pleated skirts of the Ghawazi dancers of the Dom people. The donkey boy knew that there was something skirted far below, the mistress of the winds and streams, her wandering fingers reaching out to the far coasts of all the world and drawing the foreigners to herself, sacrificing her most favoured donkey boy so that these beautiful strangers might share the knowledge she had, in sending her opaqueness, shared with him. High above them now, the upturned hull of the bababeeah casts its shadow, cutting out a curved triangle of seventy feet of blackness from the moon, while at its stern the waters thrashed and struggled, the dragoman and his crew caught in a syndicate of crocodiles; their struggles, seen from the cliff high above, appeared to be a war with a single monster possessed of tens of scaly pointed arms, mounted with leathery teeth, the whole a giant lacerated mouth biting and biting again at the surface full of sailors. While down below all was at peace as the donkey boy led the three sisters, by an invisible halter, down to meet the reason of all thought and the motive of all motors.

On January 30th, 1876, The Times of London announced the drowning in Egypt of three nieces of a prominent Recorder, the daughters of a clergyman of significance and sisters of a curate in a Devon town. While their Cairo correspondent would carefully note the efforts of divers to recover their bodies, he desisted from publicising the results of their endeavours: a tangle of hair and slime, feathers and limbs, of female bodies stretched out of all natural definition, twisted in the fierce turbine of billions of tons of water their pretty teeth now mounted in every inch of their flesh, their bellies confused with those of swans or some other kind of foreign bird, and tongues and toes, so extravagantly puckered in the cold waters as to drag them out to the length of crocodile tails; the whole mess of recreation never was satisfactorily untangled for their three coffins, but occasioned much horrid cracking of jaws, sluicing of fats and scything of heads to pack something like a young woman into each of the oblong crates.

For seven days the steamer crossing the Mediterranean with the containers in its hold was haloed in the surrounding sea by luminescent shoals, while above an unnatural star trespassed on the charts of the mariners below; in the daylight the ship's condition was much worse and its passengers were recorded in the log, though nowhere else was any word ever recorded of it, nor conversation even whispered once the cargo was released, as having stayed in their cabins day and night to avoid the shadow of a bulbous thing, trailing long glistening streamers of sinew a few feet beneath the surface of the ocean, escorting the steamer around the Rock of Gibraltar, through the Bay of Biscay and only as the Cheek Stone at the end of the Devil's Sett was passed to port, disappeared.

Chapter 12

The car ride up to the Forest Inn was an uncomfortable one. Kentish collected Mandi from a flaking boudoir where she had been left to 'freshen up'. With what? He returned rather too quickly, Mandi thought. Next time she would be brutally frank with him. In the car, making their way to the edge of the Haldon Ridge, the meeting place for the wheel rolling, were Bob and Janine, stalwarts of the Old Mortality Society who Mandi had met briefly at the meal.

It had horrified her. Slithery muscles and oyster innards tangled up in unnaturally long tentacles of pasta. Gobbets of the sauce unavoidably splashed shirts and tops, which the guests enthusiastically peeled off and threw over the backs of their chairs. Only for more sauce to dash hairy chests and pendulous breasts. Mandi had done her best to remove the stains from her blouse; as if she were some frightened and exploited intern. Not ever an enthusiastic participant, she had been to those parties; they always felt to her like scenes from spy movies where the trainee spooks are forced to humiliate themselves, so that all their fellow agents share at least one secret about them. Mandi was loyal to no one; she kept secrets for company. When asked at tills for her 'loyalty card' she could become abusive.

Trying to distract herself from the late middle-aged gangs of aspiring dilfs and milfs, Mandi had become more greasily tangled than the linguini. The movement of objects in the minestrone reminded her of a configuration of waters she had seen off the shore of the Sett. Pretty soon those who were not already moaning under the tablecloth, or banging against the table legs, sending ripples through Mandi's soup, had sidled off for sex in the ballroom's generous variety of side rooms, leaving only her and Kentish at the table. Never for a moment did he raises his eyes or offer any interest; he carefully wound spaghetti around his fork and brought it smoothly to his lips. Then sucked in the snakes of pasta, as if inhaling them. He alone was unstained.

Mandi replayed these horrors as the lanes she recognised from her taxi ride were replaced by those of a vale she had never seen before; anonymous fields and winding narrow ways bereft of signage. There was nothing to make her feel uneasy, yet the place seemed uneasy about itself. Mandi decided she should stop transferring her own feelings to the vale, but it was better than having to think about Janine, who had left the shuddering dining table before Bob. Mandi had detected a helpless lasciviousness in Bob's eyes that undermined any higher purpose he or the Club entertained. They might just as well have planted Pampas Grass on the big house's driveway.

Why this need to over-claim on the same shoddy desires everyone else had? Mandi had conjured plenty of demons under her sheets, unlocked doors to lands that boys had never imagined existed. The Old Mortality Club were fancy frauds selling the 'same old same old' as exotic goods. The market mechanism in the magical realm was malfunctioning. It needed the smack of an invisible hand upon its esoteric product?

Gazing at the dire fields, Mandi laughed out loud at the thought of Grant, Bob and Janine writhing around in squelchy congress to ritual mumbo jumbo invented in a bungalow in Stevenage sometime around 1954. She wondered how she knew that, but she was pretty sure she did. The sex might be ancient but not the liturgies. They did not come from hollow hills or blasted heaths, they came straight out of the suburbs and sneaky boredom of dirty minds. As Harold Macmillan had said at the time: "you've never had it so repeatedly" and "we're all sex-magickians now". Three generations later and they were repeating the same 'transgressions'. Vomit. Decades of wasted time! Did they think they added to a giant willow man with every fake ritual and vanity publication? Mandi's mood did not make for easy conversation. She could feel a blog post coming on.

"I'm sorry to hear of your loss," Janine offered.

Mandi gave a short, bland note of thanks. Leaving few hooks on which to hang a reply.

"Looking forward to tonight, you two in the back?" snarked Kentish cheerily. "Fifth year. Seems to get bigger every time."

"And spoiled", added Janine "it's too well known now, and the Morris Men bring their crowd."

Mandi's mood darkened further. Morris?

"Are they going to do that again?" asked Bob "I'm not so sure they do any more, you know. They can keep on saying that it's all about poachers and hiding their faces in some bucolic past they've imagined for themselves, but I don't believe 'em. They're blacking up! The local Black and White Minstrels!"

Kentish cackled and slapped his thigh, catching Mandi's knee in his excitement. Janine and Bob echoed from the back seat and popped up and down in glee. Mandi wanted to punch them all. Complacent crap. She was already sketching an easy 800 words on why Morris Men should paint their faces black, and then fuck off and die. It would have everything: race, the sneering middle class, political correctness, laisser-faire neo-nationalists in fake costumes telling invented stories about sons of the Devon soil. A stew of hypocrisies to which Mandi would bring a long handled spoon; no more appetizing than The Old Mortality Club's soup.

The pub's car park was packed.

"What will you have?" asked Kentish

Kentish was a 'gentlemen' as well as a priapic scholar. Mandi decided on a half of cider, relieved she would not have to brave the heaving bar. The winding lanes had left a blur of minestrone whirling before her eyes; through which she spotted a group of blacked up dancers holding decorated pewter tankards.

"I'll hang out here."

"Half a cider it is, my dove."

Mandi was not Ken's "dove"; she was no one's buzzard, peregrine falcon or sparrow hawk either, though she would far prefer to watch proceedings from high over the forest, particularly if she could watch Kentish rolling down the hill in a cape of flames. Her bubbling but bottled fury concerned her at times. She laughed at her inner snowflake.

The folk-revivalists had begun to circle and mass. One woman dancer stood out above the ranks, well over six feet tall. Quite a presence amongst and above the crowd; the male dancers were tiny. Folk seemed to orientate to the Amazon, swarm about her, hover in her presence. As with all the Morris Men she wore black rags and a black top hat decorated with pheasant's tail feathers, her face was smeared with shining grease paint that made the whites of her eyes and her straightened teeth glow like moonlight. Her bulk lifted her physically, but it was her piping voice that transcended her companions. Here was a confident woman, Mandi thought, as she wandered over to say hello, hoping that a conversation might add some colour to a story she had already topped and tailed in her head.

"Hi" said Mandi, confident of her reception, and told the usual lies about a web feature for the Huffington Post, "it's about issues around Morris Men blacking up their faces. Do you mind answering a few questions?"

"Morris Men?" said the tall, blacked dancer.

Mandi sighed quietly to herself.

The Amazon tore open her jacket of rags to reveal a prodigious pink sports bra onto each cup of which had been printed a foaming beer mug. Christ, thought Mandi, it is not just the swingers at the old house. Mandi waited until the woman had buttoned herself away.

"How would you describe yourself then?"

The hint of unhazed aggression in her tone was not lost on the Amazonian, who took a long sip of beer from a pewter tankard handed her by a raggedy Obby Oss.

"It's all bollocks," retorted the gangly dancer. "We black up, always have done and always will do!" There were cheers. "It's nuffin' to do with people of colour, it's to do with people round these parts back in the day painting their faces black to avoid the gamekeeper, sent to god knows where if they were caught..."

"Nailed on a post in the larder!" someone offered.

"You could get a death penalty for wearing a black face in the forest", continued the pink-bra'd Amazon. "Wearing it is a protest against the old oppression."

"Mind if I quote you on that?"

"Go right ahead, kiddie."

People of colour? Parroted from an unconscious bias course, no doubt. Mandi imagined the towering dancer on weekdays in a council office, processing forms, with breaks for indoctrination; scared of showing her bra there, Mandy bet herself, for fear of causing extra anxiety among middle management already out of their heads with stress. Why couldn't they paint their faces whatever fucking colour they wanted without a justification from fake history?

"What do you think about councils in the Midlands banning Morris dancers who black up?" Mandi asked, trying a different tack.

"Well, we're dancers, we don't want to piss people off. Bans are a bit heavy I suppose, why not look at alternatives, paint your faces dark green or whatever."

"Unfair to Pepe!" heckled a bystander in wellies.

"Maybe not brown up there, know what I mean?" She giggled. "I think we'd be open to suggestions..."

First hint of censorship and the lusty sons of the earth were toast.

"Kelly's talking shit."

Mandi turned to the heckler. A non-Morris man standing to the left of the flexible dancer. He was wearing a Barbour, chords, and black wellies. Mid 40s, Mandi guessed. Local, for sure.

"What the fuck do you know, Dave?" replied Kelly with a smile.

"I happen to know it gets harder and harder to organise this event every year with all the fucking regulations and shit. Never mind banning these Al Jolson wannabes! Why don't they ban the whole effing shebang for good measure? This and the maypole?"

Dave leaned in on Mandi.

"All we want is a bit of fun." He leered into her face. "But you can't do that nowadays without treading on some friggin' byelaw."

Despite this bullying manner, this man was speaking Mandi's language, in a crude patois. Yet she had no common cause with him; she knew what he was, straight off. She doubted if this Dave (now undressing her with cider addled eyes) bothered much about state regulation or the serfdom of the individual. He probably thought Ayn Rand was something traded on the currency markets.

"Breaking the law?" Asked Mandi, the upward inflexion handing Dave plenty of rope.

"Oh yeh," replied Dave, leaning further in, "a few of us started this whole thing back a few years. I were a kid, then. Old Bob over there were chatting with this bloke who was doing a bit of tree work for him up on the hill. The bod reckoned that in ancient times they would come up here, midwinter, and roll a flaming great wheel down the slope. Summat to do with a coven of pagans or some such shit; either they did it or it was to burn them out. He probably got the wrong place, anyway, he was a right twat. Been listening to those freaks down Lost Horizon, probably. Anyways, Bob's telling us about this at the bar and Nigel, who owned the pub then, you could see the pound signs in his eyes! He thought it might conjure a good evening's takings; he weren't expecting the whole mind, body and spirit circus!"

Dave drew pound signs in the air with his thick forefinger.

"Anyways, a mob of us helped ourselves to some old wooden cable reels up at the Palmer farm, luvverly bit o' hay, paraffin. Bunged a few quid to Help for Heroes, or whatever it was in them days, and you'd got a genuine heritage event, just like that! Tommy Cooper! Just like that! Do it around Christmas, a Yule type thing and, bang again, you've got a nice dollop of free advertising. Worked a fuckin' dream. Got a decent crowd straight off. And these hilarious fuckin' witches and wizards all got hold of it too and they made it even bigger with all their pals, brought their costumes and ukuleles, and they bring along some fair totty too, fair play to 'em... pardon my Franglais! As good as the fuckin' Wicker Man it was, till the Elf and Safety killed it! Ha ha! Got on telly and everything. Put this place on the map. That's when it attracted the twats from the council."

The twats from the council. Mandi already knew this story. She felt like a deer sinking into quicksand, dropping deeper the harder she kicked. A thick mud of words came racing up her nose, closing her ears and eyes, the background chatter, the noise of the pub crowd, the music, the din, the rooks in the trees, the distant passing trains down towards the coast all fell away. There was only the sucking and drawing down of Dave's folktale. The forms of the people around her, of Kelly Blackface and the feather crowned dancers turned into a bright darkness. That silent fug; when she could not speak and the world – or something like it – closed right in. No passing angel, just her and Dave in a cave with no walls. Him chirruping about adults scared of kids who can't make up their minds what sex they are, kids scared of themselves, something about the old religion.... But, it all felt wrong. Dave was taking her words, from somewhere, and twisting them around other stuff. He came on like an inadequate troll, but Mandi knew, just by looking at him, that he was not who he was pretending to be. He was trouble. Putting up a wall that looked a little like her. She had met people like Dave before; looked like fools, unaccountable agents of unattributable malice. No training, no station chief, no cell, lonely sole members of a leaderless resistance with enemies and no comrades. But they knew exactly what they were doing, even if they couldn't explain it. Dave started in about a Punch and Judy show on the beach, how the council made the old chap change the act to something "more acceptable to diverse audiences". Dave affected Punch's voice. His visage changed, as he squeaked, his features became more pronounced. Then, he spoke like Judy. A calm, reassuring tone, not quite a puppet voice, but female, less like a squeaker and more like something familiar. Dave was speaking to Mandi in a voice that was more and more like her own; she could hear it singing to her, very softly echoing Dave:

"Muddy Mary, mother of God,
Killed the Old Boy in his bath,
God went to Hell
And started to smell..."

Was he taking the piss? She wanted to say something. Dave's version of Mandi's voice was becoming more and more distorted inside her own head, her words all fouled up. As if at the end of a long tube she could hear herself speaking about cyberspace, freedom and men's rights, while Dave began to strut and punch the air, thrusting his hips: "wanna be in my gang, my gang, my gang!"

He stopped, his head turned as if it sat on his shoulders like a mask on a turntable.

"Well? Do you?"

What? Dave's face was changing again. His features softening. His hair less grey, a hint of strawberry, and it was longer now. And where were the dark shadows beneath his eyes, and the stubble? Now Mandi really wanted to make Dave stop, but her arms were pinned to her sides, her tongue lodged in the roof of her mouth. She tried to think into his mind, appeal to him, but the more she got inside him, the more he got inside her, operating her own voice in anxieties she had buried long ago. Hadn't she danced to Gary Glitter hits at right wing parties shortly after the paedophile's first arrest. Well? What about Bowie? She was protesting the hypocrisy, but even so, if it came out, at the wrong moment, all her work for kids' rights... something dark and powerful was trying to bind her...

"Bandy Mandi think's she's so bright
But bandy Mandi's just not right!"

Bandy Mandi? How the fuck did he know? She had forgotten that! One of the boys at Lost Horizon had made it up. Sung it again and again whenever she wanted to speak. As Dave kept singing the rhyme, his jaw opening and shutting like something run with strings and wire, she noticed a trickle of blood roll down his chin from the corner of his mouth.

"You're …"

The blood became more profuse. Dave dipped his head forward, then back, clearing his now long red hair from his bloodied face. A pause. Nothing. Just Mandi and Dave gazing at each other. Mandi and something else. Whatever it was, slowly and deliberately, lifted its hand to its red mouth and with a twist and a tug removed one of its upper front teeth. The action was so sudden and so startling that Mandi stumbled back in shock, wincing. He, she, whatever it was, held out a tooth in the palm of its open hand, offering it, with torn pieces of gum, to Mandi. Who reached out for it.

"Oi, daydreamer! Here you go! It's a nightmare in there" announced Kentish, gently touching Mandi's arm with the half of cider.

Mandi looked round. Then back to Dave. Who was sharing in some banter with Kelly Blackface.

"Oh, oh… ", Mandi stammered, taking the glass in trembling fingers; checking her other hand for teeth. She was unsighted. Kentish began to berate Bob and Janine about how packed the bar was.

"You, OK?" asked Janine. "You look like you've seen a ghost!"

"No. I heard one."

"Sure you're alright?"

Mandi made no second answer.

"Oh, she's OK", interrupted Dave, now a little worse for wear. "Me and Mandi are bessies, aren't we, love?"

But Mandi was looking at Dave with fresh eyes. On the lapel of his Barbour, raised above the brown corduroy, below a UKIP pound sign badge, was an enamel badge with a small red triangle, tip pointing downwards. She hadn't noticed that before. Dave moved away, into the crowd, shaking hands and patting backs as he went. His gestures drew many smiles. For Mandi, something like 'service as usual' returned; that High Definition illusion of 360 degrees wraparound reality. She could see the hairs on midges in the air, the veins in leaves and the residue of that horrible thing with broken teeth and shattered jaw that was stalking on her shoulder.

"Mister Kentish?" she whispered.

"Doctor Kentish!" corrected Janine. Kentish waved her objection aside.

"Doctor Kentish, can you see… something standing right behind me?"

"April, you mean?"

"Wha..?"

Mandi turned and the glamour was gone.

"This is the archivist I was telling you about."

April's face was broad and friendly. Mandi was not ready for her homely presence. When April spoke it sounded to Mandi as if it was from deep underwater. That April was one of those seals you could watch through thick glass windows in the tiled wall of an aquarium.

"I'm sorry?"

April repeated herself and this time the only words, two more than before, Mandi caught were 'teeth' and 'hyena'. Then something happened. Like someone pulled the carpet out from beneath all this crap. Everything got sharp and sensible. Mandi knew what to do. She held out her free hand to April.

"Doctor Kentish said you might be here."

"Grant rang me about your enquiry. We're going to try and help you. I'm not promising anything, but there are certainly local connections, by the sound of it. Give me a little time and I will check what we have in our stores."

"Sorry, did you just say 'hyenas' teeth'?"

Kentish and April laughed. Mandi felt her angry self-possession returning.

"Can I get back to you?"

April held out her phone and Mandi, woozily, typed her number into April's memory.

"Don't thank me", said April, "thank Grant!"

Mandi turned to Kentish, but he had turned away, his eyes following Dave's progress through the crowd.

"Wha..? O, please don't take any notice of our resident Brexiteer! Everyone round here voted that way…"

"Makes sense…"

"The community did not, of course," said Kentish. "Magic does not respect borders."

"I heard that!" yelled Dave. Though he could not have…

A great shout went up from within the trees.

"Best make our way up the hill," said Kentish. "Be a shame to miss the local sun god eating its children!"

"I wish it would!" shouted Dave, from the heart of a surging crowd of newcomers arriving from the car park. Bob and Janine honked like geese, their laughter clattering down the darkening valley from where a huge yellow-painted wheel was slowly mounting a tiny lane, its rim turning above the tall hedges. The steady flames of torches, held aloft by their bearers, flickering on its tin veneer.

Chapter 13

The driver smiled as he passed the gates of Lost Horizon. Nothing was lost on him now. He gunned the 14-year-old family saloon up the sharp incline, the old engine struggling to bear its measly load past the giant 1930s' pub that only ever seemed full for Christmas lunches.

Two miles further down the coast the road rose once again, out of one of the small coastal towns. The driver had barely noted the passage of time. Things were threaded together now. In the headlight beams he searched for the obscure turn he knew was there. As a brief suburban layer fell away, he saw the darkness at the side of the road and turned in, then pushed down hard on the accelerator and sent the car scything through a rusty metal gate; it sprang apart like a family of frightened deer. Exhilarated by his success he gunned the machine once more and it began to speed downhill, bumping along the grass track towards the cliff edge. This was his lucky day.

The driver knew the lie of the land, knew the muddy lane took a sharp right turn just before the thorn bushes and the sandstone precipice. He kept the wheel steady. He had never felt like this. Anyway, if he had, the memory was useless to him now. He was living in the moment. All the bills, failures, fuckups, belittling and bullyings, handed out and received, the emotional ice age, estranged son, mountains of pills and hours of painful consultations, humiliations handed out every minute of every day by a bastard world every bit as emotionally illiterate as he was; the whole goddam thing had vanished in the moment of his decision. Gone for good. Like him. He felt like a million dollars.

A sole moth flickered across the windscreen.

Cruising towards oblivion, he felt the car shake as it hit three deep ruts in quick succession. It reminded him of some music he had heard long ago, but… he never heard music now. He kicked the accelerator down and the wheels began to spin. Don't fuck it up now. Everything was going so, uncharacteristically, well.

He felt the left wing clip something. In the nearside wing mirror a wooden fence pole cartwheeled into the darkness. The blow sent the car rightwards across the track and, skidding now, it glanced off a grassy bank; the driver was struggling for control. Get it over with. Fast, fast. He slammed down once more on the accelerator; it felt so light, and the car seemed to float for a moment, the headlights frozen, all went smooth, but nothing moved except the wheels racing on the spot, showering liquefacted mud in giant red spurts back down the green lane. The old car halted, the more the driver powered it, the quicker the wheels turned and the less momentum he got. The abyss, so close, seemed much further away.

He rethought; but he had never been good at this. He took his foot off the pedals, let everything stop and then he started again, very, very gently. At first nothing gripped, but then, inch by inch, the car began to move slowly forward, towards the drop. If it took him an hour he could not care less; his resolve was crystalline. At last, he was moving in the right direction. Inch followed inch. Glimpses of well trodden path, a point of barbed wire, something like an airborne seed, a well of shadows, the eye of a rat, withered and ruined ferns bending their split heads... then it all went silent and fell into slower motion.

Incredible.

He was out of gas. Like, why would he need to skimp on fuel now, what would the cost of another gallon have mattered?

The windscreen, such a movie of motion and dynamics a moment before, was dull and sulky. Walking himself to the edge of the cliff had never been part of the storyboard. He stiffened. Upright in the driver's seat, staring ahead, tense. Like a test dummy.

The four angels stepped out of the darkness. White figures, female forms in tight jumpsuits. In place of wings; rifles. Moving out of the headlight beams, they paired off down the sides of the vehicle and the driver quickly wound down the front windows on both sides.

Two eyes, shadowy mascara, framed in a white balaclava.

"Can we help you?"

"I'm fine, Just leave me alone would you? I want to kill myself."

"We can help you with that."

"Who are you?"

"What does that matter to you?"

"It doesn't. Nothing matters. I'm just asking a question."

"If your brake is on, take it off. Then I'll answer."

It was not, but he checked.

"No brake. So, who are you?"

The white figure placed two white gloved hands over the sill of the window frame. "One question, if I may?" She did not wait for approval. "Do you feel that you could have done better, or others could have done better by you, or was there always something in you that would fail?"

"Something in me."

"Good."

The four white figures immediately gathered to the edges of the car.

"Wait, wait... I'd like to talk with you some more? I don't have to do this right this minute!"

The four white figures, as if in chorus, looked up; their eyes were cold. With one orchestrated shove they lifted the tyres out of the rut and the saloon began rolling over the greasy lane, silvery purple under the newly emerging moon.

Through the window the driver, 53, divorced, yelled: "who are you?"

And a voice from the pack of four white figures shouted: "We are the white snipers Brigade of the Beyondist Bund!"

As the car careened through brittle cast-iron railings and over the edge, the driver cast a last glance in the rear view mirror; unsure if the four white-clad women were waving him goodbye or were raising the right-handed Roman salute, before the saloon smashed into the blades of limestone below. There was no explosion like in the movies, only the hiss of compressed air escaping, a gentle groan of metal relaxing after impact and the quiet slurping as broken bones pushed further up into organs, while severed arteries and shredded muscles settled down into unfamiliar combinations.

The four white figures stood upon the broken cast-iron, gazed down from the cliff top as a cloud of dust bloomed upwards. From inside the car, a puzzled figure climbed, transformed, oozing a strange kind of new life, bent into a novel shape, a veil of blood folding down from his forehead and gathering on his chest. Faint, adrenalin racing through torn muscles and propping him up, soaring on broken bones, he raised his eyes as the four women raised their rifles. Red lasers cut through the night and the driver looked down at the jiggling dots playing on his blood-soaked vest and missed the wave that crashed over the rocks and washed him into the darkness.

Chapter 14

A crowd gathered at the entrance to the green lane that led up to the crest of the ridge. Beside it was the field down which the flaming wheel would soon be rolled. The wheel itself was pretty much as Dave described: an old wooden cable reel packed with straw and bound up with chicken wire. Mandi stood alongside Grant, Bob and Janine on the edge of the throng. The archivist woman, April, had run off up the lane to take photos. An unseen barker called the group to order.

"As it has been done for generations, so it shall be done! With this wheel we shall set the sun on its summer course!"

There was something comfortingly familiar in the unlikely archaism. A proportion of the crowd, mainly the Morris dancers, responded with an affirmative "aye" and raised their pewter tankards.

Dave, his arm around the waist of a distracted woman, turned to Mandi.

"That's our young Spike, he got himself a few of those "How to be a witch" books. Top job I'd say."

"Wiccan lite", Grant laughed.

Mandi looked up from her empty glass. "I'm going to grab another while the bar's quiet," she said, falteringly.

The invisible Spike continued: "And so shall it be that this eve we set the sun's fire in motion, enlivened, that she may be full this summer and gift a bounteous harvest…"

Grant leaned over to Mandi. "And all the tills may overflow with silver!"

Mandi started to wander back to the pub. What was Dave's game?

"Mary bold and bounteous be!" shouted Spike.

A pain gripped Mandi's stomach; something was in there grabbing at her insides.

"Mary bold and bounteous be!" called Spike a second time

Mandi stumbled against the oak bench by the pub door.

"Mary bold and bounteous be!" shouted Spike a third time, to which the crowd now roared a ringing "aye". The voices crowded in on Mandi's dizzied head; they pushed and shoved. Sharp elbows dug into her soft tissue. She felt sharpened blows in her stomach. She wanted to throw up. The wheel rollers had set off to the accompaniment of pipe and drums and excited chatter.

"You OK, Mandi?" called Grant.

"Yes, fine, I'll catch you up…"

Mandi was not fine. She was feeling decidedly sick, the rhyme of Dave's was whirling around her head, along with the image of the bloody tooth. Where had that gone? And Gary Glitter. In the background was a sound that Mandi felt impelled to repeat. "Mary, Mary, Mary. Mary… bold and bounteous be…" But it was more blurred than that…. It might have been "Many, Many, Many…" It was something between "Mary" and "Many"…

Mandi retched and the contents of the pasta meal she had had at the big house filled her nose and fell to the ground. Pieces of chewed vegetable and worms of spaghetti spattered the tiled porch.

"Oh dear, are you OK?"

"Oh I'm so sorry," stammered Mandi, the surprise jolting her back into reality.

"Had a bit too much, love?"

It was one of the bar staff stood over her, partly pitying, partly laughing. Half a cider is not a bit too much.

"No, I …" Mandi started to reply, but vomit was drooling from her chin.

"Hold on. Don't worry, we've all done it. I'll get you a glass of water and some tissues."

"Thank you" said Mandi, her voice now that of a nine-year-old. The nausea was passing, replaced by dire embarrassment. And something else. Not just the tininess and vulnerability of a child, but the painful openness, the naivety that let in terrifying things. Her body, so carefully self-controlled usually, had acted without her consent. Mandi prided herself that she could cleanse her system after a heavy night out and still kill a thousand-word blog post before breakfast. She had been exposed; and nothing warranted it.

"I don't know what happened…" Mandi started to explain. The barman returned with water, tissues and a bucket of sand. Genuine old school, thought Mandi. It took her back to primary school.

"… it must be something I ate?"

"That'll be it."

"I'll walk it off," said Mandi, sipping the last of the water. A little unsteadily, she wandered off towards the green lane where the wheel rollers had begun. Now, they were already high up on the hill. Mandi could hear their drums and shouts. A flicker of flame. The sun was low in the west, dipping towards the tree lined ridge. Half way up the gentle slope the lane forked, offering Mandi a choice of flaming throng or a quieter tree lined route to the summit. Her head was clearing, but the sting of infuriating humiliation remained. Not feeling sociable, Mandi chose the quieter left-hand path. When her attention was taken by a loud cheer, she turned and the flaming wheel was already rolling down the hill. From her viewpoint she could see, despite the lowering sun, that the trajectory it was following could, if forces allowed and obstacles permitted, take it all the way past Lost Horizon, over the Sett and into the sea. She partly wished it would, preferably with that idiot Dave and a few others attached to it.

"Sod you," Mandi muttered aloud.

Down below, the burning wheel had escaped its minders and leapt a hedge, careening into the kitchen garden wall of a large house, cleverly concealed by the large trees of its windbreak. The crash had brought people running – it was a fair way off now, but they looked like scientists in white coats from an old movie, then men in suits arrived – and an altercation was developing between the people from the old hall and the firewheel revellers. Raised voices floated up the hill, but any precise sense was lost in distortions of distance and the self-righteous hysteria of all concerned.

When Mandi was starting out she had briefly worked for a PR consultancy based in Slough; she had been enrolled into the company's 'Full Power' exercise. As part of which, Mandi had to take a 16PF psych-profiling test. Mandi's follow up phone call from the test interpreter had not gone well. 'Mike', probably ringing from a workstation in Shanghai, struggled through the results of her multiple guess questionnaire.

"Do you get easily bored?"

"Right now? Sure."

"Do you wish that you were more persuasive?"

"I wish I could persuade the company to stop wasting its money."

"Do you find it hard to cope with embarrassing situations?"

She told the interpreter that she was never embarrassed.

"Aren't you embarrassing yourself now?"

After putting down the phone she felt burned up with fury. Outside her window, a robin had landed on one of the lower branches of an oak and burst into song. She gazed at the robin, and for a moment it gazed back.

"What's your personality, little one?" Mandi had whispered. The robin had flown off over a hedge and away across the fields. Now, another robin squeaked a territorial demand, gave her a look and flew away. Mandi laughed, but a strange thought struck her; had the robin appeared when she was angry in Slough? Or just now when she was 'remembering' it? What if birds – or at least the timing of their appearances to us – are the products of our feelings?

A second fork in the path, just within the forest, was marked by a partially rotted way marker.

"Keep going left," Mandi thought.

The sun was now well within the tree line. Mandi knew that she could just turn round and retrace her steps, she had noted the turnings; but she reasoned that if she kept going left, she would end up where she started. Like in those old lost-in-the-desert movies. And something about not walking the same path twice. Patently she was marked somewhere on the map of ridiculous.

The further she walked, the more the nagging thoughts fell away. A sense of resignation fell over her. Not an unpleasant feeling. Perhaps all that snowflake nature folk ritual connectedness crap had helped clear her mind; it had been a strange day. She recalled an op-ed she had written called "What is nature anyway?" for some eco-modernist loons she despised, but who paid well. For their entertainment, she had called out the author of 'Last Child in the Woods' for facilitating privileged middle-class parents who lacked things to berate their poor conservative clone children about.

"It's not the kids who spend all their time in front of the screens, Richard Louv! Those are adults in the offices and the call centres and they need to get out more. But how could they, Richard? Because then who would you call to renew the insurance on your electric car? Believe me, the kids are happily connecting to nature down the park every night with a bottle of White Lightning."

It was a crude argument, but it had written itself. Mandi was paid handsomely, and it was partly true.

The path led her to a clearing. On one side was a stunted oak tree, its deformed branches, perpendicular to its trunk, reaching out over the space. There was a loaded feel to the space; as if her arrival had interrupted a conference of oaks. A gentle breeze approached, the trees on the fringes hissed at the wind as it passed through. Mandi's attention was grabbed by movement in the lower branches of the squat oak.

Curious, she wandered over. Out of the undergrowth, shockingly close up, a middle aged ruddy faced man emerged, stumbling on a fallen branch. His clothing was somewhat loose given the season. He was perspiring.

"What the fuck," said Mandi in surprise.

"I'm just foraging," he said nervously. Mandi heard the ping of his phone. Digging frantically in his pockets, he checked the message, and looked back up at her, helplessly. Unable to describe his mistake. Then he excused himself and hurried off into the undergrowth.

What had just happened there?

Looking down on the ground where the man had stood, a black carrymat was curling at the ends, froth on the lip of a discarded Starbucks coffee cup was hardening, a single black crumpled sock unrolled disconsolately and a set of car keys winked. He will be missing that, she thought momentarily. She looked up at the old oak.

"Welcome to Merrie England, you twats."

Above her the branches were festooned with hundreds and hundreds of used condoms, hanging like fruits. Some coloured, others perfectly transparent save for the obfuscations of spent matter. Each momentary crisis, maybe planned for days by text and apps, passed in seconds.

"What's love got to do, got to do with it…"

Mandi hummed, taken aback by her bitterness. Why should a libertarian care about what other people chose to do with their bodies? But this sexual detritus was simply dismal. There ought to be some sort of aesthetic merit. A quick shag on a crumpled mat in the woods with a loser from the 'burbs', not her idea of a beautiful thing... but it didn't seem to have struck these people as anything very beautiful either... maybe that was partly the 'appeal', the 'fuck you' to beauty, a perverse detour around the evolutionary imperative, a refusal of the tyranny of the attractive. Nasty. She could get that.

The sun had disappeared from the branches, swallowed by a hollow. Exhausted, Mandi slumped down beneath the condom tree. Sod hygiene.

"I really need to get over myself," she muttered.

The experience of sitting beneath a tree was markedly different from how she had imagined it. It had been a long time. Mandi shuffled impatiently, violently, attempting to find a comfortable support from the oak's unyielding substance. For a moment she was even convinced that some bastard had tossed his needles there, but the scratches were from twigs. She looked up, her lips closed tight, just in case something fell from the tree. She wondered if the latex blossoms were actually growing. Male flowers almost ripe and soon to drop their seed?

Mandi remembered her friends Toby and Jane back in DC who had a cat called Rubber. A rescue animal, the long-haired ginger tom had come with the name, allegedly because of its habitat of rubbing up against people. Jane had wanted to change the name to something less embarrassing to call out at night. She was unimpressed by Mandi's suggestion: 'Polyurethane'.

Beneath the oak, Mandi pursued a procession of thoughts. Cats' names, Toby and Jane, their kindness, those November walks in the park. Autumn leaves. Law firm offices; handsome paralegals moving like raptors. I see your lips, those summer kisses, the sunburned hands I used to hold. One thought after another. The summation of your life's thoughts. Sell your book.... Ugh, what? Robins and feelings? Well, Mickey, what if there ain't no next book...

A branch cracked. A couple of roe deer broke cover, bounding through the trees, pausing briefly to gaze back at Mandi, then on into the gloom. Mandi gently closed her eyes.

"I am Panagia."

The words fell into her.

"I am Panagia."

Something barked, far off.

Then the woods were still and the silence squeezed on her eardrums. A tinnitus-like hissing faded in and out, then settled down at wild track. Her mind, trying to make something of this audio Rorschach test, came up with its own whirring. No summation was forthcoming. Thought stopped. There was Nothing.

Mandi opened her eyes. Had she fallen asleep? For how long? It was dark, but it had been dark already, hadn't it? When did it get dark? A little to the right of where the roe deer had disappeared, an empty space. She peered into it. No information was forthcoming. As with the silence, there was nothing that her mind could make anything of. A perceptible and recalcitrant nothing.

"I am Panagia."

With the third repetition of the phrase, an image appeared. A gem in the ring of emptiness. A figure, her hands raised, pleading. At her heart, a writhing.

Another branch cracked. Footsteps. The glow of a torch. Mandi started and instinctively turned her head in the direction of the new intrusion.

Chapter 15

Bob and Janine were chasing the burning disc down the lanes with Grant at the wheel of his borrowed saloon, steering one-handed. As hunt followers, this kind of adventure came as second nature. It was a wild hunt! The flaming wheel careering down the hillside, at first within the trees, had somehow glanced off their trunks rather than come a cropper, then leapfrogged a stile with enough momentum to kick over its wooden step, plunge down a rough field steered by a quad bike track and then swing wildly through the one gap in a frost-crumbled boundary wall, climbing a pile of cracked rubble, and roll across manicured grounds before hammering in a shower of sparks and ashes into the fragile bricks of the elderly kitchen garden.

"Wow, they are going to be in such deep shit!"

Bob sounded delighted.

"Who lives there?" asked Grant.

"O, the aristocrat family are long gone," explained Janine. "It's Mandun Hall. They've taken the sign down. It's some kind of company offices now, they keep themselves to themselves…"

"Not anymore they don't," said Bob, turning the saloon into the metalled driveway, past a quaint lodge. After a hundred metres they were stopped by a metal gate with warning notices about dangerous dogs loose, privacy and no public right of way.

Grant wanted to turn back.

"It's a shame while we're here," wheedled Janine. Bob jumped out and swung open the gate and jumped back in. Grant drove through, reluctantly, without stopping to close the gate. As they slowly approached the big house it emerged from behind a massive windbreak of trees. A confrontation was already building in the grounds; a straggle of the Wiccans-lite were angrily harangued by white-coated and smartly suited residents of the big house. A parcel of crows was joining and scattering repeatedly above the affray. Fists were raised, not by the pagan yokels, but by the white-coated technician-types. Their physical prowess was likely to be unimpressive, but the flood of people from the big house had increased and the locals were outnumbered. The men in suits drew what looked like professional expandable batons from their belts and began to lay about the more aggressive of the pretend pagans.

Janine gasped. Grant braked.

Across the driveway, blocking their further progress, were four suited men in line abreast, a fifth in the centre, a stride ahead with his hand held in the traditional 'halt' gesture. At the fringes were four handlers with straining Dobermans.

"We'll be needing your magic, Grant…"

"That won't be necessary," said Bob, beginning to climb out of the car. "Dogs like me."

Janine reached over the front seat and with remarkable strength yanked him back into his seat.

"What the…"

"Do something, Grant…" begged Janine.

Grant pinched the bridge of his nose; this was the moment in the movie when the wind machines would blow all offending narrative obstructions onto the editing room floor. But somehow they were not in the movies anymore…

"O for…" and Bob began to open the door again, and again Janine reached over and placed an expanding hand over his shoulder and pulled him back into the leather upholstery.

"What the…"

Bob span round on Janine but she was already nodding to something outside, to their right.

Bob and Grant peered through the gloom.

"Let's get out of here!"

Grant gunned the car, reversed, performed a clumsy three-point turn and accelerated through the metal gate he had left open. As they turned, Grant looked up the grounds to where the wheel ceremony celebrants were being escorted lamely from the property. Among the suited men, their telescopic sticks still hanging from their fingers, seemingly in a position of some respect and power, was the unmistakable figure of Dave the joker, the Amazon Blackface stood behind him in the adjutant position. Grant was even more surprised by the swooping crow that landed on Dave's shoulder and seemed to turn Dave's head with its beak in the direction of Grant's car, sending the magician ducking beneath the side window.

"Jumping Baphomets, did you see that!" shouted Bob. "The women behind the hedge? They had guns!"

Chapter 16

Danny's day had not gone as planned. Or rather, as fantasised. Recent personal circumstances had left him bereft of intimacy; now with time and diminishing returns from the screen's cold show, desire had become a haptic affair. His choice might be wrong, but it was excitingly basic. He was driven: things would happen. The internet, ever generous, supplied Danny with locations, times, preferences, etiquette ("don't touch unless invited"). The prospect of others, an audience, a crowd and the firm slap of discipline were almost as appealing as the hope of contact. He had rifled the online encyclopaedias of England's Areas of Outstanding Natural Desire. There was even advice on disabled access!

Danny's journey to the ridge was a mixture of rising excitement and submersive self-loathing. Despite this longing, he soon decided he was not emotionally cut out for this sort of thing. He thought too much; at least he thought he did. He wanted to be like the crowd on the estate he had done a health project with. Unthinking and insensitive; they had sex on tap. How did that work? For people living "chaotic" lives they seemed to organise that pretty efficiently. Of course, he was not supposed to think that. He was trained not to think like that. But some kinds of people felt less and some kinds felt more, at least he felt so. He pressed on, the tightness in his chest and the sweat on his clenched hands did not abate. "I have not become an animal", he told himself.

The parking spot suggested by the website usefully came with GPS co-ordinates. They really had thought of everything. Danny had expected more cars, greater anonymity, he reasoned it might still be early. He turned off the engine and reached for his mobile. He flicked through his Facebook newsfeed; the happy contented lives of his friends were not what he needed right now. He reached for the ignition, this just wasn't him, but before he could turn the key, the doors of a red Honda estate parked by some wooden benches swung open and a young couple stepped out. The woman was blonde, perhaps in her thirties, confident, a young Julie Goodyear. Her basque suggested she was not there for birdwatching. No binoculars were evident. The bloke was older, well built. A builder by the look of him, thought Danny. He faltered. What if this was a set up? The guy looked like he could handle himself. The couple glanced once around the car park and then walked purposefully along the track and into the line of the forest. Danny hid his wallet under the front seat. The door of the car just behind Danny's closed with a click, the lock was beeped, and a single man, same sort of age as Danny, followed the couple at a discrete distance.

This was it, Danny thought. He wished he had left his Facebook feed alone. What was it to be? Enter the forest for a visceral and momentary thrill and suffer the shame at his leisure? No contest; something right there was always going to trump hazy prospects of future guilt. Which was why he never put himself in situations like this. Any chance that he could drive home and drink himself insensible with his self-worth intact were gone. He opened the door.

The couple and their follower had vanished. Danny followed the faint track through the ferns. Just within the tree line, the path forked. No sign or sound of anyone. He had not expected a search; just to queue. Listening carefully yielded nothing but the insistent alarm of a nearby blackbird.

"Singin' in the dead of night…"

He chose the right-hand path. The blackbird appeared from the brambles.

"Oh, hello! What do you want?" he asked.

The kindly exchange lifted Danny from the matter in hand. Into something worse. Danny recoiled and the bird flew off across the woods in the direction of the estuary, perfectly framed by the canopy and the forest floor. His earthy response to Julie Goodyear began to fade. Maybe he could pass this off as an evening stroll?

The right-hand path had led Danny up a steep bank towards a clearing. Danny sweated from the climb. Much more of this and he would not be up to a shag. Despite his work for the community health project, he had rarely bothered with the functioning of his own body; no one on the project would dare confront him about it. He had never discussed with his expert colleagues how his ego stayed so firmly in control of his state of mind, how when he got ill, it would obsess over its demise. The body, Danny reasoned to himself, does not fear death as it knows it will be reborn or recycled, but his ego's annihilation really upset him. So now it was an irony that when the chips were down, the bastard thing wouldn't let his wants have free reign. But, then, he hated his body too. So here he was, again, thinking too much and doing fuck all about it.

Danny's monologue was brought to an abrupt halt by the condom tree.

"What the fuck…"

He was disgusted. And out of breath. He loosened his shirt and sat down on a conveniently discarded black carry mat, flicking to the side an old coffee cup and a dubious looking old sock. Disgust instantaneously faded into a glorious resignation and serenity. It was so quick! He had never felt anything remotely like such euphoria. He wondered if he had sat on a discarded skag needle. He was going to be OK! He was not the creep he thought he might be, and this brought a smile so wide to his face that it hurt. All of his fevered planning, the anxious drive, that all fell away. The robotized programming of his armoured shell loosened; he began to undo the straps. He could sit right here, naked beneath the condom tree, and everything would be really, really,

really OK. He was gently closing his eyes, when he heard the pad of approaching footsteps.

His eyes snapped open. Had he fallen asleep? How long had he been there? It was still dark…

Anxiety returned at the thought of having to explain himself, a lone male, in the woods, sweating and sitting on a carry mat beneath this particular tree. They would say he was a pervert, or a limp dick. He could not win from here on in. He sprang to his feet hoping to get away before being seen, but it was too late; far, far too late.

The raven-haired woman was clearly surprised. Danny stumbled for words, but he felt he should at least try and explain himself.

"I'm … I'm … I'm just foraging…"

The words were as much a surprise to him as the appearance of the woman. "Foraging"? What was he? A hunter-gatherer? Bear Grylls, for… Without waiting, he stepped quickly away from the woman and the tree and fled into the thicker forest.

"Fuck," he repeated to himself over and over. "She's probably going to report me. I'll be cautioned by the police. Health charity worker exposed… Fuck, fuck, fuck…"

After half an hour of wandering about randomly trying to guess the right path in the increasing gloom, he found his car. Then he felt the ground of the car park cave in. He felt the forest close around him like an angry and lascivious crowd. His keys were not in his pocket. He knew – how did he know? – he knew for sure exactly where they were. Back in the woods beneath that tree. Must have fallen out of his pocket when he was asleep.

Danny picked his way back to the tree slowly, using his phone torch to light the path. He really did not want to meet that woman again. That surely would be the end of his life. What if she made an accusation? What was she doing there, anyway? He clambered up the hill to the clearing, surprised at how quickly he found it.

"Jesus, what's that?" he whispered to himself.

The torch on his phone was not so powerful, but it shone enough light into the gloom to pick out a vague figure. Danny shivered. A trick of the light combined with fatigue, maybe. He strained to see.

Wow.

The figure stood some eight feet tall, slender and motionless. Its arms, if that is what they were, were held upwards in a gesture of supplication. From the waist, twisted tendrils fell down to the forest floor.

"Fuck."

Danny stalled. He felt his mind fail. Nothing in him knew what to do or how to do it. He needed his keys.

"It's just the tree!" He shouted at the thing. "You're just the fucking tree!"

That had reasoned with it, he decided. He walked slowly forward, keeping his torch on the spot where the tendrilled figure was. As he drew nearer the vision transformed into a broken trunk, with drooping branches, weighed down with condoms, draped with a little ivy.

"Oh thank god," he said aloud, and dropped to his knees by the carry mat, head down searching for the keys. To his massive relief, he found them. He sat up and sighed. He could now go home, grab a few drinks, more than a few, sleep off this fucking nightmare.

"Danny?"

Danny looked around. An indistinct voice. Again, hushed.

"Hello?" He responded nervously.

The whisper came again.

"I'm just looking for my car key…" explained Danny, gesturing awkwardly to the earth and the trash, "and I'm sorry."

His voice seemed to be speaking for itself. "I'm sorry," it said again.

The whisper, a repeated phrase, now became more distinct.

"I am Panagia."

"I'm sorry, I need to go home. I'm not a bad person. Please, let me go."

Danny felt tears on his cheeks. He felt the massive figure in the shadows driving them down his face. He felt its terrifying, body-bending power. He was scared by how turned on he was by the thought of the mutilation of his body.

"I'm not a bad person, I'm just, you know, confused or something… please don't tell on me…"

His voice sounded like that of a child. The child he had been once. The tears continued to roll down his face, but they were nothing to the waves of memory and loss that were pummelling him. As they fell, Danny felt a huge release; as if a tumour or a stone were expelled from his belly. Something was becoming unblocked. It was OK to be Danny. It was OK to be all the conflicting and confusing wicked and desiring things that Danny is. It was OK to say one thing and think another. And not know; ignorance and knowing nothing was fine with Her. Not knowing anything really. It was OK that the world was confusing and that he didn't really understand other people or what they were there for. That it was OK to desire what you did not know, that it was the giving up on the need to begin again, turn over new leaves and break new grounds, and guilt was the first portal and he did not need to go through it… he had the keys, he should run now… For the first time in a while, Danny felt warm towards himself, at the same time he was coldly petrified by the dark figure that seemed to grow up in front and above him, sucking in all the shadows from the forest, silencing the blackbirds, and through the tears he laughed and laughed and laughed. And then he screamed and screamed and screamed.

Chapter 17

Dream Diary (Mandi Lyon, sole entry, undated)

At the beginning of the dream I was flying. A group of birds were either supporting me or flying alongside me. I felt no fear of the height. I felt very light, 'light as a feather', ha ha. I thought of this phrase in the dream, I laughed at it in the dream. Down below me, the landscape of the area was laid out partly like a 3D model and partly like the real thing but seen from a distance. From what I could see it was all very accurate, from the sea and the Sett on one side, across the fields to the foot of the hills, then the villages in the West clustered around the Great Hill, like it really is. I was not seeing this from any particular direction, but from all directions. Then it was more like a game board, or a very cheap movie set. It got more intense then, the hills were more mountainous and there were prehistoric mounds, barrows, standing stones that I didn't recognise. There were also people in the fields, and under the trees. I assumed these were from the ancient tribes who once lived here. I hadn't noticed anyone before; and these people were careful not to show themselves. Even though it was ancient times, there were lanes just like there are now; with macadam tops, so it was a bit mixed up in terms of time, but the basic geography was right. There were also beings that weren't right; black dogs with red eyes, a giant person with bat wings, hobgoblins, and walking electricity pylons and parades of trees, zombie-like trees, a Labrador made of gold (!) came running down past me, I was on the ground by now, though I don't remember landing, and a pack of animal ghosts (cats, dogs, other pets) came racing by, a hairy lurching thing with a tail following at the back with a colony of wolverines. They ran into the forest and I followed them, they disappeared and for a while I was very lonely; then I felt a presence and there was a glowing tree in a clearing, right in the middle with the moon shining down on it. It had been daylight before, now it was night. The tree was covered in white glow-worms that all began to fly and settle all over me, on my arms, in my hair. It was very pleasurable, except for one worm, on the back of my hand that began to insert itself, like a living cannula, into one of the veins, it was very painful and the other glow worms began to do the same thing. I said: "these aren't actually snakes, these are legless lizards" and the worms all laughed and pretended to be drunk, it was crazy, they were all very long now, and hanging out of my skin and lolling about pretending to be drunk, so I was surrounded by a writhing skirt of these things which felt really slippery, rather than the dry skin they have in real life. When I said "you're not wet", they replied that they had come to show me something about the sea. Then one of the worms that had inserted itself into the flesh just under my breastbone began to expand massively like a balloon blowing up and opening the flesh out; it disappeared into the hole and I bent over to look and I was looking into a cave with snakes running down the walls like water and I thought 'I can see right into myself'. What was a bit odd and didn't make sense was that although I was bending right over, I wasn't seeing the cave upside down, but right way up. Inside the cave was a part that was much darker than the rest; I strained to see what it was, but there was nothing there. Then a huge figure walked right across my vision and I fell backwards and cracked my head on the rock and the figure was standing right over me, it was female, it had huge windmill sails growing out of its back and poles with red flags stuck into its collarbones and it was protected by a guard of squids psychically controlled by this thing I knew was called "The Navigator" which was mostly a body of bones and a huge helmet with a full-face visor and it communicated with me and said "we are the true people" and I saw human people running down the lanes, nineteenth century people in clothes of that period, terrified of the squids, and jumping into boats, which didn't make sense as a way of escaping sea monsters. I tried to tell them. The animals – and this now included the squids and the black dogs and the slow worms – caught someone and they began to rip this man's arms to shreds with jaw bones and teeth they had taken from the floor of the cave inside my stomach and – this was right in front of me – I could see them peeling huge slices of flesh off this man's arms and then his chest and stomach and they peeled them down until they trailed on the ground and he looked like he was wearing a huge skirt of his own flensed fat. The man wasn't in any kind of pain, instead he was really excited, his eyes turned back inside his head and his arms were up in the air like 'happy-clappy' worship, and his mouth was a shape like "Mandi bandy up from the deep / Rode the big squid in her bare feet" and that's when I realised he was worshipping me... I looked down at myself again and I saw that I was the landscape with the mounds and hills and valleys and cave and that my teeth were broken standing stones and out of my back grew these huge pages with a title like 'The Pocket Book of Birds' and the pages began to flap and I felt an incredibly cold wind and heard a beating and I held out my arms with the flapping pages on them and on either side of me were exact copies of myself and together we began reciting a spell in birdsong and the whole forest shivered and out came the creatures, nameless things, all sorts of weird confabulations of teeth and string and blubbery heads and instead of the Sun there was a giant darkness in the shape of something that I knew, I knew really really really well, and I wasn't allowed to say, I struggled to think of its name, but just as I had it I forgot it again and I woke up with a horrible start... under the tree, draped in condoms, yeeuch, and I was so stiff from being propped up against it I could not move, but I could see a pair of feet in front of me ... and I had to really strain, hurting my neck to see whose feet they were, and a voice said "you are awake" and all the toes on the feet, there were eight on each and twelve feet, they began wriggling and wriggling and I jerked back and hit my head again and I blacked out in the dream and I woke in the real forest and there was someone coming.

Chapter 18

Mandi was not at all sure what to do. She knew movement would give away her presence. If she stayed sat at the base of the tree, however, the intruder might go by without seeing her. But the intruder's torch was scanning the ground, shining directly at her. Mandi's pulse raced.

"Jesus, what's that?" she heard the intruder say. It was a man. He must have seen her. Yet he was not letting on, despite the torch surely revealing her sat against the tree. Maybe he thought she was a corpse or a hobgoblin. He walked slowly and deliberately towards her, shadowed behind the torch's beam.

Then, without a word, he dropped to his knees.

Was he praying or something? Mandi was seriously worried now; this guy was acting like a maniac. She wanted to get up and run, but she had seen that film. That scene never went well for the woman.

"Hello?"

The figure spoke.

Mandi thought quickly. It was not a definite "hello" as if he had seen her or recognised her. It was more of a question.

He whispered something again and then more clearly: "I'm sorry."

He seemed to be sobbing now. This was way too freaky. Mandi tried to call out, but something had clicked in her lungs, she made almost no sound at all. The man continued to kneel, a few feet from her, wailing now and throwing his head back and forth.

"I'm not a bad person, I'm just confused!"

He kept repeating this. Mandi dare not move; yet her initial horror was giving way to a kind of calm. She gazed at the kneeling figure, a palpable sense of compassion towards him rose from somewhere inside her. It was not something she recognised; it was part of the pathology of her fear. She wanted to reach out and hold his head in her lap and comfort him. To have the power to soothe his brow and snap his neck.

It was now just him and her. Everything else had melted away. And he was laughing, joyously. And Mandi was laughing too.

Chapter 19

The robin was the first to sing that morning. Followed by the blackbirds. And in the top of the condom tree, a song thrush. Its percussive and insistent notes finally woke the slumbering Mandi. For a few seconds she gazed around her, empty. Then the thoughts began to rush in. She had been there all night. She was alone. She was OK. She really was as stiff as a board. Getting to her feet, carefully testing her muscles and avoiding the condoms – she could have sworn that there were fresh ones that had been hung on the branches since she fell asleep – she stepped into the clearing and gazed out on the view down to the valley. The vista had an unreal quality, the colours, so bright, were childlike; it was like looking at a bad painting or a model made with egg boxes and poster paints. The kind of place those creatures, the nameless things with weird conglomerations of teeth and sinew and slubbery-dubbery brains, might come racing out of the trees. Instead, what came was the black-clad figure of the caretaker.

"Come on, Mandi, you've been here all night." He looked around. "It's not the safest place in the world."

"How did you know I would come here?"

"Same reason everyone else comes here."

"Sex?"

He snorted gently.

"The spirit of the place."

Chapter 20

For the rest of the day, Mandi completed the arrangements for Anne and Bryan's funeral; getting everything ready before a much-needed return to London. What she had wanted to do was walk on the dunes and talk with the caretaker, but each time she thought she had everything in place, another subtlety would strike her, another detail would step out of true. She was learning about the inexact complexities of her 'pagan' tenants; the interwoven genealogies, the histories they had all somehow remembered for themselves, the distinctions that proved to be equivalencies and the equivalencies that proved to be distractions. At different times during the day Mandi had decided that they were all rare sorts striving in good faith for something remarkable, ordinary types trying to exceed their own expectations of themselves, and that they were a motley bunch of conniving and conspiratorial opportunists. What she had not expected was the importance of respectability and acceptance for so many of them; no sooner had they settled on some aspect of the service than both its critics and its proponents were looking for how to massage it into something recognisable in other spiritual discourses. Mandi wondered if, outside of church circles – she had no real idea – anyone in modern British society worried about this stuff. It was only as the prospect of missing the last connection to a London train began to loom that Mandi surrendered her hope for a walk on the sands and an exegetical gossip with the caretaker. That would have to wait. With minutes left, she rapidly packed a bag with essentials and ran to the station, past the charred shell of the slot machine parlour, and up the hill past a neat holiday home whimsically named Bedlam Towers. Sprinting up the incline she dashed through the platform entrance beside the railway house, but she need not have rushed quite so manically. The electronic display indicated that her train was delayed, due in 3 minutes.

Mandi did not want to wait, to think, to look, to feel; just to be on a train, getting away, losing herself in another kind of world. Everything around was bright, sensually enhanced, high definition. She looked at the platform and at the rift between the pinkish tarmac and the concrete slabs that formed the edge, its Hawkbit and Bristly Oxtongue rooted in the grime like miniature versions of jungle trees shading Cyclopean stop-motion throwbacks; the idea irritated her. She turned to look at a train already parked alongside the other platform in the hope of something banal; but the train was unusual. In mustard yellow livery, inside dull lights were on in the carriages, no one aboard as far as Mandi could see. The interiors were like old-fashioned offices; seats arranged in fours around tables on which sat IT towers. Mandi tried to make out the images on the screens; maps of the railway system or a blueprint of circuitry, possibly. She was too far away, and, anyway, her train was approaching; the wait had passed, she had distracted herself. The one carriage stopper – she would change at Exeter for London – sounded its horn as it passed the bend with its pedestrian crossing; where, for some reason, she knew that the original station had been sited, and something about why they moved it, something her adoptive parents had told her in a rare moment of...

"Amanda! Amanda Lyon!"

Up the steep incline, a rolling gait as if she had run some distance, laboured the archivist from the Museum. It was a strange place for her to catch the train, why not use the station in her own town? The stopper pulled to a jerky halt and the doors opened. No one got out; Mandi put a foot on the step to the carriage.

"I've found something important, can you wait, catch the next one..."

Mandi did not want to wait; there was no next one till morning, the important thing was to be away.

"You're too late, sorry... I have to get back to..."

She moved to climb into the carriage and the historian tried to restrain her, placing a firm hand on her lower arm. The guard yelled angrily from the end of the train: "Step back, that lady! Step back right now!"

The archivist leapt back in surprise. Mandi moved back inside the train, taken aback by the firmness of the archivist's grip; the guard rang the buzzer, the doors closed, and the train moved away. Mandi took her seat quickly; she expected the archivist to be left gesticulating on the platform, but she had already turned away and was walking quickly back along the platform, where a broken arcade machine, a mechanical fortune teller, a travesty of the Bocca della Verità mask in the Santa Maria church in Rome, leant open-mouthed and stupefied against the wall of the railway house.

Mandi closed her eyes, but the scary angels persisted inside her head until Exeter, where she finally managed to distract herself with the lights of a small factory and incinerator beside the canal. In a boatyard ropes and chains were holding a pristine hull as it was lowered onto the bed of a lorry; 'The Loch Ness Cruiser'. On the London train, Mandi found the trolley and drank herself to sleep for a couple of hours. In her dreams the angels swirled about in coordinated displays with a plesiosaur, creating a vast space of darkness in the gaps in their aerobatic routines. Lowering herself into that void, Dream-Mandi lost any sense of herself in a rich zone of pure feeling. Pulling into Paddington, the guard's announcement jerked her away from sleep; it was something about "Mandi in First Class coach A, you have left your destiny on the refreshments trolley, how will you find the chapel, the well and the cave now?" Awake-Mandi grabbed her bag and pushed her way past sleepy passengers desperate to get to the solid ground of the platform.

Chapter 21

JW3 is a Hampstead right rectangular prism and Mandi was happy to find a place in its symmetry. She brushed aside the idea that she had found herself in an aquarium. The giant plates of thick glass did not detain water, but drew in buckets of light, splashing them about everywhere; across shiny tables and over huge planes of wall. She eyed the self-service brunch and waited for her date.

The train journey had been uneventful. In the moments when she could escape her dreams, she had stared out across gloomy counties, into their brown-lit bedrooms and dark lych-gates, their sparsely occupied pub car parks and muddy canal towpaths; all quickly passing without any manifestation of the broken-toothed angel that had been plaguing her since she had been told to get home. The RTN ticket had exorcised the hallucinating power of the OUT one.

Back in her Belsize Park flat – a postage stamp she had blagged for a pittance from a billionaire – it was hard to believe that she had been away. Everything was neatly tucked in its place, folded and sited; prepared, anxious to be working again. Mandi had no memory of tidying the flat before she left.

She was in a kind of daze, a sharp daze, a daze filled with bitterness. "I'll come back for the funeral; let them fight it out". Crabbe the caretaker had looked forlorn; as if he had failed in some way, or missed an opportunity. Or that maybe she had. Well, those were her issues, not his. She was beyond caring for a while.

Technically, Tyrone was one of her trustees, but he had become a trusted friend; a Palladium treasure. He pulled up a chair and tossed the tiny single sheet menu to Mandi. She had never stopped being surprised by just how lonely everyone in London was. Sure, there were the handful of younger execs who had already built their nest, who plugged into their chicks for a recharge either side of the paid childcare, and then there were the older men who had long ago made their own arrangements for brightening the hinterlands of tired marriages; but mostly there was a desperate reaching out through the flood of pixels for some kind of fleshy response. In that market, friendship was a rare metal. Even so, she was surprised on her return to find an envelope slipped under the door of her flat; only the other residents and the landlord had access and this was not their kind of envelope. Tyrone's invitation was simple; he knew what would get to her. A hint of sympathy and she would have screwed him up and tossed him in the bin.

The restaurant was a kind of canteen; the menu a set of rules. If you left anything on your plate you paid extra; and you could eat and drink yourself stupid for the same flat fee. At a glance she could tell that no one there would. The counter of food reminded Mandi of some of the artists' studios she had hung out in; the ones where the artists were going back to painting. Ones you could sit for, strip for. There was something very 1920s about them – as if they had emerged from the trenches of conceptualism and one-trick ponyism, unembarrassable and familiar with corpses, rediscovering the representation of fleshy surfaces in claggy colours. It was fun to watch them fail, caught in the flytraps of hardening oil. The tastes, however, were fantastic. The first bite into the soft carrot and she was reminded of the existence of happiness.

Tyrone was still in breakfast mode; piling his plate with layers of eggs and pancakes and folded parcels of smoked salmon. He took some of the cold fish in his long brown fingers and dropped it whole into his mouth. He ate to let her talk.

She complained. That morning she had tried to make herself a latte; the milk had formed a skin across the top of the cup and she had been too... something... to peel it away.

"Something my ... something Anne would say: 'couldn't kick a skin off a rice pudding'. What am I turning into? A libertarian who's managing a commune?"

"It's a commune?"

He bit into soft pancake; but his eyes scorched hers.

"Not really. They wear the clothes. I think they would probably like it to be, but Anne and Bryan ran a tight ship, I can already tell that. Maybe it was just good business sense, I don't know, but I can sense something else there that they might have wanted to manage, or contain."

Tyrone swallowed.

"What?"

Mandi shrugged.

"They're lightweights. Lifestyle pagans, with a little small press publishing on the side. I think Anne and Bryan were different. When they could get away from the camp..."

"Stalag... "

"Stop it. It's where I grew up. In its own way, it's sweet. Yet... weird... it's horribly unfamiliar. I remember our house, but..."

She shook her head and sipped her skinny latte; but the thought of the skin on the milk in her flat made her gag slightly. She was making a fool of herself in front of one of her trustees; her response was visceral, as if the parts of her body literally pulled themselves together. She tightened.

"...they're all strangers to me. Ten years is a long time, but surely people don't change that much?"

"O, they do. People are jellies. Turncoats, chameleons... change is what people do. I wouldn't put money on anyone sticking by what they stand for."

"Not even me?"

"Especially not you."

Tyrone meant it; though he smiled and pulled another pancake from the tower. On the next table a frizzy haired young woman performed an effortless pixieness; her eyes blazed with attention to her friends. Her frequent smile was a gorgeous half-moon. There was surely art in all this, but Mandi was tantalised. It was not like her to fall for someone at first sight, but since the accident she felt as if she was inventing what she was like each day differently.

"Let me see what spring is like, on er... Jupiter and Mars...' The scat singer heading up the jazzy three piece at the end of the room lapsed into words.

Mandi was thinking about the weather on other planets. Tyrone was not.

"I don't want to be a container. I don't want to be a manager," she eventually offered.

"You are a manager, Mandi, that's what you do."

"But of a holiday camp? I don't want to screw up everything here..."

"We won't let you. We'll do everything to stop that. You're not seriously thinking of giving it all up to go back to Devon, are you?"

"Your concern is very sweet. I think?"

"You've just lost you mum and dad..."

"Not really. I don't make a big fuss about it, Tyrone, but actually I'm adopted."

"O. I'm sorry. So who did you grow up with?"

"O, with them."

"Then they were as good as parents. They were your parents."

"It's complicated..."

"I'm just saying, it's a big shock, don't make any hasty decisions, we need you. You don't need to do anything now; no one was expecting you back for a couple of weeks."

"How did you know I'd come back?"

"A little bird told me."

And he laughed, spread his fingers like crabs on the table top, and leaned over to Mandi to whisper in her ear. She was not sure how seriously to take Tyrone; he was well known in the charity sector as an operator who read the ground intuitively. There had been one or two minor scandals at organisations where he had worked and yet when they broke – nothing massive, minor confusions of interest – by then, he had already moved on; no blame was attached, but he had seen what was coming and made his excuses. He was a good person to have on your side in a shitstorm.

After the meal Tyrone suggested a walk on Hampstead Heath.

"Are you Jewish?"

"No", he laughed, "a friend brought me here. Now I can't stay away. I like it, I feel comfortable here."

"Behind massive sheets of blast proof glass?"

"Mandi, you know the sector. That's what it takes."

Climbing Arkwright Road, Tyrone invited her to spill her feelings. He had worked hard, it was the least she could do for him. As she opened up, she had meant to share her thoughts about Anne and Bryan, her regrets around not knowing them better, at her having to rely mostly on suspicions rather than memories. How weird and freakish she felt at not having a childhood to look back to, to feel that her legacy was a kind of blank from which she, Anne and Bryan were all missing. But what came out was a splurge about reviewing her position in the world, getting old (30), wondering aloud what kind of a person she was, what stuff she really believed in and what were just sticky ideas she had picked up on her shoes passing through. The last tenuous link to a family was gone and she would have to stand up on her own.

"Isn't that what you've always done?"

"That's what I thought, but I'm not so sure now. Maybe that was smoke and mirrors. There was always something in my background shoring me up. I've been trying to reach back and identify it. Maybe some really very early memory of my real parents? I don't think it's that though. It was something to do with Anne and Bryan, some link through them to a strength I have always had. Is there such a thing as a weak strength? Something that gives you power, but makes you weak?"

"Bullying? Prejudice..."

"I hadn't thought of it like that. God, is that what I am? A bully?"

"I didn't mean..."

"I didn't either. But for once I'm not going forward. I was always going forward. Not just cos' I was pushing myself, I was good. I was changing organisations, I was making space for weak people to become strong people, for clones to become individuals, for dependents to become independents, and now I'm asking myself whether I have always depended on someone else or something else in order to have that. Have I always been standing on other shoulders?"

"Doesn't everyone?"

"You really believe that? Whose shoulders did you get to stand on? Toes, maybe. No, not shoulders. No one should. So am I going to waste the next part of my life facilitating a camp full of benefit-scrounging hippies and Satanists? At Childquake I'm managing for people who have no rights at all. Children. They're worth it, right? I feel differently about compromising my principles for a bunch of ageing hippies. They already did all the things my kids can't do."

"Satanists?"

"No! Of course not! There's no such thing! It was all invented by Denis Wheatley..."

"By who?"

"Not important. The important thing is that for the first time I can remember, I have an obligation that I didn't choose to have, and I object to that on principle. I am the unwilling owner of a seaside holiday camp full of hippies. Jesus!"

"Can you sell it?"

"Sure, but I don't want to. And I don't understand why. I thought if I told you it would help, but it isn't..."

"I'm sorry..."

"It's not your fault. This isn't about you, Tyrone..."

"I am one of your trustees. I am not going to lose you. For a maverick libertarian you're a brilliant organiser. Surely, you can bring in someone to help run this camp? Delegate – with your contacts! Keep the camp, pocket the profits – you don't have to be there."

"No. I do. I have to be there. I don't know why, but I do."

"So why did you come back to London?"

He knew. She had not meant to speak about this; the conversation would not have come around to this unless he wanted it. They had left behind the giant somehow anonymous mansions on Arkwright Road and were blundering around in the expenses of Belsize Park.

"Do you know where you are going?"

"Vaguely. Why did you come back?"

"Because being there was driving me mad. Literally."

"And now that you're back? How's that?"

"I feel fine."

"I rest my case."

They had come to a junction with a main road. On the opposite side of the traffic artery was a medium-sized building, standing out from the houses, with the same kind of self-conscious symmetrical massing as JW3; except that in place of glass there were planes of brick, painted a peeling white, and in the centre a half-dome tipped on its side, its curved edges entering the brick walls as if they might continue where they were concealed. There was no sign, no number, no door that Mandi could see; it was like a giant version of a tatty children's play-garage blanched by time.

"What's that?"

"Really want to know?"

Mandi puffed her cheeks and blew a non-committal sigh.

"No worries, then."

"No, what is it?"

The bastard. He had hooked her.

"Come up here."

And he led her across the road, turning away from the odd white superstructure, striding ahead and beckoning to Mandi to follow him up the main road and away from the modernist mystery. At a line of shops he turned sharply into a wide alley and Mandi broke into a jog to keep up. At the side of the short concrete drive was a great flat slab of concrete, like a redundant altar, and at the end was another odd white building, virtually identical to the one on the main road, but more like the prow of an ark. This one had a door; a dirty grey featureless plate of metal.

"You wanna see?"

Tyrone rifled his jacket pockets and produced a key; four sides of teeth from shoulder to tip. The dull metal door opened surprisingly smoothly; Tyrone flicked a switch and dispelled the darkness. They had fallen back through time. It was something about the way that Tyrone's classic Hackett colours suddenly made no sense against the institutional paint of the strange building; Tyrone shone like a surreal slushy against the dried blood colour scheme of the antique lift contraption, sealed inside a pillar-shaped cage. A crude sign pointed to a spiral staircase: UPPER LEVEL STAIRWAY.

"What's down there?"

Tyrone threw back the sliding metal gate of the lift.

"I'm not getting in that. Is this your idea of Elevatorgate?"

Tyrone didn't miss a beat.

"You won't find any coffee down there."

"How old is that thing?"

"It's better maintained than any lift at your office. The maintenance crew are ... put it like this... they're the people who don't make mistakes."

Against her better judgement, Mandi stepped into the lift, and Tyrone slammed shut the gate and pressed the button for the bottom; once again, the font of the numbers on the control panel made her feel like they were in a time slip. Yet, there was no jerky drop into the past, but a smooth, purring descent. Mandi was flattered that Tyrone was trying so hard to impress her; their wandering route must have been part of his ploy, but she remembered taking most of the decisions. That took talent.

If Mandi was impressed by the lift, it was nothing to the sights that greeted her at the bottom of their descent. Tyrone powered up a lighting unit and overhead fluorescent tubes stuttered successively into life, illuminating a short passageway crowded by a ventilation unit with a fan the size of a propeller on a Second World War bomber, which led to a gigantic tunnel that stretched and stretched far away; so distantly that Mandi could not make out any far wall. It just seemed to end at a point. All down one side was a thick weave metal cage, while down the other was the curved metal skin of whatever massive tube it was they were inside.

"OK. First: wow. I think you deserve that. Maybe a 'sick'. But I don't think that's why I'm here. Explain yourself, young sir."

"The answer is in here."

He tapped a code into an anachronistic hi-tech keypad strapped onto the metal caging and a section shifted to allow them in.

"If would be nice if the trustees of worthwhile charities were in their positions simply because of the generosity of their feelings, but, as you well know, a generous direct debit is also required if sentiment is to be complemented by effective outcomes. Crudely, Mandi, this is where I make my money. Hard to believe, yet this is unstable stuff. Volatile; like bricks and mortar its value rises without anyone having to do a damn thing other than make sure it continues to exist."

He gestured to acres of shelving.

"What is it?"

"Information. In its crude form. The government pays my company to look after it; the people at the top ran out of trust in bureaucracies thanks to their believing people like you and your scare stories about serfdom under the tyranny of clerks. Instead, we chose to be under the lash of accountants, but hey ho..."

And he fluttered his long brown fingers as if they might turn into the fantail of a bird.

"...these are medical records, not the routine GP and NHS stuff. These are records from a humungous... by the way, we have to have our own private Official Secrets Act agreement here..."

"If you tell me you have to kill me..."

"Something like that. Though, I'm the likely victim. There's nothing security sensitive here. Nothing Joe Ordinary couldn't ask to see, if he knew it was here and how to ask for it. It's what's left of a giant HM Gov scheme from the mid 50s to the 80s which was when our state lost faith in its own benevolence. Nothing was done with any of this. But here are the records of a whole generation and a half – not everybody, but a controlled sample and massive compared to anything ever done by commercial polling pre-digital. This..."

And he threw his aquamarine sleeved arm wide.

"...is where the health of a nation unfolds, where it confesses its eating habits, sleeping habits, exercise routines, stress levels, cultural activities, units of alcohol, calories, fats, relationships, std's, regularity of conjugal relations, drugs, hobbies, access to silence, air quality.... membership of sex clubs, masons, political parties... there's a portrait, an anatomy of the generation of people who either rule us or have sucked us dry, right there, in printed, analog form."

"OK. Wow. I give it another wow. But that can't be it? Isn't there something – other than my general revulsion that any state would do such a thing to its citizens – you want from me? In relation to all this?"

"Well, I was rather hoping you'd be so impressed by my access to the secrets under London streets that you'd come back to my flat and allow me access to some of your secrets..."

"Jesus Christ, Tyrone, is that the best you can do? You said we could walk on Hampstead Heath?"

"We can do that too."

"What are we waiting for, then? Let's get out of here."

The rest of their walk was oddly romantic. After passing Triffid Alley, they walked around the plum tree under which Keats had written 'Ode to a Nightingale', turned down Downshire Hill where there was a blue plaque to two surrealists and then, after a house where a sinewy ornamental tree had almost grown across the door, the Freemasons Arms, where the pub sign triggered something in Mandi. By now she and Tyrone were walking with fingers brushing. And although there was a prospect of something else, she did feel that here was the alien brother she had always wanted.

"Tyrone?"

"Sure?"

"You wanted me to talk about my mum and dad... Anne and Bryan?"

"Only if you want to. Only if it helps..."

"Of course it doesn't help. They're dead! Nothing helps when someone's dead. I just remembered something. Up this hill. On the Heath. Something they told me. Something they thought was terribly important, or importantly terrible. Maybe that was it."

"What was it?"

"Why do you want to know?"

"I want to indulge you."

"You... well, for that, you get to hear about it, whether you want to or... I want you to."

She leaned over a low front wall and picked a few pebbles from a desultory floral border. Wiped then against her trouser leg. Tyrone mock gasped.

"Back in the .... woo... late eighteenth century, seventeen hundreds... a story older than it feels, kind of thing you imagine Victorians doing, anyway... there was this Welsh individual, no special education, but smart, way outside the dominant groups, but he has a head for power, so he invents a whole new magic story-space where he's the teller, he dictates the story. And to make his storyland he calls together a handful of other enthusiasts... Welsh nationalists in exile, o, and his name is something like Jones or Jenkins, for real, but he calls himself 'Iolo Morganwyg' ... approximately ... and they gather on the hill just up there, on the Heath. Parliament Hill, isn't it?"

"Yeh. And?"

"O, there's an and. So, he calls these people up to the top of the hill and from his pocket he produces a few poor stones, like these..."

And Mandi laid the stones in a rough circle on the nearest slab of pavement.

"And they conducted some bogus ceremony – from ancient texts that Iolo just happened to have found... or wrote... know what that becomes? The National Eisteddfod; the Queen is a bard of it! I'm not interested in this stuff, but I remember Mum and Dad talking about it... they would get very animated... everybody goes ooo Stonehenge, but my Dad called it paganism's Nuremberg Rally... Mum and Dad thought it was a wrong turn that those beliefs took, way back then – hierarchy, priests, rituals – I'm not talking about what they do there now, that's all pretty harmless, all very open and meek and mild, but Dad didn't reckon the historical practices were benevolent at all, he thought it all fell apart because it was so reactionary, which, ironically, is why the memory of it survives because it was so reactionary and put up giant temples of giant stones that never quite disappeared. But, hey, quite inspiring... Iolo not Stonehenge, a few people on a hill making things up, with stones in their pockets, eventually they get HMQ for patron..."

"I thought that was Primrose Hill."

"O yeh. You're right."

How the fuck did he know that? Mandi glanced at Tyrone; a cool black British entrepreneur in a blue Hackett suit; maybe things were a lot better than... yeh, or maybe a lot, lot worse.

Passing the bathing pools, as a screeching squad of parakeets hurtled overhead, they followed the paths to the top of Parliament Hill. The smooth upturned bowl of the hill gradually replaced by its unfolding vista of central London. The warm erotic wave that was coursing through Mandi turned chilly. There were the familiar shapes against the grey distance: Shard, Gherkin, Walkie Talkie, Cheesegrater; and off to the East was a middle-aged Canary Wharf hung out like a metropolitan Heel Stone. But it was not the triumph of the bad old ways that struck her hardest – though part of her was nauseated by the thought that after all that deregulation, all that floating free of signifiers and currencies, it had come to this, and the centre of her adopted city looked like nothing more than a mouthful of broken teeth – but that she could identify the tiny rectangle of the North-facing window of her office at Childquake, an office to which only she had access, and where she clearly remembered tidying things and turning off her pc and all the lights before returning to her flat to pack a case. That rectangle now shone brightly and shadows flitted indistinctly across it.

Chapter 22

The squadron of ring-necked parakeets that had overflown Tyrone and Mandi were exhausted now, settled into the honour guard of lime trees that flanked a curving lane up to the front of a Devon manor house. It was their first resting place since setting off from London; a flight of around one hundred and fifty miles. The old house here was once the home of one of the powerful families of the locality; it, like most of the families, had seen better days; after a time as an ice cream factory it was now an unimpressive, publicly administrated, tourism attraction. An empty jewel box in sumptuous grounds. The parakeets were uncharacteristically quiet; an occasional screech ran along the lines of green birds in the limes, planted half a century or so ago, each of the forty-two trees symbolic of a government's participation in the General Agreement on Trades and Tariffs conference in the Bay, setting the course for neo-liberal globalisation. There was no sign, no plaques; that bright dawn of free trade had come and thrown too harsh a ray on the old powers and, now, they were coming back. Holding their own conferences, unannounced, planting no trees.

High above the parakeets a grid of black-headed gulls had stretched across their airy parish; riding the thermals to hold their positions, buffeted like a vestry full of surplices escaped towards a pantheistic heaven. If these were the avian sentries, then the parakeets were the snatch squad; girding themselves for a colourful information dump.

Chapter 23

May 1876

Two days previously a small coaster had docked discreetly at Teignmouth's Old Quay; as night fell the wagon of the Bovey undertakers had clattered to a halt outside the dark warehouse there. Three solid figures emerged from the shadows, in rapid succession depositing three large oblong boxes into the vehicle, which left as quickly as it had arrived. The transfer had taken less than a minute on the timepiece and if anyone had seen it, they would have assumed, by the spills of ice from each of the boxes, that it was nothing fishier than a transaction of herring.

Now the same wagon struggled across the sands of the Sett and down to the beach. The Reverend Gurney in full regalia sat beside his younger brother Edmund, his surplice at times whipped up into his face by the rising gale; before them the Bovey undertaker and his assistant were decked wholly in black, holding beribboned top hats to their silvery pates. A small rowing boat was waiting on the strandline, oars tucked inside its gunwales.

Once halted, the four men helped themselves down to the sand and began to unload their cargo. Taking a rusty crow, the undertaker set down his hat upon the sand and began to raise the lids from the three large boxes. The assistant removed his hat and held it across his crotch in respect; then abandoned it to the sand and began, with the undertaker, to remove handfuls of ice and deposit them onto the strandline. Their hands grew red and then orange, until they looked like lobsters struggling on a fishmongers' tray. Edmund's face lost all colour and he began to fall. He was caught by his brother who spoke sharply in words lost to the savage wind.

Once sufficient ice had been removed, undertaker and assistant reached into each of the boxes in turn and recovered three shrouds, the contents of which, preserved by the cold, were stiff and light enough to handle without mishap and yet, to the numbed touch of the two men in black, seemed unnatural; smooth where they should be broken and broken where they should be smooth. Though they were careful not to say anything upon the beach, later over porter, warmed with a poker from the fire, they admitted to each other that they feared something had disturbed the bodies in Egypt or in the transit from Cairo to the Old Quay. Both professional men, they kept their imaginations to themselves, where they stewed and fermented and bubbled to the surface at inopportune moments for the rest of their sorry careers.

"Should we not check the bodies?"

"I 'udn't advise it, sir..."

"Perhaps undo the ends, in case... by some miracle..."

"Sir, them shrouds is naval. Pardon me frankness, sirs, but 'e, the bo'sun, 'e puts the last stitch straight through the big toe, there ain't nuthin' living in there. Pardon me frankness."

Without further discussion the three shrouds were loaded, looking not unlike salted fish in their frozen state, into the rowing boat. The assistant was left upon the shore to guard the wagon, holding both top hats, while the undertaker rowed the small boat into the gathering waves, Edmund side by side with his brother in the stern, the Vicar of Bovey clutching his Canterbury cap to his head while the twin strips of his stole curled around him as if he were an Anglican snake charmer.

The undertaker demonstrated considerable skill in piloting the small boat between the hillocky waves. All the time he had half an eye to the shore; steering by the obelisk on top of Mamhead Rise, the hedge on Adam's Garden and gradually aligning the two with the soft mound he imagined breast-like at the foot of the hills. Once the three had fallen into place, the giant Cheeke Stone came into view, perhaps a hundred yards from the boat, an exclamation mark at the end of the sentence of dunes. The undertaker raised the oars.

"Sirs, this be the spot."

The Vicar and Edmund rose from their seat, but the former had got no further than 'Man that is born of a woman hath but a short time to live...' before the two men were thrown forward by a prematurely breaking roller, pitching them onto the white frozen shapes. Struggling to his knees, the Vicar caught the wide-eyed disdain of the undertaker, and hurried to complete the liturgy from that position, while his brother Edmund had assumed a rictus, as stiff as the corpses, lying incapable in the bilge waters to which were now added melting ice and frothy spray; Edmund's uncontainable spittle contributing to the soup.

"Saviour, deliver us not into the bitter pains of eternal death..."

A white seething wheel of spray soaked the boat. The Cheeke Stone was beginning to recede into a rising mist.

"Hurry, reverend sir... if ye can... otherwards them words will 'ave to do for us all..."

"For as much as it has pleased Almighty God of his great mercy to take unto himself the souls of our three sisters..."

"That'll do..."

Roughly lifting Edmund aside by his frock coat, the undertaker hauled the first of the three bulging shrouds from the planks of the hull and levered it over the side. The others were swiftly and similarly despatched.

"They are delivered from the burden of flesh..."

The Vicar suddenly rose from his knees, as if inspired and roared out at the miasma of sea and sky: "...come ye blessed children of my Father..."

And here, in the mind of the Vicar rose a confusion that he would never untangle, for within that jumble the face of Almighty God had become entangled with the face of his own father, their own father, the Reverend John Hampstead Gurney, Prebendary of St Paul's.

"...receive the kingdom prepared for you since the beginning of the world..."

Barely had the final "evermore, Amen" left his lips than the undertaker was digging the oars into the furrows of angry water and the Vicar of Bovey was pitched once more into the company of his brother in the bottom of the boat. Swinging the vessel around to avoid the broadside of the waves, the undertaker promised himself not to look where the shrouds had been dropped. He could not help himself, however; and what he saw just beneath the water would trouble him in dreams and in moments of waking leisure, when he would ask himself how it was possible, how could he trust himself, and who would verify what he had imagined he saw: those three creamy sinking shapes that seemed to undo their garment and gesture obscenely, direct to him.

Two days later and the undertaker's wagon was once again in service. Summoned rudely to the vicarage, the undertaker and his assistant sat up front. Where before there had been an insouciant professionalism in their demeanour, now they were cowed and afraid. Edmund, parcelled up in a heavy overcoat, a scarf wrapped around his face and wearing galoshes, was helped up onto the wagon by his brother and their housekeeper. If anything, the weather had worsened incrementally since the burial of the sisters; repeated squalls had bathed the hills, rivers swelled, bridges threatened to collapse, cows stood up to their shins in dank red water. The Vicar was no longer dressed in liturgical vestments, but over his cassock he had drawn a huge dark brown cape; the Canterbury cap had gone and in its place a top hat. Those that did not know better might have imagined that he was attempting to pass himself of as a member of the undertaker's staff. Accompanying them, crouched in the otherwise empty wagon, was a gamekeeper from the Castle whose horse was presently recovering in the yard of the pub.

No one owned the Sett; though it seemed always to be present in some form, its shifting shape, blown and driven and swamped by storms had made it elusive to property claims and legal descriptions; without any limits or boundaries, no judge would grant ownership. So it was that the Earl in the Castle, bearing the county's name in his title, stood in for authority as far as anything in the way of disputes, commerce or crimes on the Sett was concerned. Invoking that authority, he had summoned the Vicar of Bovey there, the standing of his caste relieving him of the need for an explanation. On receiving the Earl's perspiring gamekeeper, the undertaker was sent for and the

Vicar and his brother were on their way within the hour. The wagon bobbled along the lanes under dull skies; Devon Reds bellowed, wisps of ghostly smoke were the only signs of life among the scattered homesteads; the Lovecraft villages gave way to the Vale Without Depths and the metamorphic sands of the Sett grew closer.

The Earl had summoned them to the Cheeke Stone; but before they could reach the end of the dunes, the wheels of the wagon already struggling for a grip upon the marram grasses, a gang of the Earl's men blocked their path.

"Where is His Grace?"

"'Is... Lordship ain't yer, e's gone back castlewards, we be commanded to take you to the... problem. Sirs, pardon me..."

He waved away the rest of the gang.

"It's the young Earl, see, sirs. The Countess is desp'rate poorly wi' the worry of it. It's us as found 'im. The boy."

"We don't need a great story. What class of problem has brought us here?"

"'Fraid a story it is, sir. T'ain't no other way t'tell it; for us, my men and I, we've seen things you can't class. Bit 'o a mess, sir – what would you call it, sir? Nature decomposed? It is! 'n then disarranged ag'in by devils, I'd say. The boy saw 'um and now he's unnaturally... curious. 'Scuse me, sir, but I bin in service with his Lordship full thirty year and my father..."

"Yes, yes, and? 'Devils'!"

"There's allus bin a strain in the blood yer at the Castle, sir, for years it's bin a troublin' thing to the old family. Right since the business with the young Earl and that writer..."

"O, for... that was seventy years ago, man! What possible bearing can that have on a young boy now?"

"'Tis the same blood, sir. Same... fascinations, if you know what I mean..."

"No I don't know you mean. Now, let myself and my brother through and let us attend to... whatever it is!"

"Yes, sir, I just thought you oughtta know that, cos it made the Earl sick just now, 'e's in his bed, 'e's the opposite of i'self, sir, and the boy's... wherever the hell 'e is, well, it's unnatural to be like that, that's all I'm sayin... Could it be the Devil, sir? Some say they saw 'is footprints in the snow this winter... say he ran off to Totnes..."

"What would the Devil want in Totnes? You're talking rubbish, man!"

Suddenly the gang of estate workers stirred in confusion.

"'E's a comin' back ag'in!"

Between the dunes a slight figure in green velvet breeches and jacket was scampering erratically towards the sea, a white ruff raised like the threatening display of an angelic lizard. The gang of men gave chase; their heavy boots sinking deep into the soft sands.

"Follow me," said the ganger to Edmund and the Vicar. "Leave the wagon yer. And prepare yourselves. Pray for thy sanity!"

With that he marched off after the chase. The skittery boy in his velvet suit feinting and dodging the lunges of the clumsy adults. The Vicar led Edmund by the hand; a glance revealed his brother reanimated, something in the sight of the racing boy had excited life into eyes that had been glazed for these past two days. The undertaker followed behind, reluctantly, dragging his feet. As the tip of the Cheeke Stone came into view, peeping over a perpendicular wall of sand, the massing gang of estate workers finally laid hands upon the boy and hauled him back from the brow of the dune. They led him back inland.

"'E was lookin' agi'n, couldn't help 'isself!"

Edmund seemed transfixed by the fluttering cuffs of the boy's sleeves, as they moved in abstract and meaningless gestures, as if the child were swimming in a pond. The boy's eyes blazed with outlandish desire, his mouth shaped in a cruel adult grin, a tiny self-inflicted cut upon his lip oozing a cherry of blood. Edmund swooned at the sight and the Vicar held him tighter.

"'E can't help 'isself, Ted! Tell us wot t'do!"

"Get him to the Castle." Then, to Edmund and his brother: "Keep close!" And the ganger began to climb up the wall of sand, followed by vicar, Edmund and undertaker. Avalanches of soft sand glittered and tumbled beneath their feet. At the top the four men gathered themselves, straightening their clothes as if they were about to meet their betters. Then, like sleepers waking from a dream, they saw what it was that lay before them.

The high tide, raised by the storm and the moon's new strength, was lapping about the foot of the Cheeke Stone. Around its thick red shaft and bulbous head were draped some soft ornaments. The first impression was of a window tableau arranged by a sensitive retailing hand. But as the dislocated parts of the display slowly made themselves known in their impenetrable totality, it was certain that nothing so virtuous as art was involved here. Instead, across the red stone were the remnants of the three sisters, arranged in the appearance of one ghastly jumble. Their young limbs were spread like the tubers of a rough plant, around which boiled rioting eels competing for sweetmeats. The jaws hung down like broken curtains, gaping smirks uncovering ranks of disorganised teeth, inverted yellowish triangles fringed with the something blood-like that was oozing from their shrivelled gums. Around the shoulders fluttered a godless halo of seabirds' feathers, while the remnants of the shrouds flapped back and forth above their fused heads. The whole contrary thing, woven together by a meeting of estuary tides and storm swell, was a fabricated and preposterous triptych apostasy, a demon's rood screen over the altar of the Cheeke Stone, a coverlet made from ruined girls, with a chorus of sandhoppers, conducted by homuncular imps, dancing a slow ballet around a hem made of the sisters' shredded toes.

Chapter 24

His skin was like Palladium, there was a lustrous softness to it, a fatal distraction to something greater, a calling down of the unintended, and she was drawn to its darkening and then its lightening and then its darkening again, amused by how amused she was by this uncharacteristic stupidity in the face of flesh, and the thought that in the most shadowy pigments she might find a darkness to curl herself up in, a cell to perambulate, ready to burst out and escape.

Mandi was surprised at herself. Sex was usually so self-contained. It welled up from deep within her, maybe even from some way below her, and then it spread to the edges of her. She flowered in sex. Yet, it never had much to do with the boys. It was not that she demeaned or disregarded them; she knew what she needed to do to make them feel included, but in the end, and it was in the end, on 'the plane', that was most important, it was never about them. It was not even much about her; it was about the sheets of feeling that unzipped her skin and spread her like a fidgeting counterpane. There was not much space for individuals in that place; it was all light and fields.

In the morning there was nothing special left. Tyrone was lovely, but not even more than loveliness could connect. There was some amputated limb inside Mandi that would never be satisfied by mere saintly masculinity. This, despite his fussiness, and some sort of egg with herbs on toast served in bed. She did not mean that they might not meet again, but, hell, he was one of her trustees; how many indiscretions was a good man worth? And she knew where her priorities lay.

As the lift doors eased open, Mandi knew that she was in trouble. Anxious faces at reception. She was prepared. The lights in the office over the weekend had signalled all kinds of mischief; they would only multiply if she let on that she had prepared a response. Sometimes spontaneity was all you could plan for. She checked the few tiny objects – a pin, a scrap of paper torn from the corner of a paperback, a button battery – she always placed on things that might be moved; they had all been meticulously returned exactly to their positions. Things were worse than she had imagined. No real spooks would have had the slightest bit of interest in her; which meant that some delusional soul, perhaps someone she knew, was dragging her into their messy fantasy.

Mandi swept her little tells into the palm of her hand and tossed the crumbs, pins and lithium buttons into the small metal bin she had brought from her first office, a wildflife charity. She had hated everything there except the little metal office bin, so she had stolen it. The pieces made a barely perceptible tinkle against the sides of the bin. Mandi looked around the room; it all seemed too neat, too exactly fitting; she had become a round peg in order to fit into a round hole. She was too snug these days.

She read her emails. One from the Queen Bee, red flagged. Shit. O, really shit. It was Tyrone, after all. He was the honey trap, the unknowing (she was sure) stinger for the Queen. Drone, drone. Her asset was wholly compromised; Tyrone had been part of the golden project and now they were dropping him. They had cut him some slack, once before, but not this time. He had failed to move quickly enough and this time the shit was sticking to him. They would cut their losses and let a promising man go. Before then, they were going to cash in the last shred of his value, in order to undermine her. She could expect a visit.

So, Mandi took her time. Accompanying her intern to the coffee machine and making them both thick espressos. Sipping the darkness together; power and nothingness complementing the sourness to come. She had, of course, understood instantly; there was to be a sifting of the chess pieces. She had always known the kind of chequerboard she was playing on; that there was no nuance, you were either on a good square or a bad one, and there was nothing to say which was which. She favoured the darkness, but she was only guessing.

Enter Queen Bee.

Mandi supposed that the Queen had come to play on Mandi's emotions (there were none, not in any sense the Queen understood), maybe on her loyalty (that was a shell), or on her sexual dependency (which was only upon herself). There was none of the weakness here that the Queen relied upon in others. The only really weak card in her hand was Tyrone; and Mandi had stopped the Bee dead on that account. Tyrone was gone; removed from his position on the Board of Trustees. Mandi had sacked him between two sips of espresso, and tweeted her announcement, with appropriate regrets, before the third. So, now she and the Queen could stop playing silly games about people and get down to the real stuff about projects.

It was all about medical records.

"I believe that Tyrone..."

"You don't 'believe', you know."

"... he showed you, didn't he?"

"He was trying to impress me... No doubt some confidentiality or privacy laws were broken, but I was an innocent party."

"O, this is so much more important than you, Mandi. We don't intend to allow you to get into any kind of trouble..."

That was a threat.

"OK... so..."

"Don't 'so' me, Mandi, don't 'so' me..."

"O, get on. We have a children's charity to run."

And there was the whole terrible sticky messiness of it. Mandi probably even believed that, thought the Queen Bee. So she moved carefully, hovering over Mandi, she danced a little. Shifting her weight from one foot to the other. Mandi was always a little surprised when she saw the Queen Bee's legs; so accustomed was she to seeing the Bee seated at a conference table, or chairing a board meeting or speaking at a lectern, that she often wondered if the bottom half of her body would eventually wither and drop out of public sight. Now, however, Mandi was unable to deny the little black Nakamura trousers that gently rose and fell beneath a long flowing Ono cardigan. The Queen was often draped in some kind of scarf or wrap that cascaded around her like the vestments of a female vicar. Today however, the Bee was stripped for more savage business; a tight black Fey top was dragged across her front, showing a surprisingly tense skinniness. Mandi always thought of the Queen as a slightly homely figure, but now she was all black sharpness and angles.

"Part of the challenge of leadership", offered the Queen, "is knowing how to give the same intensity to multiple situations. Specialisation is not a virtue right now. We expect you to act..."

"I don't think you heard me. I removed Tyrone from his post on the trustees..."

"You don't have that power..."

"Really, then what is this?"

She brandished her phone at the Queen Bee. Tyrone's short but obedient email made its point. The sacrifice was done. There was no real need for it, of course, they could easily have weathered the storm, a teacup would have stayed afloat, but the point of sacrifices was pour encourager les autres not natural justice. Executioner, victim, onlooker; all were weakened, except for the wizard twitching the curtain.

"That wasn't the plan..."

"Which is partly why it was so easy to do. I am not going to sell Childquake short to grease the wheels of your plan."

"There is no plan."

"There is always a plan."

"Just think this through, would you? I didn't ask Tyrone to show you the records. I had no idea he would be such a fool. I wanted him to let you know, in broad terms, what they'd got hold of there. In broad terms! Not compromise security protocols! I assume you've worked out what our intentions are?"

Mandi had worked out many things, and she was not about to let on to the Queen Bee what any of those conclusions might be. She sat motionless, and let the Bee dance a little more, swinging her expensive grey cardigan. Mandi glanced across her; through the giant glass screens she could see her staff, heads down at their monitors. She knew that her PA would be attentively watching

Mandi's reflection in a polished brass screen positioned for that purpose. The Queen opened her mouth and Mandi jerked forwards. The Queen paused; Mandi shifted a tiny snowglobe a few inches to her left, then sat back into her wheeled chair. The PA stood abruptly and the other staff began to rise, spilling out from their stations and massing at the coffee machine next to Mandi's office. For a moment the Queen Bee was mesmerised by the tiny white flakes fluttering around the Riesenrad under its plastic dome.

"Maybe we should find somewhere a little more anonymous?"

Chapter 25

The reverberations, like a gate slammed again and again in a subterranean city, were barely dying away, before the darkness crept in across the sky. From the West it came; a bloated cloud of metallic greys, glinting in the sunlight before shutting it from the seas entirely. Precipitously, the waters cooled and the animals began to die. Great animals that had swum oceans, shallow and deep, grey and blue and pink, cool and warm, now slowed, stopped and sank. The massive shapes of plesiosaurs fell backwards into the gloom, sharks froze mid-predation and left the halves of fish to hover and fall apart. The surface of the ocean smacked with the fall of pterosaurs, their leathery wings spread in belly-flops, cracking the last whiteness before all turned to black.

In the shallows small fish, crustaceans and molluscs felt about them as the sudden night ticked on and on. Every now and then a mighty body, smooth and filled with limbs would slip onto the sea floor and the first shift in the waters would be followed by an advance of billowing silt. At times the predation of the skies was such that the waters churned and the ocean floor knew no rest. Any beam of light that might have trespassed through clouds of soil dust and iridium was lost in the murkiness rising from the bottom. Caught between the two the soft and hard things of the ocean began to die. Fish stiffened and fell. Circular shells rotated and sank, in their billions. The ocean floor looked like the breakers' yards of the future, filled with tyres. Piles of corpses were rooted through by something crocodilian and uncomplicated.

Hovering, abstracted from this horror, there was something changing. An armoured cephalopod was picking its way through the writhing mass of its struggling families, some of them wildly rolling in deranged faithfulness to chance, others shrivelling and retiring from the harvesting jaws that grasped and swung, reaching blindly for survival. Nothing was satisfied. Nothing could see, and a vicious egalitarianism settled over the seething ocean floor for a while, as animals chose rather than reacted. Some dug down, below the rising monuments of lizard bones, a ruined city of plesiosaur rib cage cathedrals and rivers of mush, to their own graves. Through all this anarchic change, the armoured cephalopod extended its softest parts. It risked the sudden sinking in of crocodilian teeth, in exchange for greater sensitivity to the vibrations in the water. It followed the quiet lines of melody through the symphony of predation; a mollusc connoisseur, pushing out its pendulous globules of membranous skin, forcing its floppy organs closer to its surfaces, straining against the glue that held it to its shell.

A large shifting in the water and something armed and giant washed by, stirring up the swill of planktons. The brief bioluminescence triggered among the fading organisms illuminated the waste land on the sea floor, the grim wreckage of monsters, the spiralling decline of the soft things, the ecstatic thrashing of crocodilian emperors drowning in food. The armoured cephalopod pulled harder against the restraints of its carbonate casing; pain was turning, in desperation, into idea. The thingness of the thing pulled harder again on the thin illumination of its senses, a lushy love for a dark thing within, an intuition of a depth, a spark so hidden in the blackness it was starkly separate, like an eye floating on a tentacle, an impossible organ; yet the thing knew that there existed a thing within and went searching, diving for it, turning itself inside out. The soft arms and flanks overwhelmed its egg-like casing, the exoskeleton drowned in gloopy membrane and the thing exposed its innards, anus and valves to the jiving chaos of the fallen dinosaur world. A plesiosaur corpse, trailing scum, plunged through the black, prefiguring a bomber shot down from the matrix of a night raid, spearing into the bed of life and death curling and folding on the ocean floor, sending up a mushroom cloud of filth, the newly naked thing a few metres away, startled into squidgy alertness, fled.

The shock turned it inwards, even as it was pushed along the pinnacles of the chaos by the shock waves from the plesiosaur's fall. It reached down inside itself and the darkness went to work on its shell; as much a metaphysical transformation as a mutation of cells, the animal liberated itself in its own prison, tearing down the walls of its carbonate gaol, ripping the last of the glue, for the first time it feels a pain from inside, not from without. Its fear of fullness drops acids into itself, fizzing at the white shell, thinning its borders, all of itself collapsing together, narrow chapels turn giant abbey, inside and outside lose their meaning; meaning is pain and pain is meaning and through it comes change, welling up from the hidden and invisible nothingness that reaches beyond the ocean to the emptiness of the universe, shaping its flesh, stripping its armour, swelling and bloating its nervous tissue, rippling anxiety along sinewy paths, puckering its arms in curling motions and rushing to a central system quivering with novel distress and transcendence. Feelings flashed across the waste land; then the animal saw, in the dull glow of crashing beasts, that it was alien to all this filth of what had been and it would be the soft motor of all that could be better.

Turning from the extinction, the transcendent squid propelled its anxious limbs and wobbling head through the murk, towards the abyssal drop, the only equivalence to its hidden self in the ocean. It navigated by distress, its pain a kind of light that bathed the ruined empires of bones, broken leathery wings and fractured fins. The squid 'saw' the different darknesses, it 'saw' the shadows of danger in the darkness and the shallow hungers in the depths and as it swam it avoided its enemies, turning deeper and deeper within so that those depths rose up and along the very edges of its being and the edges ran down to the very depths of its nothingness and it was a world in its own world, a goddess of its own creation, a mother of its own future, a child of the cosmic dust, lonely traveller from the dead and distant stars. It did not know what it had become; a progeny of what had been forgotten on the traveller's journey. As it went, the goddess-squid dragged wriggling morsels to its beak, unsheathed the curled talons at the extremes of its arms, toxic juices working on the remnants of its armour just the same as on its food, swelling and collecting and melting as it went, the progress of an absurd and stellar saint, giant and soft, rolling above the devastation towards the depths of the future.

Chapter 26

Hunched over a flat white, perched on the edge of her padded chair, the Queen Bee cut a far less imposing figure than the one that had padded around Mandi's office a few minutes before. Mandi had seen this kind of performance once before, however; something would seem to break inside the Queen Bee, and anyone foolish enough to read it as a weakness would move in to take advantage, then the Queen Bee would look up like a lion breaking off from sipping at a lake or tearing bits from a wildebeest. Mandi gazed across the cafe to avoid any temptation to interrupt.

She had never taken much notice of the store logo before; it did not make much sense, and begged a lot of questions. For example, why would a mermaid wear a crown? And how many mermaids have two tails rather than one? And if you took away the band of graphics that circled the image, would the mermaid not be displaying her genitals just where it said COFFEE?

"What is the one thing that everyone knows about you, Mandi Lyon? What is... her defining feature, the single thing you could not take away from her without destroying the woman inside?"

And why was there a star in her crown? From what constellation did that come?

"Do you want me to answer that?"

"You don't need to, babe. We both know. Integrity, consistency, empiricism."

"That's three..."

"Don't nitpick with me, girl!"

Babe? Girl?

"I wouldn't insult you by coming to your office and presenting an idea that hadn't been fully thought through. And not wholly consistent with the principles of Childquake. One of which is its survival. But that will not stop me threatening you with the blighting of an entire generation of children unless you agree to my suggestions. Ha ha."

The Queen Bee placed her palms flat on the table, leaned over her coffee, in which one of the baristas had shaped a small crop circle, and smiled into Mandi's face.

Some of the sub-Oxbridge folk in her sector seemed to regard Mandi's mild Westcountry lilt as a form of intimidation. The Queen Bee was not one of them. She was a hardened survivor with every intention of taking advantage of her reputation. The daughter of Grenadian communists, she had lost all three of her elder brothers by the time she left home for university. Of the two eldest, child-soldiers on the Railton Road frontline, one had gone to sickle cell anaemia, taken by a stroke; the other got out of his depth in a row with an imaginary don of imaginary Yardies that escalated to machetes. The youngest of the three "who we never speak about" had gone into banking. The Queen Bee liked to speak of this 'loss' of her younger brother as if it were a third death, but Mandi had never bought that. Though she was careful never to share her suspicions, this third 'lost' brother might explain the Queen Bee's unfailing access to funding. Sure, she was expert at playing the system, because she had an analysis of it, but the flow of funds went beyond the rational.

At university, the Queen Bee had abruptly changed course, from chemistry to philosophy, specialising in animal rights. For a while it seemed that she worshipped at the feet of Peter Singer, and unsuccessfully applied for a PhD under his supervision in Australia. Instead, she immersed herself in sabotage of labs and farms. Allegedly. But there was little chance of operational anonymity; who else was black in the animal rights movement? Instead, she found her place in its leadership; taking over and fronting a tight little unit of activists and re-organising it into an arcane structure borrowed from the ill-fated Grenadian New Jewel Movement: a radical popular organisation, but with an elite party-within-the-party quite separate from its parent body. While unpopular with many other activists, the Queen Bee's little group was remarkably successful at using the national AR networks to propagate their structure as a model; they were adept at using pragmatic arguments to promote their particular ideological ends. But at a cost: they became the activists that all the other activists loved to hate, known for their 'superior' attitude to all other shades.

"Nor will I insult you by pretending to your face that you won't have to sacrifice some of those principles here. In order to save... maybe, hundreds... maybe hundreds of thousands of children's lives. Not necessarily while they are children; but it's your clients now who will be the ones to be sacrificed eventually."

As the first long prison sentences were being handed out to 'AR terrorists', something mysterious happened to the Queen Bee's group. Overnight, it began to organise ticket-only public debates with furriers, then with GM scientists, even badger-gassers and dogfight enthusiasts were featured and baited. Once the extremes had been pegged out, the middle ground began to wash in; no one wanted to get left out of the angry noise. After all, it sounded like democracy. Her brief history of sabotage was forgotten as the Queen Bee's group rolled out their formula to other fields. Under the name of 'The Other Channel' (all their AR-based structures vanished from public view), they became the media's go-to source for mediated but extreme controversy. They were political box office and in the age of the reality-spectacle there was no more investible a cultural currency. Not even escapism could compete with what sounded like the banging voice of authenticity. A rhetoric of "rights for the marginalised" – from reptiles to Nazis, gun owners to ritual-slaughterers – put a roof over their big tent.

The word on the street was that just after the first wave of AR arrests, the Queen Bee had received an interesting visit. No deal was done, but the division of territories was explained in the tones of civilised threat. Animals and terrorism were the business of the state, nosiness and ideas were thrown as scraps to Bee and her drones: Big Boys' Rules. Mandi had no patience with such conspiracy theories; the Queen Bee was quite capable of performing moral somersaults without being threatened. Whatever bitterness was driving it, it was her own. But something was 'going on'; Mandi had never been convinced of the sincerity of a grand project to petrol bomb the liberal consensus under the banner of libertarianism. It was serving somebody's interests, and part of the deal was that no one should ever say who. The margins of the tent were under the control of the Queen Bee; inside this big, if strangely shaped, marquee there was an inner tent-within-the-tent. Many of those who passed in and out of it were the same faces who years before had donned balaclavas, but the framing had all changed; they were PhDs, the chairs of trusts and charities, professors and journalists and lobbyists, if they bothered how they looked they dressed in MM.LaFleur and The Idle Man. If not, they looked nerdy and unthreatening. But they had not lost the lights behind their eyes. Early on, Mandi had received a rare invitation to enter the inner tent; ever since then she had been finding increasingly creative reasons to refuse.

"We want to harvest the data in the stories that Tyrone took you to see."

"I don't want Tyrone to get into any more..."

"Tyrone has gone. You're the player here. No one will argue against us mining that data if Childquake supports it?"

In 1983 the US marines' rapid deployment force had invaded the island of Grenada and replaced its government. Everyone on the anti-imperialist Left, or with access to the History Channel, knew this. The excuse for invasion was a coup mounted by the leaders of the New Jewel Movement's inner party, unseating and executing its wider movement's popular leader, Maurice Bishop, and his close associates. Mandi wondered if the Queen Bee's parents, or maybe members of the wider family, had been at least supportive of the coup, if not directly associated with it. What else would explain the Queen Bee's enthusiasm for giving the whole ghastly business model a second run? Family was always a powerful thing. Bee was re-making hers in the belly of the beast? Whose interests was it serving to be reeling in Alt-Righters, Brexiteers, Bannonites, Petersonites, radfems, trans-activists, posthumanists, sex work advocates and primetime liberals who were too cool to swot up on small group politics? And the whole thing floating on trust, charity, and government money?

"Think. What could be so important that you – you! – would be willing to relax your principles? The impact of that. Massive. No one speaks about children's lobbyists like they speak about you. You make up for what your organisation lacks in size by your intensity. And your integrity. That's the only reason I can come to you, and ask you to throw it all away. And for it to mean something. Huh?"

Mandi always suspected that woven into the Bee's whole schtick was a massive resentment machine; and yet she never showed it. Even when she was bullying she was relentlessly charming. She had found a way to make stridency a gentle art. It did not make much sense, the stuff she said, but it had an effect. Mandi felt flattered, of course she did, and she knew she was being flattered; yet, somehow the fabrication of the Queen Bee's manoeuvring was all part of the seduction.

This was not at all how Mandi supposed that she should feel. Her tiny claim to fame was her – trust-funded – walk-on part as the libertarian's libertarian, the maverick within the rebellion. She called out the spotty boys who just wanted to be offensive, who thought the world owed them a hearing, who thought they had been outraged by the disrespect of women; she called out the shock-capitalist, economic neo-liberals before they transed their principles and glided over to the Alt-Right. "I'm just asking you to be consistent" was her refrain, "if you can't apply the rights you want for yourself and your pals to everyone else then you are not a libertarian, my friend!"

She had the rare distinction of being one of a handful of people to be ejected from a 'Free Speech Seminar'...

The Queen Bee and her drones did not always like what Mandi said, but they liked her capacity to draw lots of spotty young men to come and see her say it. Her only weakness – in Mandi's own opinion – was Childquake. Her love and loyalty were unconditional. Lowering the voting age, lowering the age of consent for partners of the same age, lowering the age where a minor could be tried as an adult, lowering the age for jury service, for owning a company, for owning a gun. Childquake was the instrument for achieving the greatest empowerment of young people since the child labour laws and the Education Act; so she told everyone. Relentlessly. Hers had not been an unhappy childhood, but she wanted others to have amazing ones. Mandi's advocacy for a children's police force, for under-12 Members of Parliament chosen by an electorate of 11-year-olds and younger, and for girls' courts to hold preliminary hearings for paedophiles, genital mutilators and other abusive adults, with ratification by a higher adult court; she got repeated national media coverage. Of course, the religious conservatives and open chauvinists of all shades were not impressed, the establishment was nervous, liberals torn, but, whatever you thought of their policies, it was always educational to observe who was willing to line up with and who against Childquake. And who dare not decide.

Mandi supposed that the curvy lines falling from beneath the mermaid's crown were intended to represent her locks of tumbling hair; but they could as easily be read as two streams from the spring of her mind.

"Think of this as a lever. Not just statistically, but in each case specifically. Our data company..."

That was new...

"...will be able to identify each individual whose life you save. Add to them, their families and close friends..."

Who was she kidding? Broadcasters loved the triggers, but all of Childquake's policies were likely to end up on the same scrapheap as proportional representation, recallable Parliaments, an elected Head of State, land reform, the abolition of the House of Lords and the privatisation of the Church of England.

She had stopped listening to the Queen Bee's wheedling persuasion and was muttering under her breath some lines she had learned as a child from Bryan:

"And it's through that there Magna Carta,

As were signed by the barons of old,

That in England today we can do as we like,

As long as we do what we're told."

Terminating the conversation, Mandi promised to consider the suggestion, snatching up her laptop; after the funeral she would give her answer. In her head, while her lips had been forming the silly musical hall song, a completely other voice was singing, and it sounded horrifically like hers:

"Muddy Mary, mother of God,

Killed the Old Boy in his bath,

God went to Hell

And started to smell,

And now all the bad things are back!"

The Queen Bee was on her feet, unwilling to be cut dead, apologising brusquely for her thoughtlessness, she swished out into the London streets. The crop circle on her untouched coffee had turned saucer-shaped.

Chapter 27

Mandi laughed as the Great Western service careened through Taunton and Tiverton Parkway and on towards Exeter. All the expected hobgoblins, skrikers and opened-mawed horrors had hidden away for the day; and Mandi's path home to her pseudo-parents' joint-funeral was unnaturally uneventful. Just beyond Exeter she thought unexpectedly of the archivist woman who had tried to meet her at the station as she was getting away; Mandi rang the number the woman had tapped into her phone. No signal.

Back at Lost Horizon the lights blazed in the permanent zone of the camp. In London, Mandi had returned none of those calls she thought might be concerned with the details of the funeral; she would not be dragged into the hippies' fighting over the bodies of her Mum and Dad.

Inside the arid shell of the sentinel home, more like a husk every time she returned, Mandi lay down on a thin mat in her old room, pulled a stale duvet over her head and fell into a deep and instant sleep. Somewhere in the mush was the dream she always had; she was organising something, but the chairs had not arrived and there were metal structures that had become inextricably entangled; in search of a hex key she found her way to an inner room, hung with dark burgundy curtains and in the centre a table cluttered with possessions, maybe those of her parents, which she attempted to rationalise. All the time she was aware that she had lost the ring they had given her. On the table she rearranged grails and flutes and they clinked and wobbled, threatening to fall and smash; fabrics snagged, the whole collection began to slide to the floor. In the dream, she backed away, uncertain and conditionally relieved that there was no cataclysm yet, but could not escape the curtained room. Through a shrinking window, its lead mullions closing around her arms, she looked up into a red-tinged sky and there was a temperature reading of 40 or so, though no indication of which scale; someone had exploded a nuclear device in a cathedral city but she was unsure whether it was the Russians or the local authorities cleansing the area of the remnants of a biological strike.

She awoke refreshed and feeling guilty; but about what she had no idea. When she remembered the ring, the guilt melted away; her parents hadn't given her a ring. She had lost nothing. That morning Mandi had an appointment to visit the undertaker, maybe to see the bodies of her adoptive parents and for a chance to say goodbye; maybe that was what the dream had been about. The arrangement of limbs, the fear of shattering and loss. The unrecoverable nature of what would now always be unarrangeable, unorganisable. Other forces were in charge at a funeral, like Decay and the State.

Zak was a 'green' funeral organiser; yet there were protocols that even he was unwilling to transgress. They met, not at his premises in a nearby town, but in the vegan cafe next door, where everyone seemed to know him. Over nut milk lattes, Zak had explained that the bodies were too damaged for a viewing to make much sense to Mandi. He pulled on his neatly trimmed moon of grey beard and strongly recommended that Mandi not visit the bodies.

"It's not them anymore. Anne and Bryan have gone, you would learn very little from what is in those coffins.... your parents are what they did, not that... that is left over. But they have another legacy. Please don't judge them by their residue, but by the lives they lived."

It was odd, thought Mandi, it is as if the undertaker knew her parents and yet their daughter did not. It was an oddness that rang true.

"There's nothing for you there... your parents are what they achieved, the heights they reached! Not that... void..."

Nevertheless, reluctantly, he led Mandi to the mortuary area where the bodies lay, sealed in willow coffins. For a moment she thought that they were in wicker baskets, but a chart of options on the wall relieved her concern; she was glad that whoever had chosen – was it her? – had avoided the steam train journey, the piano keyboard that looked like a sinister grin or the daisies.

Mandi walked twice around the coffins, once anti-clockwise and then clockwise. She had never felt so self-conscious, so theatrical. She was desperately feeling for authenticity, but the room was distracting her. Unlike the curtained-room of her dream, there was an airiness, a naturalness, a cooled ease of the processing of things; it came on like an animal trap. An impression exacerbated by the thick cords, tied in Gordian knots, that now sealed the coffins shut. Even if Zak had not persuaded her otherwise, they would have struggled to get into the coffins anyway.

"So, your kind of ... pagan undertaking ... sorry, I have no idea how to correctly... will it involve anything unconventional with the bodies? Do you do anything unusual?"

Zak invited Mandi to take a seat in a large lawn-green armchair, seating himself opposite her on a red sofa. He leaned in towards her in a posture of intimacy; but what he said, sincere or not, felt oddly obfuscated. As if God were listening and Zak were fearful of cracking out of turn and spoiling the whole operation. He spoke of the integrity of bodies, of beliefs about the body's survival in the spirit world, of the body as symbol of a greater system, and he spoke passionately of murmurations of starlings and Platonic ideals and the illusory nature of belief that is belief in itself. Mandi half-followed his argument, but could not grasp its relevance to her, Anne or Bryan.

"Too often" Zak bemoaned, "when you question folk, good pagan folk, sincere Wiccans, the magickians, even some of the very holiest ones, you begin to hear something else inside their words, which is simply the words talking to each other. The ideas have created a feedback and become a thing separate from the speaker, generating a whole new bunch of thoughts in the person's mind, an inner empire if you like, and this then creates new desires, new idols, if you will; so, crudely: "wow, the solution to my problem is serving the goddess, but to do that I really need a statue" or more subtly "wow, the solution to my problem is greater devotion to god, but I really need to be more pious" or most subtly yet "wow, the solution to all my problems is enlightenment", which traps the meditator in a dark cave of materialism because enlightenment has become a thing for them. The new desires, new idols, feed the machine, so more surplus is created to meet and make new desires, and the vicious circle of big ideas loops round and round. Your parents were not like that. They saw through the curtain of words to what was behind it... they believed in what was real."

"The more I talk with people about them, the less I think I know them."

"Know who?"

"My parents...."

Zak seemed thrown.

Mandi helped: "My step-parents, Anne and Bryan..."

"Yes, yes, of course... good people. But I've burbled on, I'm sorry, I have a tendency. Would you like a moment alone?"

"No thanks. I've no idea what you meant, but I found it strangely comforting. It's weird isn't it, how in these moments, and don't take this the wrong way, that kind of banal things, things you would never even dream at any other time of taking any notice of, are exactly what you need to hear?"

At the door of the wood-built office, Mandi offered her hand and Zak shook it. He was trembling. Taking a step outside the front door, he glanced quickly up and down the street and then up to the skies.

"Don't ignore the lumps and bumps and contingencies in everyday life, Amanda. The certainties that we serve..."

He broke off. A herring gull clattered down onto the pavement opposite and began to pick at a discarded plastic wrapper.

"If you truly want to have a moment in touch with... both parents, then trust your feelings, not any big ideas that anyone else has about them or anything else. Trust your feelings and trust what you can touch, find yourself in the right place and what has happened will make itself plain and the angels will come."

Mandi felt that she ought to burst out laughing. Instead, she kissed Zak on his pale and bristly cheek and ran towards the waiting taxi. As it pulled away, she looked back to give the thoughtful undertaker a thankful wave, but he was already in earnest conversation with his young assistant, who wore an apron around his waist and a tense look across his face, and who Mandi had heard from time to time pottering in a distant room.

Chapter 28

They were never friends. Maybe back in the old days, as kids, holidaying together. Since the one thing that brought them together, was the one thing none of them would talk about, none of them seemed able to remember in any detail; they had no idea why they kept in touch in spite of their indifference to each other. Perhaps it was their shared failures. Despite avoiding all the major addictions – drinking, skag, the slots, illegal sex and porn – they had each of them somehow found ingenious ways to royally screw up their own lives and the lives of everyone around them.

Teresa slept with a loan shark and he had dragged her down into spiralling debts, she had lost her council house after falling out with her neighbours and spent her daylight hours travelling between one sofa and another.

Eddie had been misdiagnosed early, doped to the eyeballs, and had learned to keep his head down so low that he barely registered on anyone's radar until he left school without sitting, let alone passing, a single exam. He signed himself up to an agency and for fifteen years had stacked shelves, dug graves, collected dirty linen in hospitals, stacked more shelves and swept pavements until repeated managements and colleagues would eventually lose patience with his invincible self-absorption. He had long ago passed requiring meds, but still took them out of habit.

Kayla did puzzles, compulsively. Where most puzzle-solvers and crossword-addicts were either in it for the escape, the pleasure or the intellectual challenge, Kayla had become caught up in a global conspiracy in which her efforts were required to keep the world turning. No sooner had she completed one book of challenges than she set off to buy the next. These were not the cryptic crosswords, not the real brain-friers, but fairly simple posers. She never asked herself why she never tried anything more challenging. After a while she started using pencil, writing very lightly; with a rubber she would erase the answers and place the used magazine at the bottom of her pile. By the time she had worked her way down to it, and as it in turn had risen to the top, she had forgotten the answers, or always known them, and she could begin again without any extra cost. She had never worked. She had had two episodes of psychosis and been sectioned three times; the latter occasion was an undiagnosed visions of angels.

Ethan was strangely empowered. He generated energy like a power station. His hair stood up on end, he crackled across synthetic carpets and made metal handles and rails in shops spark. At times he glowed like a superhero, but the problem was that it all hurt. It had really kicked in as his hormones began to bubble, around about twelve, and at first he had imagined that it would all gradually dampen down. Instead the pain got worse and he barely left home now, slept on a woollen mat under cotton sheets that he neglected to wash regularly. He had ripped up the floor coverings and walked on wood and tiles. After his parents died in quick succession, Ethan had turned off all the power to the house. His only ventures outside were to fast food outlets; the ones that wrapped things up in paper or Styrofoam. The staff knew him well and bought the food out to him on the pavement so he would not need to brave the metal counters before dodging lampposts all the way home. He ate for England, sugary fatty food, yet he looked little more substantial than a dried cadaver.

Every few months – the longest gap had been two years when they were all in their early twenties and embarked on various failed romances – the four would meet up; partly now to talk about Jade. During one of her episodes she had wandered off, triggering a massive search of snowy wasteland on the edge of Birmingham. Old industrial buildings had been opened up and searched, tunnels and sewers examined, junkyard owners and car dealers had wasted their Sundays opening their yards to inspection. In the end she had been found, frozen as stiff as a board, prostrate in a ditch in a tiny strip of wooded land between two industrial estates. There were no signs of foul play. The coroner had delivered an open verdict. Now, when they met, the four survivors would give over the first hour or so to wondering aloud, between long pauses, about what they might have done to save Jade. They always came to the same empty conclusion.

This time, the conversation felt even more redundant than usual.

"Why are we even doing this?"

"Fuck off then!"

"What the fuck else have I got to do? Got a big fucking meeting 'ave you?"

"Cunt."

"Wadyousay?"

"Nothing, cunt."

"Fuckin' charming. This ain't your place. Eth', mate?"

But Ethan had not been listening. He was arranging crisps from a non-metallic packet into a shape on the floorboards.

"Eth'!!!!"

Shocked, he gobbled up the crisps like a dealer hiding his stash at the wrong knock on the door.

"Kin aida! Eth', we know what you're up to down there. Don't need t'ide it from us, tittybaby!"

Teresa started to laugh hysterically. "Tittybaby! Tittybaby! I ain't 'eard that in..." And she leapt up on the coffee table, stained with countless spilled instant coffees, and began to bump and grind like a stripper.

"Squirty Mary up from the deep,
Rode the big squid in her bare feet,
When she dropped her guts
She gave birth to fag butts,
And her secret hid under her creep."

"You remember what The Creep is, right? That road under the railway tracks where we'd go to get the buzz..."

Teresa began to twerk in a series of ass claps.

"Work it, girl!"

But she stopped dead and spoke quietly.

"When the expresses went over.... the big roar was like a maniac was in yer ear, and the air sucked out of your tits in the dark..."

"Yer don't breathe with yer tits!"

 "It were like being deep down somewhere...."

"Shuddup, Tre, everyone's 'ad you! School bike!"

"Shuddup yerself, Kayla!"

Ethen spoke, spitting crisp bits.

"Damp place, black mould, I remember it... before you get to the dodgems..."

Eddie, who had been silent suddenly piped up. "Those are gone now."

"How do you know? Have you been down there again?"

"No. I just know I know."

"He knows he knows; how's he know he know he knows, eh? Ha!"

Eddie, again.

"I want to... go..."

It was the first time in years that any of them could remember him speaking three times in succession.

"We all want to, mate! Course we all want to! So how come none of us is ever going to fuckin' go?"

"You really want to, K? I thought you hated those people?"

"O just do yer crisps!"

Two of the legs of the coffee table snapped with a crack like pistol shots. Ethan ducked, Eddie's mouth dropped open, Kayla slightly pissed herself, and Teresa headbutted the wooden floor and bounced into the skirting board. Slowly raising herself, her mousy bob was embroidered with fragments of Cheese and Onion.

Chapter 29

The funeral was a large, grand and well attended event. And an epic farce. The entire community of Lost Horizon was in attendance, along with a number of faces unfamiliar to Mandi, but who – by their dress and manner – she assumed to be members of the various strands of alternative pagan and 'pre-Christian' beliefs that were popular in the county. Cassandra had told her that although only a couple of thousand had claimed pagan faith in the most recent census, the local Confederation of Pagans reckoned that at least ten times that figure were practising pagans, many of whom kept silent, worried at the prospect of discrimination, making theirs the second most popular faith in the county. A position that Mimir insisted came with certain responsibilities. A need to keep up appearances in the sight of the non-pagan world.

This other world was well-represented at the funeral. There was a gaggle of middle-aged men and women who Mandi had down as holiday camp owners and managers from The Sett; careful to stick close together in a Roman tortoise. Less defensive, and more surprising to Mandi, were the Christian clergymen and women in dog collars, a few in cassocks, and for a moment she thought she caught the purple flash of a bishop's clergy shirt. These mingled with white-robed witches and black-suited late-middle-aged Goths as if the occult battles of the past between Good and Evil were about as relevant as the Singeing of the King of Spain's Beard. Grant Kentish was splendid in a peacock green suit with what looked to be a black rose in his lapel. Mandi had no faith in any of the various nonsenses, but there was something about liberal relativism that got up her nose like nothing else. Is that how these pagans wanted to be regarded? Was that the standard by which they wanted to be judged?

The funeral was held in the distinctly unmagical setting of the canteen-ballroom of the Sunny Glades camp, just a five-minute walk from Lost Horizon. The procession of pagans along the connecting road had raised a few eyebrows among passing motorists on their way out to the city for football or shopping. The ballroom had been dressed with forests of dried ferns and berry-laden branches, posters of various affiliations had been blu-tacked to walls; images of pentacles and crystals, stags' heads and white doves glistened down on the congregation who sat on cushions and mats around the edges of the room. In the centre were the two willow coffins, no longer tightly bound. Mandi was concerned for a moment that there might be some opening of the lids as part of the ceremony; she was relieved to see that Zak the undertaker was among those who were directing events.

There were a few words of welcome to the congregation, which were shared between Cassandra and one of the female Anglicans. Then the coffins were blessed by representatives of different faiths, holy water mingling with sprinklings of oil, red ochre and wafts of incense; while an undertone of mumbling from different parts of the hall greeted the actions of the different representatives. Mandi was unsure whether sections of the congregation were joining in with their leaders or objecting to the presence of those of other orders. Finally – Mandi wondering if every aspect of the ceremony would be repeated so many times so as not to leave anyone out – these officiants withdrew and members of the Lost Horizon community, seemingly at random, stumbled up from their beanbags and retreated from the hall. Moments later they processed back in, each of them steering through the double doors a painted polystyrene megalithic stone. The sight was absurd and magical as these huge objects entered horizontally and then floated up vertically, almost brushing the roof of the ballroom and then one by one landed softly in a circle with the two coffins at the centre.

The community members retreated from the 'stones' and the ceremony proper began with a middle-aged woman who Mandi did not recognise stepping forward. Dressed in white robes and with long red hair, the woman seemed nervous, yet the moment she rose from her mat, an intense hush fell over the congregation. The woman carried a long stick, around which were curled and tied freshly cut spring flowers; each waft and poke of the stick was followed eagerly by the mourners. Mandi had no idea what the gestures signified, but so hypnotic was the woman's tentative presence that she neglected to attend to the words she was speaking. It was a poem, Mandi thought. Unfortunately, this growing intensity was punctured from time to time by late arrivals. Each time the doors at the back of the hall were opened, the draught of air would unbalance one or more of the polystyrene standing stones and their guardians would rush forward from the outer circle and steady them. An unintended ritual dance resulted and Mandi found it affecting; eventually, rather than keep moving and distracting, all the guardians stood and moved to hold the 'stones' in place. Culminating this part of the ceremony, the woman in white held her stick above each of the coffins and invoked something – the name of which Mandi could not catch – to preserve and protect the bodies of Anne and Bryan "in the otherworld". At the mention of "bodies" a small group of dissidents in torn jeans and black t shirts – "angry gnostics" was how Mimir had described them – heckled limply. Mandi had seen them around the camp; they lived in two caravans at the very edge of the camp and kept themselves to themselves; Mandi had checked the books and they paid their rent regularly. They were not wholly inattentive to the material world.

A casting of petals over the coffins was the signal for the synthetic stones to rise up and float horizontally across the hall and out the double doors. Once the traffic jam in the corridor outside had cleared, the community members returned to their mats and were followed into the hall by a long procession of gothy folk, some dressed in character; a bagpipe player with an aqualung mask, a drummer whose face was entirely hidden by coloured ribbons that fell down to the back of his knees, two children in imp masks, and a red haired middle-aged woman, the complement to the first priestess, dressed in purple robes and carrying not a stick, but an apple in one hand and a transparent flask of water in the other. Bringing up the rear was a tall man in a goat mask, carrying a flaming bowl of accelerant which he struggled to control, presumably as the heat suffused the material of the bowl and his unprotected fingers. Finally, and gratefully, he laid the flame at the feet of the purple-robed priestess who stepped back abruptly to avoid becoming a human torch. No one in the congregation seemed to appreciate the danger; Mandi looked around and even Zak appeared distracted from the events.

There was something very appealing about the mixture of danger and clumsiness that made the whole event... 'real' was the only word that Mandi could think of. She remembered Zak's advice to "trust your feelings and trust what you can touch, find yourself in the right place and what has happened will make itself plain and the angels will come". That was what was happening. She had been to three funerals in her time in London, funerals of colleagues, some of who might even have called her a friend; cancer, suicide, car crash, and none of them had been 'real'. Either badly briefed Anglicans misrepresenting the dead into odd pre-cast shapes, or a sincere humanist resolutely warding off the mystery of the void. Somehow, even though she knew the words were mumbo-jumbo conceived in a 1950s suburban villa and the gestures and costumes were largely borrowed from movies and graphic novels, these pagan liturgies felt appropriately consistent with her weirdly intimate and remote relationship with the two people whose broken shells lay inside the willows, just a few feet away. The ceremony was making the distance, the absence, the loss and the hopelessness real, for the first time. Mandi was surprised by her tears.

Through her misted vision, the imps and goat and skrikers danced to the beat and the skirl until the sounds died away and the magic animals became once again children and adults in masks and took their places seated against the walls of the canteen; for a moment Mandi had a vivid memory of a childhood drawing she had made that Anne had spirited away from her while she was asleep and then denied knowing anything about. Until that very second she had probably thought of the drawing at most once or twice since she found it screwed up under a layer of carrot peelings in the recycling bucket. She had called the drawing "the everglades" and the name had made her mother scream.

The last arrivals were led by Cassandra and Mimir, two by two, white queens with green knights; the men carrying drooping poles and fallen branches with withered leaves. The women formed themselves into a single full-breasted white blob, while the men waved around their feet, until, presumably from under the dress of one of the queens, a huge stuffed but articulated black swan was produced, the women raising it over their heads and the wings spread in a huge fan, as if something black and coal-pure were escaping the coffins. There was a single angry shout of "truth!" drowned out by a huge collective beat as everyone in the hall but Mandi slapped or stamped three times on the polished floor and the pipes groaned and surged. The swan flew like a dark feathered halo above the women and out of the hall through the double doors, striking the edge of its wing on an exit sign and two black feathers, caught in the spring light from outside, fluttered slowly to the parquet.

The willow coffins were lifted by the remaining queens and processed – with Mandi directly behind, ushered forward by Zak – directly out of the ballroom and into the camp car park where, but for the intervention of the Sunny Glades staff, they would have been gently laid in the back of a white hearse. Instead, the men in their chocolate brown Sunny Glades uniforms were impelled to assist, so the loading of the coffins came somewhere between fist fight and assistance. Despite this hiccup, the hearse pulled away sedately and headed out of Sunny Glades, up past Bright Sands, Golden Haven and, finally, Lost Horizon, before turning along the coast and off towards the city. "Everglades, everglades, everglades..." muttered Mandi to herself as the white limousine disappeared into the trees at the edge of Lost Horizon. "Everglades, everglades..." but, other than Anne's uncharacteristic behaviour, the words evoked nothing but a darkness where a memory might once have been.

Chapter 30

Mandi strode up the beach in a vain attempt to clear her head. She had been surprised that the caretaker had not attended the ceremony. Perhaps he felt he needed to keep an eye on the camp, given that, for once, all its residents were absent. Mandi would enjoy bumping into him now; arguing over the meaning of the latest heap of flotsam and jetsam to wash up.

The ceremony had been followed by a buffet and mini-wake in the canteen. The ceremonial instruments were put away and guitars and violins appeared; folk tunes wafted over the gathering. The vegan caterers had excelled themselves; there were even foraged flowers to eat. How they had found these at the time of year was puzzling. The tastes were rich and strong. Yet, the wake was remarkably restrained and ordinary. The same embarrassed anonymities and dislocations that Mandi had felt at other drinks and nibbles after other funerals. Except that this time she was the focus of the sympathies. The only wrinkle was when the caretaker suddenly popped up to throw out a kid in a hoodie, drawn down over his face, nothing to do with the funeral, stealing food, Crabbe had said. In the scuffle the kid had dropped a black disc badge and the caretaker had thrown it after him.

Once it was decent to do so, Mandi had worked the room, saying her goodbyes and dishing out thanks, before escaping to the beach. There was no one else around. Not even dog walkers. The light was just starting to fade. The sea was flat. Mandi checked up and down the dunes, but there was no sign of the caretaker. She resorted to throwing stones into the waves.

"Everglades, everglades, everglades..."

There was something in the water. Twenty metres or so from the shore; a dark shape just beneath the surface. Mandi watched it carefully, occasionally obscured by the white foam of a wave, but there was certainly something there. At times it seemed to show a wide reflective surface like the body of a seal or a large mammal, but there was no head lifted up above the surface, and what looked like the limbs of starfish spread out from its centre; then it would roll in a wave and the whole thing would appear more like a large bundle of rags, soaked through and close to sinking. It was hard to tell if it was moved by the waves alone or was treading water. Mandi took another stone and threw it so it landed a few feet from the shape. For a moment it did not react, but as another wave came tumbling in, breaking more as the shape approached the shore, it turned and for a moment Mandi saw what she thought was a jaw and three eyeholes, before it twisted again and slipped out of sight, replaced by what might have been a large filthy sheet or dark sail.

Mandi was still wearing her good shoes; she had not changed since the funeral. She looked around for a piece of driftwood to try and hook the thing and drag it to shore, but there was nothing long enough. She scanned the dunes once more; she was still alone. She would wait then. And ten minutes later the shape was within reaching distance. Mandi took a short and solid piece of wood and leaned over the water to drag it in. By now she knew what it was; a body.

Probably a man's by the clothes. Once she had it out of the water, in some crazed hope that there might still be some life in it, she turned it over. What had been a face was pale and bloated, tiny crabs and sea slugs were escaping from the gaping caves in it; not just the eyes and mouth, but new openings. The police came very quickly. They sealed off the beach and the body was spirited away in an ambulance.

A young constable assured Mandi that there was no question of foul play; from the clothes and what remained of the contents of a wallet they had already identified the deceased as a missing person with a long history of psychiatric problems. "It's a crying shame," he said, "you have no idea how many of these poor souls wash up along this coast... we don't make a big fuss about it obviously because of the holidaymakers... people don't want to think of these poor fellahs washing up where they're sun-bathing..."

"How many do you mean by 'no idea'?" She really did have none. "Ten a year?"

The young policeman did not react.

"Ten a month?"

"I better be getting back..."

"How did you know to come so quickly?"

He nodded towards the dunes.

"The gentleman from Lost Horizon alerted us..."

The caretaker in his usual black was standing on one of the sandy brows.

"But... when I got here there were no footprints near the body..."

"Says he saw it from the tops, Madam. Recognised the pattern, when the sea leaves a body. You should know that these poor sods are very unhappy individuals, they have their own reasons for what they do and they deserve some confidentiality... I'd be grateful if you didn't share our conversation. Just for good practice."

Another snowflake.

Chapter 31

It was a surprisingly well attended meeting. Not simply in terms of numbers, but the side streets were cluttered for an hour with BMWs and SUVs. The Bay Museum had been hosting these events for years, or at least the organisation that hosted them was nominally the same – the Bay branch of the Hexameron Essay Society (an otherwise extinct entity, originally established as a conservative discussion group in the mid-nineteenth century by a Corpus Christi student opposed to the decadent ideas of the aesthete and author of the notorious final chapter of 'The Renaissance', Walter Pater) – but in recent times the society had received an infusion of younger blood. Publicised as a local historical society with a detailed interest in the work of local nineteenth and early twentieth century thinkers, along with the predictable bookworms and retired academics, the meetings now attracted a new generation of local entrepreneurs, technologists from the two nearest university labs and from anonymous industrial estates, and dealers in intellectual property.

Business, on Hexameron afternoons, was a forbidden subject, however. Discussion focussed solely around ideas and their local histories. The Society's aggressive championing of the role of the county (particularly its Bay area) in the pioneering of radical ideas in information technology, psychology and industrial design had at first created ripples and then loyalty among the more regionally patriotic of the small local village and town historians. Approving articles appeared in the nostalgia sections of local newspapers, then in their mainstream features; trade magazines and free sheets quickly picked them up and the Society's name was mentioned at Rotary Club dinners, freemasons' lodges, trade associations and Probus Clubs, filtering down through board room chatter and shop floor recommendations. Mostly male, mostly white, the shining faces that eagerly greeted the arrival of the chairman and speaker were now a familiar sight at the Museum. At the back of the room, staff from a local hotel, Russians in smart black and white uniforms, were discreetly clearing away the last of the champagne flutes and canapé crumbs.

"Good afternoon, gentlemen – and lady! – I am very pleased to welcome you all here today. There is no society business, so I suggest that we move immediately onto the main item on the agenda, and introduce you all to..."

The speaker, who in common with the chairman wore a black disc badge, glanced down at his notes, and paused, allowing a group of four young women, dressed in startling white shirts and dark grey flute knit skirts, to ease themselves in through the back doors, navigate the Russians, and take their places in four reserved seats on the back row. So silently and lithely did they enter that barely a head turned. One that did was that, for the time being, of a young CEO of a big data shell company that had spun off sensitive work to the anonymity of a rural address. He had the four down, on first glance, for a local women's business leadership group; the kind of set up he could not have been less interested in. But there was something about the self-possessed demeanour and the faultless grooming, not to mention those skirts; they could not be Diane von Furstenbergs! He had not expected to see many of those in Devon. One of the four shot him a warning glance and he span round in his seat, surprised by his guilty nervousness. As he reconnected to the speaker, he found he had missed some introductory remarks and that the talk was already imbedded in illustrative anecdote. The audience laughed, then looked at each other and laughed again. Something about a cabbage and calculations made by steam. He tried to focus, but the look he had received continued to bug him. Female aggression usually excited him, but the deep coldness of the glance had thrown his expectations out of gear.

A new image was thrown up on the screen. Like something from an old telephone exchange. Ah, not cabbage, but Charles Babbage, the inventor of the analytical engine and father of the computer, this really was ancient history; a local lad, apparently.

"Let me illustrate the significance of organised affective information and its politico-anthropological sensitivities, by sharing with you a brief if traumatic episode, a cautionary tale, from Charles's life..."

The speaker had the knack of referring to historical events as though they had just happened outside the door and that he was a personal friend of those involved.

"... his own fault, actually. He had cultivated a habit of poking his nose into public business at every opportunity and developed an instinct for great injustices and intervening with great force at those points where the issues were most ambiguous. Where angels feared to tread Mister Babbage rushed in, a genius-fool you might say. On the occasion in point, he was prey to an enthusiasm – a favourite of Jews, Mohammedans and other Puritans – for iconoclasm. Babbage's target however was an idiosyncratic one, for he chose music, which is mostly acknowledged as having no real representational qualities other than a squeaky similarity to the call of birds and other animals. Nevertheless, our predecessor had made up his mind to wage war upon pavement musicians who were in the habit of regaling unwitting pedestrian audiences close to his home. When Charles's letters to the London Times elicited no response from law-makers, he wrote his own piece of legislation outlawing a variety of instruments including penny whistles, doom boxes, cheap German saxhorns and bombordons, hurdy-gurdies and – most particularly – bagpipes."

Laughter.

"This move was wholly consistent with his work in the British Association in which he fought manfully to remove all romance and metaphysics from science. Now he would take from the general mob all temptations of art and other fancies. Using his considerable influence he pushed through the Act, which now bore his name among the populace, and it turned out to be a bullet! For the rest of his life he was chased by an inexhaustible chorus of disgruntled whistlers, bangers, grinders, clangers and gut scrapers. They would form impromptu bands to serenade him from under his windows, they pursued him along the streets in musical crowds of up to two hundred strong."

On the screen, from 'Punch' a Harry Furniss caricature of Babbage's predicament.

"Repeating ad nauseam the same chord sequences, a few notes again and again, all with a blatant disregard for traditional tonal hierarchies; the effect was of a superband formed by Arnold Schoenberg, Philip Glass and The Adverts!"

Great hilarity; and some nervous checking to spot anyone unsure who The Adverts were. To help the slower ones, the speaker clicked up a video of the band from the Bay playing on Top of the Pops.

"The eye receives the messages,

And sends them to the brain.

No guarantee the stimuli must be perceived the same

When looking through Gary Gilmore's eyes..."

With another click the frame was frozen and Gaye Advert stared out into the Museum meeting room from thickly darkness-lined eyes surrounded by a lightless anti-halo of jet-black hair. A chair was scraped unsteadily.

"They pursued him even to death, accompanying his coffin, banging and whistling, to the grave."

A crossfade to a grotesque engraving of the chaos at Babbage's funeral. The speaker had begun to enjoy his own parade of effects; he built towards his conclusion.

"This, gentlemen, and lady... ladies..."

Realising his mistake, instantly, he shouted at the top of his voice.

"TROLLS!!!!"

Heads that were beginning to turn, span back.

"Yes, trolls! The first instance of collective informational and communicated trolling! To protect the fundamental freedom to make a nuisance! The irony, of course, would have been lost on all parties, but Babbage's inventions would create the best possible instruments for the right to cacophony and the buskers' deregulation of tonal structure would arm the modernist shock troops soon to bring down the temples of romanticism so despised by the founder of cybernetics! Those who do not learn from history...

and remember, Charles was a member of this society.... and some say TV Smith is too!"

The speaker mimed looking around the hall, but quickly stopped himself.

"My little joke... Charles was a signatory to the elevation of our greatest member, the father of modern archaeology, William Pengelly, to the Royal Society. Those who do not learn from history are destined, like bishops, serial musicians and one-chord-wonders, to repeat it. Forever!"

Knowing amusement all around.

"Let no one dare silence the cacophony, but rather, by subjecting its complex systems to our analyses, and extracting from it the serial music of psychometric patterns, let us benefit by the more effective programming of our machines. Thank you."

The young CEO so wanted to sneak another glance over his shoulder. Despite the strange fear that still sat at the pit of his stomach, his curiosity was stronger, fuelled by his fear. For a reason he could not explain, he believed that he might understand better the meaning of the talk if he could see the four spooky females' reactions to it. He waited until the applause was done and the audience were filing from their seats. However, the four seats were vacant; their reservation notices had gone. A kid in a hoodie making a brisk exit – probably a 'homeless' looking for somewhere warm, he thought – caught his attention; no women in white shirts. He pushed his way out through the lobby and into the street in the hope of catching a glimpse, but there was no sign of them. He made his way back through the town to his Jaguar XF; unsure, as it floated along the lanes back to the edges of Newton Abbot, quite what it was he had seen and heard. Later that night he received a visit at his hotel.

On the way to his car, flinching at the sudden cold, though neither knew the other, he had passed Mandi on her way to Museum.

Mandi was surprised at how crowded the town was. Perhaps the local sixth form college was between classes; there was a great emission of young people racing off in divers directions, hanging upon each other's arms, vaping, texting and swinging along in groups of six or seven abreast, blown by gusts of a freezing wind. Mandi did her best to anticipate the dodges required to navigate the horde, using the shaft of the crossing beacon as a convenient protective barrier. She took a moment to scan the street; it was a clone town. There was nothing in the familiar shopfronts to suggest there was a harbour only a few metres away; at The Sett the proximity of the sea, the dunes, the sand affected everything. Here, nothing seemed to notice. Mandi watched the traffic lights change up through the colours, an approaching car slowing, and she prepared to anticipate the illumination of the green man, when a young lad, by age and appearance probably a student from the college, threw himself headlong into the bonnet of the first braking car.

For a moment Mandi thought the boy might have tripped, but there was something in his trajectory that was agentive, willed, demonstratively self-destructive. The boy lay before the wheels of the car, his body slack. Pedestrians on both sides of the road paused. The boy suddenly rolled twice from under the car and over into the opposite lane. Fortunately for the boy, nothing was moving that way, but now he was exposed to whatever turned the corner. Mandi stepped into the road. She did not enjoy a public role. Participating in a spectacle of communal spirit and responsibility always felt bogus and over-performed to her. But this kid was going to get himself killed unless someone did something. Mandi stood over the boy's prone form, holding up her palm to a warily approaching van. She was shocked when the car against which the boy had just collided abruptly pulled away and speedily disappeared up the street. She was unsure of her next move; how well-placed was she to safely coax a clearly distressed boy, now curled up in a foetus shape, to the pavement? What right had she to save him from himself? And how pissed off was she that no one else seemed bothered enough to share in her discomfort? Enough to walk away?

She would be shocked again; the van she had halted, now gunned its engine, swerved around her and accelerated into an adjacent street. Whether it was a genuine assault on his own well-being or a cry for help, there seemed to be a general mood of indifference and spectatorship to the boy. This was immediately contradicted by two middle aged men who, separately, put down their shopping to come over and crouch over the young man, encouraging him to come to the pavement. Unexpectedly, the boy, without speaking or responding in any other way to either of the men, pushed himself up on his feet, and, folding in upon himself, wandered to the gutter and out of the road. Mandi breathed an irritated sigh of nervous relief; which turned to cold concern as the two men picked up their shopping and reintegrated to the passing crowds; they had done their duty to keep the highway clear.

For a moment the boy swayed from side to side, then ran headlong at an information board and struck it with his forehead, staggering backwards. Mandi felt the shock ripple through her stomach and ran towards the boy, who was still reeling. Did she have the right to touch him, to restrain him? Fuck the right, was she going to endanger her.... what? Livelihood? Career? ...for laying a hand on a child? How old was he? Sixteen? Thirteen? Jesus and Mary, she was caught in the web of her own invective, she had to think clearly, tactically. If she lunged at the boy he might run into the traffic which had resumed its busy progress. Yet, she dare not leave him.

So, she marched by his side, unspeaking, as he set off up the street. The boy darting angry glances at his unwelcome guardian. In this formation they made a hundred yards or so, neither saying a word, the crowds now petering out, both eventually staring ahead, Mandi primed at any moment to grab the boy if he ran for the wheels of a passing bus. She had no plan for how to bring this drama to a happy conclusion; no idea what to say, how to comfort, whether to be involved at all. Across the road, a pair of policemen were arresting a bearded male, who was arguing his case and swinging his arms in woozy gestures. Mandi ran to the nearest constable and tapped his arm. "I think there's a boy, young man, he's in danger of his life, of losing his life..."

"OK, OK, madam... we are just attending an incident here..."

"No, I think this is urgent, he just threw himself at a moving vehicle..."

"How badly injured is he?"

The constable looked around for a wounded body.

"He wasn't really... but I am scared that he's going to do something stupid and really hurt himself, unless you do something."

"Well, what would like me to do?"

Mandi breathed in; an unintended inspiration. She was surprised that public safety had become quite such a laisser-faire operation; she had assumed that there was some specialisation in such matters. That it was not just a case of: well, guess for yourself.... that there was a procedure.

"Show me where he is."

"He's... He was proceeding..."

She winced.

"...fast, that way. I can't see him now."

She stared intently, but there was nothing individual or distinctive in the stream of pedestrians. The wind had risen again, cold was descending, the grey of the sky soaked into the populace.

"Can you describe him?"

"Er, mixed race, maybe sixteen or seventeen, maybe much younger but I assumed he was from the college, black hair, black trousers, I can't remember the colour of his top, like a sweat shirt I think, he was hitting his head on metal boards back there... I didn't see his eyes, the colour of, quite short for a boy..."

"Thank you, I'll phone that in straight away. Thank you for your help. Your concern. I'll phone that in right now."

And with that he turned away; Mandi unsure whether he really was phoning it in or just trying to get her off his back. She thought of going back and pulling rank, "do you know who I am?", dropping Childquake's name. No, she had done her best. Possibly. At least all that was required of her. More than the scores of others who saw the same thing as her and chose to do nothing. Or the least imaginable, and then deserted the scene. She would not even write of this. It was personal.

Mandi stumbled on with a grey contempt in her heart for the people all around her. In a way it was quite comforting; it felt like a return to the simple feelings she had had as a child. The world was evil and she would fight it. She glanced back; the constable was in conversation with his colleague. No sense of urgency. Mandi wondered at how she had been made to feel like a crazy person; she wanted to race back and berate the coppers, but then she would look crazier still. She wanted to know what this general indifference was; it wasn't just racism, surely, it was something even deeper than that and she was going to...

But what she was "going to" was quickly forgotten as Mandi realised that she was standing outside the Museum. Absorbed in the wash of passivity and the sharp elbows of anxious minimum wage consumers, she had forgotten why she was in the town. It was not to deal with the area's suicide problem. Getting her bearings, she glanced up and down the street before leaving the rumble of the rising gale for the quiet of mummies and rhino teeth; opposite was a dull multi-storey car park, its upper level draped with wire nets to deter jumpers.

Chapter 32

1912

From the undulating miasmas of the Great End, rising through the seething waves that coursed through pillars without base or capital, came the aethereal numen. In life it had borne the name 'Edmund Gurney'; now it had assumed a more anonymous and universal appearance. A centre parting still organised its hair, a thickly knotted tie hung loosely from its stiffened collar, and a large thick coat disguised its limbs; only the moustache, stretched like a pair of horsehair wings, had grown more eccentric and ornamental since the shuffling off of its mortal coil.

The numen stepped nimbly and carefully from the maid's bedroom and began to make its way through the curling sheets of smoky vapour; spectral manta rays might have been swimming along its corridors in aqua-acrobatic displays. As the numen floated by the open door of the tiny 'master' bedroom, Smith was bent over a bowl of heated oil, driving billows of sickly effluvium with a giant cardboard sheet. The numen twitched; the last chance to check the balls of soft paper blocking both its nostrils. The elderly Smith waved it along the corridor impatiently.

Outside, the narrow street was effectively blocked by a line of landaus driven down from the great houses and palaces high above the Bay. It was incongruous in a street of such mean if respectable lower middle class types to see such a display of shining surface and glittering particulars. Only around the rims of the carriage wheels was the grimy evidence that, just to get here, the procession had passed – silently and with curtains pulled tight – through that part of the town where dead babies arrived in brown paper parcels and the bakers' loaves were corrupted with sand.

Inside the house, the spectators were arranged in two ranks. In the hall, around the walls of the parlour and at its door hung the members of the Hexameron Essay Society, two junior members on guard on the modest front porch. Under the pretence of protecting their lungs from the ectoplasmic odour now seeping down the staircase, the Hexamerons covered their faces with scarves and kerchiefs in private and professional embarrassment. Not only were they exposing themselves to public ridicule, but inner ruin too. Those that had brought with them technical sensors, gridded charts and other devices by which to monitor and measure the reality of it all, had quickly squirreled them away in deep coat pockets.

Within this academic crust, the inner circle consisted of the great and the susceptible. Since the tiny coastal valley, once a den of mountain lions and nomads, had been ruined, first with cottages, then palaces and slums, concert halls and baby farms, the resulting layer cake had attracted from the Continent the last ailing remains of hereditary monarchies and aristocracies, the most wealthy of the domestic industrial classes and the hardened skin atop the nation's literary Eton Mess. Representatives of each stratum were present and uncomfortable; palms flat on the cheap and greasy tablecloth. In the dim illumination of smouldering tow and Bengal fire, adding to the fug, it was hard for the impatient princesses, dukes, knights, magnates and belles to tell the patterns apart from the blooming stains of supper. Imperious Victor Bulwer-Lytton, jealously protective of his grandfather's fantasy, lifted his dark eyes, swept a mop of ginger hair from the top of his aquiline nose, and bared his teeth as if to bring the whole thing to a halt. A princess giggled; one or two Hexamerons pulled their scarves a little higher.

"Now, I am here!"

The medium, Mrs Willet, sprang from her prone position, head down on the table, and jerked with a straight back into her chair.

"Urrrrrrgh!"

She exhaled with unnatural force; the patched curtains shook and the flapping wings of large birds could be heard outside. The flames in the room flickered.

"Good evening, your royal highnesses, good evening, my lords, ladies and gentlemen..."

At the mention of such titles, the sculptural indifference of Bulwer-Lytton's features fell away to reveal a surprising vulnerability for a future Governor of Bengal.

"That's Gurney!" whispered an elderly lady in the inner circle; the inadequacy and age of her best dress revealed that, rather than one of the modern witnesses, here was someone who had been on the spiritualist circuit for some years. "Welcome, Edmund! I can attest, ladies and gentlemen, and your royal... um... this is absolutely and without doubt the voice of our spiritual mentor, Edmund Gurney, brother of the three tragic Gurney sisters! Emily! Rosamund! Mary!"

Silence, but for the creaking of floorboards outside in the narrow hallway.

"My sisters are gone forever, the darkness of the Nile has swallowed them..."

Gasps passed from princess to lord to common shopkeeper.

"There is no return for the lost, but there is life in the hereafter. I promised I would come and come I have..."

There was something gruff and scratchy in Mrs Willet's voice, but later the lady in the cheap evening dress would remark loudly on how closely her articulation had followed that of the living Edmund. A few strands of Mrs Willet's black hair had fallen across her brow, a tiny trickle of perspiration was reaching out toward the bridge of her nose. Her nostrils flared with excitement. Though not far from beginning the journey into middle age, hers was a handsome face, on a figure more statuesque than homely, but there was something else; a kind of smoothness in her manner that promised all kinds of accelerations and sudden mutations from one thing to another.

"I have spoken before, but tonight I will act. In the world of the living I made this plan, and now from the dead I will realise it!"

A sound like that of a breaking cello string rang out and died quickly away. The curtains shifted. A chill wind moved into the parlour. Smith, with a stiffening back, pulled himself in through the bedroom window, having given the signal for his assistant to open the back door to the cold of the meagre yard and outhouse. There was an acidic sharpness in the spiritual nip as it made its way to the parlour.

"In life, many of those who took the ordinary path felt authorised to demean my careers, but in the beyond, I have achieved everything that life denied to me. Now I will endow my spiritual line, the inheritance of my new supernal nobility, upon a child of your world. Conceived in flesh but forged in spirit; not since the time of the miracles have the two worlds been so close as now; the spiritual realm has answered you, my dear friends, it has seen your suffering and chaos, it has witnessed across time and space your crises, abolitions and overthrows and it is coming to your side. The saviour of the world is at hand!"

A voice from the top of the stairs shouted: "He is here!"

A hand placed firmly in the middle of the numen's back. A shove. The numen began to descend the creaking steps, one at a time. One of the Hexamerons in the hall gasped as a limy glow filled the space behind the numen, while another Hexameron turned and ran, spinning through the front door and sprinting off down the deserted street and into the night. The greenish light began to fall inside the parlour; Mrs Willet's face lit up like a mermaid's. The Hexameron in the hallway backed into the room and all inside shrank back. A further "phutt" of limelight and the air was full of sparkling lights as if strange gases were escaping from the other world into this one. With the hallway free, Smith skipped quietly down the staircase, following the numen and adding new chemicals to the burning bucket. Green was followed by yellow and then red.

Around the parlour wall, the various scientific dignitaries had lowered their scarves, their mouths dropped open. A natural philosopher whispered to the populariser of the aquarium: "it's not a fake!" The inner circle, their hands still flat down upon the tainted cloth, were swivelled round to watch the door. Slowly a figure, at first no more than a dark shape, began to edge into the opening. Yellow and orange gases broke over its head in waves. One or two of the inner circle glanced down to check the illustration of Gurney, a pencil sketch, provided with their invitations. Now girdled by the doorframe, the concealed bucket released a further surge of illumination and the occupants of the room collectively cried, shrank and exclaimed. Emerging through the fug, came the unmistakable wing-like moustache and the signature centre-parted head of Edmund Gurney.

Slats in the walls were heaved back, wallpaper tearing in angry shouts, and beams of limelight shone from the cavities, which momentarily blinded the occupants and illuminated the numen in startling detail. Motionless for a moment, the room holding its collective breath, the figure then shuddered for a moment as it received a gentle tug from the hidden Smith. It lurched backwards and the door slammed shut with a crash like the crack of doom!

Everyone in the parlour, including Mrs Willet, jumped and screamed. But Mrs Willet topped them all, throwing herself into a fit upon the table top, as the royal princesses turned to the woman in the cheap dress to come to her assistance.

"Hold her down," commanded a male voice.

"No, you fool!" yelled the experienced spiritualist. "She's in a trance, you could kill her!"

The men fell back, and Mrs Willet rose to her feet, her face on fire and in exultation.

"The annunciation is over," she declared, "the séance has begun. Follow me."

Outside, the sinister black box of a Brougham was turning into the street. A reading light shone within, an austere, corrupt and excited face looked out. The top-hatted driver, mindless of the parked landaus, drove up the side of the street, the carriage's pair of black stallions shaking their heads, their staring eyes swivelling in their sockets, clanging and bumping the wheels of the parked landaus. The drivers of the landaus began to shout, but were silenced by the two Hexameron guards who had not left their posts at the front door of number 19. A flame or two from an ignited lamp began to appear in the top windows of the terrace. Outside the house, the Brougham came to a halt, the guards leapt forward to open the carriage and a figure familiar to society stepped down to the grimy surface of the street. He wasted no time in bounding up the impoverished set of steps and into the hallway. Mrs Willet was awaiting him, poised halfway up the staircase.

"Good god, what have we now!" exclaimed Bulwer Lytton.

The starry multitude hushed and shamed him.

"Who is that man?" whispered a princess, and the woman in the cheap dress replied.

"That is the prime minister's brother."

The thin, dark suited man, with a hint of wildness in his upturned wings of hair, climbed quickly up to Mrs Willet and offered his hand. Together they turned and climbed the narrow staircase toward the master bedroom, brushing aside the webs of smoke and vapour. As the inner circle rushed up the stairs to follow them, pushed from behind by the Hexamerons, torn by disgust at the depravity and desperation to see and know, they entered the layers of hot air, created by Smith and his buckets of pyrotechnica. In a moment the heavy coats and shawls, necessary in the chilly parlour, were discarded, thousands of guineas of fashion lay in piles along the edges of the corridor, while in the bedroom, Mrs Willet, seated on the bed, the thin man standing over her, was quickly divesting herself of all her undergarments, arranged to fall away quickly for the occasion. Once more the layers of the séance were repeated, as below so above, as in the parlour so in the bedroom: the inner circle of bare-shouldered princesses, wescot-naked lords and sweating spiritualists, while around the edges of the room and squeezed at the door were the shirt-sleeved denizens of the Hexameron Essay Society.

Twenty minutes later, the Brougham pulled away from outside the house, heading back towards London. Ten minutes later and the procession of laundaus was broken up and spread across the Bay. The few upstairs lights in other houses went out one by one. In the parlour of number 19, the spiritualist in the cheap dress served tea from a large pot, while the remaining Hexamerons sat around the table, an exuberant and flushed Mrs Willet at their head.

"I feel that it has happened. Everything that Edmund has promised is come down to us. A saviour is coming, a great leader, and the world is about to take a new shape."

As she spoke, Smith's assistant was helping his tired and ragged master up a small ladder beside the outhouse, and in a moment the two men had rolled over the low wall and dropped down into the back lane, making their way to the street where the single Brougham and the row of landaus had been replaced by a house-painter's cart.

Smith leaned in to the three men in overalls.

"Must 'ave been quite a party, guv'nor!"

"And that's the last you speak of it..."

He placed a hundred guineas on the footrest. The foreman gasped and reached for the notes and they burst into flames, vaporising in seconds. The painters reeled back in astonishment, wide eyed and slack-jawed. Then a narrow anger began to return to their features as they realised that their bonanza was gone; an anger met full-on by Smith.

"Unless you want to see the rest of it go up in smoke, keep yer traps shut!"

And he slapped another hundred on the cart.

Chapter 33

Inside the lobby, April was waiting for Mandi.

"I've been expecting you!"

"How did you know I was coming?"

"I saw your missed call."

But there had been no signal. Something must have got through eventually.

"I've got something very exciting to show you. But first, I would like you to meet some people who may be able to help you. Local history people..."

April led Mandi through the cluttered lobby, walls hung with venerable awards, plaques to patrons, a giant female Egyptian goddess and a small cabinet of oddities; on its middle shelf, a tray of small bones, claws and mostly teeth. Inside the hall, the Museum's Engagement Officer was morosely stacking chairs while the representatives of the Hexameron Essay Society were extracting memory sticks, packing away their projector and tidying up the notes and minute book. Mandi noticed how April waited patiently for the four men to conclude their conversation before interrupting.

She had a wide and ordinary face; almost moonish and plain. She gave no impression of depth or definition. There was no requirement, Mandi assumed, for archivists to be dull, but perhaps the attention to minute detail, the isolation among the records, the repetitive searching and recording of similar things might inevitably lead to an ironing out of temperament. She wondered if there were many volatile or angry archivists? Were there storerooms and records offices where the archives were regularly hurled at the walls in frustration? After a minute or so, the four men concluded their discussion and turned as one to Mandi. As though April were invisible.

"Yes, my dear?" The Chairman smiled, a little creepily; but not as creepily as Grant Kentish might have. "How can we help you?"

"O, er..."

Mandi turned to April.

"So sorry to bother you gentlemen, I've been helping this young lady with an enquiry about a manuscript and I noticed that you were meeting here today. I think her enquiry might have a local historical angle."

Young? April seemed no older than Mandi; yet she spoke of her like her grandmother might. If Mandi ever had had the luxury of grandmothers.

"Well, that's what we're here for," volunteered the lunchtime speaker. "What is the nature of your enquiry?"

This was all so tweedy and antiquarian. The manner, the turns of phrase, the sports jackets and the politesse; out of kilter with the state of the art projector, Iron Man charger, the micro-recording devices, the Sonos One speaker, the fitness trackers, tablets, the Kaiser Encores and 4G phones. One of the younger ones dangled the keys to a Lexus.

"I think Mandi might be interested to hear any reflections you have on the history of the Lovecraft family in these parts."

"That would be the family of H. P. Lovecraft, the renowned American writer? Well, I think his kith and kin were long emigrated before he came along... but he was a strange character, obsessed with monsters that he would very successfully fail to describe properly; many-tentacled things lurking under the ocean, globular subterranean creeping things with eyes that came and went like rashes, if I'm not mistaken..."

"It was more the original family, the ancestors before emigration."

"Ah well...."

"I think the last one was in an asylum at Newton Abbot. These were not sophisticated..."

"I think the great grandfather was a choirmaster – or maybe leader of the church band, was it? – in one of the village churches close to the Great Hill..."

"Yes, that is correct, and either he or... hmmm.... not sure, but one of the family was landlord at the beer house there, or it may have been an inn in those days... but if you are considering drawing some conclusions from our remarks, I suggest that you travel to New York, ride on the metro, visit Brooklyn... what this Lovecraft fellow feared was not our county, but the new urban technology, the rushing lights and racing winds of the New York subway, and.... of course, the African-Americans... those were the inspiration for his monsters."

"It was an ordinary family with its own troubles; some dispute or other sees the great grandfather prised out of his position as head of the band... perhaps for low churchmanship, high churchmanship, they were major issues then... and some of the locals held eccentric views... I'm pleased to say that many of the most esteemed members of our Society have played a significant part in expunging the superstitions that once spoiled the county's life..."

"I have been working on the finds from the Old Grotto..."

The lunchtime speaker turned on April as if she had impugned the Society.

"That man was a rank fool! Widger!! God! If only he had turned to Pengelly earlier! Instead, he spent twenty years digging up the most fabulous finds in order to prove that the Deluge was real!"

Mandi assumed that they were talking about a contemporary detectorist; she was amazed later when April explained that this was fury about events that happened a hundred and fifty years ago.

"Have you been able to make any sense at all of them?"

"You would have to ask Theo..."

April and the men turned towards the distracted Engagement Officer, who disappeared behind a stack of chairs. The men turned to April.

"O. No, not really. Unfortunately, as I think you know, there are no charts to explain where the various artefacts were found, or when, no markers on the finds themselves, so we have no idea at all at what levels of the cave floor the objects were found..."

"Then they are meaningless. Throw them back in the cave! That was a treasure trove of finds; ruined without some grid, the objects themselves are senseless... worthless... what could have been a space of learning and discovery is now just a black hole!"

April touched Mandi on the arm. It was a strange touch; a steely localised numbness like that immediately after a Lidocaine injection at the dentists.

"We are talking about the man who dug up that tray of bones in the lobby."

"Was he a Lovecraft?"

"No! Though, I can see how you make the mistake! He was no less tortured by a fear of hobgoblins, poor man. No, Lovecraft was a secular materialist, in that way a modern individual, but one who liked to stare into the void left by God. Our amateur excavator..."

"Who was he?"

"A nobody. A draper's assistant. Not a man of either learning or evolved intelligence. Combining – somehow! – a fervent belief in the literal meaning of the bible, that the universe was created at some time on a Thursday afternoon six thousand years ago, with whatever anyone told him at the pub. He was so terrified of the world, that in the end he took to getting home by running across the fields and vaulting the hedgerows rather than confront the hobgoblins that his fellow drinkers had told him lived in the lanes. In the end he gave up his job and spent all his time either at home or in the cave... twenty years..."

"Twenty years of destroying the archaeological record!"

"I hope, madam, that when you come to write up your research..."

"O, I..."

"That you place these men – Lovecraft and the draper's assistant – in the correct context of the county. Not only were they wholly unrepresentative, not only were they from the lowest strata..."

"Like judging psychology by the values of a Viennese dustman!"

"This town was once the watering hole of the royal families of Europe, we had our own symphony orchestra, with premieres of new English symphonies..."

"And will again, Brian, now..."

"...and not only do the scholars of today dwell on them like lower animals fascinated by the faecal droppings of their own kind, but they have contributed nothing to the great progressive project of men like Pengelly, Froude...

"The engineer."

"And the other...

"...Heaviside the prince of electro-magnetism, Babbage, you know obviously, Peacock and propulsion..."

"All members of our society..."

"And the great Cattell..."

"At one time and another..."

April broke their flow.

"Would you like to see the hyenas' teeth, Amanda?"

"Then we'll leave you to your bones and wish you no harm! By the way, we are members of The Hexameron Essay Society, this branch established 1865, our aim to preserve and promote the most progressive ideas in technology, philosophy and psychology intuited and developed here in the county. My name is Toby Jugg. You would be most welcome to visit us at our new headquarters."

He offered his hand.

"If we can help you in any way with your studies, please don't hesitate to call us."

And he fished in his jacket, while the others, as if at a signal, plucked their goTennas from the table. The Chairman produced his Samsung Galaxy.

"Bump?"

"Sure."

Mandi and the Chairman bumped phones and transferred their business card data. Then in a disturbingly short space of time, in a move like a credit card unfolding into an Ian Sinclair knife, the four Hexamerons gathered up their gadgets and, smooth as any Roman unit, rolled out through the double doors and were gone.

"Theo!"

There was no sign or sound of the Engagement Officer.

"O, let's just go down and look at the teeth."

Chapter 34

It was the Jaguar Man who, much to his surprise, was making his way up the lanes from the anonymous industrial estate to the former monastery. Two weeks before, he had attended his first lecture; now he was an agent of the Society and on his first assignment. Things moved quickly in the Hexameron world. He might not have been so amenable to this sudden promotion but for the encouragement of his boss. He had not quite worked it out yet, but there was some connection between the company's global harvesting of information and the fine detail of this tiny local Society's philosophies. Maybe they were providing the unambiguous solutions for the algorithms?

His briefing, however, had nothing to do with data and everything to do with "tradecraft", the working up of a credible legend and the possibility of some kind of cosmic steganography; in other words, his target might be playing games; there might even be a signal woven within the fabric of everything, stemming from this one individual, which was driving the whole air loom!

Jaguar Man assumed that that last part was a test of his credulity.

Over the tall Devon hedgerows, up on the tips of his Berlin brogues, he caught glimpses of bulbous towers with exclamatory spikes. Yet, at the top of the hill, arriving at the entrance to the site, all sense of its former use seemed gone. There was nothing very holy about the functional buildings immediately inside the gate. Pleasant and well kept, enough of a 70s office feel to make him feel at home. Perhaps their thinking was the same as his boss's: no one asks questions about dull places. The complex was now a residential home for seniors with good liquidity, and he was less than likely to be welcome trespassing beyond their PRIVATE sign. Yet, there was no one at the main office. What were they going to do to him? Beat him with their bus passes?

He was sure to meet someone on the paths snaking off to different buildings. Some friendly old dear would direct him to Mister Balfour-Willet.

There was no one on the paths. Although the weather had become increasingly and unseasonably mild, a cold spell had set in. Perhaps the elderly were keeping warm inside. The layout of the complex became clearer once Jaguar Man had cleared the reception area. There was a larger and older set up of ornate spires and large grey halls to his left; they presumably constituted the former monastery and convent. He had no idea how that had worked; unisex religious houses fell outside his experience. He was stronger on social psychology and contemporary consumer trends. On his right were the more recent flats, a bank of small but expensive homes replete with glowing windows and smart interiors, but no signs of life. Should he knock arbitrarily on a door?

Frustrated with himself, he elected to forgo the flats and press on through a patch of trees beyond an ornamental lawn, in the hope of something more inhabited turning up on their other side. The man he sought – Balfour-Willet – had served in the British security forces, so he might not be easy to find if he was avoiding visitors. To add further mystery to the man's cv, it seems that in the 1960s he had become a monk, moved in here, joined the closed order that occupied the place at the time – closed by their own choice apparently – suitable for someone used to a clandestine lifestyle, he supposed. When it all folded and the nuns and the other monks moved on, he had left the order and stayed here. Something had hung onto him, or he had hung onto something; the guy was good at hanging on. Unless the information was all screwed up, he was well over a hundred years old.

Jaguar Man wondered if he had been allowed to keep his cell, while everything around him was transformed into swish retirement flats, or whether he was in one of the warm flats and maybe even watching him now. He felt the chill of a man watched. The documents acquired by the Hexamerons indicated that Balfour-Willet had left holy orders, but might still wear a habit. Did he still believe and was he maintaining some kind of religious life here; even though the monastery had been closed for almost thirty years? He would have already been an elderly man then, perhaps he never fully understood the changes? So what comprehension would he have of the Hexamerons calling in their debts after a century? The man, as a child, even as a babe in arms, had played some role in their past, but how much was he likely to remember of that? Jaguar Man would tread carefully; best that the shock did not kill Mister Balfour-Willet! That, surely, was not the Hexamerons' intention? So why send in Jaguar Man?

Rather than the thin windbreak he had expected, the gathering of trees was thick and crowded, the paths obscured by huge and bare Rhododendron bushes and a large tin shed. Instead of a further block of housing, he came to the old wall of the monastery grounds and a long plot of graves, marked off by a cast iron fence. Inside, the graves were decorated with crosses made of the same metal; Benedictine cross molines, the points of which ended in something like forked tongues or the wings of moustaches. One or two of the crosses had lost a limb and looked more like giant fishhooks. Another cross had sunk up to its arms as if the ground below had collapsed and it was trying to climb out of the grave.

Jaguar Man turned back and retraced his steps to the shed.

"Hello, Deirdre!"

The voice was somehow both vital and quavering. It sounded almost feminine.

"Come in, you silly little fool, come in! Don't skulk about out there with a face like an early Christian martyr!"

On the edge of the tree line, looking out over the open fields beyond the monastery grounds, was a hooded figure, its back to the Jaguar Man. It was seated in a folding chair. By its side was a small easel on which sat an oil painting in a state of incompletion.

"Excuse me, sir..."

"Why, what have you done now, you little scamp?"

"Are you talking to me?"

The hooded head turned and Jaguar Man caught a flash of a white moustache, just as the first flakes of unseasonal snow began to dodge through the tree tops.

"Of course, I am, you damned little fool! Do you think I'm delusional? Don't you dare ever try to steal my savings again! I've got my eye on you, young lady! I know your tricks!"

"I think you might have the wrong person."

"No, you idiot, I know who I am! It's you who has no idea who you're dealing with..."

The old man broke into a hacking cough. He had turned his face back to the fields. Jaguar Man walked down to where he was seated by the easel and moved around to catch his face. He was not a monk; or, at least, he was not dressed as a monk. Despite the white moustache and the frail voice, the face under the hoodie was almost cherubic. A large patterned rug of red and black was pulled up to his chin. It was unclear quite how he had manipulated the palette and brushes that sat on the small table next to the easel.

"That's better. Now I can see you, get an idea of you. What fool's errand are you on today? Let me guess. You've come from those buffoons in the town; another of their wild goose chases. O, Deirdre, why do you do it? Why do they all do it! 'Deirdre' was the first to come and I've called every single one since by her name. Poor Deirdre! Poor all of them! Do you really know who they are? No, it's not your fault, poor benighted lass! Have you come about the messiah?"

"Who?"

"O, what are they calling him now? Shiloh? The prophet? The Bagwan!"

This time the coughing fit doubled him over and Jaguar Man saw the explosion of long white hair that fell, shaking, from the hoodie until the attack had receded.

"I do beg your pardon, young lady! But we get so little opportunity for entertainment here that I always look forward to the arrival of a new Deirdre!"

"I've come to meet a Mister Balfour-Willet."

"Have you? You've just missed him – he's gone to Bristol to visit his parents!"

The fit returned, the old man doubled, and the long white hair, like the claws of a hermit crab creeping from its shell, showed themselves. Jaguar Man was becoming impatient.

"I'll leave you, if you're..."

"O, leave me, will you. Big threat! O, Deirdre, dooooon't leeeave me! Hahaha! O, Deeeeirdreee! Hahahaha! He gave his soul to Mary, you fool! That's what I told Deirdre, that's what I told all the Deirdres. Did none of them report back to station? What unreliable assets you have all turned out to be. Pengelly must be furious! How can you expect to meet with Mary if you have not been trained in her craft? If you have not been initiated, my sweet one! Mere novices, my God, Mary will eat you alive! She has girls like you for breakfast! With toast and marmalade! With her boiled egg! Hahahaha!"

"Where can I find this Mary?"

"You are a seeker, are you?"

"No, I'm not. I don't know what you mean. Frankly, I haven't got a clue what the fuck you are talking about, you old fool, but I've got to speak to Balfour-Willet and if he's with Mary I want to see Mary."

"Well, dear girl, if you think you're ready. She's in the chapel, waiting for you."

"Well, why the fuck couldn't you say that in the first place, you old bastard?"

"And deny me my fun?"

"Fuck off."

Jaguar Man climbed the grassy incline and turned down the path, making Berlin brogue-shaped tracks in the dusting of snow gathered there. Behind he heard a cough. Not an involuntary one, this time. Reluctantly, he turned back to the aged cherub, who was turned towards Jaguar Man. For the first time he noticed the painting. He had taken it for granted that the hump of green represented one of the distant hills. Now it looked more like a sea creature.

The old man fixed his stare, and then nodded his hood at the land above the path.

"You mean the shed?"

The old man's laughter filled the trees. The flakes grew bigger. Looking up, snow landing on his nose and catching in his long eyelashes, Jaguar Man thought that he saw seagulls mixed up in the clouds.

"O, Deirdre, you really are a gas! If only we'd had girls like you in the service! We'd all be speaking German by now! Yes, in the shed, you little fool! She's in the shed!"

Turning back to enjoy his painting, the old man sang under his breath:

"Squirty Mary up from the deep,

Rode the big squid in her bare feet,

When she dropped her guts

She gave birth to fag butts,

And her secret's hid under her creep."

The shed was made of corrugated iron and painted a shade of green that reminded Jaguar Man of found footage movies set in deserted psychiatric institutions. Three wooden steps led up to a gothic door with two tall gothic windows either side. The shed itself was remarkably narrow, and he had assumed it held gardening tools and plastic sacks of insecticide and fertiliser. Above the door was another window, shaped like a clover leaf within which the mullions formed a triangle bisected by circles and parts of circles, always in threes. Either side of the narrow building were open but roofed wings with benches. He climbed the steps and knocked on the door.

If there was a reply it was softer than the falling snow. He tried the door and it was unlocked. Immediately inside was a small white chair, stood out in the darkness. For some reason he thought to turn and through the gothic frame of the open door, among the trees, the old prankster was waving a paintbrush over his easel. Jaguar Man turned back and felt breath fall out of his lungs. When he inhaled again the air was ice; a freezing sensation ran along his chest and down to his fingertips. Goddam weather forecast! An unnaturally bright statue of the Virgin Mary stood on a Mediterranean blue altar, stained glass lights radiating from around her head. She was dressed in a dazzling white robe with a blue stole. Under one foot she trampled the thorned stem of a rose, while from a chocolate-coloured rock a great rush of warm blue water gushed in breakers and white horses.

Jaguar Man felt the need to sit.

Walking around the white chair, he was puzzled by the cork interior of the chapel, draping down the walls like bark tentacles. He sat in the white chair, less than a metre from the Virgin. He felt he ought to look up in adoration at her face, her eyes lifted like his. But he could not raise his eye line above the blue gushing spring, which seemed to move and curl and run. So rapt, he was, that he did not hear the grey wooden door close gently behind him; he only noted how the light around Mary was intensifying. He sat stock still, as outside the snow began to mount and the paths disappeared, filling the footprints of the old man and the lines in the snow where he had dragged the legs of his easel.

One of the residents found him. Walking her dog, she had looked in to check that the thaw had caused no damage. At first she thought to leave him; that perhaps he was a visiting relative deep in contemplation. When she returned and he was unresponsive to her polite enquiries, she fetched reception, who came and then rang the emergency services.

No one could understand why the young CEO of a thriving big data spin-off might choose to walk to a tiny chapel in the middle of woods and sit until he froze to death. There were no signs of foul play, no suicide note, nothing in his emails or texts to suggest that he was anything other than an ambitious operator, with prospects and no interest in religion or spirituality, keen to improve his wealth. They had no inkling that Jaguar Man was just the latest victim of a spiritual skirmish that was about to escalate.

Chapter 35

April and Mandi set off from the doors of the Museum as the snow that had begun to pile up around the chapel in the trees also began to fall in the Bay. Two weeks before they had made the arrangement to walk together after their first meeting. Then, after meeting the officers of the Hexamerons, April had taken Mandi to see the boxes of finds turned up by the hobgoblin-pestered draper's assistant.

It had turned out that there was no "down" to go to. The stores were on the ground floor, behind a large yellow door that anyone might have pushed their way through. The collection of small bones, bear's claws and teeth of hyena, of lion and of deer were stored in small tray-like boxes made of thick cardboard and stacked in piles on high density mobile storage shelves. While it felt privileged to be in there, handling the teeth and claws, the Hexamerons were right. The parts told no whole; until April pulled out a larger box, just as flat, but much wider and longer. Peeling back the lid and peering in, Mandi had that same feeling she had felt in the Museum lobby, catching sight of the small tray of the draper's assistant's finds.

Mandi had imagined that the uneven base on which the pieces of ivory lay was velvet; but now she could look more closely she saw that it was actually paper, the thin kind of paper that some designer clothes still came in.

"Is this paper something that the draper's assistant would have put in?"

"I don't think we know. Do we?" She turned to look for the Engagement Officer...

Mandi tried to take one of the claws from the display, but the fragile paper began to come away with it and she she laid it back down.

"Do you think he might have been attempting to record something by this arrangement?"

"Without some information about where the pieces were found inside the cave, it's hard to see how it would help very much."

"Was this what you wanted to show me?"

"No, no! Something far more exciting! I just saw that you were interested in the Widger finds... Come here!"

And April began to wind violently on the crank of the folding shelves. Mandi jumped back as sections clanged and closed and others opened until a new metal ravine was revealed.

"Here!"

April took down one of the uniform flat khaki boxes and handed it to Mandi.

"Read that and see what you make of it. Wait a moment."

She dug into a drawer and took out a pair of white gloves.

"Just to be..."

And she handed them to Mandi, who, warily, drew them over her fingers. April held the box to her chest, opening the lid slowly, tilting it up like in a heist movie when the characters gather round to finally get to see the bank notes. There was a large brown envelope inside. Mandi took it out, pulled back the flap and from it slid, neatly into the palm of a white glove, a number of foolscap pages, paper yellowing to a light brown. On them was a text written in ink in a scratchy hand. The ink had probably looked black once, but it was now a brownish purple, a darker version of the colour of the pages. One day the two might become indistinguishable from each other.

"Read it."

'That traces of an antediluvian civilisation with its attendant flora and fauna can be so readily found in the obscure lanes, fields and woodlands of this part of Devonshire has long been known to the coarse laborers that dwell in this lugubrious place. That this foetid and extinct civilization should, through blasphemous dreams...'

"Christ, is that my Lovecraft thing?"

"So it seems. It's word for word the same. Not, unfortunately, a story by the world famous writer H. P. Lovecraft, but some kind of testament of Joseph Lovecraft, H.P.'s great grandfather. At least that is what it says on our manuscript; the paper itself appears to be early 1800s, first half of. It may not be a new horror story, but bringing our attention to the existence of the document may contribute to a new understanding of why HPL wrote the kinds of stories he did."

"But my copy isn't worth anything – you already had the original."

"That's right, but why would your parents have a copy? They weren't collectors were they? Or Lovecraft fans?"

"To be really honest with you, April, I'm not sure I know who the hell they were. They were always talking about these little expeditions they would go on. To stone circles, prehistoric tombs, that sort of thing; they looked after a community of New Age types. Which is now my responsibility, can you believe? But everyone there has a different opinion of what my parents believed in. So, for all I know this may have been something that was very important to them, but I don't know."

Now, a fortnight later, Mandi and April were setting out to look for the places in the manuscript. It didn't seem likely that there was any money in it, but maybe Bryan and Anne had discovered something in those sites that was of more importance; maybe some real connection to the writer? In the meantime, Mandi had been reading his stories, and at night she had had the same dream. But it was not of Shoggoths or of Deep Ones or of the Elder Things of his weird and obfuscated tales. Instead it was always about the tray of finds of the draper's assistant. Each time the dream was like a shot, maybe the opening shot, from a movie. The camera moved over the lip of the cardboard tray and then slowly, very low to it, snaked its way around the crumpled purply-brown paper, like a drone filming between rough hills; the rucks and bunching in the packing paper appeared like the 3D map of the hilly terrain, while the teeth and claws seemed to point the camera to destinations on the tray, first to one tear in the paper, then another and another, until... she would awake. The dream was the same each time, the details differed slightly, the routes taken might occur in different orders, but the routes themselves and their destinations were always the same, the dream never varied from the parts of its overall structure, and she would always awake while the camera was still looking out for the final location.

As they left the museum, with the intention of walking out of the Bay and into the Lovecraft villages, the snow had begun to fall. At first a few grains, but within minutes large coagulated flakes began to chunter down, settling everywhere. Immediately the whiteness opened up emptinesses behind the once bright facades of the town. April and Mandi peeped around hoardings and through the gaps left for chaining large wooden gates, to see great voids of the town's foundations held up by expanses of concrete wall. They followed an alley that climbed behind the rears of the buildings. Already, they felt like explorers, stepping carefully on the rising layer of snow.

The alley took them to a spiral set of concrete stairs. Mandi had always been aware of the faded glory of this town, but now the cold seemed to expose its bones. On one side they could see into one of the white voids, in the centre of it a curve of upholstered seating filling up with snowflakes. Hanging from a buddleia growing from out the concrete was a tree of clothes; unwanted garments hurled over a wall. Under part of the concrete stairs was a small recess. Someone had written with a sharpie on its cream pages: RABBIT PORN, SEX IS LIFE. Then drawn a face made up of genitals, a floating eye, a crude pair of breasts (one of them veined like the eye), a stoned alien and a dragon with a hard-on; all this, among the more usual claims about so and so's mum, suggested a richer life of obscenity for the town than Mandi had imagined. At the top of the stairs April and Mandi were tempted by the entrance to a lift, its shaft stood like a small temple building above the valley, in front of which an abandoned leather sofa was already thick in snow. As well as the usual up and down buttons on the lift, the arrow on one pointed sideways. The walk to the villages was a long one. They decided against pushing the sideways button.

"For now..."

A moped driver was slithering in shrinking figures of eight; eventually, he parted company with his vehicle and left it, disgusted, at the kerb. April pointed out the yellow house, now converted to flats, of Edward Bulwer-Lytton, nineteenth century author of 'The Coming Race', a fantasy novel about a race of super beings living in tunnels beneath the surface of the planet, waiting to take over. She was explaining to Mandi that after their climb they were now on top of the Sticklepath Fault, a flaw that ran North dividing the county, when they came to another writer's house. Though still alive somewhere, his house – a hotel he ran – was boarded up and beginning to crumble. From the centre of one of the woodchip boards, covering what had presumably been a large lobby window at the hotel entrance, a chunk of the composite wood had burst and fallen in a torn wound onto the pavement; given how efficiently sealed the whole place was, it was odd that the fragment seemed to have been knocked out from within. Someone had drawn, in chalk, first a symbol of a fish and then a crucifix-shaped cross, above the tear; had they imagined they were warding off from the town something that hid inside?

As they walked beyond the nineteenth century heart of the Bay, April explained that she had wanted Mandi to see the derelict hotel because the writer who had lived there, whose followers would gather there every year to celebrate him and his works, had made his name writing stories in the style of, and often with the same characters as, H. P. Lovecraft.

"The family may have left, but there is still a connection..."

"How do you know all this stuff?"

Mandi did not go in for competition with other female professionals. Not for the sake of it. She wanted to beat everyone, certainly; she was an equal opportunities vanquisher. The gender made no difference. It neither increased nor decreased the pleasure of prevailing over another. Only repetition would do that; had done, she feared. Now, she was quite happy for the archivist to set the pace, choose the route, and make most of the interpretations. April's idea was to explore what she called 'The Lovecraft Triangle'; a few square miles of countryside and tiny villages – most of them, she said, no more than a few cottages – which would have been the full extent of the known territory for most of H. P. Lovecraft's eighteenth and nineteenth century ancestors, before they upped and disappeared into a gargantuan continent. What would get into a family to do that?

April said that there was more chance of spotting things on foot. This was a new concept for Mandi; she had never really thought about doing much of anything on foot. It took too long. Taxis or tube if you wanted to keep up in London. And "things"? They were not for "spotting"; they were for paying admission to see, or accepting gracefully even when you knew they came with a price of their own, for buying and selling, for avoiding and lusting after. But not "spotting". There had always been someone else to do that; a travel writer, a tour guide, an app. What would there be to spot? Surely, any old things not already in a museum or a private collection were either worthless or too ruined to be recognisable?

April suggested that they start in graveyards.

"I have given my life to learning about this little area of the county."

Mandi laughed at April. Her thoughts had been ticking round in her head; now she looked up, April was a statue almost, a moving marble thing. She was covered in a layer of snow.

"You look just the same!"

Mandi used her phone – it had come back to life – and she was an ice maiden too.

"Come on, we're walking stereotypes, let's behave like them!"

And she took a selfie with her arm around April and posted it across her platforms. In the image, beaming, April looks as young as Mandi. But when she looked at April now, dappled by flakes of white, cringing in a sudden gust of Siberian wind, Mandi saw an older woman; the years kept from her by a lifetime in archives, shuffling cardboard boxes and wearing white gloves to handle claws.

Long past the fringes of suburbia, Mandi had barely noticed the large farm buildings they had passed and then their submerging into the tiny lanes. Nor the gentle transition from the smaller fields and the busier landscape, to something less definable. A kind of easing out, a couple of villages that April dismissed as "Saxon" and then a lonelier and yet more present kind of space, of folded hills and quiet curvy lanes. Here the fields were not so smooth, but punctuated with patches of gorses, jumbles of stones and wet dips that the farmers neglected to plough. Not a wilderness, this was managed land, but the human hand was looser here.

"What's that?"

An old man with a green beard and white eyebrows was hanging through the hedge.

April laughed.

"A simulacrum."

As they drew close, the angle to the old rotted stump changed and the eyes and mouth disappeared into the blackened wood.

"You're in good company if you can see those. The draper's assistant who found all the bones and teeth, he was so prone to spotting those things – hobgoblins, he would have called them – that he took to.... o, but you know that story. You're becoming an expert..."

As they walked in silence for a mile of so, Mandi looked out for further figures and faces, stretching arms and drooping tongues, and, surely enough, the more she looked the more she saw that they were there, everywhere.

April turned off the metalled lane, just after passing a kennels in the middle of nowhere; the hounds came running up to the fence, only to turn and ignore April and Mandi, who stood for a while watching the dogs hoovering around the grounds.

"The Hunt."

"Ah."

They walked on down a farm track between two tall blade-battered hedges. Such was the sharpness of the incline that Mandi could see over the tops, to smooth whitened hilly fields, over which the sun now fell, the clouds parting, and already the melt began to drip from the ends of the broken hedge twigs. The fields were topped with huge trees, their last few leaves loathe to let another year pass. The further down the lane they walked, the greener grew the fields and the wetter the path. At the bottom they crossed a stone bridge over a stream that was beginning to flood, water turning an earthy red; a dead and dried crow sat on guard against the gate, and beyond that April and Mandi crunched their way up the last of the snow towards what seemed like a lone thin tower emerging from the tops of trees at the summit of the hill. It reminded Mandi of the freestanding lift shaft that had loomed over the Bay. Large red cows ignored them as they laboured up the slope.

As Mandi huffed and puffed, wondering if sex was really the only exercise necessary to keep fit, she asked April if she thought that there was anything odd about The Sett.

"How do you mean "odd"?"

And Mandi told her about finding the body of the suicide.

"I've heard a lot of stories like that, more bodies than they say... that's the general consensus, that there are a lot more unhappy people here, people with serious problems, a lot of exploitation, low wages, seasonal work, people on benefits who think a seaside place would be easier but find it even more lonely, a lot of voids, cold and empty spaces behind the facade that the tourists don't stay around long enough to see, the false smiles and the dying inside. They're up on the cliffs pumped full of sleeping pills or walking out to sea with their pockets full of pebbles. That's what everyone says; I even heard a whisper that some of them have bullets in them... did yours?"

"It was in a hell of a state... must have been in the water a while..."

"There's a pattern, the locals seem to accept it as a series of one offs, not really connected... by the way, this church..."

As they climbed they were passed by a self-absorbed figure; a young man in a hoodie, his haunted eyes fixed to the trace of footpath in the chewed grass.

"Probably one of the meditators from the West Ogwell Retreat House; they're told not to acknowledge passers-by."

They reached the top of the hill and under the trees was a nave that fitted to the tower. Halfway across the field the meditator turned and lifted his head, watching April and Mandi disappear around the side of the church; then with a nervous glance to the blue sky he hurried down the hill. In the tree tops rooks were calling and fussing.

"...it's deconsecrated, but we can go in..."

Inside the rather anonymous skin of the building, the void was simple and neat. Old fashioned high-walled pews under a sharply curved roof, and at the end a simple altar with a low wooden rail. On the altar in the centre of a white cloth stood a brassy metal cross.

"I thought you said it was deconsecrated?"

"I suppose they like to keep up appearances... there was a horror movie shot here recently. Quite Lovecraftian... a giant serpent lurking in the earth beneath the altar... o!"

April pointed behind the altar. There was some kind of fetish there; a piece of twig around which were tied fragments of cloth and dried flower.

"The Christians are trying to keep the serpent in the hotel, and the pagans are trying to let it out of the deconsecrated church!"

"It was just a film, right?"

"Mandi, it is a mystery what people intend by their marks... those graffiti scribblings on the concrete steps, back in the Bay... is that just kids scribbling rude things?"

"Probably."

"Yes. Probably."

April, laughing, led them out of the church, not through the porch, but by a tiny door in the South wall of the chancel, explaining that in the movie this door had led the exorcists directly into the mouth of the monster.

"Attacks on foreigners, a couple of murders," she continued as if there had been no interruption, "these bodies wash up on the beaches, someone sabotaged the cliff railway and it may not be ready for next season. There are attacks on tourists; they get reported as fights outside of clubs, vandalism in cafes, hotels, and so on, but there was a death, no one was arrested and the body was returned to... somewhere rural in one of the ... Kazakhstan, somewhere like that, maybe. There is never any information about the assailants... even when they take place in quite public places, and when tourist places get wrecked there are never any witnesses. They don't even put out the usual calls for people to come forward. As if there's an acceptance, that since, you know, Brexit and everything, that that's how it goes now. I'd call it a general... I'd call it a silent war... against the weakest, not just foreigners, but against anyone not secure on their patch... weird thing is, a lot of these actions... have you ever heard of the Ferguson gang?"

"What? Like organised crime? Or..."

"No, no... they were... upper class, young... philanthropists, I suppose. Early conservationists. This was the 1930s, started late 20s, went on even through the war. They were a bit wild, in a respectable upper class way. They had a lot of money and when they heard about a medieval barn or an ancient monument, if it was going to be ploughed out or knocked down, they'd collect big money from their connections and they'd buy it and save it. Usually they got the National Trust to do the actual work, they collected the cash from their rich friends – and I mean cash, they delivered as cash, like a criminal gang. And no one knew who they were, mostly still don't after almost a hundred years. They would always appear in masks, they used fake names like Bill Stickers, Sister Agatha, Red Biddy. Anyway, I think I've found evidence for a similar kind of gang, same kind of time, but not well off, comfortable I suppose, middle class, young, plenty of time on their hands, they were based out on the Sett, you were asking about anything odd out there. Well, back then, there's no sign of it now, but there were houses that stood on those dunes..."

"No!"

Dropping down from the church a long view opened up across the thawing fields, with only a farmhouse dotted here and there, miles from one another, right up to the tors on the Moor still topped with thick snow. The wind, when it blew, stung their faces bright red.

"... yes, there were sixty or so houses, built by locals out of wood, no foundations, I've no idea what they did for plumbing and sewage, probably threw it in the sea; anyway by the mid-30s some of them were damaged in a little storm and many of the folks got scared and stayed away, so this gang moved in. I mean there were no property rights out there... it was just shifting sand, it didn't exist legally..."

"What did they do?"

"Nothing very much, nothing constructive like the conservationists. They sailed around there, kayaking, braving storms, taking stupid risks, they were rather sexually progressive for the times, which might have been the influence of a couple of young German women who were part of the group, all very 'Health and Efficiency', 'Kraft durch Freude', wearing shorts and doing gymnastics on the sand..."

"Just sounds like everyday Hitler Youth having fun..."

"Yes, that's what they were. Small scale, sweet and innocent, but they seem to have been preparing for something, which is where the secret gang thing comes in. I have no evidence they ever did any of this stuff, right, but they wrote about it, in their innocent little books about sailing off The Sett and pamphlets about fishing and swimming and wild flowers…"

"Wow, they were real subversives…"

"They keep dropping comments, promoting a sort of green fascism or green terror, they make jokes about blowing up the railway line along the front…"

They had crossed a wide field, the pockets of snow almost melted or blown into the hedgerows. Beyond the gate at a corner of the field was a large white rectangular sign: KEEP OUT. GOVERNMENT PROPERTY.

"…about keeping the tourists out of the area, about closing down all amusement arcades and modern entertainments, which they seemed to think was very un-English, though that doesn't stop them being very keen on German town planning, they liked things to be hygienic, as they called it…"

They had taken a sharp left and very quickly a village was all around them, the stumpy tower of an old church up ahead and an odd arrangement in the middle of its central crossroads; a stone cube-shaped building with a pyramid roof and on top a large metal teardrop with a light bulb inside.

"…and it's all done in fun, of course, and yet it's not funny, in terms of what we know…"

"And what do we know?"

"The Holocaust and…"

"OK."

"In the 1930s there were camp coaches in the sidings at The Sett; ordinary train carriages but converted into rooms where you could stay. There are still some there. The gang made jokes about trapping the holiday-makers in the coaches and then transporting them to prison camps…"

"Very nice…"

"Yes….let's look in here."

And April turned into the grounds of the church. It was old. Many of the stones were keeling, covered in mosses, the inscriptions obliterated with grime or smoothed away by rain and wind. As they walked April scanned the names.

"Apart from the German women, they were locals, sons and daughters of the doctors and vicars and small businessmen of the Bay. They considered the holidaymakers from the industrial Midlands an inferior race that had invaded. Invasion was their right and the Brummies had stolen it from them! I don't know how seriously to take them or how seriously they took themselves…"

She paused, transparently. They had stopped before a grave that was unlike the others. Not an upright stone, but a construction of three layers of rectangles, largest at the base, smallest at the top. There was no visible ornament except the shining splurges of white and yellowy-green lichen that ran over every surface.

"But?"

"Well, at least one of them – called Raymond Cattell – became a world authority on the human mind, a psychologist who was listed and quoted in more academic papers than Freud. Not a household name, but someone whose work has permeated advertising, education, prison design, social policy... terribly respectable, a hundred awards and honorary this and that... he moved to the States and that gave him a world stage... like this family... check the inscription."

Mandi leaned over the austere symmetry.

IN MEMORY OF WILLIAM LOVECRAFT...

"How did you know?"

"Which other one would it be?"

April looked about the graveyard. Mandi followed her gaze. It was true, there was no other likely candidate among the regular monuments. But that was not what Mandi was feeling most; a sneaking disappointment that this might be the end of the journey. That she would not, tomorrow and the day after that, be walking down thawing lanes and across softening fields and adventuring with this vague and humdrum archivist. She could not place the feeling, but running through her was the desperate desire to be and stay in April's company. As they had walked her voice had become more startling, her face sharper and more well-defined.

"Could this be the one who wrote my letter?"

It was hard to discern the exact date. The original leaden letters and numbers had mostly fallen or been prised away, but the holes for the pins that anchored them could still be read approximately.

"Died eighteen something five... sixty-five? Or eighty something... Aged seventy-nine, that bit's clear... could that be him?"

"I think this is probably the great uncle of the writer; he could have written your letter, if he wrote it young enough, but the name on our manuscript says 'James', yours just says 'Lovecraft'. That doesn't necessarily mean James was the author, rather than, say, a witness. We can go and look for the cave if you like? I think it may be the same one as our draper's assistant found all the teeth in..."

"You're shitting me?"

"I don't know for sure, but I know where it is..."

"Have you been there?"

"No, but it's not a secret. It's on maps. It's on the edge of some farmland, but I don't suppose they'll mind. I can take you straight there, it not a long trek – and we can check out the look of the cave against what's in your letter. Did you bring it?"

She had.

Chapter 36

1814

The analytical engineer was deeply uncertain about his supporters. They had responded generously when, after his wonderfully successful lecture at the Royal Institution, his responses to questions and his condemnation of government and scientific societies alike for the common weakness of their support for the invariant iron laws of the universe had turned general approbation to violent pockets of scorn. Goaded, he had denounced the entire absence of any real scientific culture and compared the parlous state of the national thinking with the solid materialism to be found elsewhere. By unseen agents he was denounced from the corners of the lecture room as lacking in patriotism, and the defence of his thesis in public disputation – which had led to accusations of blasphemy and his excusing from all examinations at Cambridge – was raised in some detail.

When the Hexamerons had rushed to his aid, just as violence had seemed inevitable, first forming into a thin line of protection across the centre of the room and then mounting an honour guard for his triumphant exit from the lecture theatre, Babbage had imagined that they must be some student offshoot of the Analytical Society. Certainly the invariant derivatives of differentiation – velocity, acceleration and reaction rate – were uppermost in his mind as they rushed him from the room to safety.

Now the same unflinching certainty informed the momentum of his colleagues as they marched him through the gates of Bedlam between Raving and Melancholy, the two Cibber sculptures in soapy stone, the image of stupefied joy even more awful than that of pained contortion. The Moorfields building was a parody of itself; buckling walls and uneven floors and streams of water gushing between the storeys from the roof. It giddied Babbage and his little band. His comrades seemed little different, in the mathematician's mind, to the armed warders who patrolled everywhere; when he had refused to come they had threatened him with revelations concerning his secret membership of The Ghost Club.

God damn them! Who had blabbed?

"In here!"

The warder held out his hand and one of the Hexamerons slipped a folded note into his palm. A nod and the chains were unlocked from the door. On creaking hinges it was swung open and Babbage ushered in.

The cell was mostly bare. The walls cushioned almost to the ceiling. A single chair sat in the middle of the room and on the ground before it a large sheet of paper with a design of some kind inked in. Babbage was guided to the chair. He looked up at his companions.

"Tell us what you think? Will it work?"

He turned and bent over. The sheet measured something like five yards by three. In a spidery hand, someone had drawn upon it a series of connected shapes: boxes, tubes, pumps, gears, pistons, barrels, organ pipes, rotor blades, levers, drawers and giant eyepieces.

"Where is the engine? What is supposed to drive this mess?"

A curtain that covered the entire far wall of the room trembled. Babbage saw it and looked up.

"Is there someone else here?"

He addressed his companions, but he was answered by a thin voice from behind the curtain.

"Pne...m... ic Ch...mi....y..."

"I beg your pardon?"

A figure slipped from behind the curtain and moved along the side wall, sliding the back of his coat down the padding as if he were trying to make himself invisible to those in the room. The knee length coat was filthy, but somehow he had managed to retain clean breeches and westcot. His feet were bare, his wig awry, but there was some species of frilled cloth pinned at his throat.

"Pneumatic chemistry!"

Pushing off from the wall, the patient performed a kind of dance; an illustration of the movement of fluids and gases that would eventually populate the machine he had imagined and saw before him and inside him and throughout the whole world. The machine that was running the Jacobin galaxies.

Babbage laughed.

"There!" shouted the inmate, "you can do it! You're a pneumatic chemist! At last, they have sent me the man I have been asking for!"

On bare feet, the patient approached the mathematician, his toes crackling the chart as he trod carefully from part to part, modelling the flow and velocities of the fluids, imitating the rate of the reactions. For what seemed to Babbage an eternity, the man gyrated, marched, pirouetted and gestured as he followed the design's strict choreography. Nothing was improvised; he kept to the plan. His exposure of the grand plot was exact and conscientious.

Finished, he stood before the chair.

"They have lobster-cracked, they have lengthened my brain and worked me with the nutmeg grater, but I have scientifically memorised their treachery.

These men" and he gestured along the row of Hexamerons "assure me that you are the inventor of an analytical machine, the antidote to this infernal influencing engine of the Jacobins... is that true or are you another impostor come to draw more wool over the eyes of society?"

Babbage paused, then drew in a deep breath.

"Careful, sir, the weave is in the air..."

"Something is in the air. To be sure. But there is nothing in your machine but air! Hot air! I am sure you are sincere in everything you say, and I am certain that there are particular men – as we all have these – who wish to organise the world in such a way as to bring us down in it. However, your map, your blueprint, is not how these things are done!"

"Are you sure?"

The patient looked, appealing, to the line of Society members. Finally, one took a tiny step towards the seated figure of the inventor.

"Sir, are you sure there is nothing in the plan? Look again; on your words hang our future."

Babbage was uncertain whether he meant the future of his Society, of which Babbage was now a part, or whether he meant that "Society" of which all living persons were members, including the deluded and dream-haunted idiots in bare feet and frock coats.

Babbage looked again at the paper. He stood. Bent over, then skirted it, followed by the inmate, as though they had both seen something new, and were chasing it to a destination. Babbage performed a full lap of the blueprint, bended; then rose to his full height.

"Absolutely nothing in it. A mess of line and tubes and whatever. It may have the appearance of a machine, but if you were to build it, there would be no life in it, mechanical or spiritual. No more life than a coffin would."

"Idiot!!! Idiot!!! Madman!!!" roared the inmate and tore a handful of cloth from his breeches. The Hexamerons instantly formed a ring around the mathematician and began to usher him solicitously to the door, screaming for the warders. As the door swung open, complaining rustily, Babbage had only a moment to look back before the door swung shut and the chains refastened. In that moment he saw through the frame the scampering inmate leap halfway up the curtain at the end of the room and grabbing handfuls hauled the whole thing down in a dusty confusion, cracking his skull, with a sound like a broken bell, on the uneven wooden boards. Light streamed through the giant barred windows that were revealed and covered the entire far wall, and, though the dust was beginning to form into a miasma, what the inventor saw beyond was a panorama of the great metropolis and how it was made up of a series of connected shapes – houses and warehouses like boxes, chimneys likes tubes, factories full of pumps and gears and pistons, breweries shaped like barrels, cathedrals like organ pipes, pub signs swinging like windmills or rotor blades, one person pulling on another like crowds of levers, banks full of drawers and everywhere the constables lurking like blue uniformed eye-pieces. The whole capital no more and no less than a lunatic's plan and just as lacking of an explicit engine. Yet it ran!

As the Hexamerons raced him out between Raving and Melancholy, despite their blackmailing ways, he had committed himself to their crusade; he, with them, would harness the chaos in his machine.

Chapter 37

"For my sins, I downloaded a couple of Raymond Cattell's papers."

April paused at the wooden gate. Beyond it stood a large house, and then a field of sheep grazing, indifferent to the seriousness of the two women.

"Sophisticated stuff, all the findings apparently based on experiments and observations, charts and graphs, peer-reviewed... some very attractive ideas around risk-taking but behind it all, like a ticking metronome, is the same basic idea that they were laughing about on The Sett in the 1930s..."

"Which was?"

"Survival as the final test of ethics.... natural selection among groups, and the acceptance of direction by qualified elites. The drive to create a better humanity in conformity to evolutionary ideals..."

"Is this OK, coming down here? Isn't this someone's lawn..."

"It's a public right of way. The sign's fallen down."

"If you say so. 'Survival...'?"

"Of the fittest to... culturally develop."

They had cut away from the winding lane, and along a driveway, approaching and then skirting a large house called 'The Old Rectory'. Or something like that; Mandi had forgotten it no sooner than looked at it. At times the terrain seemed very real to Mandi, brighter and sharper than she had seen fields before; then a moment later she was in a fuzzy infatuated space hanging on April's words. It was like being a character in a film, it was like being a child again, like being a soldier without enemies, or an artist without reviews.

"Of course, Cattell didn't say 'race' in the academic papers. Not very often. I think he did on The Sett, I'm sure he did; later these people were waiting for a time when they could again. The papers sometimes say 'class', mostly 'groups'; that's all they need to say for those who think that race and class is everything. He'd use 'intelligence' a lot; when he was being provocative 'evolutionary development'. The declared intentions of the work were seemingly idealist and humanitarian, Cattell even calls it a 'religion', it has a name – 'Beyondism' – improving humanity in preparation for the end of chaos, the abolition of progressive taxation, and the epiphany of the free individual, but you can hear the ticking like a bomb under a pier or behind a slot machine, or in a crushing comment from a teacher to some working class kid in Birmingham, or savage punishment in the kind of correctional facility where incarceration is designed to deter breeding. Worst perhaps, in the offers of genetically engineered intelligence to poor working class families as treatment for their foetuses... all of that happened because of his ideas... thing is, Mandi, all these suicides and attacks on tourists and the fire in the arcade down on The Sett the other week and the attack on the funicular railway last year... it's like they might have all been carried out by the eugenics-mad Ferguson's Gang that the gang on the Sett aspired to become..."

"O, you! O, you! You had me there right up to the punch line!"

"I'm serious..."

"I was taking you seriously! Before you got to the ghosts bit! O, come on! There've always been bastards, April, they didn't go away because of a few documentaries about the Holocaust; they adjust, they re-present their state control mind-fuck steel fist in the kid glove nanny state as scientistic business-as-usual... that's what you're saying, right? I see these people every day! Fake libertarians – one minute they're rolling away 'unbounded social welfare' and the next they want.... what was it? 'Acceptance of qualified...'?"

"Elites..."

"Exactly. The fascists faded back into the system, some of them looped themselves into libertarianism, to share their hierarchy-crazed mumbo jumbo by other means; and I can just about buy that.... but a gang of ghosts? Conspiracy theory is a conspiracy against thinking. I was enjoying our talks..."

"Sorry..."

Mandi laughed at April.

"Yours isn't even a conspiracy by living people! Most people do me the decency when pitching a conspiracy to at least have it run by living people..."

April shrugged, almost coquettishly.

"It's a story by Lovecraft; about a big nasty thing that doesn't die, but sleeps and calls from underneath..."

Up ahead, trip-trotting down the path, a woman on a tall white horse. Her hi-viz top decked in blue and white chequers, and the word POLICE...

Mandi and April looked twice. No, POLITE.

That was a weird thing to have on a jacket.

A pair of rooks clattered across the path of the horse and swung into the tops of the trees that stood far up on a rise. The gentle folding of the green fields had been broken now, the land was flattening out with sharper rises and hints of limestone faces and snatches of small cliffs to either side.

"Going for a walk?"

"That's right."

"Looking for anything in particular?"

April jumped in.

"We're following public footpaths, visiting churches, looking for some of the old names, tracing the history, getting a sense of the past... we were thinking of some lunch?"

"The pub in the next village does a decent ploughman's. So I've heard."

"That's good enough for us! Just out for a ride, are you?"

"Nice day for it... so it's turned out, anyway!"

"Enjoy yourself."

The woman swung the horse around and rode off in the direction from which she had come.

"That's the Hunt," explained April. "They didn't take kindly to our stopping and looking through their fence at the hounds; thought they'd check us out for sabs."

"God. Really?"

"I'm guessing."

"Did you notice the 'POLITE' on her thing? Thinking we'd be lazy enough to read it as POLICE? Cheeky, eh?"

They pressed on. Mandi, a little wearily now. April, unfaltering.

The horse rider, once out of sight, turned into the first field. Tethering her horse to a gate, she stripped off her riding gear and dressed from a saddle bag in the kit of the white snipers, slipping an anonymous hi-viz top over that, slinging a rifle and case over that. Then faded into the trees.

Chapter 38

1888

The steam engine, a devil billowing red and black within its vented cylinder exhaust, raced along the line set down by Brunel's navvies. A coast defiled; a shoreline made where none had been, and tunnels cut in desert dunes that had stood solidly for three hundred million years. In places, the seas had been driven back. For this evening's passenger alone in the first-class carriage, the splash of spray against the window was unnecessary; his thoughts were already boiling around the vehicle, the highest development of human genius against which nature threw its basest power.

The man felt a shiver, not his own, as the train passed the Sett and then the Red Rock. Even in the bright sun of the late afternoon, he caught the shades of primitive beings in conference with unsophisticated monsters on the beach. Yet, these thoughts came as a relief to him; the letter in his pocket burned like a white-hot coal against his heart. Inflammation spread like an unholy frost around his fragile frame; barely middle-aged, the trauma of his losses had eaten into and disturbed his cells. His complexion was grey and getting greyer. Sadness and suffering had never damaged his generosity; now, however, he was dragged by the flaring engine towards a scandal made by the meanness of others, threatening to drag down all the chapels of hope, and he was obliged to do his best to save them from the scoundrels.

At the tiny station at the top of the Bay, the fireman had over-stoked. The passenger stepped out into the choking cloud, escaping the platform and coughing his way down towards the coast. Without looking up, he passed familiar modern villas and respectable guesthouses where he knew there were friends dressing for dinner; and parlours where preparations might be in hand for a séance or two. Though he was confident that his unexpected arrival would be greeted as a boon at all these doors, he marched solemnly on in the knowledge that all of that, every strand of the web of friendships and spiritual adventures reaching across the best of all societies, from the threatened capitals of glittering and tumultuous Europe to experimental societies formed around the kitchens of humble cottages, was now fallen and under threat.

As a gentleman of a certain delicacy of sentiment, grateful to the services of young men (and a few young women) barely out of childhood, bound to their openness of spirit – if that is what it was – he knew how he and others were always vulnerable to gossip. He feared – indeed, if he were honest with himself and less ready than usual to forgive, he knew – that others had been quicker than him to exploit the intimacy necessary to their joint endeavours. Now there might come a fatal exposure and the re-telling of their entire adventure in the sordid terms of a brothel.

Eschewing the porters, the man marched his small suitcase to a line of villas perched above the stilled waters of the Bay. Sat on a stable fault, it was a home for solid industrialists and even more solid novelists. Dropping just below this rank of small palaces, among them the yellowing mass of Argyll Hall, the man presented himself at the reception desk of the Shedden Hall Hotel. Perhaps it was the unfamiliarity of the place, or the proximity to so many living rooms that would usually have been so welcoming, that alerted him to the spiritual dowdiness of the place. Even in the hotel's new wash of paint he felt its future desecration by addled folk, desperate spirits struggling to escape, in its rich brocades he felt the uncomfortable nervousness of the worship of mediocrity and the heat of the arson that would threaten the hotel's timbers. An officious manager checked him in. For a moment he considered leaving a false name, but only unpleasant absurdisms – "Ambrosia Homunculi", "The Dishonourable Peter Rast" – came to him; in their place, he wrote "Edmund Gurney".

Once in his room, Gurney sat upon the bed and waited. His suitcase was unopened. After a while, he thought to check his timepiece, but it mattered little how quickly or how slowly disgrace came. Accustomed to the grip of emotional suffering, these minutes were of little account to Gurney in the greater book of his life. What did weigh on his heart, though, was the prospect of the sinking of the entire ship. The bringing low of so many fine souls. The losses of his childhood had driven from him the duplicities and simple crudeness that he observed in both the upper and lower orders; and he knew that he was a thin-skinned and thin-souled man who felt too much to act with the ruthlessness of the middling sort. The world was going to hell and he was restraining the handcart.

Eventually there was a knock upon the door.

"Come! Please come!"

The maid – somewhat filled out in figure from the mere slip of a girl he remembered – gingerly opened the bedroom door and then closed it, silently, behind her. She spoke quietly.

"Sorry, sir! I weren't allowed to get away. Keepin' you waiting!"

"Think nothing of it, dear child. Here, sit down, and tell me what is troubling you. Take your time."

He cleared the suitcase from the chair and beckoned the maid; who seemed to shrink in height as she approached him. Seeing that she was nervous to sit while he stood, Gurney resumed his perch on the edge of the bed, unconscious of his shifting very slightly from buttock to buttock. Their slight vibration, an uncontrollable shaking of the bones, quietly squeaked the hinges; Gurney contrived an appearance of superficial calm.

"Very sorry, sir, to bring you here, but I could bear it no longer, a ruined conscience is a terrible thing to live with, and what with leaving my post in Brighton, the upset..."

"Yes, yes. I have no ruined conscience, but go on..."

"I'm sorry, sir. I didn't mean to imply..."

"How could you? Now, proceed quickly to your complaint. There is a late train, I might just catch.... Is it about Smith and the boys? Is it Podmore?"

"No, sir! Everyone knows about that!!"

"Oh... do they?"

"Yes!"

He had come on a fool's errand. The sudden lifting of the cloud dazzled Gurney. He felt a dizzying exhilaration, as if he were floating from the bed, his head among stars.

"It's about what... what I was persuaded to do."

Gurney's soul came plummeting back onto the bed. The room darkened. The heavy wallpaper moved in on him. The furniture leaned over.

"I should never have agreed, but 'e were such a lovely man; 'e dazzled yuh! I wanted to help, be part o' it all. It were like being actually in the magic, sir, like being in a pantomime! Or Arabian Nights!"

"Good Lor'! Is that what he told you it was!"

"No, sir! That were just my feelin's! I were a foolish young thing. What did I know of the ways of the world, back then? Let alone of the next world..."

"Of course not, of course not, how could you? We were all innocent then. You acted as best you could, I'm sure. Gentlemen must take responsibility for the young.... but why do you wish to raise these matters now? To call me here? So many years after?"

"I have recently attended the Roman church here, sir. I've bin prepared for my first communion, and as I'm sure you is aware, what that requires? Confession?"

"Ah! I see. But surely... you need not confess the sins of others, whether you were a victim of them or no..."

"I weren't no victim! I knew exactly what I was a-doin'. I knew my right from wrong, even then. I ain't never been anything special, but I 'ave a conscience."

"Of course you do."

"Every day it 'as preyed upon me, comin' like a creepin' thing in the night, in the day waiting for me in cupboards, spoilin' all my dreams. I'm so sorry, sir, I 'ad to tell you. I should never 'a fooled you all..."

"Fooled? What do you mean?"

"Smith, sir... I were in on his schemes. Part of his 'set up'. None of it were real..."

She stopped and looked hard at Gurney, intent on reading his face.

"I knew! You never guessed! Smith said you was just playin' along, but I said 'no, you was a proper gentleman'! That you 'udn't never make such a fraud. Never a one t' cheat at cards."

"I don't play cards. If you are alluding to Smith's dishonesty at Brighton, Annie, I knew all about that at the time. I saw the mechanism. I challenged Mister Smith and he confessed everything – the rehearsal of the boys, your own manipulation of the strings, the use of fabric and chemicals, everything. Mister Smith was as appalled at his behaviour as I was; he wept! Poor man! He explained that in his belief in his own inadequacy faced with such grave affairs, and import of the dead being heard, he was afraid of letting us all down and so had given nature, and supernature, a helping hand. To emphasise the truth, rather than... well, you know... invent it. As his tears fell, he made a solemn promise to me, sworn on the memories of my three dear sisters, that – whatever the goodness of his intentions – he should never do such a thing again. We are all frail, Annie; the chaos is always nibbling at our heels, along the way we sometimes stumble, but..."

"It were all of it play-acting."

"What?"

"From the start to the end on it! After Brighton the same as before Brighton. The boys always rehearsed. Like it was for a play. Trick properties and effects. Smith taught us words; nought was writ down. There was strings the first sitting and the last and Smith were always behind the screens poking at things to make 'em move. I'm so sorry, sir. 'E taught us 'ow to conceal things after the witnesses 'ad checked the rooms..."

"All of it? Every single..."

The maid nodded. A tear dropped from her cheek and burst on the blackness of her uniform.

"Nothing was real?"

In a moment he would be sure to wake up, and the whole thing – the letter, the journey, the meeting – would all sink back into the dream.

"Nothing, sir."

From the pocket of her apron, Annie produced a handful of ectoplasm, a scribbled prompt card, a linen mask that Gurney recognised, shockingly, as the likeness of the face of his youngest sister, and a retractable tin claw. Annie laid these out on her lap; as if they were the sacraments of an obscene ritual.

"Ye gods!"

Gurney shook for a moment and then fell back onto the bed. The maid leapt up from the chair, scattering the sacraments of hoaxing.

"Sir!"

"She leaned over, fearing that the visionary had suffered a seizure. His face was fixed in a rictus, his eyes glazed. His lips began to move. Annie bent, putting her ear close to Gurney's mouth.

"Go to confession. Confess all. Leave now."

The maid straightened, gathering up the bits and pieces of her past, and fled the room. As the door clicked in the frame, Gurney sat up straight like a vampire ghoul in its freshly-opened coffin. Then, as if in a trance, he fetched paper, pen and ink from his suitcase, sat at the dressing table and began to write.

It was almost a day later when the manager gained entry to the room, concerned that their recent guest had failed to appear for either breakfast, lunch or dinner. Gurney lay, dressed, upon the bed, just as Annie had left him, except for a cloth upon his lower face, the last vapours of chloroform still hanging lightly around it. His eyes were glazed, his lips did not move.

When, two days later, a detective called at the hotel, he was surprised to hear from the manager that he had already handed over the two letters, found upon the deceased gentleman, to "the first 'tec, a right proper gentleman copper he was, dead posh, from London". The manager felt that it was impolitic to communicate to this ordinary detective that the letter summonsing the deceased had come from a member of his own staff. The authorities had both letters and if trouble came it would come soon enough without his encouragement. Of the second letter, Gurney's, all he would say of it was that it was "mumbo-jumbo".

The detective excused himself, in order to pursue his enquiries, furiously, at the local police station, where his investigation quickly ground to a halt. The manager, however, had not been wholly frank with him. In fact, the manager had carefully read the letter that Gurney had written. While he did not understand it all, he had caught the gist of it, was glad to be rid of it to the first person who asked for it, and would not be mentioning its contents to anyone in the near future. This is as he remembered it:

> "My dear good friends, distinguished colleagues and fellow
> seekers, our Olympus is wholly destroyed, and all of our
> endeavours, so it appears, are at an end. I have received this day
> testimony – and examined incontrovertible evidence – from an
> impeccable source who stands to gain nothing by the revelation,
> that all of our experimental works have been tainted by
> pantomime. Not a one of them was true. Smith, in whom I
> invested so much faith and forgiveness, has cheated us entirely.
> All his hypnoses were thespian, his boys mere scenery. We have

played fool to his knave. I take full responsibility for exposing the Society to his charlatanism. Our work is dead. We are back at the beginning, with our suspicions. One small hope, only, remains: such has been the nature of my losses and the depth of my suffering and grief, that only the prospect of a reunion, in flesh, with those who went on in haste, has kept me from the logical course of self-extermination. Now, it is with the same hope and prospect that I destroy the bodily part of me in a last throw of the dice; a gamble on a desperate solution to our Great Problem.

Friends, in the years of our labours the physical world has come to chaos. Even in our Society there have been those who strove to turn our chapels into bordellos. Those of our friends in power avert their eyes from the cesspit in their charge. My simple exit will be an unimportant and a trivial one if I cannot aid those of good to bring the beast to heel; so it is that I propose a final experiment. If I find myself upon the 'other side' and in good company, I will organise in that blessed place a Story to be communicated in many spirit voices, transmitted by mediums, and assembled upon earth. In that blessed place, I will also arrange for a Plan; I will do what I failed to do on earth and father a child, a mystic child, a leader-prophet engineered by the finest biologist-minds in the hereafter. My soul will father it upon a medium; I leave the exact details to you. This child will rein in the bestial Chaos and restore Man to the road of progressive evolution that He has departed from in order to court decadence, and thus raising Man to perfection by selection.

If, however, you hear nothing.... then, my friends, Darwin – though even he refuses to accept his own 'findings' – is right, and there is no Purpose; mutation and meaninglessness rule and only Nothingness in the blasphemous majesty of darkness awaits the dying. In such an event, individual existence having ceased with the death of my body, I ask this: that our Society adopt a new objective, in lieu of salvation, and that is the quickest possible extermination of the entire race itself.

Your friend in hope of a progressive result,

Edmund Gurney (deceased)."

Chapter 39

"You won't find any lunch there!"

Left alone by the Hunt's outrider, April and Mandi had followed the drive and then its becoming a muddy path until that in turn met a winding lane bending across the flat valley floor; under the shadow of the Great Hill. At a sharp corner of the lane was a gate and April indicated that they should enter, shutting the rickety structure behind them. They passed the low remains of small stone buildings and jumbles of roughly stacked rocks, leftovers from quarrying.

"What's that? That weird sound?"

"Hah! Skylarks!"

To their left, beyond a barbed wire fence and the valley bottom, a wide green field was grazed by Devon Reds, the lane edging its far side before the land began to rise to the dominant hill.

"The Great Hill, that is," said April.

"Ow!" shouted Mandi, sweeping a wasp from her arm. April rummaged in her pockets and produced a small tube of ancient-looking cream, squirted a whirl onto her fingertip and began to rub it into Mandi's arm, until Mandi began to feel inexplicably discomforted. They set off again. Mandi stumbled on the loose rocks, steering close to the low cliff and away from the field and any possessive eyes.

"Should we have asked?"

"I already did. I rang the farmhouse. They claim the cave's now inaccessible, overgrown with brambles, and dangerous. None of which is true. They're just trying to keep people off; probably anxious the Old Grotto will attract cat stranglers and Satanists..."

"I thought you said it was a cave?"

"It is. A natural cave; but there was a dig in the 1960s and they found medieval artefacts – possibly earlier – and remnants of a chapel that had been destroyed and the entrance blocked. Similar to one up in the north of the county dedicated to "wicked Eve and naughty Diana..."

"Don't mess with me..."

"I'm not. That's true."

"I thought you said the shop assistant was a fundamentalist Christian?"

"It's all mixed up, isn't it?"

"What's that, now?"

Mandi had frozen mid-stride. April turned back.

"What?"

"That was definitely a hobgoblin. I saw it move and hide. That was no tree stump!"

"Where?"

April joined Mandi and they scanned the line of trees and scrub above them, along the rising diagonal line of the low cliff.

"See anything now?"

"Five, six, seven goblins, at least."

"Me too."

They laughed it off and carried on. Yet there remained an uneasiness. Above them, the scrub faces and tree trunk legs shifted back into the bright camouflage of green and yellow shadows. They scaled the piles of quarry cast-offs and scrambled through a gap in the cliff face, inadequately obstructed by a large wooden plank, a recent half-hearted attempt to keep intruders out. This tiny opening brought the two out a little further along the stretching cliff face, above ruined sections of wall and the entrance to the cave they sought.

"Is this it?"

"I think it must be."

"And these walls were a chapel?"

"The walls were the nave, the cave the chancel..."

"If it was Christian."

"Maybe at that time everything was 'Christian'?"

April did that stupid thing with the rabbit ears fingers. Mandi ducked into the cave, though the mouth was tall enough to take her on tip toes. Inside it was quickly dark, but dry, with light enough for Mandi to make out some long tentacular accretions of solidified lime that had formed as ribbed limbs on the walls. It was like standing under a rock octopus raised up on the points of its eight legs. Mandi quickly scrambled out again under the pretext of telling April, who was scrutinising the remains of the low wall.

"This is the cave the shop assistant dug out, right? Didn't keep any useful records of his finds? You don't reckon this is the same one as the Lovecraft thing is about, do you?"

April glowed, and opened her mouth, but the shout was someone else's.

"You won't find any lunch there!"

It came from one of a group of hobgoblins in hi-viz jackets that had begun to move in from three sides. Burly men in jeans down one side of the cave mouth, men in suits and hard hats down the other side, while across the field, scattering the herd of Reds, a howling farmer.

"Trespass!!"

April recognised the men in suits as denizens of the Hexameron Essay Society. A different section from those who organised the talks at the museum. But she explained them that way to Mandi.

"It's the club from the museum, is all."

"What right have you to be here?"

Mandi bluffed, cracking in ahead of April.

"What right have you?"

"We're here at the pleasure of the landowner."

"Get off my land, you two! You're the woman that rang'd!"

"There is a public interest in this site," explained April, coldly. "I am researching the historic Widger finds from this cave..."

"Who are these two?" shouted the farmer.

"I have no idea, sir. I am a trustee of the museum and I can tell you that neither one of these women is a member of our staff."

"I am a volunteer," stated April. Mandi turned coldly to her. "And I have dedicated my life..."

"Well you can go an' dedicate it to somewhere else!"

Mandi looked at the red-faced farmer stood in his field, legs wide apart, battered trilby askew, and then at April who had become oddly middle-aged and frumpy. The vivacious virago was gone. Mandi went instinctively to April's side, unnerved by the theatricality.

"Whatever your association with the museum, you have no right to use its authority to make trespass on private land. Before I call the police on behalf of the landowner here..."

And he gestured to the farmer as if he were a visual aid.

"... I suggest that you allow our security officers to escort you to the public highway and then be on your way?"

The Hexameron suit, a neatly trimmed beard that seemed to sit dead on his face like Astroturf in a stadium, pointed a manicured finger back the way that April and Mandi had come. The farmer in the field echoed the gesture with the similarly unblemished digit of a similarly smooth hand. A cowed April turned to Mandi as if looking for permission to persist, or an excuse to surrender. Mandi was a blank; in full lockdown. April looked beyond the fingers; a pack of younger Hexamerons, galoshes over their Ted Baker trousers, stumbled in a line, then the jumbled squad of security guards shuffled themselves into a random order, while, last line of defence, a step back within the treeline, were the four white snipers, yellow hi-viz tabards for disguise; their rifles, in their cases, hung over their shoulders.

At the broken gate, held open by one of the overweening security staff, the Hexameron elder held up his palm in salute.

"You are welcome to our lectures and any other public events we choose to hold, but the private projects of the Society are strictly members-only affairs. Any future actions on your part that threaten the confidentiality of our business operations will invite a legal action. If, however, you choose to do anything that effectively prejudices or inhibits the actual aims and objectives of the Society, then you stand to invite a less... formal and more expeditious response. I hope I make myself clear?"

"And don't come back!" yelled the farmer. "Loony bitches!!"

April and Mandi walked off, down the lane, without looking back. Almost a mile on and they had walked through a small gathering of houses, a smooth-skinned church and a beer house with a sign that both April and Mandi noted – a romantic pseudo-medieval lady mounted on a horse carrying an upturned sword by the blade to form a Christian cross and riding across water – then out the other side, towards a sun low in the sky. Mandi had photographed the sign and later, online, an image-search identified it as a copy of cover art for a 1980s Arthurian romance, written by a paedophile authoress, about the overwhelming of paganism by an invading Christianity, turning its goddesses into Christian virgins and martyrs.

It was another mile before either spoke.

"You OK?"

And another mile before Mandi replied.

"Anything I can do to get back at those bastards, just let me know. I... loathe being told off!"

When April turned to look at her companion, Mandi saw that she was abruptly young again. She laughed.

"That wasn't a real farmer. That wasn't who I talked to. A while off, I met the couple who farm that land and they're not like that. Security guards? Out here? I've never seen that before. To protect a cave? I didn't recognise any of the Hexamerons from the other day..."

"Nor me."

"The whole thing had the feel of a... charade. Like they were all played by actors, and they almost fluffed their lines! We're just so used to shit drama that we take that kind of incompetent crap for reality..."

"I really don't like being told off. I don't like it, April, and I don't accept it. But if you're telling me that we were just reprimanded by a team of extras, then I... whuh?"

She had tried to ask 'what's that noise?' There was a loud gulping and wheezing sound running up and down the hedgerows. Mandi looked around and then above, before she realised that the sound was coming from her. That the tears running down her North Face and spilling onto the lane were her own.

"Are you sure you're OK?"

"That was the.... woman from the Hunt, yeh? Up in the trees?"

"I don't think they know who they are..."

"Ditto. I swear I remember something about being told off by someone really important to me and I was really tiny and who was that? Who was that?"

It was an hour or more before Mandi felt able to explain. Her cold fury at being told off had triggered a memory of a time before Bryan and Anne; a reverie of being chastised by someone or something else, something more real than false, but she had forgotten what her disobedience had been and who she had disobeyed, but both things felt important and wholly obliterated by 'stuff'. The more she tried to remember and recover the faint trace of the something, the more the intimation retreated back into the cave.

"What did you say the name of the shop assistant, the digger in the cave, was? Wager?"

"Widger. James Lyon Widger."

"Jesus."

Mandi Lyon had stopped dead in her tracks. She stared ahead and then swivelled to search the dark eyes of her companion. Mandi felt a rushing impulse to take a hold of April and seize her, squeeze the truth from her, dissolve into her.

"You better not be fucking with me..."

Chapter 40

October, 1938

"You are telling us... what? That the texts experimented on each other!"

"They talk to each other. Yes! Whether that is because their original sources were communicating in the otherworld, or whether it is in the nature of messages in this arrangement to do so..."

"Whatever the reasons, sirs, the result is... enigmatic."

"We have only their shared references – Tennyson, Blake... as clues for a meaning."

"Perhaps", facilitated the least furious of the Hexameron elders, "that is the message?"

"No! If we accept this argument, then the message is Tennyson's 'The Idylls of the King'! And I believe the world already has that!"

The wind howled through the many tiny apertures around the foundationless house. Sand kicked up in the lobby.

For an hour a small group of porters had lugged crates of manuscripts across the sands of The Sett. Even before the storm had got up, the wind was fierce and lashed the four men with stinging particles; like test subjects in a brutal experiment in natural philosophy. On arrival at the tentative wooden villa, sat on the very brow of the dunes, they had unloaded the thousands of pages, and the three women and one man, the Interpreters, had begun to arrange the manuscript around the house, using every room except the water closet (which stank); a snaking tail of papers that thickened here and there into bellies and thighs. Rather than for reading from left to right, the papers were often laid beside and over each other, as if the whole were some bestial child of palimpsest and crossword. The completion of the pattern conjured puzzlement; for its creators and its audience.

Matching the four porters and four Interpreters were four senior members of the Hexameron Society. A fifth member was waiting, in hiding far away, in case some mischief befell the four at the meeting. Together, these five were all that remained of what had been a remarkable regional force, a dynamo driven by industrial and agricultural forces, feeding back to them the most developed technological, mathematical and bio-engineering concepts; spreading their influence along the furthest tendrils of the British Empire. Yet, their entire enterprise had foundered on this one experiment, the results of which would be received now. A gamble on death as a mirror, as a scrying surface of knowledge beyond what is known, to bring an advanced technology garnered beyond plain death into the world of day; now ended in a cry of despair.

"There's nothing there!"

In a neighbouring house the next generation waited; eager to replace the séances, automatic writing and experimental spiritualism with the psychological reprogramming of a scientific religion. The choice for the four Hexamerons was stark; to harvest the fruits of intuition, the merest echoes of distant ghosts, and find some formulae in their ambience, or take the metallic frame of a brutal and competitive psychology and strap every human to it, twist and bend them till they rose to a new stage of being.

Listening to the Interpreters, the four Hexamerons were sunk deep in their armchairs, held down by the weight of their responsibilities. After half a century of effeminate mediumship, during which they had shed almost their entire scientific membership, were they about to jump horses and embrace the terrible cotton gins and vicious spinning jennies of Social-Darwinism?

There was still a chance that the dead would come through, surely?

They could all hear the waves. The dusk had been ugly. The only lights on The Sett were in the two houses; one for the Interpretation of the papers, the other a waiting room for the Beyondist youths. The other fifty or so villas, many damaged beyond repair, were in darkness; no one holidayed in this cold. There was a greyness to their wooden walls; salt had made them all dull. The moments when the moon had broken through, earlier in the evening, had only made matters worse, smearing a milky gruel on everything. In the houses, some modelled on ships' bridges and American ranches, there was only the failure of ghosts and missed opportunities, a whole village of things that never happened. Souls so lost they had not the energy to haunt. Instead, they existed beside the treacherous void they baited, its sudden sucking down ready to spoil a promising athleticism or a literary career in a single drag.

"'...the kingdom has gone to the beasts...'"

"That's Tennyson?"

"Yes."

"A beast, you say, has the whole kingdom?"

"That's before Arthur comes, he solves that..."

"A child of obscure birth, son of an unidentified father..."

"And three mothers... queens in light..."

"What is this?"

"Brought by the waves... remember this is poetry..."

"We are no longer concerned with poetry. What is the interpretation? Hurry!"

The four Interpreters sat upright, like vampires, in spite of the soft upholstery of their chairs.

"This is the language of the dead! This is how they communicate, by quoting the poets..."

"We are in a lunatic asylum! Let's retreat next door! To rationalism!"

"Wait! A babe was brought by the waves, according to the poet... does that ring any bells? A babe found on a beach? Recovered by a wise man, a magician, a seaside entertainer?"

"You think that these..."

To animate himself, the youngest Hexameron rose and removed his smoking jacket, casting it over the back of his armchair.

"...intimations, through mediums, might concern the young Balfour-Willett's boy?"

"Young? He's a grown man now! He's a Trinity man for crying out loud!"

"If he is the messiah..."

"A typical boy of his social position, joined up with the Welsh Guards!"

"He won't save the world with them! He should be in the wilderness!"

The four Hexamerons, all on their feet by now, were pacing around the script, making figures of eight to avoid disturbing the puzzle in which they were all steadily losing faith.

"Well some folk might say that joining the Welsh Guards is not unlike going into the w..."

"Shut up! Shut up!"

The Hexamerons coagulated in despair. They cast a collective gaze over the tables and floors of the Devonian dacha carpeted with the pages of automatic text; sometimes a single phrase on an otherwise blank sheet, other times finely scribbled text almost obliterating all gaps and with them any sense. Lines of narrative were suggested, dramaturgies of epic conflict were here and there prepared for, strands roused into choruses, conundrums pushed themselves forward. For a while each of the four Hexamerons pursued their own lines of intuition, peering intently where one paper had landed over another. As before, when the interpreters had led the Hexamerons from room to room pointing out the echoes, the allusions and shared references, so now the Hexamerons followed their own hunches, until these, in turn, led the four men back to face each other in the centre of the main room.

"They haven't got it! The bastards!"

"We have spent twenty-five years of the Society's patience and hard cash, investing our faith in you... you curs!"

"Then you were mistaken. We are not saints, we are psychic literary scientists, and we have spent those twenty-five years labouring honestly over these papers in the interests of peace and keeping the world from chaos..."

"And the result is?"

"The Gurney Plan failed."

"I am not convinced, on the basis of this.... presentation... that any Plan ever existed!"

"Don't try and deny it! Your Society had every faith in it!"

"Hah! A Plan formed in the spirit world..."

"How in the name of hell can that be a Plan?"

The youngest of the Hexamerons kicked a few of the papers into a dust devil.

"Please, please... This, this is precious..."

But the interpreters begged to no avail as their four employers began to set about the mystery with boots and fists. Pages were kicked up into the air, sheaves of writing hurled against the walls to shower down the lampshades, sending flocks of shadows across the wooden boards.

"Sirs, this mystery was our bulwark..."

"Against what!"

"The black tide of materialism!"

"Against the goddam truth, you mean! I do not question the sincerity of our former directors, but I question yours! This paper chase was your bulwark, yes! Your funk hole and cash cow! What have you done to us! Bled us dry!"

Another of the Hexamerons sat with his head in his hands, muttering to himself: "O damn, our elders sold the Society for this?" A third collapsed in an armchair ranting about "Uranian affinities" and waving his arms like a demented windmill.

"But we have felt the spirits so close..."

"Whatever you felt it was not the spirit of truth! If you heard anything it was the voices of each other!"

"But we delivered Edmund Gurney's child!"

"An incarnation of divine effulgence..."

"And no one felt minded to tell him! You left the messianic avatar in ignorance of his own destiny, so that the Secretary for Ireland could continue his affair with Mrs Willett!"

"Certain respectable discretions were necessary..."

"So while we fretted that our Interpreters were running their ghosts, it turns out the ghosts were running a brothel!"

A terrible silence filled the house; so deep it seemed to push away the crescendo of surf massing outside.

"At least", began the folded man in the armchair, "this avatar is ignorant of Gurney's Plan and unable to destroy us. We can deny it... let us destroy the papers, pay off these ponces!"

"Please, no!"

"Burn them! Whatever is in these papers is a form of Chaos. These idiots have conjured an Anti-Arthur! Used science against science and opened the door to a monstrous force of ignorance and lust! Burn it all!"

"Porters!"

The Interpreters summoned their bearers; the men drew brass knuckle-dusters from their pockets and fixed them to their fists. Outside the wind roared among the shutters. Something thumped the front door. A thin sheet of water shot over the door mat and foamed across the polished boards in the hall, pushing at sheaves of automatic writing, and lapping against the jamb of the living room door. The gathered meeting were now all on their feet.

"Save the papers!"

Confused porters ran between the rooms gathering up the pages, hurling them into cases. A second thump on the front door was followed by a further burst of foam into the house. A porter ran to the back door, clutching a case of papers, holding the door back for the Interpreters who screamed at the porters in chorus – "Save the papers!" – just as a third thump threw in the frame of a front window and sent water cascading over the sill, spilling over carpets and rugs, knocking over lamp stands and occasional tables and sending candlesticks cartwheeling into boiling foam, extinguishing the wicks and plunging the rooms into deep gloom.

"The Beast is here! Run! Run! Alert the Beyondists!"

"Nature plays us like toys!"

"O what have we done!"

Pushing the Interpreters aside the Hexamerons plunged through the back door, down the porch and onto the sands. Up to their shins in froth they raced toward the second house as a third, a little lower down the dunes, crumpling with an oddly muted crunch and a brief shattering of glass, was swiftly buried by a breaker. Before the Hexamerons could reach the second house, the Beyondists appeared on the front porch and threw their kayaks into the rising masses of spume. The two men in one, the two German women in the other; they quickly paddled the few yards to safety, racing up the side of a dune that was already beginning to slide into the sea. Reaching the top of the dunes, secured more solidly underfoot by thick marram grass, the Beyondists stopped to help the four struggling Hexamerons to the brow.

Already the porters were well ahead of everyone else. They rushed their cases across the tops and towards the Creep. Beyond, at the railway station platform, a 'special' waited, already under steam. Beyondists and Hexamerons stood shoulder to shoulder as the sands began to shift beneath them, and the dark waters before them turned twenty wooden villas around and around like dull Catherine wheels. The Interpreters, their divine sparks extinguished, were taking their chances among the flotsam that was swirled about in the maelstrom of disorder; lampshades, model boats, family Bibles, paddles, flags, name-signs, tennis rackets, a stuffed dog, an aspidistra, a chess board and its pieces were turned about and then dragged out towards the deep dark sea.

Somehow the four Interpreters fought their own way through the waist-high waves, the women's skirts lifted up to the surface, spread like open parasols, and then clambered up the surrendering sands, until they stood on the firmer ground beside the Hexamerons and their young allies. The three groups, awed in different ways and drawing different conclusions from the sight of the weekend palaces dragged one by one below the surface of the foaming water, began to tramp in the porters' footprints; four broken, four isolated and preparing for a long retreat, four bright with hope in the rise of new regimes of hygiene and coercion. All twelve chastened to different degrees by the drowning of a false god, resentful that the job had not been left to them. The veil between this world and the next had been torn back and there was nothing to be seen but tattered veil.

Muffled snappings and splinterings were momentarily drowned out by the howl of the special's whistle and the crunch of its pistons as it began to lurch forward onto the main line, throwing up pillars of smoke.

Chapter 41

The possibility that Mandi might have some connection to the drapery assistant's limestone cave – if her adoptive parents were Widgers, and Lyon her given surname – dominated hers and April's conversation as they walked north, stopping for tea at Hill House nursery. Then out again into the lanes, which at times had seemed to fold around and then loop back inside themselves, past deep white clay wounds in the hills, blue pools still as ice, the metal footbridge over a major arterial road, the industrial pottery steaming and churning as streams of cars, vans and lorries roared beneath them, and then on towards a small town. On either side of the bridge were concrete podia to help riders dismount, lest their steeds leap the bridge and eviscerate horse and jockey in the traffic flow.

What if the narrative at the Museum was untrue and there was a meaning to all the teeth and bones and claws; that something had survived through the rituals and practices of the 'Old Grotto', through Diana and Eve, and passed along in the tales of the old Lovecrafts?

"You think perhaps there was some kind of 'Blessed Darkness' or 'Great Dark One' they worshipped in the cave? That naughty Diana seduced the Perfect God and exposed him as a bungling male Demiurge, seducing him into becoming flesh and giving birth to all the material unevenness and mutant chance of animals and plants? That's what the medieval Gnostics believed; that God made a mess of things, botched the job... and now the only way back to the beginning is to end the flesh and transcend into pure knowledge..."

"What do I know about that stuff?"

"Your parents were... into that sort of thing, I thought?"

"Do you think they might have driven into the path of the oncoming car?"

"I didn't know them..."

"No, nor me... not sure I know much about anything anymore..."

They had been following an overgrown canal. It came to an end at a silted-up basin. By the side of the stone terminus was a set of railway sidings; rather than metal rails these were of the same granite that the trucks had carried down from the Moor. In the mud-filled basin, someone had left a carved clay object the size of a large dog in a milky puddle. It had a wide curved back and shoulders, a smooth domed head and a face in which the eyes and mouth had run into one another in a single broad sweep; its arms were stumps. Two rock chips had been placed in the mouth, broken molars. At intervals glass marbles were pressed into its body; alive with eyes. Shoved into crannies in the bank were clay models of a mouse (wrapped in spiders' webs), a bird, a snaky thing with a giant eyeless open-mouthed head and a pair of balls.

"I hadn't expected that their dying would pull the rug right from under my feet. I feel like I'm walking on air all the time. Not connected... maybe it's Devon; I need to get back to London..."

"Is that any more real?"

"O yea, it's real. Things have consequences there; people get stabbed, get poor, get rich real quick, get stoned, overdose, get clean, get to be boss, lose everything and make it all back; in Devon they just play at life."

"So real for you is... consequences?"

"Not for me. Real was never for me, really."

"O, so you don't believe all that Vatican-inspired nonsense about the Big Bang? Of a convenient event horizon across which no useful information passes? There is no mystery for you..."

"It's all a mystery for me. But no one can live like this... I've been happy sorting out the camp. Checked all the leases; I can set up a management there, so I can oversee things at a distance. I thought that dealing with the pagans would be a nightmare, but it's not. I don't know if I said this, but they're all pagans there – white witches and chaos magicians, Goths, crystal-huggers – but they're decent enough people, reliable in their own way. That part's been unexpectedly easy. It's the other shit that's difficult... the human shit..."

Without noticing, Mandi and April had reached the edge of the town and the wall of a rather grander graveyard than those in the villages. They entered, still imagining they were looking for H. P. Lovecraft's relatives, though their walk's purpose had moved on. Distracted for a moment by a monument to JAMES BOND, excessive lichens and a row of gravestones shaped like spearheads, they quickly fixated on a single monument: on a tall plinth three large white angels arranged in a triangle. No one had dared to strike their heads from their necks. Epic, huge, chiselled and detailed. Mandi was first taken by their faces; moonish, responding to each slight alteration of the thickness of the clouds. The smooth yet sandy particularity of the stone got to her. The star above each forehead was buoyed on waves of sandstone hair, the haloes, the fulsome sleeves of the carved garments and, most of all, the way the tips of the feathers of one angel's wing were woven into those of the others'. Together, two wings of separate angels made something that resembled a single cephalopodic head, their haloes become two plate-like eyes, and where the tresses of the sisters fell down by their sides these were like the diminutive feelers of the body of the marine thing.

The three young ghosts were conjuring a fabulous stone sea monster within the symmetry of their wings.

Mandi turned to point out the illusion to April, but she had gone. Mandi searched the churchyard, assuming that she had been drawn by one of the other monuments. She circumambulated the church, pushed at its locked door, zig-zagged across the graves, and then, in a less than rational desperation, explored around the three-angel monument – noticing now where the names of three sisters were engraved, faintly now, on stones sashes: Emily, Rosamund and Mary Gurney – checked the shrubs, and then peered over the low boundary wall, as if April might have fallen over it or was stooping to hide or examine something. A sharp tug checked her search. Spinning round, there was only the trio of sisters. Mandi felt a faint influence; she couldn't pin it down, but there was something about them that, rather than sink immediately into her unconscious, had stayed above the line. They impressed her. Mandi checked her phone; no signal. It was starting to get dark and the darker it got, the more the three angels' wings merged into the single squiddish head, the more their curling hair crept and sucked and the more the haloes blinked and stared.

Mandi walked backwards out of the cemetery, then, running down the pavement, she made for the centre of the town, in search of a bus stop.

Chapter 42

The birds relentlessly circled the shadows under the sea's surface. The nagging suggestions in the tiny implants drove them; but they struggled to compute the meaning of the darkness beneath them. Hour after the hour the crazed aerial dance went on; occasionally a curious human walking the beach or far off on the other side of the estuary paused to take it in. Quickly bored by the repetitions of a black sky shuffling, they turned their attention to something else. So no one quite appreciated the significant duration of the wild circling. As the dusk murk rose, the puzzling distinctions of shades of darkness began to join more profoundly into a singular suggestion of surge and flex, without borders or gaps. The birds gave in. What autonomy remained, something in the profound freedom of their flocking, escaped their digital commands and the birds formed up in a clattering muster, cawing and gibing at each other. There was a kind of fury in the beating of their wings; as if they sought to shake something off. But the chains were tied too deep inside their chemistry; and when they tried to steer by their natural pigments, their digital masters re-coloured their vision and steered them back the way the masters wanted.

Dropping downwards, the birds left the sea and cruised low over the beach and dunes, crossed the lagoon and golf course, then the road where the headlight beams of a few early evening journeys were playing over mobile homes and holiday camp signs. Then they flew over a confusion of low scrub, a junkyard, and into the vale, where the fields grew lonelier, the lanes darker and narrower, and where the tiny lights – spread far, far apart – in cottages, farmhouses and the odd caravan parked in the corner of a hedge were incapable of burning out the dullness of the emptied evening. The muster's progress shuddered for a moment as the birds reacted to a procession of shadowy giants; the blotting out of light by the unreflecting spiralling bodies of massive sweet chestnuts, mostly dead now. The crows swept by and the cyclopean cadavers seemed to stiffly bend toward them and then ease back as if they felt the magnetism of the birds, and drew away, repulsed.

Undisturbed by a perfect dome of green grass, the muster raced just above its blades, unnaturally low, and then bent to the incline as the hill rose towards a stately pile, an aristocratic hall, its wings thick and wide, its main part undistinguished except for a grand central entrance, its huge door wide open. The crows piled through the front door like blackened leaves blown in by a gale, then raced up the grand central staircase before veering unanimously to the right and settling on the carpet of a large, almost empty room on the first floor. Anxious Hexamerons came running down the corridors.

The machine at Mandun Hall, manufactured in the late 1970s, influenced by the fiction of a local anarchist, Hyams, who lived at Hill House among the Lovecraft villages, a place that had drawn down the wrath of the stormbringer in the 1890s, had always included living things. At first they had been ants. The cultural blueprint was Hyams's scatological sci-fi novel *Morrow's Ants*. Modelled on the most sophisticated development of an analytical machine, the Hexamerons' latest recruits then – now the elders of the Society – had brought desiccated cybernetic skills to bear; trapping the ants in mechanical systems that turned their instincts into numbers, their organisational unity into computational power. In crude terms the individual ant was left to its own devices (if it had any) but the actions of the nest triggered the electrical levers that were instantly converted into information and fed back to the ants in an endless reshaping of its prison.

The results had been remarkable and before long the technology that would later allow speechless humans to transmit imagined words into artificial language was tested at Mandun in a series of unsupervised and often grisly experiments; electronic levers thrashing about in the brains of Labradors, foxes biting into sparking cables, octopi swarming across the landings in psychotic and self-destructive panic. These wild frontier days were quickly done with; the animal data, synaptic and chemical, secured in the mainframe. After that, the cages were removed and the servers were installed. Where stinking mammal dormitories had once run wild with tsunamis of acrid evacuations, now the immaculately restored Axminster carpets, designed by Whitty himself, were a wild savannah only for cooled thinking machines grinding binaries.

The exception to this was the Erithacus Portal; the great Cobra Mist adaptation that hung within the loft space of the old hall. In its fiendishly complex web, the quantum collapses and entanglements of various flocks, bevies, tremblings, wakes and scatterings were caught up and processed as psychic geography. Battlefields and embassies and secret bases were no longer surveilled but thought. There would be no more secrets. The final web, to make the birds the Facebook of the skies, the avian-algorithm invasion, was almost in place; only the belligerence of the herring gulls, and one or two related species, had so far defied and delayed the mapping of humans' innermost desires. But they would succumb, in one way or another; just as the Hexamerons had carefully primed the conspirasphere with whispers about a "Company" manipulating the birds, so they had ruined the reputation of the herring gull, preparatory to its decimation.

The crows marshalled on the carpet; the algorithms were reaching out to them. There was a dark sharpness about their manoeuvres on the blue luxuriance of the Axminster, traducing the designer's symmetry of urns, viols and fronds. The roomful of 'operators' at their screens could make no sense from the chaos of data that flooded from the 'reports' of the bluey-black messengers. Screens began to flash, oscillating between a flood of positions and blue death, a new tsunami of positions, then blankness. Young white coated technologists raced along the cushioned corridors to find the elders; two uncomfortable-looking female technicians exited the control room and made themselves scarce.

A single crow escaped the first room and followed one of the white coats; one who knew his way to the outer layers of the Hexameron hierarchy. Though the young man had no mental picture of the layout of its six layers, he had seen enough to know how to access the lowest stratum. The 'monks', as the younger bloods called them in private, were seated in quiet thought; in recent years they had affected a hood and long flowing cape worn over their business suits. These costumes were not seen outside the grounds at Mandun, but they had become the distinguishing mark of the leaders of the higher caste. Useful signifiers in an organisation that recognised no status other than merit.

The crow barely registered as anything more than a flurry of shadow as the flustered technician alerted the elders to the collapse of their system. Rising from their seats they swept back along the corridor towards the control room, the crow running across the carpet in their tracks. Unlike the young Hexameron it did have a mental map of the hierarchy at Mandun Hall; the birds were beginning to learn how to manipulate, crudely, the algorithms to their own ends.

The control room was not an impressive affair. It might have been the office of an estate agent, were it not for the eclectic collection of eighteenth, twentieth and twenty first century landscapes by Michael Honnor, James Tatum, Francis Towne and Yves Tanguy that hung upon its six walls. The "machines", as the Hexamerons persisted in calling their bio-electronic vehicles, dominated all the larger rooms and hall. Where society had once danced its cotillions, electrons now jived and jitterbugged, leaping between one and zero, spinning on the spot and jumping back to one. The young operators stood back from their desks to let the leaders see the chaos for themselves. The flashing of the screens ceased, replaced by streams of code.

"What does it mean?"

None of the boyish operators was willing to take a guess.

"Sirs, I think I may have an idea."

The crusted faces of the elders, survivors of a generation of Hexamerons recruited from the early Cold War codebreakers, apprentices of Turing and his amateurs at Bletchley Park, turned to the door. The young woman, a stranger to them, was standing in the frame; she wore a white coat, like the young men, but there was a crow sitting on her shoulder.

"I think it has something to do with subjectivity..."

"Go on. Come in..."

The young woman moved into the centre of the room. The Hexameron elders gathered in a circle around her, as if in preparation for a Roman assassination. The crow flew from her shoulder and off down the corridor.

"I think it's a mathematical problem around nothingness and binary codes. With any set consisting only of ones, a single zero will negate such a series. If we assume that this is a universal law, and that the only way anyone has found to contradict it is to exclude all empty sets entirely, then all sets are conditional on an energy – let's call it a zero event – which has none of the properties that make any other thing discernible as a set. It has a meaning-negating force, so to speak; and without it there is no meaning. I suggest that what has happened is that..."

She looked over her shoulder at the gaggle of male programmers in the frame of the doorway, but her eye was caught by the Honnor seascape, the waves like cracks in a desert floor. She turned back to the elders, still and expressionless, like statues of justice, signifying much and exuding nothing.

"... in the attempt to programme a complete social-psychological system we have left out the destructive subject force that creates small pockets of emptiness for itself. In other words we have programmed nothingness out of the system, so when the birds encounter the zero event of this destruction, in the natural world, they faithfully reproduce its effects in systems that are incapable of recognising the event's reality without denying their own. We have constructed an electronic model of the fabric of reality that cannot tear, so that when it does, out there in the natural world, rather than us being able to repair it, to close down its aperture, block up the sinkhole, our model dissolves into an infinite number of sinkholes. In trying to repel the beast, we may, unintentionally, have created portals for its materialisation everywhere..."

"Do you boys agree with her?"

"What's she's talking about, sir, are what we call 'not-well-founded sets'..."

"So do we, my boy. What is your point?"

"That she's talking nonsense, confusing binary codes with structuralist language signifiers; using metaphors to confuse the maths with ontological jargon and ending up in metaphysics..."

"Unless you hadn't notice, Mister Wang, that is exactly what we do here."

The programmers jumped back, the elders swivelled around. In the doorway stood a middle-aged man, a dead crow in his left hand. It was the Chairman of the meeting at the museum. His dress was identical to then; nothing had been changed in his hairstyle or complexion. Yet, the uncomfortable modernity of his presence in town had disappeared; in its place he smiled the smile of a clever feudal thug, tossing the crow's cadaver into the arms of one of the 'boys'. The elders circled him, just as they had the white-coated young woman a moment before. Suddenly excluded from the magic circle, the woman began to edge towards the door.

"Where are you going?"

She froze. The Chairman moved towards her with such lupine alacrity that she tripped and fell back against the William Morris wallpaper, supporting herself with her palms against the thick green pattern.

"Make sure you wash your hands, my dear. That green was made with arsenic mined from the other side of the Tamar. Many workers died so that their socialist proprietor could make such wonderfully bright medieval patterns. Similarly, we too are reversing history here; perhaps it is not so surprising when the past tries to bite us back? My dear, I like your theory very much, but what if... forgive me, for stealing your thunder... what if the arrangement of data that you describe is opening a portal not to zeroes, not to nothings, but to... to coin a phrase from one of our earlier members... a coming race?"

A door slammed far off; then an echo as if an angry demon had stormed out on the caverns of hell. The cathedral-like ripple of sound halted the Chairman mid-speculation. Before he could complete the loop of his thoughts he was inhibited by a clatter of running feet, as if the coming race itself had escaped the tunnels and was running, en masse, to seize the Hall.

"Sir, sir! The Erithacus Portal's down! Something's coming through!! Quickly, you need to come and see this!"

The speaker was at the rear of a group of middle-aged men who had come to a stuttering halt outside the door of the 'control room'. Pushing his way through his colleagues – all dressed in jeans and t shirts, none of the white coated mummery for these controllers – and beckoning to the Chairman as if to a recalcitrant poodle.

"I think we should all see this. Peter?"

One of the elders manipulated a hand held device and bleepers began to go off all around the many wings and sections of the Hall. Doors swung open along its corridors, which quickly filled with a stream of technologists and theoretical scientists, administrators and monk-like elders. Though its head hung limp from the hand of one of the programmers, something deep in the crow continued to pick up the traces of the hierarchy of souls in the Hall. Even in the surging of the staff it intuited the statelier progress of a spectral crew. The mob of Hexamerons had collected in a single rush, halting only for a moment, beside a closed door, from behind which came a thump of music, excited howls and another urgent rhythm.

"Leave them."

The crowd moved on, swarming down the grand staircase and assembling inside the old ballroom that stretched to the very rear of the Hall and then sank beneath a glass ceiling partly comprised of the glass floor of an outside ornamental pond. There they came to a halt, faced by the Hall's security guards – the four White Snipers – guarding the partially curtained gold doors on one side. At the command of the Chairman, the Snipers stepped aside, pulling back the brocaded drapes, and drawing open the doors to let the crowd, led by the elders, into their Society's 'holy of holies'. Despite its modest proportions, most of the staff were able to cram around the edges of the space, a former private chapel stripped of all its symbols except for a Perspex cube, the size of a shoe box, in the middle of a round oak table at the centre of the space; the same shape and material as many of the elders wore for a lapel badge. The remainder of the Hexamerons hung on the door frame or stood on tip toes staring in. The White Snipers chased up a hidden staircase and appeared on a small balcony looking down on the room, training their rifles on the Hexamerons below.

For all except the elders, this was their first time inside the 'holy of holies'. The crow cadaver felt the tightening of the fingers, the sweat breaking out of the palm, began to make pictures of expectations; of the giant airy and cool halls receding one after another into a sea of servers and big data, of electronic war rooms, of a factory floor of air looms, of a conceptual space without physical form. It had felt the disappointment as the bare stone chapel was uncovered, the simple and unvarnished circle of wood at the centre and the rush of cold discomfort at the figures seated around its altar as they were uncovered one by one by the hands of the elders, lifting thin white gauzes from the shoulders of the candlestick shapes.

Mummies; emptied, dried bodies, preserved and propped up around the table, dressed in faded period clothes: frock coats, blazers, cassock, overalls, tweedy tea-stained jacket, shirt and tie and academic gown. What had been the flesh of their faces now ranged from a uniform grey to a blotchy purple and red. Marbles for eyes. Beneath their seats, under domes of glass, were their scraped skulls.

Each one of the elders stood at the right hand of a mummified predecessor; as if they knew which place to take. The last brain activity of the dead crow sought out the names of the ancestors: Bulwer-Lytton, Babbage, Coombe-Tennant, Froude, Gurney, Cattell, Pengelly, Hyams... and felt a nervous guilt, as if not all had been recruited here by their free will. As if it felt a force of persuasion and a persuasion of force. A spirit of reluctance hung over the cube. Mummies, elders, young bloods, programmers, dead crow, and whatever was present, waited for something else to act. Slowly, something inside the cube began to move; very subtly, the elder's badges began to cloud.

Chapter 43

The bus dropped Mandi off outside the station at Newton Abbot. Her return ticket from the Bay was valid from there, where the two lines met. But before she could get to the barrier, a feverish Grant Kentish pulled her aside. His face was running with sweat. He panted like an old dog, his eyes were red and his hands shook violently. His grip on Mandi's wrist crumbled and she shook it off.

"Thank Baphomet I caught you... don't get on the train!"

"Get off me!"

She could see the railway woman at the gate becoming anxious for her, so calmed her with a raised palm, and turned back to Kentish.

"For god's sake, calm down. You'll get yourself arrested..."

"What difference does that make? I'm a dead man!"

"Calm down, what is the matter with you? If you don't speak calmly I'm going to leave you here."

"No, please, please... OK, OK, but the idiots! They think they've created something – they've invoked it!"

"Invoked what?"

Kentish's mouth fell open. He took a step back, looking Mandi up and down, in terror.

"I can't say that here!"

"Baphomet?"

"No, no... listen, Mandi, please, talk to them for me? Explain, you were at the house, there was no magic, you saw that, didn't you? Just old friends, some new acquaintances, with common interests. Good old-fashioned decadence!"

He tried to laugh, but the chuckles became caught in his gullet and he chirruped like a toad.

"You'll tell them, won't you? Promise me?"

For a moment it seemed as if he were about to get down on his knees. He began to bend, but it was only in a faint. Mandi caught him by the forearm and he recovered. As his look cleared and his stare grew sharp and penetrating, he pulled back.

"O no, no... you've joined them. I can see."

He glanced down at her filthy trainers and trouser bottoms.

"You're involved. I've said too much! Too much!"

He turned and sprinted away, his belly flapping under his cape as he shot through the car park, abruptly turning at the pavement as Mandi saw her train pulling in. She flashed her ticket to the barrier woman who tapped her card to let her through.

"Mandi!!!!"

Kentish's scream stopped all the passengers dead, but it was only her attention he wanted. As she turned he made a ritual gesture of distress. Mandi had had enough of all this bullshit. She turned and stepped onto the train and as the automatic doors were closing behind her she heard him scream again:

"Tell them, please! Please! It was only a sex club!!"

In her seat, against the glass, chosen so that she could see the water on her way home, Mandi smiled to herself at the sneaky glances she was drawing from the other passengers; basked a little in their jealous disdain. Humans were strange animals; disgusted by their own instincts; what other beast was like that? It was the burden of stinking culture.

At Teignmouth the entire carriage got off and a small group of men swiftly took their seats directly behind Mandi. She had the impression that they were obliquely interested in her; maybe a group of men out on a stag 'do' or a rugby club bender. She studiously ignored them and fixed her gaze to the sea as the railway line turned left along the coast towards The Sett.

She began to feel uneasy. She had laughed off the encounter with Grant Kentish. He was a drama queen. All the smoke and mirrors at the Italian Gardens, trying to get into her knickers. Like he said "it was only a sex club", but why would he say that unless he was lying, unless he believed the opposite? Mandi realised that she had never really come to terms with what had happened in the room with Kentish, the effect that the reading of the manuscript had had upon her. She had carried on imagining it as a dusty historical artefact, like one of Widger's hyena teeth. But then, maybe they were not so dusty either...

Mandi checked her phone, for once there was a signal. Emails from work, she ignored. Queen Bee she ignored. One from the Chairman of the Hexameron Essay Society; a picture of a black circle or disc. A black sun. No text, no explanation.

Mandi put her forehead to the windowpane, a hand up to shield her eyes. The moon was above the water; from under the waves came a scattered glint like that off hundreds of upturned eyes. At the final stop before The Sett the other carriage emptied. Mandi kept her focus on the long expanse of sea. It was only two minutes to The Sett from here. She would soon be home; she could shower, there was a bottle of dry white in the fridge, she would sit and drink and think what to do next. If there was a late train, part of her was tempted to get to London that night; another part wanted to sleep forever. She could see through the windows of the front carriage the house that had been built on the platform at The Sett to replace the previous one destroyed by an arsonist; as the train grew closer she could just make out the edge of the old 'Bocca della Verità' fortune-telling machine that had been discarded there, leaned up against the back wall... then the picture swung violently, as if it had just been swiped across a handheld screen. Her carriage lurched sideways, the view to the sea had gone and the lights in the carriage failed as it came to a gentle halt. On both sides they were now surrounded by the old carriages; the ones converted into holiday homes by the railworkers' association. Although it seemed a little early in the year to have opened them up, Easter a few weeks off, the lights in the carriages were blazing away, affording a view of several moving tableaux; youngsters crawling over bunk beds, mothers cooking tea, men reading sports papers and sipping cheap beer from cans. Everything was right, except for the period ambience; as if she was seeing into the past? Or were people still living there?

One of the men – she had forgotten about them – got to his feet and opened a switchbox by the automatic door. He turned a key and the lights flickered back on. Mandi blinked. The man looked directly at Mandi as if it were her turn to act.

"We've come to apologise. We had no idea who you were."

The speaker was sitting behind Mandi, but now he got up and moved in front of her. Sat down at the table diagonally opposite to Mandi, another man slipped into the seat beside her, trapping her in. The man at the switchbox sidled over and a fourth man leaned over the head rest just behind her. The four men were dressed similarly, but not in uniform; their little cube badges and expensive suits gave them the look of upmarket missionaries.

"Please tell me you're not Jehovah's Witnesses?"

This made them laugh a lot.

"No, no, no... you know who we are, you met our people at the museum, and then at the cave; there was a misunderstanding and we have come to put that right. Our people were disrespectful. We had no idea who your parents were, otherwise there would have been no question about you visiting the site. You are welcome to any and all of our projects! You get wonderful references from London!"

"I haven't applied for anything."

"You can't. Ours is a 'by invitation only' Society..."

"Which is why there are no women in it? Or black and ethnic minorities... I don't see any need for you to respond to directives about diversity, but let's say, you look a little... homogenous to me?"

"That's partly what this... apology is about."

He held out a ticket, the size of a thin paperback book: CELEBRATE THE 200 MOST INFLUENTIAL WOMEN IN THE COUNTY.

"Come late; the event is a scam put on by a free sheet; they name a lady from every company and charge them a fortune for tickets to hear themselves being congratulated by each other. We host an after-show party. We'd like you to come and meet the women with real influence in the county, none of whom you will find in any magazine, or receiving any award, but all of whom are members of the Hexameron Ladies' Essay Society..."

"We believe in the right to autonomous organisation, Amanda..."

"Were the African-Americans ever stronger or more progressive than during the Black Panther period?"

"Not so good if the autonomy is compulsory, though..."

"No! Of course not! That would be apartheid! Autonomy of groups is a natural right, not a requirement. Take away state-sponsored feminism and multiculturalism and the natural tendencies of the group re-emerges; and before you think that our ladies' section is a second-class Society, come and meet them. You'll see who really runs the Hexamerons!"

The other men laughed, then laughed again, this time ruefully.

Then one of them cracked: "Sometimes nature needs a little helping hand."

"You don't really think I'm going to turn up to that kind of bullshit, do you?"

The laughter stopped. The men relaxed; as if actors in a movie had heard "cut". One of them loosened the knot of his tie. The man beside Mandi lifted the ticket from her fingers and tore it into four pieces.

"We were very much hoping not. But not everyone lives up to their references. How much do you know about the Hexamerons, Mandi?"

"Nothing."

"Well we began as a campaign to champion rationality over decadence, our first members were eighteenth century experimental scientists and technologists, in their words 'natural philosophers'; in the 1930s with psychology's break from the hocus pocus of Freudian and gestalt guesswork the Society embraced experimental psychology, scientific behaviourism, and an approach called Beyondism; a blend of Darwinian laisser-faire and natural selection that operates among groups as much as individuals. We continue to promote those ideas – flat rate taxation, respect for the specialised abilities of private elites, risk taking, and so on – but now we apply them in the field of the information rather than the industrial economy..."

"Congratulations. What do you want? A Blue Peter badge?"

"We want... we need your help. Around the turn of the last century, the Society succumbed to what at the time seemed to be technologically acquired evidence of life after death. Photographs, sound recordings, automatic writing. It would be easy to be scornful; but many in the cultural elite were similarly duped. For generations the Society wasted its energies and shed its members, only to re-find its mission in the 1930s."

"Gold Blue Peter badge?"

Mandi was losing patience. She gazed out of the window at the brightly illuminated families. Only too aware that she had no memory of a childhood as bright as these...

"What did you mean about my parents?"

"We understand that they may have passed on to you certain traits..."

"My biological parents?"

"Yes."

"I don't know who my biological parents are. So how come you do?"

"O, then... perhaps there has been some mistake. Perhaps the traits are cultural?"

"What the fuck are you talking about?"

"Amanda, certain of our members, during the bad times, have left us with a... supernatural legacy. A combination of the weak and the conniving – our members Edmund Gurney, a desperately bereaved man, Frederic Myers, George Albert Smith – a theatrical fraudster – a medium named... let's call her Willett... and others contrived a plan to create a World Saviour, with Willett operating as a sort of ersatz Virgin Mary..."

"Yeah, well I heard plenty of tales like that from my adoptive parents, there are more attempted World Saviours than you might think; now I haven't been at my camp all day and I need to check that things are..."

The Hexameron sat directly opposite her placed his hand over hers and eased it back onto the table.

"They succeeded."

High stakes move.

"Crap!"

"They created their messiah, their avatar, somehow they... combined esoteric information, god knows how, with magic lantern shows and biological engineering, of a crude and early kind, and... they made their superman..."

It was the detail about "magic lantern shows" that stopped her from pushing her way out of the carriage. It had the smack of the farcical nature of real life.

"...of course, flesh is weak, the mother forgot to tell the son about his mission, in order to pursue the affair that had fuelled the whole charade, and so... decadence continues, the world is not saved... and just now, just as our Society has acquired or... developed, rather, the technology that is required to realise our principles, this False Messiah, the fruit of the Society's failings, has reappeared, posing as a mad monk, up in the old monastery on the hill just before Newton Abbot..."

"That old people's home?"

"They're retirement properties. He's up there, one of the residents, threatening to work his magic on our headquarters and interfere with our servers. We want you to go up there and tell him to stop..."

"Tell him?"

"Assist him..."

O, not "terminate with extreme prejudice, Willard" then?"

"What?"

"Because you think I can see through New Age bullshitters and Wiccan messiahs? Because of stuff I learned from my mum and dad, right?"

"Well..."

"How old is he?"

"A hundred and something."

"I might kill him with a sarky comment!"

"He's the messiah, he's dangerous... he's the most dangerous man you're ever likely to meet, ex-special forces, Mandi, you are the only person we have identified who might have the occult pedigree to... understand where he's coming from..."

"You are all stark staring fucking mad! That's the fucking craziest thing I've ever heard! Anyway, I'm supposed to be going back to London tonight to sort out my charity... Hell, I was looking for an excuse not to... this is so fucking crazy it's probably the only excuse the trustees will believe..."

The caretaker was waiting for Mandi, just as he had on her first night back.

"Where have you been?"

"All over, I'm totally shattered!"

Then she noticed the police car.

"What's going on?"

The door of the car swung open and the officer who had come to collect the suicide climbed out.

"Is this the young lady, sir?"

"Yes, this is the one."

"Everything alright, m... madam?"

"Sure..."

"You're feeling fine? Nothing untoward happened to you?"

Mandi suddenly felt scared; she didn't know how much people knew about her anymore. It seemed like random information about her was being passed from stranger to stranger.

"I'm absolutely fine. Nothing has happened to me."

She threw her arms wide as if to present her unwounded body.

"Then, I'll be going. Good night, madam. Sir."

And he climbed back into the car, gunned the engine and left the grounds of Lost Horizon with an angry swerve.

"What was that all about?"

"I was worried what had happened to you..."

"Jesus Christ! It's about half past nine! Who are you? My father?"

She turned angrily, let herself into the house and slammed the front door. She stripped off her muddy jeans and trainers and threw them at the washing machine; cracked open the dry white, turned on Sky News 24 and threw herself on the bed. "They've fucked that up", she thought to herself, they had the dates screwed up. She opened up her laptop and her inbox filled up with angry emails: where was she? Well, screw them! She might appreciate a little compassion on her compassionate leave! She thought to Google the names of the sisters on the monument, Emily, Rosamund and Mary, but before she got to their stories she noticed the location and went to "maps"; her impressions of the day were starting to run into each other, wet recollections beginning to drip over the lines, one colour mixing with another. They had walked a very long way in an afternoon; too far for even two days walking, maybe three... she tried to remember taking a bus... the last thing she was thinking about before she fell asleep, the announcer already in some nightmare about a chemical gas attack and something about children and the powerful, was that she must prepare herself in some way, wash herself, exercise, something, before she... she met the messiah... that couldn't be right...

Chapter 44

She had made it back to London. But it felt like 'only just'.

In the morning she had taken a taxi up to the retirement home above Newton Abbot. It had been a troubled night. In her dream she had returned, alone, to the cave, following a map made with the bonelines from the Museum. She recognised some of the landmarks from her walk with April. All the time she was scared of dropping the bones in case the route was lost; but she was distracted by figures with machine guns dressed in white hiding in the trees above her. At the mouth of the cave she stood and listened hard and she could hear the sound of waves and beating wings and she understood from these sounds that time was passing very fast and that there was something she had to do that was urgent, that there was some link between the angels in the graveyard and old seas. This all came in words and ideas and it made the place around her very fluid, as if she were stepping through a portal into a new dimension of the adventure. Inside the cave it was warm and very smelly; she had looked down and she was surrounded by hyenas, swarming around her like waves breaking around a rock. April was standing at the back of the cave. Behind her, frozen into the wall, was a figure wearing goggles and a diving suit. April was holding a drowned bird, seawater dripping from its feathers. Water began to rush into the cave and Mandi felt herself being washed away and the hyenas swirling around her. She tried to save herself by hanging onto their coats, but she was being sucked towards a giant plughole at the back of the cave. Just before she fell in, Mandi caught sight of a rounded green hill through the cave's opening, with black dogs and hobgoblins massing around its base, and a single tree on its summit, its branches full of white birds dripping with water. She heard April call out to her and she struggled to free herself from the hyenas, but they were pulling her down, she reached out for April's hand, but could not quite reach her fingers and as she fell with the pack into the darkness she saw April turning into a green parrot-like bird with a broken beak... a door opened and she was in a wood-panelled room like a court room. The jury, dressed in wigs and eighteenth century frock coats, stood and like a choir recited warnings about a "dangerous place underground" which they associated with stories of another world and a superior race "that you shall not stand in the way of!" They began to accuse her: "we let you into our confidence and you have betrayed us!" Suddenly she was back in the cave, being swept along in the opposite direction, out of the cave and into the field, not by hyenas but by weird robot-like soldiers in black uniforms with red triangle badges who kept tripping over Mandi – "get out of our way!", "she's in the way again!", "take her to the leader!"

and they grabbed hold of her and began to march her up to the retirement home, while others began to strip a church of paintings and tear down statues of female saints and smash the lower parts of their faces with pliers, while all about them the mouths of tunnels were opening in hills and men in black uniforms were pouring out, these ones with giant heads and swollen skulls and long hair turning blonde, while the figure at the back of the cave began to weep huge tears through its goggles. The soldiers pulled Mandi away from the cave, telling her not to look, not to look, but she had to... and then awoke, howling, her face soaked with tears.

When she had come to climb out of bed to shower, Mandi found that she was still fully clothed. Her knees were stiff. Her trainers and trouser bottoms were caked with a red mud that had barely dried. She had thought that throwing her dirty clothes in the wash was the last thing she had done before falling asleep, but that was a dream as well, then. In the shower, she felt terrified that the cubicle would become a cave, the water would wash her down the plughole and the shouts of Lost Horizon children outside were the snickering of prehistoric hyenas. That dreams and everything else were the same.

Booking the taxi and packing her things straightened out her thinking. By the time the taxi pulled up outside the retirement properties, she was back to the Mandi who no one messed with, the London Mandi. She would complete the business and be on her way. Outside the old priory, she asked the driver to wait for her, offering to pay the fare so far; he waved it away, turned off his motor and pulled a paperback from the glove compartment.

Mandi found the manager at Reception, a helpful woman who – though she was just knocking off and on her way home – took time to explain where Mandi would find the former monk and accompanied her to the edge of the trees.

"He likes to be by the chapel. He's impermeable to cold!"

Mandi was troubled all the way, following the helpful woman's instructions, to the chapel. Had she really meant "impermeable"?

She had not seen the avatar, at first. The woman's directions, unlike the Jaguar Man's intuitions, had brought Mandi to the back of the corrugated iron chapel. In its shadow was what appeared to be the dried and shattered trunk of a lightly-coloured tree. As Mandi got a little closer she saw that it was growing from a square plinth; it was the bottom half of a statue. The imitation of the folds of a garment and the results of an assault some while ago had left its surface with the appearance of bark. Making her way around to the front of the statue she was confronted by the half-figure of a priest or monk dressed in a decorated robe, smashed away from around the top of its chest, the head wholly gone and part of only one shoulder, topped with the remnants of a clerical pellegrina, remaining. Mandi felt her foot brush up against something and bent down to pick the rusted head of a hammer from a scatter of statue fragments, the wooden shaft almost wholly rotted away.

"Have you come to visit the chapel, Deirdre?"

Mandi, with difficulty, climbed through the rhododendrons laced with brambles. On the edge of the tree line, below a path and above the bright green fields, was a hooded figure, turned to Mandi in his folding chair. The darkness of his face beneath the hood was accentuated by the line of his white moustache. At his side was a small easel on which sat an oil painting of what, at a distance, looked to Mandi like an aquatic centipede climbing onto a beach.

"I'm sorry to bother you, sir!"

"Sorry? You damn well intended to! Come in, Deirdre, come in, don't be shy, let's have a good look! Yes!!! Lost your way, have you?"

"No, sir, I came to see you."

"Did you, dearie, did you really? What? Never mind. Go and look at the chapel then. You might as well now you're here, get this over with! O, listen to me! Indiscreet again, Deirdre, what will you all do to me! Blackball me? Excommunication, is it, this time? Think I've been playing fast and loose with my CX bulletins? I left the service. Once in the service, always in the service! Quickly, dear, have a look in the chapel while you still have the chance."

Was that his trick? The best he could do? Distraction? Incoherence?

"You know they sent me to... shut you up. I wasn't told in so many words, but... I thought I should come and warn you; that you are in danger."

"Why, Deirdre, why on earth would you do that? You already know that I already know. So, why not be honest with yourself, and tell me why you really came here."

Christ on a stick, how did he know that?

"Tell me who I am."

"The same as us all, my dear. We are the children of our parents. But you already knew that."

"Your father was a ghost..."

"Yes, yes..."

The old man was flustered; he flapped his papery hands and Mandi worried. He did not look like a man who had often been taken aback.

"You're not my... Dad, are you?"

The avatar howled. He was bent over in the chair by his guffawing. Hilarity shook his ancient frame. Mandi thought she must have killed him this time; that unconsciously she was carrying out the bidding of the Hexamerons.

"O, that would have been far better! A dream come true! Hahaha! No, my only relation to you, dear girl, is that I was a great admirer of your mother. If you want to find out who you really are, Deirdre... why don't you do as you're told and look in the chapel?"

It was a strangely appealing building. A shed of corrugated iron, painted a shade of green that reminded Mandi of the prefabricated chalets at Lost Horizon. Why not? She turned back to the avatar, still with half a mind to demur and get back to the point, but the old man was already hard at work on his painting. She was relieved not to see him stricken by a coronary. Well, she could afford the extended taxi fare; expenses would cover that. She climbed the three wooden steps and let herself in through the gothic door.

She had second thoughts.

"Did you smash that statue?"

"Yes!"

His brush was poised above the sea.

"A long time ago."

"Why?"

"It is of Thomas More. The idiot! His hair shirt was here, you know, when it was..." He twisted in his chair and gasped slightly. "Despite all appearances, Deirdre, being is not suffering. O, bad things happen to people, I've made a few happen myself, but life, existence, being as only suffering? No! To the weak, maybe. And to fools who seek to increase their own. Go into your chapel, Deirdre. You will find everything you need in there. Then you won't need to go running after Utopia like the rest of them..."

He was back at his painting, dabbing at the waves.

Mandi was struck by how narrow the chapel was; the two wings either side had created the illusion of breadth, but inside it was more like a short corridor than a hall. As she stepped across the threshold, it felt as though she had dropped into sea water; a huge shock of cold ran up and down her body, her nose was crammed with saltiness and the cork ribs on each of the walls stood out like precipitations on the walls of the Old Grotto. So taken by the strangeness was she, that she did not notice the slight darkening of the chapel as the grey wooden door closed gently behind her.

Mandi grabbed for the back of the small white chair to steady herself, tempted to sit down, but, conscious somehow of the consequences of passivity, she pushed herself up again, into the swirl above her and grabbed instead at a flash of blue stole. For a moment, Mandi thought that in her instinctive reaching out to the figure, she had brought the icon crashing over, smashing it in half like the statue behind the chapel, but instead what she felt in her hand was not plaster, but the softest, silkiest of things and when she looked down at the material it was hanging from her own shoulders not the statue's. It fell below her waist; beyond its blueness was the whiteness of the chair. Confused, trying to get her bearings, she looked around her and was dazzled by multi-coloured daggers of light bursting from her own hair; trying to escape the brightness she caught sight of a rose beside her trainers, its trampled stem flattened yet snagging on her pants, and a chocolate-coloured rock below her feet from which the swirling tide of blue and white was relentlessly spilling. O Christ, she had smashed the statue, its pieces were at her feet, it was ruined! She was the assassin! In a hopeless gesture, she reached down to pick up the pieces, stepped forward into the striped toothpaste colours, and felt the thud as she head-butted the altar. Reeling backwards, she sent the white chair over on its side. Recovering by fierce mental effort, she reached down and, righting the chair, placed it back in front of the altar. Mandi looked up. Who was she? The statue looked away, untouched and unmoved. What had she not understood? Tears gushed from the wells of her eyes, and in the blur of vision she imagined the old man in the hood stood behind the chapel and striking the statue of the priest with a hammer, hacking off its head and chest.

Snap.

The blurred vision was gone. The walls were cork. Mary was a plaster saint. Mandi felt for her tears, but her cheeks were dry. There was something wet on her legs; pulling up her trouser bottoms, there were long thin lines of blood on her shins where she had forced her way through the brambles. The old man had sent her into the chapel to learn something; but it was no clearer in there than in her dreams. Perhaps this was when he would explain.

She opened the grey door, half-expecting an unnatural resistance.

The first thing she noticed was the painting. While she had been in the chapel, the messiah had been hard at work, painting out the sea monster. What remained was an unremarkable landscape; a coastal scene painted with some technical skill, but no great spirit. It was the old man's final act of disguise. Or maybe she had imagined the monster.

She knew he was dead. As she left him to go into the chapel, she had felt him pass something – the torch, a poisoned chalice, a mystery – on to her. He would not be there for her – in the nature of all fathers and messiahs – to provide the answers. She stood for a moment beside the stiffening figure, crumpled deeper now into the folding chair, and looked out over the fields he had not painted, to the coast that he had, hidden behind the rise of the last hills before the water.

"...great admirer of your mother..."

The truth was staring her in the face and she chose to look away. Retracing her steps to Reception, Mandi interrupted the taxi driver from some intricate terraforming on Mars and caught the London train from Newton Abbot. On the way to the station she had sent an email from her phone, thanking reception at the retirement complex for their assistance, remarking on the old man's remarkable talent as a landscape artist and leaving her contact number at 'Lost Horizon' in case the old man "remembers anything further to my question". In a few days' time, she would be sad to hear of his death, but privileged "in a strange way", as she put it, to have been the last person to talk with a man who had lived such a long and remarkable life.

The landscape to London was devoid of angels and monsters; things were settling down. By the time the train was pulling into Paddington, past the modernist landmarks with their Hong Kong feel, Mandi had an opinion piece ready for her editor, combining a swingeing assault on the curlicues of small town thinking with a more savage one upon the asses of white-flight metropolitans filling up the Exeter hinterland. There was something to infuriate everyone.

Chapter 45

The morning had gone well; despite the two-day delay in her return to the office, everything was in order. The systems Mandi had set in place were as evident as ever; her appointees demonstrated every bit as much aptitude for improvisation and autonomy as when she had left them. The annoying projects of the Queen Bee had remained a thing of disinterest to the Childquake office; as they should be.

In the afternoon, Mandi called the staff together for an office meeting; mostly to pat heads and share hugs all round, but the long walks in Devon had taken a physical toll and somewhere in amongst the going around the table to take verbal reports she had begun to lose focus and to struggle with an intrusive string of violent fantasies... pinching her ear lobes, biting her lips, digging her nails into her thighs, breathing in short snorts, pulling the short hairs behind her ears; Mandi did her best to stay... but faded.... and when she snapped to she was still in the business meeting. It was unclear to her how long she had zoned out for, but now everyone around the table, wide-eyed and straight-backed, looked terrified and subservient. When she asked if anything was wrong, they assured her that everything was fine, yet no none would tell her what, if anything, had happened while her concentration was abstracted. In every other respect her colleagues were extremely co-operative; concluding the meeting to her advantage, the office clicking back into its routine innovativeness....

"Here, Mandi..."

She hated Toni for treating her like a trained dog; the day had transitioned through after-work cocktails and slipping into the uncreasable midi dress from Warehouse in her handbag to a flat warming in Hoxton. It was all work related.

"... you must meet Jonny, he's... they's... that thinking-woman's alt-righter I was telling you about."

A thin figure turned on its axis, a hand fluttered up to a sharp cut of black hair, flicking long tendrils over the shaved patch above the ear. Jonny smiled like a snake and the air in the room seemed to shudder for a moment. Mandi looked him directly in the milky almond eyes, the creases at the far edges somehow had naturally bent upwards, like a working-class girl's make-up. A cheap fox is what he or they was; except that for a brush Jonny wore a thin skirt, slit down one side and leggings that showed off chopstick straight legs.

"There's no thinking on the alt-right, Toni" – Jonny spoke of her, but looked at Mandi – "just bile spat in the wrong direction, so we all get covered; they're manipulated, a smokescreen for the pathetic warding off of the death throes of neo-liberalism..."

"I soooooo agree, babe", and Toni dropped a hip, earnestly. "Trying to ward off real authority, real control...."

"Oh", Mandi smirked, "take control of our lives, our own courts, take control of our own borders? Not an intellectual Brexiteer for once?"

"'Mere bagatelle'", Jonny quoted slyly. "Can we not play for higher stakes than that? We need agreeable masters.... and mistresses..."

"See what I mean?" chipped in Toni. "Orgasming woman's alt right..."

"The Fourth Reich will be social democratic, my dear, more social than democratic..."

"I'm a libertarian", pronounced Mandi.

"All the alt-right started as libertarians..."

"Only on the tin. If you want to find out what I really believe you'll have to open me up..."

Why? Flirtation bored her, nauseated her, she had written long, anti-puritanical rants against it and then binned them.

".... intellectually. Men can't do that anymore. Especially young men. Young men have forgotten how to turn sex into ideas. Young men talk to women as if words were foreplay; their vocabulary is so limited. Five words, if you're lucky and none begin with 'v'. There are no intellectual orgasms to be had anymore."

There it was. The gauntlet thrown down. Like some pilgrim knight battering at the gates of a lonely castle, asking after the Grail.

"Is that why they call you Taleb's representative here on earth? O yes, Amanda, I know exactly who you are. I am not like other 'young' men; I do my homework before I step out socially. I am never over-dressed or under-prepared; just a hint of foundation and only enough liner to be ambiguous. Look at my hands; see how feathery they are? Now, hold them."

This was more like 'Night of the Hunter' than 'Sex in the City'. Wow.

Jonny's tiny hands were no bigger than hers, but the bones just under the skin were like handcuffs. It felt as if they had her bones in a judo lock. She felt claustrophobic.

"Without discipline there is no social ecstasy; everyone says the 1950s were the most exciting time, sexually; all the private lesbian clubs, cellar cinemas with damp seats and long coats and the suburbs writhing with door-to-door salesmen, don't tell me that the sex those two in 'Brief Encounter' might have had wouldn't have been fabulous!"

"You've been reading too much E. L. James..."

"Erika? Have you ever met her? Bataille, babe, I'm one of Bataille's Babes, ha ha! Now he can write about 'pussy'! I don't like decadence, Amanda; it's disrespectful of real transgression; there has to be something serious. That's why I like the fifties, shot in black and white; a paper party hat with the promise of a trivial venereal disease. Francis Bacon drunk and in bed with George Dyer, the ever-present promise of queer East End hoodlums. The smack of firm government; while the rest of us get on with partying. I read your pieces on green politics; I think we share some uncommon ground... let's burn all the coal we want, and close all the power stations..."

"You make me sound like something I'm not..."

"Deep green? I think there's something deep inside you, Amanda..."

"Yes, and it won't be joined by you, Jonny-o..."

"'Vertigo'? Nice – "only one man in the world for me, Johnny-o...." O well, and I thought we might at least publish something together? Something mathematical to prove a correlation between the right to perverse pleasures, resilient feminine survival in the urban jungle and the persistence of the unhuman planet. Kali dancing and shitting and fucking everyone, giving boons and lopping off heads. Multi-tasking - devouring us and birthing us. Something about Slut Earth rather than Mother Earth. She's my fucking girl, Amanda..."

"There's your meme," said Toni, unnecessarily.

"I have tickets for the NFL at Wembley, do you like sports?"

"No."

"Pity."

Jonny turned on their high heels and flounced away to the canapés; just before reaching them, they swivelled and mimed throwing a quarterback pass to Mandi. She did not mime catching its spiralling mirage; but she watched it. Toni saw Mandi twitch as the ball smashed into her chest.

"Stupid cunt," whispered Mandi.

"God", said Toni, "you're really wet for him."

Mandi spent the rest of the party expertly navigating the bores and predators, drifting from icy brilliance to slushy brilliance, going with the floes, in the helpless search for her equal. But it was Jonny she kept coming back to; as feminine as he was masculine, attractive from whichever direction she approached. Eventually Mandi asked Jonny back to her flat, just to see who they might turn out to be.

Sex with Jonny was ambiguous; there was always something existentially stimulating for Mandi about her other's uncertainty. It was less about fucking, more about being. Mutability made everything, even foreplay, crucial. Flesh was suspended in moisture, a weighing of bodies with sums that never tallied, each within the other now, their multiple senses drilling down to a single touch. In each other's arms they were deep sea creatures, or divers, feeling their way down to a black gnosis articulated in rippling gills and a second touch that seemed to come from nowhere, as if there were an extra limb in the bed. Bubbling, they fell back into the pillows and slept. An hour later, they were wide awake and arguing; that was the most erotic part of the night. With their bodies open to each other like unfolded OS maps, the legends no longer fitted the territory, they rowed – in the manner of lovers – until 5am, when the relative virtues of Jordan Peterson and Cornel West, Butler, Baudrillard, Taleb, Rorty and Camille Paglia abruptly lost their appeal, stolen by blackbirds. Mandi and Jonny had abandoned their prejudices to each other and taken chances on sincerity. But there was something more; she had begun to adore Jonny, there was something of April's gentle courage and fierce intelligence there and the ability to surprise Mandi with new versions of what xe was.

A low kind of dawn slumber overwhelmed them. Even yet though, the buzz of their intimacy throbbed like a dying battery. Sometime between Sun and alarm, Mandi felt for the light down on Jonny's shoulders, stroking a finger without thought along xyrs shoulder blades to the wheals she had seen there; they felt more, she didn't particularly want to admit this to herself, puckered and very slightly moist, like an arsehole, but there were two of them; she lazily but tentatively pushed a finger into one of them and felt something soft, dry, like a feather duster on a stick, which emerged, pushing her finger away, and straightened upwards. Jonny seemed to unfold inside a pair of arms, as if by denying masculinity, a hyper-masculinity was achieved; Jonny's body erupting into multiple erections...

When she awoke, Jonny had gone, but the dream remained. It had folded into more sex, or maybe it had sexed their dreaming, one way and another. Mandi was soaked, cold, a single layer of her clothes sticking to her body, a mass of goosebumps and hard nipples pushing against the fabric; she was an initiate, shivering in procession under a giant arch on her way to the heart of the gargantuan city of rotting concrete. She lay back in the pillows and closed her eyes; tiny bits fell all around her, crystal and ivory, shards from the cyclopean towers fluttering down in sparkling showers as the alarm repeated its insistence.... she awoke again, with a start. The dream had been different this time; she had again woken inside the dream, but this time Jonny had been impassive, cold, motionless and unresponsive to her touch. She had left Jonny in their bed. Getting home from work she had found that Jonny had died, xyrs body had rotted and all that was left under the duvet was a map of bones like that in the Bay Museum. Except for two places on the map that were missing. The cave with its darkness and broken teeth, the chapel with the whole statue and the smashed statue and the graveyard with the three angels were all there, marked by bones, but one of the blanks was in the centre of the body, above their groin, perhaps the bellybutton, and another was far to the edge of the bed. This one might have been a hand thrown outwards, Mandi thought, but when she looked closer it was where the head had been severed from the body. To complete or heal the figure, she must return and find the unvisited points.

Properly awake and alone, she pondered where the two places might be.

Chapter 46

The old white van slid crazily down the tiny lane. On the pitted road surface raindrops the size of shotgun cartridges cavorted, like hobgoblins composed of Glacier Mints. Streams of red soiled water ran across the road ahead of the van, as if it were driving beside a wounded animal.

Pulling into the small gaggle of buildings that impostered as a village, the driver leaned his nose against the inside of the windscreen, then sat back. Despite the greasy smudge and stippling rainfall, he could make out the tall gothic tower of the church; the farmhouse he sought was sat directly in the shadow of the tower and he fired the engine and turned carefully into the yard.

No one answered his knocks. Calling at the pub, an old church house with a mock-Arthurian sign where beer sales had once financed the inflated ecclesiastical construction turning green in the unrelenting rain, the driver – after subjecting himself to a variety of opinions and directions – followed a track up to the cow sheds and shouted the farmer's name over the gate until all the Reds turned their heads in useless curiosity. Bitten by one too many farm dogs, the driver left word with the patrons of the old church house and then deposited his cargo of fertilisers in the porch of the church.

The rain fell in ghost-like sheets across the graveyard as he scuttled back and forth to the van. The tower appeared more than usually modern in the storm; against the purple sky a concrete rocket at odds with the castellated nave. Having stacked the sacks inside the porch, the driver swept the water from the shoulders of his jacket. Sweat streamed down the bridge of his nose and mixed with rain and catarrh. Sod this for a game of soldiers. Something carved in the white stone of the ceiling caught his eye; in the brownish-green light he could barely make it out. Four distinct figures; three had their faces smashed, one remained. He wasn't interested in this. Turning to run back to the van, he splashed into the incoming tide of rainwater that was inching its way up the path. O for... There was no way he could leave the sacks now. He tried the church door and was surprised when it sprang open. He grabbed the sacks and dropped them through the door, and against the stained whitewash wall. Around the walls of the nave, saints glowered in bold colours.

Pausing in the porch to pull up his collar, succeeding only in sending another dribble of rainwater down his neck, he glanced up at the pale figures in the ceiling. He could see now that there were patterns made partly of ribs and partly of feathers. He rose up on his toes to get a better look at one of the vandalised supernaturals; its hands made an oval, its body ended at the waist in what looked like the bubbles of a Jacuzzi, its wings jutted almost perpendicular to its body then curved to form a notional circle with those of the other three; inside the broken face were two still eyes, blemishes in the stone, and a white beak.

He turned on his heels and skid-ran down the church path and through the lych gate. Gunning the van, he raced it through the brown tide covering the lane, sending a backwash into the roots of the hedges, and disappeared from the village. In the church house, the handful of locals finished their pints; someone would tell the farmer that his fertiliser was in the church porch.

Chapter 47

In the morning, Mandi submitted herself for psychological assessment. She had gone to the party straight from the office; not bothering to look at her post while Jonny was around. Now, she had an hour to get herself across London for the appointment, or risk losing her Remington Model 700.

"I have three years yet to run on my FAC..."

"It's a random check, Amanda, concerning your mental health."

"You're a GP, you're not a psychologist, Doctor Khan."

"I'm surprised you of all people put your faith in psychologists..."

"Read my blog, do you? I don't put my faith in anyone."

The doctor swung her chair around and scrolled through Mandi's notes on the practice's pc. Then swung back to Mandi.

"Have you ever had treatment for a mental health problem?"

"You know from the records. No."

"I don't mean recently..."

"I don't know what you're talking about."

"Cross-checking, Amanda. The wonders of the digitization of records; nowadays they talk to each other. Your name has come up in the notes of a whole group of other people, children, back when you were a child."

"I'm in their notes?"

"Not their usual notes; this is a very recent thing. A release of documentation that wasn't on the system before. I can't give you names, obviously, for reasons of confidentiality..."

Dr Khan shifted some of her pens around on the surface of her desk.

"But you can drag me into this rubbish at short notice..."

"Amanda, as a member of a gun club and a gun owner, your name came up in these files as someone that the children associated with... potentially dangerous activity. It's fuzzy, children can say strange things but the children in the files all say the same strange thing. Separately."

"Say what?"

"I can't tell you that because it would probably reveal their identities..."

"Well, I can already make a guess..."

"Don't, please. Let's leave it there, I simply ask you to re-confirm that you yourself have had no treatment or sought no treatment for mental health issues. Counselling, for example..."

"Counselling?"

"Or advice."

"Dr Khan, the state of my mental health is a matter between me, my id and my clitoris and I am not interested in what any files or any counsellor or advisor might have to say about it. No, I have not had, nor sought, any treatment of any kind for mental health issues. OK? But just this once, let me lay things out in a little more detail for you. At least more detail than I really want, and that you, probably, really want – or ought – to hear. So, when I was a kid I was adopted and I lived on a holiday camp that my new parents owned. During that time something happened that was so unimportant to me that I can't even remember a tenth of it, but whatever it was there were unsubstantiated accusations made against my parents. This was the satanic abuse scare time, do you remember that? Maybe not, you look about the same age as me."

"I know what you're talking about... we studied it."

"Well, as sure as I can be, my parents were a bit hopeless, a bit inept in bringing up a teenage girl, and a bit too nerdish for me to cope with in my twenties, but not in a million years were they are any danger to me or to any other child. Capeesh?"

"The issue is not your parents. The danger came from you."

Mandi looked about the doctor's room. It had all the usual family memorabilia, worthy charts and preachy posters, greetings cards, paraphernalia for on-the-spot tests and a view onto a tiny garden; everything she would expect to find in a GP's surgery. And a second door.

Mandi got up, went to the second door and pulled it open. A tiny cupboard of shelves, a few files, more equipment and wipes, gloves, disinfectants and what looked to be Dr Khan's lunch, one of those worthy rice concoctions in Tupperware. What had she expected? The Queen Bee? Her own staff crouched around the keyhole? A contrite Tyrone? A giant hall full of servers?

"Fuck you. Fuck you, Doctor."

Mandi shut the door and grabbed up her coat and bag. She left the practice at half-jog and twenty minutes later she was filling in the forms to check out her Remington from a firing range deep beneath the central city streets. "Hunting. In Devon," she explained to the club's security officer. "Devon" seemed to reassure him; he had never heard of anything bad happening there.

After the officer had checked her rifle and ammunition, Mandi secured it in its rectangular carry case and locked it in.

At the offices of her charity, Mandi secured the rifle in its CPD Pelican case in a locked cupboard in her private office. The staff meeting had begun, her people had barely noted her arrival so rapt were they in whatever the order of business was; this was just as Mandi had requested. After fielding enquiries about the funeral from two staff members who had missed the previous day's meeting, the planning for a new project resumed as if not missing a beat. Mandi found no difficulty in maintaining her full attention; she even contributed a few ideas which were politely received and massaged into the model. Childquake's response to Edubirdie's use of influencers; re-thinking the notions of cheating and entrepreneurialism: nutrition and attention. This time, there was no zoning out for her. They had her attention; more than intrigued to know how much they all knew about the system's access to the files under Belsize Park. There were two possibilities; that little trip underground was always about her, about Mandi, about prising at a chink in her armour. They had already found the information about her, and the whole meta-health thing was smoke and mirrors. Or, much worse, the files were already in digital form and Childquake's was a post hoc smokescreen for big data irresponsibility. Either way, someone, maybe everyone, in the room was responsible for keeping her in the dark, until now. So was the appointment with Dr Khan a slip up or an intimidation?

Mandi called 'time out' on the meeting and the human flies clustered to the water cooler and coffee maker. Mandi locked herself into her office and went out to stand on her balcony. If she had less self-control she might have yelled at a passing cloud; if she had no control she might have taken pot shots at a couple of pigeons... where were the pigeons? Mandi looked up and around the marbled sky. A grid of starlings split from their symmetrical formation and began to murmurate half-heartedly before disappearing behind one of the neighbouring office blocks. Mandi stared directly down from the balcony and the map-like streets seemed to make more sense than usual; all the streets led to somewhere, all the blobs of organic passer-by were on their way to something important, everything had meaning. Nothing random or unfit for purpose and that suddenly worried Mandi as much as the absence of pigeons.

In the corner of her eye, she caught a flap of wing, coloured like mother of pearl. She looked up in hope, but it was the reflection of an angel the size of the Shard in the ocean of glass on the office block opposite; it stood, legs planted between the various icons of the skyline, titanic and juggernaut-ish, and Mandi instinctively knew it was not an angel, but a social-psychotically induced spectacle, a product of all the sentimental mythemes of the programmed found-souls racing down the tracks of their Tron-esque lives below. They had collectively ordered the birds into matrices and distorted the sun's reflections into the shapes of their own derivative fantasies. This was the mob's idea of scary; they just did not know the half of it.

Mandi looked down again. She saw the screens blinking in unison. She noted the absence of children. She noticed the way the insects moved politically.

"I think there's something sinister going on," Mandi told the meeting. High stakes. All in. She was firing with the wrong ammunition, but she had nothing else. "I've been approached to allow our name to be used in order to free up a massive cache of research information on medical histories for the use of the state in long-term planning of services, dietary advice... the usual nannyish stuff, but also as guidance for free-market research groups towards what's needed rather than what's profitable. The medical gains, the illness and genetic problems that might be eradicated before they even appear, obesity, addiction, depression... all the dark sides of pleasure... that could be considerable. No one knows, but it's likely. On the other hand, it would be a massive betrayal of the trust of the participants, a massive infringement of privacy and a massive shift of information-power from independent researchers to the state. Consider the possible consequences. What if the data was used to slow down millions of cases of dementia and at the same time allowed... facilitated big pharma and deep state to manipulate mutations in different groups in different ways, in the interests of some of those groups and against the interest of others?"

"But you already gave permission for that?"

"What?"

"You emailed us all more than two weeks ago to say we were giving it public backing..."

"Have we made that public yet?"

"No."

"Good. Don't make any public statement. Can you forward me that email?"

"Sure..."

Mandi went to the window and looked down. There was a ripple in the order. A knifing perhaps, or a robbery. A disturbance alien to this part of town. Maybe someone had dropped their coffee, broke their phone; a small rip in the fabric. They would soon haul up the backdrop. There was no sound from below, but hers was not the only face in the windows, staring down. At street level there were men now, in white shirts, surrounding a woman possibly, something different, maybe... not an insect, but someone in a costume like an insect... they were tiny, they all ran off as if at a signal, the faces in the windows were closer, but unidentifiable... Mandi's mind was wandering... it was as if she were looking at the future.

"Ugh? What?"

"I have it here."

Mandi's PA was holding up her tablet, showing her inbox.

Mandi took the Underground, in the interests of anonymity; her Oyster card would leave a trace on the system so she got off a stop early and walked through Paddington, navigating the new Exchange flats that flanked Paddington Basin. At the corner with Praed Street a Tesco delivery lorry had pulled up, on its side was a map of the UK made up of its products, on the Art Deco pub on the opposite corner giant ceramic Satans, all with breasts and large green penises, gazed down goggle-eyed as Mandi hurried by.

Chapter 48

In Devon the rain persisted; early morning news programmes reported record rainfall. In the tiny village with the rocket-like church tower, hours of lashing rain had loosened something in the church roof and during the night rainwater had begun to run down the walls of the nave, saturating neat piles of Hymns Ancient and Modern and forming a pool around the sacks of fertiliser deposited by the jittery delivery man. The sacks had sucked up the water through tiny abrasions from being dragged from porch to nave. The chemicals within were greedy for fluid.

As the miserable morning light began to filter through the sheets of rain and stained glass, a thin miasma gently rose into the roof of the nave. Watched by the unreal saints in the rood screen, the gas settled for a while, and then gently fell again, reacting with the walls. Swirling patterns emerged, curling and crashing like the tumbles of waves or the vortices of whirlpools, blue and purple, with highlights of pink and white, fading again as the sun rose, the air in the nave warmed, and the gas dispersed.

A fresh breeze sprang up, the rain clouds that had been hanging over the county were finally blown away, and the sign on The Old Churchhouse Inn began to sway, animating its unlikely image of Nymue, the Lady of the Lake, seated high on her horse, knee deep in the water she was the maker of, a swan at her side and a king's sword held upside down, her fist unharmed by the blade it wrapped around.

Chapter 49

Mandi fled back. She knew now that there was a curse and that somehow she had to 'lift it'. It was no good running away; it followed. She must track it down to its source. "Attack the enemy where it thinks it is strongest"; that was what the aged messiah had told her. She had never thought of it as a curse before. As the train pushed its iconic nose through Wiltshire and then Somerset, easing back the landscapes, she scoured in vain the shadows of village lanes, the edges of woods and the grass between the limbs of white horses for any sign of a demon with bleeding teeth. For any sign at all. A whole hunt of devils would have been a consolation after the confusions of the night before; it had left her a little more bruised and scratched than she had appreciated at breakfast, as if she had been screwing a sentient thorn patch. At first, she thought the wounds were the remnants of her fight with the brambles at the retirement home but these were deeper and more emotional. The flesh would quickly heal, but her union with crumbling edifices of flesh, with giant urban towers and her immersion in the peristaltic sewers would take longer to resolve. How had the delightful ambiguities of the night before become this: like out of date cream on a hot body under theatre lights? She felt she had been peeled and left raw to the metropolis.

Outside the carriage the world was remorselessly ordinary and secular. Landmarks she had noted as spooked and off-kilter were now forbiddingly 'quotidian'; a word her poncy snowflake opponents preferred to 'everyday'. She liked to crucify them for stuff like that, but right now she would have valued the company of a few snowflakes to enlighten her about the blizzard she was caught in.

Mandi tried to visualise Jonny, how ze seemed to her at the party; how she had watched hir in mirrors after their initial conversation, but when Mandi looked in her memory there was nothing there. She felt much; she had been in a kind of darkness, or maybe she had simply reached behind her, she remembered that this moment happened later, somewhere between the party and her flat, she had reached for something out of sight; she could not see the thing that she had touched or that had touched her. Choice and power had been fuzzy in that darkness. Wherever it was and whatever it had been, it had been alive, damp and heavily muscled. Yet Jonny was not like that; ze was light, vivid, elegant, with a dry wit and a dancer's deportment and a great haircut. Mandi felt back into her memory and touched the thing again, recoiling from the recollection. There were still the ruins from last night not wholly lost to her; a dream landscape in which waves broke on black rocks, the crumples of a bed like a wasteland full of burial mounds and dark valleys, a flat purple sky stretching for miles and miles, and yet, the whole thing was in a cave, a massive cavern filled with thick wriggling things, the life of the world was all inside; she had felt an urge to reach her hand into the mass of living rope, to break the knot, to pull apart the rat king and scoop up the whole fucking thing she knew was beating with the disgusting mess of life. And it was only then that the thought struck her; that it was not Jonny, whoever ze was, that had scratched her, that there had been something else in the bed with them. Something that, if Mandi could just for once be honest with herself... she subtly punched the table in front of her, and the passenger in the seat in front turned quizzically... she already knew, she had known for a long time.

A gathering of trees stood darkly on the top of a smooth hill. A flat valley bottom stretched away from the train, punctuated by sheep. There were walkers silhouetted against the sky, up on a ridge path, consumed by their own conversations. Nothing addressed her; the ordinary beasts of the landscape lumbered along as if her trip were of no consequence to them. Where a tree had fallen in the winds, ripping up its roots, it had dragged up a great sheet of darkness, a plane of featureless black moss and Mandi fantasised about falling into its spongy arms.

Mandi had hoped that somewhere just after Taunton a trio of drowned angels would be waiting for her at the county border, ready to look after her. Dark fields and clumps of woodland flashed by; it was getting dark. Soon, even when she cupped her hands around her eyes and laid her forehead to the carriage window, there was nothing more than the odd pinprick of light in the sea of Devon.

Approaching The Sett she tried the same trick for the river and the lights on the far bank of the estuary, but there were no celestial objects afloat. Instead, at the tip of The Sett itself, the sandbar beyond what little remained of the second world war wreck of a broken-back coaster, Mandi made out four white figures goading a large stumpy object which oscillated in the dimness. Mandi checked around the carriage but no one else was noticing, stuck to their screens or nursing empty bottles of Chardonnay. She crammed her face to the glass and the scene was ongoing.

At the stop she stowed her bag behind a fence and set off at a run across the sands. She could not leave the Pelican case; that had to be in her possession or in a locked and secure place. The dunes, in the intermittent moonlight, rose up like the bumpy heads of submarine fiends. The marram grass scratched affectionately at Mandi's shins. She was approaching the wasteland part of The Sett at the very end of the spit where it faced off to the holiday resort on the far bank of the estuary. So far, so familiar, but as she got to the final rise of dunes before the bleak end beach, she laid down the rifle case and wormed her way to the brim.

It was not the head of a giant blubber-thing; but it was just as mis-placed and unreal. Somehow, by the erosion of the sand or maybe some shifting of the harder rocks beneath the dunes, a monolith had been thrust up through the end of The Sett, twice as tall as a person, the thickness of an old telephone box, the shape of a rough coffin. Around it four figures in white fatigues, hooded up and armed, were not goading the thing, but seemed to be guarding it. Mandi eased herself up over the edge of sand to get a better view beyond the fringe of marram; despite their white uniforms the figures were still shaky, but Mandi recognised the shape of military issue rifles, the kit of snipers. What the hell were they doing out here? She was still straining to detect any badge or insignia on the blank fatigues when a tiny eruption of sand burst up from just beside her hand and another a few inches from her face throwing grains across her shoulders and hair. Mandi flipped like a seal and rolled behind the rim of the dunes.

Unbelievable. They were firing at her. "Yey! Ceasefire! Friend!" she shouted. Further spurts of sand and tiny screams of sound followed. There was little thought to what Mandi did next; she knew these moments were traps. That everything hung on her judgement and that she was far too strung out to make any kind of choice. She went with her fear, snapped open the case and loaded the Remington. This was not going to end well however it ended. She cocked the rifle and fired before she aimed. She got off the round which – without the silencers used by the figures in white – cracked open the quiet of the night. It zinged past the stone and headed off towards the resort on the other side of the estuary chased by ringing echoes. The four figures in white responded like an old mechanical pier machine, clicking into a routine of dives and rolls; they were on the beach and launching their tiny black inflatable before Mandi could get to her knees and reload.

Mandi lay on her side, letting the grains of sand make dents in her cheek. Who the fuck were they? She had to report this, but... They would take her licence away, for sure. She got to her feet and looked about her, brushing away the sand from her clothes and skin; the white trail of the inflatable was far off now, heading West. There were no lights from other boats. No one on the beach, no one she could see on the dunes. Could she get away with it? Say nothing; hope the white gun toters were a group of... what? Gun nuts? A stag party on an illegal hunt who mistook her for a rare migrating duck? Were they likely to come back? Not given how they left when she returned fire. And those shots in the sand? Was she lucky or was that expert provocation? In that light it would take a crack shot to get so close without injuring someone. If they were that good, it would make very little difference what she did now; if they wanted to get her they would. And if they were just a bunch of jerks, what business of hers was it? They had missed; why cut her own throat and do their work for them? She would keep this quiet.

She quickly packed away the Remington, careful that no sand got into the case. Then she walked it over to the stone.

It towered over Mandi. It was wet, not long out of water. In the thin moonlight that struggled through a tracery of clouds to make much impression on the dark, Mandi had little hope of identifying the kind of rock it was. It looked dark and it felt smooth, but it was riddled with ridges and defiles. Mandi pushed at it. It was solid; it might have been there for a million years. Yet, it had not. Mandi's queasy memories of childhood were sufficiently coherent to know that this monolith had been no part of it. It was an arrival. A sign – like the weird patterns in the London streets – that things were accelerating and would overtake her unless she was able to get ahead of them. Make some of her own moves.

That night she was on the bonelines again.

She tried to follow them to the dark space at the centre, but the map flung her out to its edges. Then she was back on the Sett again, with the monolith; except that rather than standing on its own, an isolated exclamation mark in the sands, it was the centre of a village of houses made of wood and mist, a trace of a place that had something of Russia or the wilds of the US about it, cabins in the woods, but all gathered together around the stone. There were no people there, only ghosts, and they fled into tiny boats and paddled away using saucepans and serving spoons when the caretaker appeared in the lane between the wooden villas. There was a crack like a rifle shot and the houses were reduced to splinters and trash, gathered not around the rock, now, but around the caretaker. In the dream Mandi looked at him, his black clothes, his face was a question mark. "I didn't do this," he said. She felt the Everglades rise up inside her. "Well, you did something," Mandi replied and woke up, sat up and was shaking and gasping for breath.

Chapter 50

Idiot! Her Pelican case was sat at the foot of the bed. She threw the bedclothes aside and took the case and locked it in the tiny room Anne and Bryan had used as an office. She skipped coffee. At least she had managed to get her clothes off before falling asleep. Chewing dry toast did not make things better. London was no longer a retreat, that was infected too. The Sett had its own standing stone. The messiah, the saviour of the world, had died on her watch. She had taken her rifle without proper storage and she had discharged it at another person. She was no longer seeing angels.

She considered calling April. In the end, she chose Grant Kentish. There was something about April... but with Grant Kentish, Mandi knew exactly where she stood. Her life had been full of Grant Kentishes, but she had never met another April.

She was still deep in thought when the taxi, which she had forgotten ordering, arrived. She grabbed her coat and pulled on her boots. It was the same driver who had taken her to the Italian Gardens the first time. Mandi made it clear she did not want to talk and curled up on the back seat; this time she wanted shot of the long expanses of green between each homestead. She caught the top of the Great Hill; the cave must be close. As they pulled up, Mandi asked the driver to wait and offered him a portion of the fare. He took it.

Just as before, there was no answer at the front door. The hand painted sign THE OLD MORTALITY CLUB was gone. The Italianate poise of the portico was coy. Mandi rang again, nothing. She pushed at the door, it did not shift. Mandi made her way down the high side wall listening out for the sounds of ritual, orgy, electronica or cocktail party. When she stopped and listened hard there was only the birdless wind in empty trees. She remembered how Mimir had described the Club in confused terms; perhaps Mandi had underestimated them? How would they react to Kentish's betrayal? Did they even know?

Inside the wind, like a signal hidden within a signal, Mandi could hear a muted track of whistle, washing machine and synthesiser jamming with the leaves. Far off the deep bass rhythm of a train dawdling or a lorry labouring up a hill. But no one greeted her this time. She expected the door to the garden to be shut fast in its Romanesque frame, but it was open and Mandi stepped cagily into the gardens.

There was no steam, no cocktail. The pools were dry, the tarpaulin roofs, tubes, heaters and generators were all gone. There was no sign of the Old Mortality Club. Not a wine glass, not a cork, not a discarded undergarment. The absence was overpowering. Mandi wandered for a few minutes through the gardens, looking hard for a dropped cigar butt or a condom hanging in the leaves of a shrub. Nothing. The paths were raked, the lawns immaculate and cropped. The stone sides of the bathing pools were disinfected, there was nothing to suggest the ageing naked bodies that draped and entwined around each other. Any residue had been burned away.

Mandi found the stone jar with the impish face into which she had tipped her poisonous cocktail; she held it upside down and then felt inside it. There was no sticky revenant. Either these people employed a director of detail or the whole thing had been a mirage. She recognised the tiny granite pillar, but there was no friendly wren. The gardens were a blank, a place with dementia. The shaggy clumps of ivy had been trained, the soft cushion of mosses scraped away and the oranges, yellows and reds of the lichen were more orderly. There was nothing to climb the steps for, nothing to be defended in the miniature castle, no posturing sybarite to be held up by the half-baked Roman arch; it was as dead as an English Heritage site. No porn to these ruins. Just a base instinct, a meaningless malevolence; the place was soulless and yet mechanically alive. It had pulled Mandi in and as she made her way back quickly to the Romanesque door in the high outer wall she was scared that it might slam shut and lock her in.

Back in the taxi, Mandi told the driver "all done" and lay back down on the seat and closed her eyes until they were pulling up inside the gates of Lost Horizon.

She needed a new approach. She sat on the edge of her adoptive parents' bed and thought things through. She had been increasingly convinced that the three drowned sisters were attempting to communicate with her through the angelic forms in which they had been 'immortalised' in alabaster. Yet, either she was wrong or they had been unable to get through to her and given up. Or something else was trying to contact her and she did not recognise it. Perhaps she had been trying to make too direct a contact, maybe they were all making the same mistake; or it was too oblique, everyone being too clever, too symbolic? Maybe the secret to making contact was right there in front of you, so simple, it was not all the stories, statues, representations, paganism, magic... it was just the place, just the place. If she could get out on the water where all this started...

She was not surprised to see that the standing stone had disappeared from the end of The Sett. She was more surprised by the eerie trace of the houses. Leftovers from her dream.

Mandi commandeered one of the primitive kayaks that had been drawn up on the shore and began to paddle out to the site of the three sisters' watery burial. The sea was choppy and Mandi had to work hard to make headway against the wind; comforted by the thought that it would quickly sweep her back to shore as soon as she was done. It was better not to look back at what you were leaving, better to fix your eye on the bow and the angry stretch of water ahead. Chugs of wind smacked at Mandi's face, water spat at her from the ends of her paddle. She bent into the rising wind, as different regiments of waves marched in from opposite sides and slashed each other to pieces, grinding the bow of the kayak in its tattered ranks. Something soft and heavy slapped against the side of her boat.

Mandi looked over each of the two sides. Parts of the same huge shadow lurked beneath her, they sullied the sea all around her. She looked to shore for a bearing. The mist had hardened, most of the houses were boarded up but one was hung with bathing towels and flags, tennis nets and fishing trophies. On the sand outside a young woman in a black gym kit was yelling in German to two men on the veranda and waving a salute to Mandi's boat. Although they seemed a very long way off, Mandi could hear the conversation on the veranda.

"Is it really too much to ask that someone at least let off a bomb beneath the pier?"

"And that dreadful squealing cliff railway! Like a caterwauling coon-singer!"

"We've been invaded! Rather than Hampstead types belly-aching about the so-called sufferings of wogs occupied by our well-disciplined troops, what about us? Don't we have our privacy invaded every summer; the vandal hordes crowding out our best restaurants, shoulder-barging us off the trams! Dropping paper bags and god-knows-what-else wherever they damn well please!"

"I am thinking of starting up a secret society of county people and the first point in the constitution will be the duty of each member, every day before lunch, to seize at least one of these visitors and smother them with a pastie! That kind of treatment the industrial classes understand!"

"Let's get up a navy! Redeploy the ammunition presently used on innocent folk and rain it down on the tourists, blow their moronic amusements and their civic flower beds to smithereens! And their concrete steps! Can't the buggers climb rocks?"

"That'll stop their jazzing and Jews!"

"Survival of the fittest!"

"Come on, you Saxons!"

The men's humour was picked up in the laughter of female voices. Mandi felt her body twist, the young woman's body in which she was lodged, dressed in the same black gym costume, jerked its right arm stiffly up to the sky, palm-straight, and gales of encouraging laughter swept her up into the clouds.

"It's human nature to defend your own!"

"Damn human nature, its scientific neurology, it's in the mind! We are the flesh machines obedient to our best selves!"

Mandi suspected that these were powerful men. She snapped back into herself. A storm was rising. On the shore, just visible through the flying froth and watery mounds, she could still make out the spectral community, foundation-less, drainless, paying no taxes, represented by no one, but only just. Their romantic anarchism had frightened her; their pirate flag grinned at her. Such were the ghosts that had been left. She felt sick. She heard complacency and entitlement in those voices. They were different from her! She would not have made their mistakes.

Her rifle...

The waves came like calculations, as if they computed her, spreading her inside out across the surface of the sea, condensing her down and extracting the core. "Who are you really?" they seemed to be saying. "What are you hiding that is important? Give us your three main drivers!" Why was an ocean interested? Who was so powerful they could employ a storm for a therapist? Her ordeal at the hands of the waves was being conducted according to strict principles.

Mandi looked down into the solid swell and she was looking down into herself. She felt the sleeves of squirming waters move inside each other, the parts parting so she could slip down between them, into darker and darker darkness. She felt herself unfold, she felt the burdens unpeeling from her shoulders, her thoughts like flocks of birds beginning to move in tumbling cascades, fluttering in lace-like shapes, then jerking in mind-changes to left and right. All her separate parts were feathers in one wing, their black parts murmurated like memories; she waited for her feet to touch the bottom of the ocean, and for the dim dome of light above to unfix itself.

"Squirty Mary up from the deep,
Rode the big squid in her bare feet,
When she dropped her guts..."

The song faded as she fell deeper and deeper into a bloated bag of soul. No line to catch hold of, she looked at her fingers and they were curled like hair in a gale. She was losing her grip on surface realities, sinking into the wriggling being of her self, inside the struggling sinking thing she had become, inky and thoughtless, closing down, shutting out, the sinking of the fields...

"Muddy Mary mother of God,
Killed the Old Boy in his bath..."

There it was again, just a refrain and then gone. Where had she heard the song before? She struggled to look down inside her darkness and fish it out. She saw the muddy Mother rising up to meet her, spreading Herself out across the Bay, a massive stain beside the bleached dunes. Mandi tried to haul the memory up; if only she could shuffle the fields while sinking. Then the whole kaleidoscope would work for her... and she would never need... again.... she wallowed and something salty tried to force itself into her throat. The colours were too bright for real darkness she realised, the spiralling strings of ideas were holding her like seaweed tangled around her ankles and she shrugged them off and dived for the wordlessness, there was more than one force down here, and she threw off the paddle, let go the line, the silhouette of the kayak began to dissolve as the shape of the sun had done before it, she gave in to the darkness and the darkness raised her, slippery and immense, a black and red football field of gooey beakless fleshiness, rising like an undulating platform, fierce tissues flexing and contracting beneath its leathery sac, and pushing her back...

This was not the time...

She fought it. For a moment it was her adoptive mother, enforcing some simple rule. She thrashed out with her fists.

Wait. There will come a time...

She didn't have time. She wanted the darkness now! The darkness refused her and with a final spasm spat her out onto the surface, where she coughed and retched salt and water and microbeads and tiny living things.

The sweet, calm ocean had gone. Dark brown waves, sloping and kicking, rose all around her. Where was the boat? She was in the water! She had no memory of falling in. The wind ripped at her face with broken nails, a wave smacked into her back, she ploughed her arms in a crawl up the side of a wave, trying to get her eyes above the fuming soap suds, in quick succession two waves broke over her head and a third drove her sideways until she could reach around and drag herself upright with her forearms; she was grabbing for a hold on mounds of water, when she was abruptly borne forward like a surfer on another thick wave of foam. Waves broke in a circle like a gang of maddened drunks, then they fell away and she could see the kayak twenty yards off, its sails kicking wildly against the gale, her paddle jumping and hopping close by. Mandi struck out for it and a solid mass of icy fluid pushed her forward, then dragged her down. She surfaced quickly, a rip tide pushing her back up. She struck out again, though the kayak seemed farther away, pushed another ten yards in a few seconds. For minutes she battled, the tiny lurching and flapping target visible only in glimpses through the valleys of furious water. On the point of exhaustion, the kayak finally seemed blown towards her; snatching the paddle from its mount on the top of a white horse, Mandi pulled herself across the last few feet of water by her one free arm and grasped the edge of the boat. She tried to pull herself in, but her arm was now so cold and the muscle so acid-bound, she could get no leverage. She threw the paddle into the bottom of the kayak and tried again with two arms, but a slipping grip and exhausted biceps meant she could do no more than hang on. Then her fingers failed, one by one they were peeling from the topsides as she began to slip slowly back to the deep.

A deep mound of water lifted the kayak. Instead of breaking the last two fingers of Mandi's tenuous hold, something swelled and lifted her higher than the boat and laid her down, gently at first, then her midriff crashing onto the gunwale. The chance would not come a second time and – simultaneous with a sudden draught of water and the movement beneath her of something massive and red and black – she pushed off from some numinous thing and tipped herself over the side and into the bottom of the boat as the waves foamed white around her feet. For a moment the waters around the boat turned the black-red of just dried blood and then faded again to the same watery brown as whipped waves. Mandi allowed the tiny boom to pass back and forth above her, like a crazed metronome. Tick, tick. Bang, whoomph. Cracks like rifle fire. The squall had come like a gunshot from cloudless heavens dragging a curtain of grimy vapour over the dome of sky.

Recovering her composure, grabbing the boom, Mandi lowered the sail and beat the waters with the paddle. She seemed, as she had hoped, to be riding an incoming tide; despite the giant breakers falling in temple ruins around her she was soon leaping into the raging white shallows and dragging the kayak out of the sea and hurling it sideways onto the strandline. The sail escaped its cleat and unravelled, crestfallen, as if it wished to race back to a master it had failed.

Mandi lay back on the sand, dragging herself up the incline of the beach like a giant turtle; her limbs leaving long curved scrapes. Out of reach of the waves, Mandi felt self-possession returning; whoever had been playing with her out there, they had made a mistake; they had given her an insight into who they were and from what they had come. More than that, they had introduced her to something she felt was their enemy; not just the thing she had intuited, felt barely, sensed was all, but that was immense and just beneath her, out of reach this time – but there would be another time for that – strongest was a feeling that it was all in the exactitude of the place. Some enemy was responsible for the boat – she cast an angled glance at the glorified kayak, its tiny mast dug into the sand, its sail flapping helpless now like a landed eel – but she had steered it against their will, she had felt their resistance, she had provoked them almost to killing her and that meant that she was doing something that they intended to keep her from: the exact sea burial spot of the three sisters. There was something about this precision, and presence, the being there of it, the precise just being that had somehow triggered the power of the place; something with more power than a storm.

"What were you doing out there?"

The caretaker, breathing heavily, was stood over her.

"I needed a bigger boat..."

He smiled briefly.

"You didn't have a boat, you swam out..."

"What?"

Mandi sat up; everything inside her hurt. There was no kayak on the sand, no flapping sail.

"I borrowed it from a guy in plus fours and a smoking jacket... strange accent... natty moustache... fancied himself... he kept it in one of the ho..."

Although it tore and hurt, she swivelled around. There was nothing on the dunes but marram grass, the red officious markers of the wardens and the standing stone.

"Do you mean wooden houses?"

"Yes, sure, I mean.... they're not here now but..."

"There haven't been any houses on here since they were blown off in a storm in the 1930s."

The winds died unnaturally. An eerie calm settled like a large mammal sinking to the ground. The wild roaring of the water became an irritable lapping of waves on bleached driftwood.

"And what the fuck is that?" Mandi pointed to the monolith.

"That's the Cheeke Stone. The high spring tides have uncovered it for the first time in over a century. Once upon a time it was on all the maps of The Sett."

"Who's screwing with my mind, Mister Crabbe?"

"I have no idea, Miss Lyon, but that's not a good place to be swimming."

"I got that impression..."

"I mean historically bad. A few years back a kid was trying out a new snorkel he'd got, just playing really. Summer holiday stuff. The tide was right out, shallow compared to now. Anyhow, kid pulls up a small cannon from the mud. Everything goes wild, Time Team get involved, a lot of excited talk about the defeat of the Spanish Armada and a sea battle... after all the fuss died down, and the more serious people got involved, turns out it was probably a Venetian slave ship, not transporting slaves but crewed by them, people captured in North Africa, they went down in a storm in their chains... their bones are still out there, indistinguishable now from sand and mud... whatever it was that was luring you, it knows the geography of bad places..."

"Is the sea a place, like that? I mean the stuff on the bottom vaguely sticks around, if it's a cannon or something, I imagine, but tiny flakes of bone? That stuff surely gets caught up in all the washing back and forward of the tides, how is that a place? It's all flow and currents and – the thing about rivers... never stepping in the same water twice... in a sea, it's the same, churning, mixing, disappearing..."

"Heraclitus. What if everywhere's like that?"

"No! Fuck!"

Mandi lay back on the beach, grabbing at the sand in great fistfuls. The caretaker stared into the grinding waves. The brown expanse was breaking up into fluffy white clouds. There was flow and there was something else. Something that moved more slowly, something older, even than galleons, older than slavery, something very old that had put down markers, or roots, or something... and was trying to talk with her, tell her something... but without a mouth, without any vessel or organ of communication... it was coming through to her in the form of events.

As if to taunt her, sails of blue began to break through the murk above, the wind that whipped foam on the rise of the waves was driving the storm away towards the obscure horizon. Mandi began to struggle to her feet. The caretaker offered his hand and Mandi took it, levering herself up. Where Mandi had lain the shape of her body formed one part of a vast arrangement of flotsam and jetsam: seaweed bound by fishing line, grey barkless logs, tins, punnets, tampon applicators, hollow crab shells, rust-orange aerosol cans, the lid of a boardgame in Arabic, a faded blue Sulley figure, large floats, a lobster pot and jumbles of plastic packaging.

"What does it mean?"

"That's what I've been trying to work out."

"But you made it! I saw the others... didn't you?"

"No," said the caretaker, "I find them, but I don't make them. I do, however, think that they are parts of the message. Maybe a warning. Of which you, for the first time, are a part..."

"A message from who?"

"From something that is possibly indifferent to us understanding."

"Why would it warn us then?"

"Well, if it's indifferent to us understanding, it wouldn't need a reason, would it?"

"Fuck you!"

"Don't speak to me like that, Amanda. Please."

And he began to weep; not expressively, but tears ran down his cheeks. Mandi was taken aback. She was always the first to rush forward to comfort (or to stick the knife in, at an assassination), but this was so unexpected from someone so composed.

"I'm sorry. I think it's the stone. If you must know... o, fuck it..."

And they laughed at each other.

"I do know what the messages mean. The same as the stone. The camp's gone, Mandi. Finished. I'm sorry. I had hoped I could come back and help secure the camp, but look at the erosion here, despite the best efforts of everyone. It's just going to go. It's nature, or at least it's the nature we've invoked. It swept away the houses on here years ago; something made it mad and it came for them. Well, something's made it mad again. I've seen the storm predictions; you can check them out online. We haven't had the highest spring tides yet, not the half of it, when one of them coincides with a big storm, like the one when the railway was all washed out five years ago, it will take Lost Horizon. It won't leave a stick. There's nothing we can do except get the people to safe dry ground before it happens and see if anything can be rebuilt after it's over. Maybe nothing; maybe it's coming back to reclaim what is rightfully its territory, and we shouldn't try. Brunel and the railway took away a lot of land from the sea..."

"Christ. You're not shitting me?"

"No," he laughed, "I'm not shitting you, Amanda. It's so, so angry right now." And he looked out to sea and Mandi followed his eyeline to where the giant shadow of a cloud was making its way between two sheets of silver ocean. She felt inordinately fond, suddenly, of this old and dying man. She snuck up behind him and put her arm around his waist. She feared that he would flinch away, but he continued to stare out to sea.

"You come from a difficult, but wonderful thing, Amanda. Let's get you back to the camp, you need a rest, settle back into routine for a few days, I've found another of the camps that can take our people, on higher ground. They'll be safe to move there when they need to, but we need to warn them so they can take their most precious things. Be good if you came round with me, saw people, gave reassurance, avoid a panic. We don't need to do that for a day or two. Have some time out; I'll drop some bottles off tonight, I know you like a drink, won't do you any harm now, and I'll make some food, there'll be a stew on your front door step, so you don't need to worry about cooking or shopping for a while..."

"Who are you, my father?" she repeated, fondly.

And the two turned their backs on the Cheeke Stone and walked slowly and painfully – both with their own kinds of tumours – back to Lost Horizon.

Chapter 51

Mandi focused. The preparation for the espresso she had forgone a few hours before took far longer than usual. For once the anticipation was better than, or at least as good as, the satisfaction. It was as if she could place life, dunes, shadows under the sea, snipers in abeyance, put them on hold. Keep them on ice.

Sips of the black gold tasted of hibernation; warm and safe and deep.

Her wet clothes were whirling around in the washing machine. She was dressed in a weirdly pleasing combination of Anne and Bryan's clothes. The time that had passed and the days of mourning were slowly dissolving those images of fractured windscreens and flesh and skulls. In their place old memories had begun to seep back in; of picnics at megaliths, slow passage through museums, cinema visits to see the first three 'Spy Kids' movies.

Mandi sat. She never did this. For an hour she just sat. She let thoughts click over her eyes, like counters. Some she noted for further attention, but mostly she let them come and go. It was only when she lifted the cup to her lips and the dregs were cold that she realised how much time had passed. It had been a full day already; she reviewed her swim. There was some logic there; something about that area of sea and water-buried sand that connected to all of this. But there was also vulnerability, poor judgement, a troubling irrationality that was expanding and a reliance on a man to sort it all out. She felt a pleasing bitterness seep back into her. She would not let the caretaker take care of her.

Jesus. The rifle. She was supposed to check it regularly. It was behind a locked door but one that probably did not conform to the Firearms Licensing Law 2016. She must re-enter the office. It had mixed connotations for Mandi; it had been a no go area for her as a child, a repository of confidential and commercial information, the only place in the mega-trailer that was special to Anne and Bryan. Even their bedroom was less private than their office. It had been where they had felt themselves as most individual, rather than as father and mother, where Mandi felt closest to them as Anne and Bryan. Anne with her old-fashioned veneer and her underlying outrageousness and Bryan in his determined search for things that would never be found and his love of Sumo wrestling, perpetually frustrated either by his lack of money or technical understanding to get the right channel.

She retrieved the key from under the carpet and let herself in.

The Queen Bee was seated at Bryan's desk. Flanked on each side by two white snipers, their hoods back and their young, overly-made-up features brazen in the dull lights of the trailer. Mandi's Remington was in pieces on the carpet, expertly disassembled. At a glance Mandi knew that every tiny spring was there laid out; the entrails had been read.

"We've been waiting for you."

"How long have you been here?"

"Long enough to smell your coffee. Must be hard to get a decent blend in these parts?"

The white snipers shifted angrily. No guns were evident, but Mandi noted that each had a Ka-Bar knife strapped to their thigh. They were female. Mandi's 'stag do' guess had been way off; not even binary reactionary, just plain old assumption.

"We missed you in the Smoke. You came back and everyone was happy. Then you ran away again. What's going on with you, Mandi?"

"I have t..."

"Don't answer that. I have a far more important question. Or pitch. Our proposal for a series of debates has been accepted by the broadcaster, we want you to mediate on screen, that includes a book deal based on your blogging – it's Random House – and there'll be a social media team assigned to you. You'll never need to write your own tweets again."

"You know the answer."

"Yes, but I needed to test your integrity. You're such a one-off, Mandi, no one is sure about you. They always need to be reassured about you. Why is that? I find it fascinating. Don't answer. Nothing is ever contained in itself, but is a ladder we pull away in order to go higher? A boat to burn to encourage us to go further in? Stop denying it – you are one of us!"

Mandi bristled.

"You think we are playing at controversy? I always saw your scepticism. Your lack of faith in our determination to put a philosophical bomb in the heart of the communal being. Right?"

"You were going to tell me who I am, but you've got sidetracked into telling me about yourself. How did that happen?"

"The two things are inextricably linked. People are very pleased with you, Mandi. Quiet, powerful people. You liberated medical files for tens of thousands to the future benefit of millions; this will collapse so many assumptions about what 'human' is, you've retired The Old Mortality Club, and the troublesome messiah seems to be no longer... troublesome..."

"I did nothing."

"Like I say, what you are and what we do is inextricably linked."

"And what are you inextricably linked to, Bee? What's your relationship with the Hexamerons?"

"No secret about that. I am a member of the Ladies Essay Society..."

"They're a bunch of racists!"

The Queen Bee turned to the white snipers.

"Would you ladies excuse us?"

The four women began to file towards the door.

Mandi stepped backwards and blocked the frame.

"Who are these people? They shot at me!"

"We are quite capable of answering for ourselves."

Mandi was impressed at how similar the women looked; blonde hair, elfin haircut, immaculate La Praire make-up, mid-twenties, high cheek bones. Ladies College accent.

"We are the Pavlichenko Brigade of the Devon Beliye Kolgotki. We honour the name of Ludmilla Pavlichenko, the greatest sniper of them all, but our allegiance is to the county."

"We are Devon girls."

"We honour Pavlichenko because of her accuracy, not her politics; our first brigade, The Fair Toxolites, was formed in the country houses in the 1860s. We were renamed after the Second World War in honour of Ludmilla's visit here in 1942; our weapon had been the long bow, and then a war bow that could shoot a heavy arrow a quarter of a mile, but Ludmilla changed all that..."

"...whatever our weapons our principles have remained the same."

"Which are?"

"To support the aims of The Hexameron Essay Society."

"By any means necessary?"

"By any means appropriate. We follow the teaching of Edward Hyams; that in those exceptional circumstances where an individual endangers the well being of the general good an equally individualised act is a justified one."

"You kill people?"

"We give democracy a nudge."

"And how exactly were you nudging democracy on The Sett last night?"

"We never discuss operational matters. Now, if you would excuse us, we will let ourselves out."

And they stepped forward. Mandi stepped aside. What intimidated her was not the knives but their effortless authority and their beauty. She recognised 'class' and she hated it, and she hated herself for stepping aside for it; but she was trembling from head to foot. The best she could do, as the four women tramped through her living room, was to shout after them: "you might have re-assem...embled my Remington!" She stumbled, even over that.

"Are you going to take my gun?" she asked the Queen Bee.

"A black woman with an unlicensed gun in Devon? I think not. Let's talk racism."

"OK..."

"We are well aware what the Hexamerons are..."

"They're Beyondists! They believe in evolutionary struggle between groups. To you, me and the gatepost, that's a race war."

"It's more complicated than that... But, sure, it isn't any better. If anything the truth is even worse. The Hexamerons are rich elitists who like to takes risks with technology. They were in at the birth of computing, they pioneered the mechanisation of mass destruction, the first telegraphic communications with the dead. They are reinventing themselves by the power of their giant servers. They've come full circle in a Nietzschean nightmare sort of way; except they don't mind the nightmare, they embrace the nightmare. The nightmare is what they do."

"So what's your interest in them?"

"Not them, the nightmare is key to this – they won't outlive it, they are in practice the living contradiction of their philosophy – they say they wish for dominance but what they really long for is destruction. Self-destruction. Those four women – psychopaths to the last one – that's what the Hexamerons are. Always have been; the death wish in the accumulative heteronormative anthropocentric economy. They have survived by failing; and now, by succeeding, they will disappear and we will pick up the pieces."

"Who are "we" and what are the pieces?"

"That's why I love you, Mandi! You save so much time! "We" are not who you think "we" are. "We" go back a very long way. But there are only a very few of "we" left. So, although we work for the many, we must work through the few."

"Giving the revolution a nudge."

"Neo-liberalism is at an end; read the runes! It has run out of energy in the margins of its own popularity. A new wave of authoritarianism will replace it, rushing to an equally toxic extreme; neo-liberalism's extreme concentration of wealth wed to authoritarianism's extreme concentration of power. The wealthy and the powerful have become a small, identifiable and vulnerable elite. They will fall at the hands... not of the masses, but of their immediate subordinates, their security guards, their accountants and lawyers, their generals and their housemaids. And then it will be our turn."

The Queen Bee laid out for Mandi, as carefully as the dis-assembling of her rifle, without a spring forgotten, the conspiracy of which they were both a part; the subversion of the last remnants of social democratic consensus by luring jaded neo-liberals and clown-demagogues into a libertarianism of anti-identity so radical they would effectively disappear as human beings. Just as the English countryside, following the death of Christianity, had, Queen Bee explained, effectively disappeared as a meaningful locus. The fields were still green, the paths still red, but there was no real ecology there. The New Right was vanishing quicker than democracy in a liberated Iraq, its policies lead to social chaos and the evaporation of the individual, a vacuum opens up...

"So what?"

No wonder they valued her brevity. The Queen Bee was a windbag.

The Boss, focused now, explaining how an elite of digitally-savvy social intellectuals was situating itself in scientific, media and religious organisations, in lobbyists and charities, accountancy firms and consultancies, political and academic organisations – ready and prepared to intensify each coming crisis to breaking point, so that when the New Right failed they were adroitly placed to advocate a violent response to its failures and usher in a new kind of digitised transhuman world.

Mandi laughed at the arrogance.

"Am I the only real libertarian left?"

Mandi could match the Queen Bee for arrogance and raise her.

"But there's more... you mock yourself and your family, you laugh at what and who you are."

"Who am I?"

Like everyone else she had asked in the past few days, the Queen Bee ignored the question, launching instead into a lecture on two schools of anarchism: helplessly pacifist and violently terroristic.

"The terror-anarchists were the most influential world political movement through the end of the nineteenth and beginning of the twentieth century..."

"You're going to tell me that African-Americans never had it better than when they were in the Black Panthers..."

The Queen Bee did not skip a beat.

"...they destroyed tsars, they blew up parliaments, they engineered the First World War, but in 1917 they were decisively defeated. In the aftermath of the revolution in Russia, they contested the leadership of the revolution with the Bolsheviks and suffered such terrible defeats at the hands of militarised collectivism, the worst at Kronstadt, the mutiny put down by Trotsky's Red Army... that kind of anarchism never recovered. Yes, Baader-Meinhof, Angry Brigade, and some Middle Eastern nationalists borrowed the tactics, but the real last gasp was in Catalonia, and the Communists came for them again and finished them off. Then something happened. A small number of the leading terror-anarchists – the 'aristocrats' of the movement – finally... finally! ... accepted the scale of their defeat and went undercover, prepared to lay low for generations while placing themselves in positions of influence, particularly in newspapers, mass media, intelligence community, communications, arts and the social media industry..."

"Right wing conspiracy theory... Marxist culture war..."

"...with a view to tempting and compromising and exposing and destroying the dominant political forces..."

"What I said..."

"...preparing the vacuum which they will one day occupy.... do you know what their name means?"

"Whose?"

"The Hexamerons."

"No."

"The 'Hexameron' is the six-day creation of the world. They don't mean the biblical creation..."

"Pengelly and..."

"They believe they can create a new world in six days."

"How?"

"Well, not by persuasion, is it? By blowing up the data."

"And you have generously allied me with this bunch of delusional racist digital megalomaniacs?"

"Our heritage is to take risks with the world, that's what we do. Your grandparents, your adoptive grandparents, the parents of... er... your parents? I get confused with all your family complications..."

"Anne and Bryan?"

"Yes. Er, Anne's parents. That's right. They were part of the movement inside the establishment. Your parents were less interesting, more flaky, but we managed to track you down, monitor and nurture you, recruit you away from deviationism; ready to take your rightful place in a revolutionary aristocracy. You have come home to the movement... accept the contract, you'll be notorious!"

"How big is all this?"

"Tiny. Has to be. Very few of the genuine anarchist families survived the Soviets, the Nazis and the FBI. We are all of the same tempered blood! I can trace my ancestry to the Haitian slave revolts and Toussaint L'Ouverture, but also to Prussian bomb-throwers. Unlike the paganism of your adoptive parents which goes no further back than Dennis Wheatley and the News of the World – we closed that down, you know! – we have real heritage, real continuity... blood and roots... not that any of that counts for anything, but our ideas are magical. Don't you feel their rush through you?"

"How far do you think this conspiracy goes?"

"No, no, no... There are no aliens, no Illuminati, just a few of us who respect an idea and pass it on mother to daughter... sometimes it skips a generation... waiting for the moment. When two people agree is that a conspiracy? Everything valuable in life is a conspiracy. To plant a forest, to shoot a movie, to fall in love. There are the plebs of conspiracy and then there are the aristocrats."

Mandi was deeply grateful to the Queen Bee, in a way. Not for spilling the beans; they pretty much echoed gossip she'd heard before in the media world. There were different versions; but each person always put their heritage – self-made man, war hero, poet – in the driving seat. None of them understood how driven they were. Bee and her senior colleagues had once been part of some headcase animal-activist set-up that had dissolved so as to re-emerge as media butterflies. Like the Hexamerons, the pagans, the political parties, the Church of England for god's sake, they all had their imaginary heritages and their delusional aims and utopias. What really met Mandi's need now was the chance to think clearly and critically about all the bullshit. All of it! The last few weeks – the trash in patterns on the sand, the weird walk with April, the standing stone that emerged on the dunes – had been resolutely unsusceptible until now. Listening to Bee she knew exactly what they, and she, were not.

The end of the conversation came remarkable quickly. Once Mandi indicated that their encounter was over, Bee did that thing again and made a pretence of calling the meeting to a halt. Mandi promised to consider everything that she had heard, thanked Bee for her generous offer. She would clear things up in Devon and then get in touch in a week or so for a meeting to discuss her decision and the details of her future involvement.

A car was waiting for Bee outside the trailer. Not a taxi. On the porch, Bee put in a parting shot. That she would see to the issue at the gun club; Mandi knew that was a threat. Bee then handed Mandi a book taken from her shoulder bag.

"Read it."

The book was entitled 'Soil and Civilisation'.

"Edward Hyams?"

"You heard his name a few minutes ago. The anarchist author whose 'Killing No Murder' inspired the first members of the Pavlichenko Brigade of the Devon Beliye Kolgotki. Stay alert. We observed you having tea with that peculiar archaeologist at his home: Hill House. I want you to study his ideas, not for their content, but for their pattern. He was a Hexameron member, collaborated with Far Right members of the Soil Association, best friends with Lady Eve Balfour, daughter of Gerald the father of the Hexamerons' failed messiah who you... well... exceeded the best efforts of the Pavlichenko Brigade of the Devon Beliye Kolgotki, shall we say? Hyams wrote dystopian sci fi novels, they predict the exact particulars of the coming Beyondist authoritarianism... how did that matrix form? And why here? It's not black magic, so what is it?"

The Queen Bee gestured helplessly, then turned her back on Mandi, just before Mandi could turn her back on the Queen Bee. As Mandi shut the front door behind her, she heard the slam of the car door, and as the copy of Hyams' book crashed into the waste bin, she heard the gunning of its engine, the crunching scraps of gravel, and its speeding off towards London.

Chapter 52

That night Mandi dreamed she was in a church; in the village she and April had rushed through after visiting the cave. 'Maybe this isn't right at all', she thought, inside the dream, but the dream pressed on. It was cold inside the church, and noisy, a choir of five singers were in the porch, holding a single deep note that resonated in the building. Mandi slammed the door to the nave and there was a dead silence which somehow contained the swoosh of a snaky belly and the slurp of slithering olms dragging their torsos over dusty stones. The doors in the centre of the brightly painted rood screen – reds and blacks and whites and oranges and more reds – were madly opening and shutting; each time a figure of God enthroned on one panel crowned the Queen of Heaven on the other. Mandi was surprised at how sexy Mary was; dressed in a poster paint red dress, her long gingery-blonde crimped locks swimming down her back. Was it OK to fancy the Virgin Mary? Well God had, she supposed? It's a funny kind of virgin that has a kid. These people could never stick as one thing. The doors slammed shut, the Queen stayed crowned, and God – who looked a lot like the Old Man at the retirement property – grimaced.

"Why did you break the statue?" Mandi asked and the Old Man replied, as if they were a comedy double act, "because he wrote Utopia, I took a hammer to him, haha!" and the doors began to flap again, flinging Mucky Mary back and forth, crashing the crown into her skull. Blood and teeth flew. Above the altar – which had a keyboard like an old cinema organ and was churning out thundering chords – two rising chains of angels throbbed with purples and orange tinges and deep sea blue lights, up and down like decorations on a pinball machine; red wingtips glowed, and two angels with shocks of white hair threw up their hands above four feathery mantles coloured green like bathroom tiles.

"What have you done?" shouted Mandi.

"That's up to you," said the Old Man sat on the ponderous throne of heaven.

Saints began to peel off the panels of the rood screen; the male ones couldn't get themselves properly free and they flapped like plastic bags stuck on barbed wire, except for Armel... how did she know this? ... who led a dragon on a chain to drink at the font. The women were more like two-dimensional stickers from a girl's magazine, flatfish floating about in a waterless tank; Barbara carrying her own wall which she disappeared through into a mountain gorge, Margaret climbing into the mouth of a dragon and digging her way out through its throat with a crucifix, Apollonia (were these real names?) pulling teeth with giant callipers from the mouth of a dark cave, and Helena digging the true cross from the ashes of a wooden Temple of Venus, burrowing, excavating.

"Why aren't you all building Utopia?" Mandi asked them.

The Old Man laughed: "you haven't got it yet, have you?" And he pointed with his free hand to the darkness between the legs of the god in the stained glass into which the dove, white wings aflutter, was rising. Mandi leaned forward towards the darkness and the rood screen doors creaked gently open. Straining to see what it was in the darkness, Mandi bent forwards, towards the altar, fearful that the doors might swing abruptly shut and trap her head.

The light outside was failing; shadows crept across the windows. The great East window began to fade, the angel lights fizzling out in a shower of sparks, then blanked, black nothingness began to crawl up the insides of the murky barrel of the nave. Mandi, determined to know the darkness of God thrust her shoulders through the rood screen and with the last haunting of its image, Sidwella, perched on the wing of the congregation of saints, leaned in and sliced off Mandi's head with her spectral scythe. The head rolled along the carpet of the dark chancel and came to rest in a sea of teeth.

"Now," thought Mandi's head, "I will receive a great secret."

And the rows of teeth jingled as they replied: "treat everyone as you would want them to treat you."

"O, for fuck's sake," thought the head, "after all that, the same old hokum."

Mandi rang the Bay Museum. April was unavailable; out at a dig. It was the Lack of Engagement Officer. No, he could not divulge volunteers' phone numbers.

The Chairman of the Hexamerons had sent an email. The same image as before, but now angled so that the black sun looked more disc-like. A black frisbee. Mandi replied "wtf?" There was no response.

Coffee, for once, did not help. The thrill of authenticity of those first hallucinations had faded, the purity of initial contact lost. Mandi wanted April's practical help, though she suspected she was meant to do things alone. So much had been going on that she had forgotten to get drunk enough, deep enough, hopeless enough. Sure, she could admit to herself now that she had been in a bad way even before Anne and Bryan had died, but since all the drama in her head she had neglected to neglect herself; she had turned the world grey and sad and controllable. She wanted her scary angels and slimy monsters back.

Perhaps there was something in the house she had not found yet?

For hours she turned it over. She considered reassembling her rifle, but she had none of the vices, keys and other tools she needed. She had hoped to find some of her own clothes; maybe if she dressed as she had when she was seventeen, she could recover some of her wounded surliness? She took out all the drawers of the unit in which she had found the Lovecraft manuscript in the hope of finding something she had missed, she pulled up carpets and peeled back the edges of the 90s wallpaper. She scribbled down lists of the cans of food and bottles of booze, in case there was some exotic code at work in the order of their storage. She lay on the floor to look for messages on the ceiling. She had almost given up on finding anything when, flicking through the empty pages of a scrap book, she found a collection of drawings she had done as child. They were folded in half and wedged into the gutter of the book.

Mandi pored over the pastel drawings. They must have been drawn when she was six, maybe seven; a house, an elephant, an island with palm trees, an aeroplane, a sky with clouds. Mandi arranged them on the floor. Perhaps they were like a jigsaw puzzle? She poured herself a drink from an opened half-bottle of whisky. She contemplated cutting out shapes and making a collage. It seemed too brutal, too violent, but she did it. Not that it helped. The elephants were no less banal in juxtaposition than on separate sheets. If Mandi ever had good reason to cry, it was now, but she was not prepared to be swayed by reason yet; she was looking for something buried, not something you could think through.

She threw the whisky down the sink. She swept the paper creatures, outlines and machines into a pile, screwed them into a ball and lobbed them into the fireplace as tinder for a future blaze. She swooped on the remnants of the oily drawings, gathering their thin and floppy frames; hills, beaches, gateways, caves... drooping between her fingers... she paused and then carefully laid out the pieces once more, moving the leftover parts around, connecting the river to the sea, the house to the hill, the chapel to the cave. She opened a new bottle of whisky.

None of anything fitted, really. She knew she was making things up. The colours contradicted each other, the lines never matched, there was no flow from one scene to another, no continuity. She had bent the roads and paths and ladders into a writhing mess. There was a patchy geography; the clumsiness and ill-fitting junctions were like they were in real places. Real... places. Was that the pattern she was missing; that there was no pattern; how weird was that? There was always a pattern. But instead, she just had a mess left behind to find her way back through. A childhood has places, it happens somewhere and that somewhere had never been in this trailer home. Mandi had made another place, other places maybe, for her early years. God, the whisky was helping her. She had – this was typical of her – she had, even then, built the space of her own childhood. Her pattern was never – never! – the one made by her parents. The memory was still hazy, full of holes, but somewhere out there, beyond the camp, not far away she was sure, were places that she had found and adapted to her own... pattern... places where she had hidden herself and hidden things, gone to and done important stuff that her parents never got to find out about. These were places the whereabouts of which she had concealed so carefully that she had eventually forced herself to forget; anxious that she would not be strong enough to keep from giving the game away.

She still had no clear picture of routes; only a jumbled sense of unwanted and unloved spaces that she had occupied and nurtured, like the tangle of offcuts on the carpet. Damp and abject spaces that she had savoured and sunk into; safe spaces protected by their general unattractiveness. She was remembering fast, but the line of brown liquid inside the bottle was sinking alarmingly. It was coming back now, she did not have much time left. She had learned fast how adults, even most kids, would stay out of certain kinds of dark and dirty spaces, soft slimy spaces, spongy and odorous spaces; it was there that Mandi had built her incubators and chancels, and it was time to see if they were still there.

She crept through the holiday camp, skulking at the edges of the unoccupied trailers as though she were not their owner anymore. The car of one of the permanent residents turned into the camp and Mandy dived behind a barbecue flat-topper. Veering towards the permanent section, the hatchback's red brake lights flickered on like a blinking demon. Mandi emerged. Small things scared her. She was remembering now how they – who were 'they'? – had built ritual dens around the fringes of the camp, and told stories to each other of their own lives and their own world, without a heaven but a place for the dead that was just like this one, hidden in the woods inland and guarded by an angel army commanded by a blue lady, and where there was long grass as soft as the kind of bed that was advertised on TV. There were scary things too – how could she not have remembered all this before? – but they were basically the same as the good things. Yes, now she knew where to go.

The 'Everglades' stretched from the backs of the junkyards to the grey stream that crept along the edge of Lost Horizon. New water management systems had not affected it much; its waters refused to obey the usual laws of hydro-dynamics and rather than seeking lower ground they were loathe to move on to anywhere else, they hung around the Everglades for as long as they could. Seeping into the mushy loam and gruel-like humus they hid like an outlaw band in the spongy floor of the 'Everglades'. Where she got that name from she had long forgotten. Some self-deprecating humour on the part of a previous resort manager, maybe, or the bitter gibe of a visitor repeated by successive waves of guests. Maybe.

Black pools hung around the base of moss-ruined trees, the air stank and seemed to loaf, suspended, like rags on a fairy-tale beggar. Or scalded skin peeling from a shinbone. There was nothing inviting about the 'Everglades';

kids in the camps had whispered about leeches that could crawl inside your pants, earwigs that nested in real ears and drove people mad with pain. The less the strip of land was visited, the more inhospitable it became; the soft silky mud a few inches beneath the surface of the stream under the over-sized run-off pipe was full of tiny bugs with razor teeth, so thin and silvery was the silt it would drag you down and under in seconds; the cruel and mocking roots reaching from its vertical banks just daring their victims to grab at their rottenness.

On the other side of the grisly interlude of decay, various cast-offs and retired mannequins from carnival floats cluttered the fence of the junkyard, its wood long fallen away and replaced by broad rusting orange and blue wire meshes draped in tarpaulins. Ropes held a mass of cast-off things together. Posters drooped from their boards and signs from floats dissolved into pulp alphabets. Painted masks peeled and leered. The front quarter of a Bedford van had been strapped to the side of a shed. It was unclear whether any of the yards constituted actual businesses. Or were hobbies run out of control.

Streams of vapour would occasionally rise from hardboard vents or tin can chimneys, but no one from the yards ever looked over the fence into the 'Everglades'.

As Mandi picked her way between splintered stumps, their shards shredded by dissolution in the heavy air, a rhyme, sung in a freakish falsetto, drifted through the trees.

'Muddy Mary mother of God,
Killed the Old Boy in his bath,
God went to Hell
And started to smell,
And now all the bad things are back!'

The singer had been expecting her. Calling to her. He stood, his feet apart, hands clasped behind his back; he might have looked vaguely military if it were not for his obvious discomfort.

"Did you call me back to here?"

"No.... did you feel called?"

He looked about thirty. One of those adult-children; although his clothes were not absurd, they hung on him like parasites. He had the kind of frame that could make an Enzo D'orsi suit look ill-fitting. His eyes were muddy and watery, his lips full and clumsy, his hair had been disciplined by an angry barber and the grey-brown mud had crept up to his shins.

"I had to come... my ... there was an accident, I had to arrange the funeral... who are you, that you're so interested?"

"Don't you recognise me?"

"No. Help me out, why don't you?"

"We played here as kids. Twenty years ago, exactly. Right here. Do you remember now?"

"No."

She made to tell him to clear off, that he was on private property, that they didn't need stalkers and creeps and that he was lucky it was winter and there were no holiday kids around otherwise she would be calling out the police on him. But a dark blankness opened up and it smelt of the same decay as that underfoot; she tried to fix on a single childhood memory. She knew that if she could, the memories would roll out like scrolls with befores and afters, in a long line of days. But the anchor point, the catalyst refused to come; the silence sank like wings folding over the past.

"My name's Edward Mann, but I was always called Eddie then. Most people do that now, actually, even though they know (he said "now") I prefer Edward, but I'm stuck with Eddie."

"Well, Eddie, I don't remember that name or an Edward..."

"O, I wouldn't have been an Edward then..."

"Well, I don't remember an Eddie, so I reckon that gives you two minutes to convince me and then let's say we leave the reunion for another twenty years?"

"You were a magician, Amanda, not a stage one with tricks, but a... real thing, actual spells, a whole myth you discovered in the Everglades..."

"You know it's the Everglades?"

"You remember?"

"I do actually... why would we have called this place the Everglades? It stinks."

Eddie shrugged, his anorak hood stood up like an exclamation mark above his head.

"You really came here twenty years ago... or so?"

"From Dudley." (He pronounced it "Dud-lay".) "The whole family, but I was the only one to play in here. Of our family. There were other kids from other families. We came here three years on the trot, then... something put my folks off and we went to Minehead after that. No Everglades in Minehead."

Mandi could hear the angry calls of birds above the treetops. The thick canopy obscured what kind of birds they were. They sounded like her London bosses; yelling at the tops of their voices because they were too permanently freaked out to do anything quietly powerful. A greenish steam lifted off from the surface of a caravan roof visible above the dummies and tarps; a moth-eaten pirates' flag fell limp against its cricket stump pole.

Eddie Mann described the rituals through which Mandi had once led him and the other Brummie holiday kids. He began to describe "the big picture" that they had all believed in back then and Mandi dimly recollected something like that; a myth they had concocted from overhearing stuff from parents and other kids she had spied on from the Everglades.

"I do remember that we put together some wild story..."

"No, only you, Amanda. Only you put it together. The rest of us were your magpies; the rest of us kids were, some of us, channelling bits of something, but you had the lot – the whole thing down. Like a religion."

"OK. I remember some of this. You have another ten minutes. Pitch it to me."

Eddie Mann settled against the rotten stump. He grinned.

"Are you sure you (he pronounced each "you" as "yow") don't remember this?"

Mandi screwed up her face; for once she was choosing a long silence.

"OK, well... it was our beliefs, right? Our manifesto, if you like ("loik"). We were kids. It went something like this. It didn't all come at once. You learned it off of things we'd heard, things we saw, things adults say when they don't think kids can hear. You used to hide in these woods for hours waiting for some couple to come walking by, repeating stuff they'd heard. Then you told us. You stitched it all together. We brought some of the bits, but you made the whole story out of them."

"I don't remember that. I remember being here, I remember the dens and stuff. But stitching together, what did I stitch together?"

"You ("Yow" again) made it into one big story. How God was murdered by his mother..."

"What!"

"Yes! That's what you told us."

"I told you God was killed by his mother?"

"Murdered. You were quite clear about the details. He was in his bath. She grabbed Him by the ankles when she was kissing His toes; He never knew what hit Him, the shock made Him breathe in the bathwater and He never came round. They hung Him up on a post. When the ropes slipped they nailed Him to it, but He rotted and began to slip down."

"That's sick. How come his mother did that?"

"She heard that God had turned aeroplanes into bombs, light had gone bad like old bananas and that was His doing as well, she was crazy, because He had put messages inside soaps..."

"Like microbeads?"

"Like in Corrie, and Eastenders..."

"Ah, that kind..."

"God's mother said she was going to wash God in darkness, and when He refused to let her she murdered him. Jesus went crazy and tried to get rid of the body in Hell, but that scared all the demons and the criminal masterminds and the torturers and the Moors Murderers and they ..."

"Stop right there. The Moors Murderers? They weren't dead in... whenever it was you were on holiday here, 1999 or whatever..."

"Who said anything about Hell being only for dead people? You told us it was mostly the evil living. And they wanted out, God's corpse was stinking out the place, so these portals started opening up on Earth and the evil started coming through..."

"This doesn't sound much like a message of hope..."

"Ah, but it is! Mucky Mary, the murdering mother of God, lived in a swamp..."

"Mucky Mary?!?"

"or Muddy Mary, or Murdering Mary... she lived in a swamp... called the Everglades, under the mud, near the posts of rotting flesh, one with the flat top and one with the point, but she couldn't escape because the mud was a kind of quicksand, and the more she tried to get out the deeper she sank down and down into the darkness..."

"This is not uplifting! But great story anyway!"

"It's not a story. It's a place. The Everglades is real. The story is about here. It's the spirit story of this place. In the same way people have souls, you were told the spirit story of here, like some people are a medium and get to hear the stories from dead souls. You told us that Mary was still here in the mud, and that she still had a call on the angels and she sent them to take down the bombers from the sky. But it all went wrong, the bombers crashed into a city and the wrong people died. The angels screwed up. Even those on holiday were crying; they left the beaches and went to the bars to watch the TVs, the same programme over and over and over again. That night everyone sat outside their cabins, because they were scared that the planes would come for them, come for their little buildings. Everything on the planet changed. The angels covered the portals to Hell with their wings, to stop any more evil pilots getting into this world; even when it meant leaving their burning skeletons across the mouths of the portals like bone cages. Every time a bomb went off, it would have been much worse but for the angel that had wrapped itself around the bombs; they were picking up flesh and feathers for months after. Thanks to Mucky Mary and her angels, the Earth was just hanging on, but the demons, master criminals, Moors Murderers and evil pilots were always trying to break through from Hell..."

"That was about twenty years ago... Hell is below here?"

"No. Here is good all the way down. There are good places that are pure springs, you told us. Even though they don't look like it. This wasn't here until you started hearing the stories, and then here... developed. It works both ways.

Story is a kind of place, you said, made by imagination, story made this place from deep in the planet like a spring makes a well; and the place made the story. The floods came one year and the camps were all like lakes with water up to the doors and inside the kitchens, and the next year they dug out the stream and the Everglades were born, between the stream and the junkyard. Even though it had been here forever, in a way, it needed the floods to give it... birth... physical shape! You said that we can map these places out. And you said that they were growing; Everglades type places. The more that people believed in pretend stories, the more pretend that was shown on the TV, the more confused people got between the truth and the lies, the bigger our places would grow, the deeper our mud would sink and the more that Mucky Mary would be recognised. Mucky Mary who loved children so much she would eat them and they would re-form in her belly and she would spit them out as angels. The more children that are hurt, the more Mary searches for them, to turn them into angels, with real feathers."

"Wow. I made all this up?"

"You didn't make anything up. You were told. Or you heard."

"This Mucky Mary? Do you think that was about a real person?"

"Not a person. She goes back a very long way; further back than people. You told us she was very, very, very old, and yet she was also very sexy. Way back when the bread was real and there was water in fountains, you said, she seduced ... you didn't say that word exactly, but that's what you meant... my mind has changed, I've become a... a adult, since... she seduced the old rubbish God, the original one, who made everything symmetrical and full of rules, corners were all like the corners of a square and everything was perfect, except for people, who were either monsters or disabled, and flowers and trees which were monsters too in a way, there was no beauty even though there were perfect rules. The rules ground up everything into mincemeat. Mucky Mary introduced curves into the universe and winding rivers and worms, snakes, dragons and intestines and ever since then God has been mad on science and proving everything he did was real, and trying to put the tubes back in the bottle. Mother Mary hid in the sea. I don't know what you meant by that, but "trying to put the tubes back in the bottle" is what you said. You have any idea?"

"None. This universe?"

"Yes, God was really furious with it. The angles kept turning into ladies..."

"Angles? You mean angels?"

"Ah... now... I forget parts... I've told these stories to myself, repeated every word every night now, before sleep, since the holidays back then, but I do a lot of other things, now. Ufos. Aliens. Steam locomotives, I'm part of a voluntary... I go to a day centre. I like football. I get mixed up."

"Can we forget aliens and steam locomotives for a moment?"

"Sure. No aliens. No steam trains. Because everything you ever said has been true."

"What do you think this Mucky Mary looks like?"

"Like you, maybe? You said that when the stories begin to be more important than the news, when people become confused and hypnotised, when real and not real are mixed up, then She will come back again."

"And I came back, here, and you think..."

"I don't think. I repeat. I'm only telling you what you told me. Except that you said that Mary would come from the mud and she would have eight arms and eight legs."

"Right..."

Mandi threw her arms wide, palms out, as if to say: "and where's my other six?"

Eddie shrugged.

"That was then, when she was the Deep's thing. Now, whenever someone tries to revive the old God, and make rules of pure consciousness, She rises from the depths and wraps her legs with tearing teeth round them and pulls them in pieces. That is what you said..."

"And I was how old?"

"You were standing right where you are now, and me right here. 1999. All of this, in one big story just like today, and you said at the end 'don't forget that' and I never did, so help me Mary, cross my heart and I hope to die."

"Why did you come back to The Sett, Eddie?"

"I stopped liking it in Birmingham. People at the club talking about this amazing time to come when we're out of the Common Market and I just thought 'Mucky Mary is not going to like this, Mucky Mary is not going to put up with this' and I thought I better get down there and show her that I'm not like the rest; I'm the same way pretty much as you made me in 1999."

As Mandi picked her way back to the camp, balancing on the slippery run-off pipe across the stream, she thought she heard Eddie speak; turning, precariously, she saw he was down on his knees. He was too far away for his words to carry clearly, but she thought they were these:

"Hail Muddy Mary, full of dirt and scum, the Old Boy is dead. Blessed is you number one among all the old girls in the earth; blessed is the crab apple from your guts. Holy Muddy of Mud, pray for us, the disconsolate ones, now at the hour of our earthing. And amen down there."

What unholy mess was this?

She went back across the pipe and collected Eddie. She found him an empty caravan and let him in, promising to return with hot food and whisky. She was as good as her word, and through the evening Eddie and Mandi talked of what exactly the thing under the mud might be like.

Chapter 53

Mandi poured a third coffee from the filter jug, its dark contents mixing in the morning's fogginess. She needed to get to town and find somewhere that would sell her a Smeg espresso machine. She flicked through the book April had lent her: 'The Iron Age in Devon'; a thin tome, on the cover an aerial view of "Clovelly Rings" (it said). Inside were numerous plan views of hill forts; as the caffeine took effect she felt herself dropping down into the middle of these, the contours were the uneven ripples from her fall. Mandi wondered how plan views would strike the people who built the forts; thin black lines on flat cream paper from monumental structures of earth?

Mandi stared into the murky coffee. She was out of her depth. Archaeology, ancient history. Sure, she had a broad picture, school, documentaries, Mary Beard and over-excited over-groomed young women who seemed perpetually surprised that studying Classics had led them hyperventilating into ruins chased by a cameraman. She was already structuring the blog post. Mandi knew the progression of ages, approximately. Stone, Bronze, Iron, which made no sense; bronze sounded so much more progressive than iron. Anything she knew had been sieved through the preoccupations of her bonkers parents and their repurposing of hedges and barrows, mounds and forts to fit their version of spirituality. Mandi had become nostalgic for her parents' speculations; where others saw monuments eroded almost to nothing, such smoothed shapes were 'blindingly obvious' to Bryan. But that was not April's archaeology.

Mandi played them against each other. On the one side, April speculating on the beautiful and mysterious layering of bones and different soils, her father ardently numbering Druidic rights and their duty to repeat the rituals of the sun. Mandi warmed to the way April always stopped short of a conclusion; as if she were drawing Mandi into making one of her own, until Mandi turned away, and then the dance would move on. Their tentative waltz in stark contrast to her father's certainties. The career archaeologist seemed much more at home with mystery than the mystics.

Thinking of April was something that Mandi caught herself doing a lot since their first meeting. Did she fancy her or something? It was an unusual "fancy-ing" in that it had no component of physical attraction, infatuation or identification. She had no fantasies of bodily intimacy with April. In surveys she would always leave the 'sexual orientation' box blank; in her head she was fashionably rather than authentically bi. Sheer weight of bodies suggested she write "boys". But Mandi found herself delighted at the idea of being with April, delighted by their conversations, delighted by the delicious things that April shared with her; she caught herself inventing ways that they might meet more often. For a moment she thought of Googling "crush", thought the better of it, did it anyway and recognised herself in every stupid detail.

Mandi looked at her phone. She counted the texts they had exchanged. She scrolled back and re-read some recent ones. Aware that she had done that last night as well. Looking for signs that April liked her. It felt so weak. A hand on an arm when April was excited to show Mandi something. The hug at the end of the last walk. Was there a secret trade in their confidences? But this was ludicrous. If someone liked you, in that way, it got explicit quickly. Sometimes brusque, sometimes charming, but always obvious. And there was nothing obvious about April. Christ! The woman was an enigmatic work of art! Fuck, thought Mandi, had she maybe been "friend zoned"? Which, of course, would be fine. Which, of course, would not. Because she didn't fancy April in that way, but because she did fancy her in some other way.

"O, get a fucking grip. Grow up."

She finished the coffee in her cup; optimistically pouring away the rest of the jug. She put whirling thoughts of April to the back of her mind and started to look forward to meeting up with April later that day at the Museum's archaeological dig near the Great Hill. Whatever it was she thought about between the last gulp of caffeine and arriving at the site, it vanished into the glowing blue sky and the phosphorous green fields above which floated a massive bulbous figure. Mandi saw it clearly. Distantly at first, moving slowly over the folds of landscape that stretched southwards from the hill fort. The air still; the birds holding their breaths. The figure was about sixty feet tall. Female and naked. Its breasts and belly were grotesquely exaggerated. Not a good look, Mandi thought. As it approached, she saw that the head lacked a face, just horizontal rows of dots. The legs were shrivelled and pointed. It would not stand upright in the fields. It floated closer to Mandi. It was out of place. Made by human minds and hands. It was not meant to be here. It was not meant to be at all. How did she know this? The people here had once rejected this figure. But here it was again. Now looming close to where Mandi sat. When the waters began, flowing down the insides of the figure's legs, stained red, they poured onto the green fields, washing away the trees and topsoil, revealing a whitish limestone. The waters persisted and ate away at the stone, burning grotesque cavities out of the reluctant bedrock. Fizzing and gurgling. Caves were formed; and from the caves, Mandi saw swarming creatures: eyeless pink salamanders, emerging unblinking into the light, their skin scorching in the sunlight.

"This is yours, Mandi?"

It was not. Mandi felt keenly, indignantly, that this was not hers. She looked up into the branches of the hazel against which she was resting, to see what bird had spoken out of turn.

"Mandi, your hat, you must have dropped it."

April threw the broad brimmed straw hat into the air and deftly caught it, before skimming it into Mandi's lap.

"You were well gone."

"Must have been…"

April sat beside Mandi. Mandi felt a creeping silliness come on and feared it.

"Great view from here. I was talking to a colleague about the idea of view sheds. Like a watershed, but instead a boundary formed according to how far you can see. You can use it to think about what natural boundaries we might share with former cultures, other cultures, no need to get too linear. About time?"

Mandi started to come round. The caretaker had dropped her off at the hill fort; he had borrowed a truck from one of the pagans to fetch a new tow bar. Mandi had walked to the meeting point and dozed off.

"You're worried about linear time because I was early?"

"Well, sweetie, I know you have temporal issues. Maybe if you thought of your appointments more in terms of nested events, different durations, some quick, some slow, hugely slow… the longue durée…"

"Nested events? What are they when they're at home?"

"Traditionally historians think in terms of discrete periods of history, with beginnings and ends…"

"That's how I like meetings. With an end."

"Think bigger. Bronze Age, Iron Age, Medieval Period, so on. There's a temptation to see these as absolutely fixed…"

"Is there?

"Among the old school, there is. In popular discourses, absolutely. It's so convenient! The different periods all have features by which they can be defined. Time's arrow! They all follow one another along a single trajectory. No one is arguing with that per se; well some eccentrics… but what if that trajectory is only ever one layer of the reality? Within each grand period there are shorter events; Athelstan kicking the Britons out of Exeter, Athelston having lunch…"

April smiled. How old was she? Mandi looked at April's shining face and it flickered. She had seen her do that before; like a screen when the signal scrambles. She could be early twenties or almost fifty. Her face stapled together different kinds of experience, different "events", the same as her theory.

"Then there are longer time scales. The longue durée of, say, human cultural development around the Mediterranean over thousands of years. Or the duration of human consciousness? They both enfold us… we are part of immediate ongoing processes, the two us right here, that also take in the folk that walked these fields fifteen hundred or two thousand years ago."

She is both older and younger than me, thought Mandi, she stands on both sides of me at the same time. I am being triangulated.

"Like music?" Mandi offered, not knowing where she was going with this.

"What do you mean?"

"I'm not sure..."

"Go on, it might be interesting."

"Well, music can be seen as a melody, right. Or melodies... as notes following each other. That's like what you're calling an old school linear view of history. And sure, there are probably repeating phrases, refrains, the same tempo for a while, but basically, it's one note after another. What you're saying is that there are harmonies too. Not just the journey along the horizontal, but there's a vertical dimension... layer, simultaneously... that resonate, above or below the melody are other notes, which heighten or disrupt the effect of the melody. And... not sure where this is going... but all the notes are parts of the larger structure of the whole piece? Sonata or symphony or whatever... You study the individual melody, but unless you can hear the harmonies, or the atonal whatever it is..."

If this wasn't love, why was she being such a fool?

"...the relationship between the note, the event, the whole and how it resolves, lingers across a wave of longer time ... what did you call it? Have you heard Morton Feldman's four-hour pieces? He said that beyond a certain point everything loses meaning but time itself..."

"I'm sure his audiences agree!"

"They probably do!"

Mandi didn't quite know where this had all come from. Or indeed what she really meant. OK, the Morton Feldman reference was unnecessary. She wanted April to know that she was not shallow.

April smiled.

"I'm not sure I follow? Say it again?"

Mandi flustered. For fuck's sake, she always knew exactly what she meant. Crystal Clarity could be her stage name. Now she was rambling. About music, the sum total of her knowledge of which she had condensed into her first attempt...

Her adoptive father had always wanted to be known for knowing. He idolised "the great writers". Crowley of course, Waite, Levi, Gardiner, Fortune, Valiente, Starhawk, Cunningham, Spare, and, latterly, Hutton. He liked to talk about them as if he were on nodding terms; probably wanted to be them, be as eloquent as them, do things they did. It was important that others regarded him as an expert. Thing was, Mandi could not be certain that he would not have been just as happy to be an expert in model railways or dog breeds; the important thing was being "the expert". Yet he never published anything, words always failed him. Before she found her own hectoring voice, she had idolized great thinkers in the fields in which she moved: Goldmann, Hayek, Rand, Camus… more recently, Wendy McElroy; McElroy was Mandi's 'Ronald Hutton'. She was fiercely proud of her understanding of these geniuses. It put capital in her bank. To not know. To fail to understand. That was unthinkable. Later on she realized that the real trick was not letting on that you knew, but appearing to come up with these ideas on your own. To act the individualist you had to become one. Sure, she couldn't pretend to understand the further reaches of physics or whatever, but she was a Right Woman. She might make a mistake now and again, but she was never wholly Wrong. Rightness defined her, drew her boundary; her Rightness. She was the expert in the Rightness of Mandi Lyon, and April was simply not getting it; and being April, she wanted to get it. So it was that Mandi found herself, on a hill above a deep pink excavation site pitted with oozy cavities, talking shit. It was embarrassing.

"Oh, it's just… it's j..j..j…"

Mandi stammered. She didn't even know she could stammer. Why was she frightened? Was she frightened? Having mostly forgotten what it was she said in the first place, she was struggling to know how to say it in a different way.

"It's …"

April leant in to listen; her chequered shirt billowing. A long white feather fell from her shoulder.

"Hey, look at that," said Mandi. She picked up the feather; relieved to find a lever to change the subject.

"Must have picked it up on my walk up here earlier," said April, taking it back from Mandi.

"It's lovely, what kind of bird is that?"

April shrugged and flickered.

"Let's have a wander down to look at the dig, eh? I can introduce you to Charlie, the county archaeologist, and some of the more… grounded volunteers."

The excavations had been triggered by a find in a field close to the base of the hill fort. An ornate bracelet turned up by a detectorist; local controversy had ensued. The well defined line between professional and amateur shivered for a while: the pros fretting over people just doing what they wanted, amateurs waiving codes of conduct and excited by the chance of getting one over on the Academy. An old story revolving like a prayer wheel. The modest bracelet, originally assumed to be Roman, marked a Dumnonian settlement on a Roman road; it was, to a degree, re-writing what archaeologists knew not only of the extent of Roman occupation west of Exeter (Isca Dumnoniorum), but also of the entwining of occupiers and occupied.

"Nothing was ever written about the Devon Dumnonii by the Romans," explained Charlie, peering over a pair of half moon glasses he could have picked up at the BBC Drama costume store; an academic from Exeter, clearly excited by the prospect of new discoveries. "So all we know we have to deduce from finds like these."

"And what do they tell you? About who the people were? The D... Romano-British, what did you call them?"

"Dumnonii. That, of course, is the name the Romans gave them; what name they gave themselves we don't know. Whatever their name, they were the people who were here when the Romans arrived; how long before? Hard to say; the assumption once was that these people arrived as a result of a single violent invasion, sweeping out the previous inhabitants, but that was an assumption based on our own colonial habits; the evidence suggests some quite complex arrivals and settlement; perhaps as a result of a climate-based agricultural failure. A few travellers arrived, found a land with a plenitude of empty space and few locals, the word was sent back to Europe and more people came..."

He shrugged.

"We don't know. After the Romans left, the Dumnonii continued as before, building the same kinds of homes, on the same sites, until the Saxons arrived. Thanks to them, and their religion, what remnants of the old Dumnonian culture that might have survived within Celtic-Christianity, so called, were probably... he shrugged, well we don't know. The one thing you can say for sure about the Dumnonii is that we don't know much about them.... They left their marks in the landscapes, the hill forts, so called, they are a bit of a mystery, no evidence that they were actually forts, possibly more like market places or holding spaces, store rooms... or I hate to say it, ritual spaces... the fort here..."

He nodded to the trees that hid the fort on the top of the Great Hill.

"...has two large burial mounds within the fort, but they were put there by the people who were here a thousand years before the Dumnonii. The Dumnonii seem to have honoured those graves, didn't destroy them, yet they built none of their own, don't seem to have gone in for ritual buildings or monuments... left very few artefacts. At least, we haven't found many. Hardly any jewellery, no coinage – they didn't have a currency, money-free! – the bracelet we found here..."

Mandi noticed that the lone detectorist had been submerged in Charlie's narrative.

"...is an anomaly; a copy of a Roman design, made by Dumnonii probably for sale to Romans."

Mandi thought of the Dartmoor Pixie figures she had collected as a child.

"Given its position right on a Roman road, this might be the late Iron Age equivalent of a motorway services. But then that's the kind of dumb, populist analogy that can hide what was unique or distinctive about the Dumnonii. Works on television, though."

He smiled at April.

"Charlie's been working on a documentary for BBC Four…"

"Here. Have a look at this."

Charlie handed Mandi a plastic bag with some rough looking sandy coloured pottery pieces. With Charlie's encouragement, she extracted a large pink shard with a simple jagged line.

"This is theirs."

"From two thousand years ago?"

"Give or take a few lifetimes…"

Holding the simple ceramic Mandi felt sensation running up and down her forearm; as if the zig-zag pattern in the clay had translated directly into vibrations in her body.

"Contrast that with some of the Phoenician ware we've found."

The piece of Mediterranean pottery Charles held up was smooth and subtly decorated. Marks of a culture that could afford, and value, surplus in design. April took the piece of Dumnonian pottery from Mandi and, rather than the tingling ceasing, Mandi felt the ripples released from her forearm and running into the tops of her legs.

"They are a mystery," chimed April. "They minted no currency. Built no temples. They lived in dispersed settlements, not even villages. They perhaps had either no, or a very loose hierarchy, were possibly suspicious of displays of wealth…"

"I often wonder," Charles embroidered, "if one of the reasons there is so little tension with the Romans, for there's no evidence of them ever fighting each other, is that when the Romans taxed the slightly better off Dumnonii, the other Dumnonii were rather pleased about it! That's very British isn't it? We hate success, don't we! We like to pull down our idols…"

Mandi recoiled a little. She did not hate success, she cultivated and nurtured it. Charlie's clichés neutralised her thrilling. She thought momentarily of debating him, but not with April there. She didn't want to appear too strident in front of her…

How was April doing this? How could a Right Woman let anyone down by expressing herself?

The county archaeologist and April continued to explain things to Mandi, but she only heard their words in fragments that she tried to piece together later. She felt herself falling into a spell around April's voice rather than what it was saying. A mental picture of a Dumnonii who were like proto-hippies intruded. Mandi half remembered the cover of the Incredible String Band's

'Hangman's Beautiful Daughter' that her adoptive parents had in their room, but seemed never to play; those raggedy folk were Mandi's Dumnonii now.

"Fancy a wander?" April asked.

The two said their goodbyes to Charlie, who was poring over some old maps with a group of local volunteers.

"Have fun, it's a funny old place this one," he called as Mandi and April left the dig and started down the lane towards the villages.

"It is a funny old place," April said to Mandi.

April stopped and began to outline the location of the villages in the distance, identifying them by their church steeples. Then pointed out each one on her ordnance survey map.

"The thing that always gets me with this landscape, is how difficult it is to find your way round. I've been coming for a few years, and I still have to think really, really carefully how to get from, say, Denbury to Broadhempston. Worse still, how to find anywhere in Broadhempston itself! Nine roads in, eight roads out: that's what they say. I can believe it. Years ago, some 'League of Gentlemen' fan scrawled "you'll never leave" beneath the village sign. These places are so 'un-Saxon', so unconceptual, unpatterned, most of them lack the simple cross layout. And time is odd here, too. You can wander these lanes, or do a bit of field walking, and you'll utterly lose track of time. You never see anyone, either…"

"Unless, they're the hunt policing you…"

"The hunt 'politing' you… That was a moment! But there have been other days when I've walked here and not seen anyone hour after hour. And then there's that feeling you get sometimes…"

"What feeling?"

"Well, more than a feeling, but I'm not sure I know how to… it's a little weird, I haven't told anyone this…"

"Go on, you can't say that and not tell me!"

The thought that April would confide in her… to have something of her that no-one else had. That was like a relationship thing, wasn't it? Or a psychopath trophy bodypart collector thing, maybe? The squiggle on the pottery was enough for Mandi. She had very little idea of what "relationship" was, other than knowing that she had probably never actually had one. All her 'relationships' were events; there was never a longue durée.

"On a few occasions I've been walking this place and it's prompted these… Promise you won't laugh? The best word I can give you is 'visions'. It's not a mystical thing, but I sometimes slip into a dream-like state…"

"It sounds pretty mystical to me."

"Shuddup!" April laughed. "Thoughts occur, that's all. And many of them are of, and this is where you can laugh… goddess figures. Fat, unsexy… according to our values… archaeological artefacts. Sometimes, a bit sinister."

Mandi did not laugh. She wanted to immediately agree. To wade in and tell April all her visions. To shower her with the details. She held back. Did not want to do that "wow, I get that too all the time, we're obviously so…" thing.

"Sometimes they are like the Venus of Willendorf or the Venus of Hohlefels, these huge bulbous figures floating over the fields."

"No way, I…" O fuck.

"At other times they are vague feminine forms, shapes in trees that suggest a yoni… you know, those Hindu, yeh…. the trees up on the hill fort are full of them. And then, alongside these figures, I also get the sense of a dragon-like being. Not the Disney, 'Hobbit' type, but more like worms, slithery and tentacular. Moist things I see slipping in and out of the caverns."

"Freud!!"

"I know!! Whichever one I see, the Venus ones or these creatures, they always end up disappearing underground. And there's always water. Water seems very significant around here. As if it were exerting a huge influence on the imagining of the place. Does that sound too weird? It does, doesn't it? I would never tell Charlie."

Mandi was quiet. The place was giving rise to identical dreaming. Or April and she were.

"One line of thought," continued April, "goes that the Dumnonii get their name from a goddess called Domna or Dumna. Which roughly translates as the goddess of the deep. It could mean deep earth, or it could mean deep oceans. In my most un-archaeological moments, I wonder if I am picking up a subtler trace of something in this place. Something specific to it, its genius loci, a tutelary deity like the Romans had."

"You think it's Roman?"

"No. I think it's something the Romans might recognise, more than many a modern archaeologist would. Nothing in the standard training suggests giving any credence to fancies like this, but there are phenomenologists, non-representational theorists, it's not so out there, with the Ley hunters and the earth energy people. I am a human being, I'm here, I'm feeling. If I said I'm an archaeologist, I'm here, I'm analysing, that would be OK with more people in my field. So I do that. Feeling walks into my work, it does into everyone's work, but I'm recognizing it, honouring it. I think to myself 'I know this feeling, I know what this is'. I have to share that. My thinking and writing and publishing and teaching is becoming entangled in the moving of the detail and the vision. But I really worry about it, I try to keep focus, try to hold it all down in analytical patterns; that works most of the time, but some finds, some terrains only open up to feeling. This place is one, I don't know, you can only go so far with analysis, this place needs something else, but when you go further than analysis can take you, you, yourself, become something else…"

The two walked further, Mandi took a deep breath
"Can I tell you something now?"
"Something nice and straightforward?"
"Well…"
"O…"
Mandi paused, April leant slowly over towards her. Mandi shivered.
"Look at that again!"
April picked a large white feather from Mandi's back.
"Ha, now we both have one!"
The strange intensity was broken.
"What was it you were…?"
"Oh, it doesn't matter now, because, look at that view!"
Mandi and April stood now beneath an old oak at a crossroads. The sun
was low in the west, painting everything red: the distant church towers, glowing
fields of barley, the Great Hill.
"It's weird and beautiful," said April
Like you, Mandi was thinking. She wanted to hold April. Hold her hand,
her ear, any part of her. Just to hold on to her before she slipped away. Wrap
her arms around her, run her fingers through her hair before she evaporated,
like she had in the graveyard. Mandi had not dared to ask April where she had
gone. A kiss would not work; she needed a hold, a purchase. Mandi felt a huge
pressure on her chest, as if something were pushing right through her from her
backbone, a shove as solid as the granite tors. She looked up to where they stood
in the distance, the peaks silhouetted in the last of the sunset. She looked about
her. Where the hell had they come to? It would be night soon; there were no
signs, no one else about, like April said, there was nothing here; just her and
April. She couldn't do this. She was losing her head.
"C'mon," said April, "It's turned. We can walk down to the village and get
a taxi from there. I can get a train back from Newton Abbot. It's been a lovely
day, thank you."
A lovely day, thank you. Friend-zoned, totally. Why couldn't she say
anything? What the fuck was the matter with her? The village appeared out of
nowhere. Pub. Phone. Taxi. She had never been like this with anyone. Nine
roads in, eight roads out. If she wanted something, she always asked and she
could always take a "no". Now, she couldn't. April's train pulled out of Newton
Abbot; Mandi would rather say goodbye here and get her own train home.
April had given her a gentle hug before leaving, and promised to catch up with
her soon. Mandi asked when this might be, and immediately felt like the
mostly obviously needy woman ever. April said she would be back down in the
Bay area in a few weeks, and would text her. She sat alone on the platform. She
could think of nothing but April. She replayed over and over things April had

said, for a clue, a sign. It was desperate. "I'll text you in a few weeks". That was not good. A few weeks was an Iron Age, no small nested event. Pushing things would end in disaster, the knockabout democracy of tiny human beings. "I do like you, but…" She didn't even fancy April, but she absolutely wanted to connect with her. And the point of which was?

She reached for her phone, drafted a text to April and deleted it. The station PA announced the imminent arrival of the next train to Exeter; an express going North. April had caught the slow stopper; the express would overtake hers at The Sett. Mandi could catch this one and arrive in Exeter before April.

The train pulled in, Mandi got on. What was she doing? This was the sort of Hugh Grant thing from shitty 90s romcons before he got caught with Divine Brown at the kerb in LA. She tried to find an excuse – for herself, not Hugh Grant – by replaying April's descriptions of her visions. If April could describe the same visions as Mandi was having, maybe that was their connection; as characters in a metadrama still in development. She had to alert April, share her visions, tell her about the angels and the sea creature and the kayak and the flotsam shapes. To know if April knew more. If she was infatuated, so what? This went beyond that. This needed to be discussed. Now. Not in the next archaeological period. Feelings were a conspiracy, it dawned on her.

Seventeen minutes later, Mandi disembarked at St David's Station and hid in St Clements Lane, just outside the Brunel façade. April caught a taxi. Mandi was too nervous to take another and say "follow that cab". She wasn't even sure if the drivers would do that anymore. She hung about in the lane, checking her phone; no problem with a signal here. Almost a city. After twenty minutes April posted on Facebook; she was eating out at a vegan cafe, the Well. Mandi took a cab, flashing the café's homepage.

During the five-minute drive Mandi considered texting April to say she was coming up to see her. Passing under a daunting 1960s' municipal statue of a saint with a scythe, water bursting from beneath her feet. It was the same as on the Mary statue, when the messiah had tried to kill her. She had no good words, because there was no justification; no way to explain what was happening to her that was not a stupid romantic gesture. She would see the thing through.

The Well had an air of newness; the faces of the customers were bright, but uncertain. There was no routine. The smell of coffee and flowers was strong. Beyond the tables was the old well of pebbly red octagonal sandstone, set within a gaudy installation of plastic plants, animal murals, sparkly pond and glittered rabbits. It made a change from fish tanks and jam jars; not a good one, though.

April sat at a table, with her back to the door; Mandi went and stood directly behind her, hoping she would turn.

"April," Mandi said, her voice stuttering, "I came to tell you something…"

April turned. She didn't look in the least surprised to see Mandi.

"Pull up a chair, my dear, I wondered when you'd be here. You could have shared my cab. I've ordered you some food, they do a lovely Seitan burger. Do you like…"

"How did you… "

"I just did Mandi. It's OK. You have come here to tell me about your visions. Your visions of goddesses and angels and monsters. Of course you have. And you've come to tell me that you are strongly drawn to me and that you don't know why. And you'll find it really hard to explain yourself. I understand. Like when you tried to explain folded time earlier today, and you had started so promisingly… I'm trying to save you time and breath. Mandi, you'll make no sense in this conversation, and you'll end up running out of words. And if I tell you this, right now, hopefully we can sit quietly and enjoy our food? Right?"

April reached over and took Mandi's hand.

"Thing is Mandi, things are not as they appear."

The cafe might have been empty. Empty of people. Empty of sound. Empty of everything. Everything was now April. She seemed to fill the space into the corners and up to the roof. A feather fell to the table. Then another and another.

"I am not as I appear. I don't only see visions, I am part of them. That's why you feel you know me, that's why you feel so strongly connected to me."

Mandi lifted one of the feathers between the thumb and first finger of her left hand. She held it up to the electric light. In the light it disappeared, in the shadow it was there.

"An angel?"

April nodded.

"How can I be sure that what you are saying is real? Lots of people – gurus and people trying to sell books and conspiracy freaks and deluded people and mystics – they all use language like you; how do I tell if you're different from the other stuff?'

"Would this help?"

And with a grinding and cracking of bones, a splitting of gristle and a rending of cloth, and a sound like a driving gale, two giant feathered wings spouted from between April's shoulders and unfolded in great hinged sweeps, sending empty chairs clattering across the cafe floor, customers scrambling for the door and staff cowering behind the counter. No visionary wings, but actual ones. Feathers made of keratin. Wings that worked. They stretched to their fullest extent, sending filigree cracks through the plate glass in the building-length front window, knocking the generic works of the "local painter" askew and sending napkins and newspapers fluttering like small gatherings of white birds. The coffee aroma smelt better than Mandi had ever smelt coffee before; like when you read about coffee rather than drank it.

April smiled, and gently cupped Mandi's cheek with her right hand.

"Sidwella."

Mandi knew. April need say no more. The table at which they were sitting was swept away. Mandi stumbled backwards. April's wings began to close and warmth ran through Mandi's body; the great fans of feathers, bearing many wounds, about to close around her, whisk her away from her quest and transcend its mistakes and wrong turnings. A sharp shining burst of light issued from the chest of the winged priestess; despite its brightness Mandi felt no pain or wish to close her eyes. Instead, she looked into the angel's eyes, there was no light there, no light of any kind that Mandi recognised; instead there were small wells of darkness like coffee, the best coffee, coffee that was something, coffee that tasted and burnt and fed. Suddenly, the great wings shook like two white waves breaking against the foot of a cliff and they closed, with all their wounds, and a sound like the beating of giant arms upon the surface of the sea.

"Are you one of the Gurney sisters come back?"

"We are not envelopes, we are the message."

"You are their spirits?"

"There is no 'their' – we pass through 'their' and we are the passing through."

And then she had gone.

Mandi looked around, expecting to see the cafe returned to normal, but the cracks in the glass were there, the chairs were on their sides, the papers strewn, and the staff beginning to reappear over the counter top.

She heard April's voice: 'They will all tell the story according to their assumptions; some will have seen angry youths, others a raid by criminals, the worst will remember foreigners and unintelligible declarations. Only you saw me. Now you know that I am real, you know how you can see me again."

But the angel-priestess had gone. Only her chair, and her untouched cup of black espresso, somehow unspilled, though their table had slid to the opposite side of the room. Mandi waited for the accusations, but April was right; the customers and staff argued among themselves and soon none were sure what they had seen; beginning, even, to blame each other.

Mandi left three twenties on the counter and picked her way through the disorientated diners. She knew she had to make a journey. Now. There were three white statues in a graveyard. But she must find something new, somewhere new. The fourth place on the bonelines map. She had no idea why; the triple-nature of the sisters she had somehow grasped without being able to explain why. But there was something more. A fourth, closer to home.

As she left the cafe:

"Call the police."

"A bomb's gone off!"

Chapter 55

The long grey land was quiet. Only the dry winds whispered and spoke with the sea. In reply barrelling turquoise waves tipped their white peaked caps, but the land, in repose, was silent and still. The sun baked its greyness, but the land held its own. Mountains gleamed and valleys echoed with only a dim innuendo of water far away. If the surface cracked at all, the infrequent storms swept any dust into a hungry expanse of aqua and left the land perfect and barren again. Nothing rooted, nothing moved.

Beneath the waves the clouds of silt, longing for the bottom, were rarely left in peaceful descent. Long slithering shelled things fought in groping bouts, while heavier complexes clanked about, stabbing their tender-pointed spines at other armoured things. Sex echoed in dull jolts of water; things moved on. These beasts did not know their origins; aliens every one, their parents were unrecognisable. Their ancestors might be viruses, those aliens over there, or the last thing they ate... It was as if each family, each species could not rest from one generation to another, but birthed monsters every few years; weird things that were monsters even to monsters.

"It was ever thus" was the thought that communicated itself in the writhing of limbs and the reading of a giant mind that disappeared within them only to rise like a fleshy bulb refusing to flower, age after age, aeon after aeon, generating limbs on limbs, lophophores on lophophores, thinking and thinking, a bubbling, steaming heap of sulphurous sensitivity, a soft city, periodically writhing over an ocean floor at astonishing speed, throwing up clouds of distraction for the giants with tiny scratchy legs, cantilevered jaws and articulated tails. Softness could only prevail by incisive thought and environmental obfuscation; the patterns were laid down, like sediment, by the cephalogods.

Chapter 56

Like a bowed sentinel, the caretaker stood on the dunes and waited for a sign. An hour after giving up hope, but not determination – he knew that hopelessness was the best he could expect from this relationship – the caretaker lowered himself gently into the tall grasses as a single feeler shook itself in the foam at the water's edge. Its barbs were tangled with fishing line, a tampon applicator, faded crisp packets, kelp, a sprig of sea grass and a length of bright blue synthetic rope. The tentacle thrashed and the detritus was flung about the beach. Then it rose up like a cobra, menacingly. The caretaker knew what this was, and raising himself from his position, setting off orange avalanches, and raced across the hard sand towards the recovered and repurposed art.

The limb glistened; under a gelatinous membrane its colours circulated and its organs winked. It seemed to flop uncontrollably above the mess of flotsam; then with two swipes the lines of barbs flung the parts about and re-entangled them with each other; then the limb withdrew across the sand, through the breaking waves, and back to whatever mass it was a part of.

"I still love you!" shouted the caretaker at the wake left by the limb's submergence. "I know you are coming! I know you are writing to me! I'll wait for you!"

The sea was as silent as the Cambrian surfaces, even the tiny waves paused. The millpond sheen was grey and featureless. No dolphins played, no cormorants hunted. Nothing broke the enigmatic dullness. It would not last for long, the caretaker thought to himself. His premonition was shared; shared by the place. The spit where he had stumbled on the mermaid-angel-priestess thing and fallen into its arms, fins, wings and feelers. The sands onto which his daughter has been born. He looked down at the mess of rubbish and pollutant. The message was clear. He looked to the horizon. One more day and then all the power and life out there would come to wash this place away.

Chapter 57

1352

The priests and monks had appeared as the sun was rising over the Great Hill. The storm from the night before was still washing down the valley and fell in tired sheets over the face of the small cliff. The first smudge of dawn buffed the bright colours of stowaway flowers in abandoned fields. The priests roused the vicar from his cot and dragged him to the small wooden church that was warping already in the first beams of sunlight. Throwing him down at the altar, they insisted on mass immediately; watching and listening like sparrow hawks as he recited the Latin, elevating the host, mixing the cup, alert to any hesitation or alteration from the orthodoxy. The body and blood duly transubstantiated and consumed, the vicar was despatched to the fields to find volunteers – his vestments feared in the fields as vehicles of plague – and an hour later the staggered crossroads that linked the cluster of homes with the farm at Tornewton, the religious house in the valley and the old Roman settlement at Ipplepen was busy with disgruntled but curious labourers, fearful of the arrival of the powerful farmers, already furious and out of pocket with the falling away of labour under the Death. None came. Instead, an enervated priest in cloak and vestments, flanked by broad-shouldered monks in habits and cowls, harangued the men in an untranslatable Cambridgeshire accent about their wives' devotion to "proud and disobedient Eve and unchaste Diana", excoriating the men of England in general and the Torbryan labourers in particular for their love of "heathen Latin and Germanic deities". Then the monks, pushing the Devonian labourers in the back, horded them through the farmstead and past the church to the low and sulky cliff of shining limestone, sparkling in the sunlight, receding to barrenness where it dried, the old Cambrian wasteland returning. In the valley a solitary cow wandered, lost and unattended.

As the men were shuffled off along the valley, their wives and eldest daughters were led, no less roughly, into the church, where, beneath the complaining beams, the vicar demanded confession. The women hesitated, then refused as a weird grumbling grew from within them, ready to blame each other for the sufferings of their neighbours. Their mouths seemed not to move, and yet a chorus of complaint began to fill the dull wooden box. The lower clergy from the bishopric stood guard at the door. Outside, a group of monkish enforcers were preparing the instruments of shaming. A fire was lit and fed from the wooden grave markers in the yard. The vicar insisted and the women stiffened; Catharyne, who was prone to moments of mystical ravishment, fell rigid as a door, crashing to the trampled earthen floor, a trickle of treacly ooze escaping from her rictus. The women began to swirl, like a crowd in a vortex; a dance that decussated the solid form of the church, their feet in swinging patterns, arms aloft and then sweeping the ground, Catharyne stiffly at their centre, as around her the other women flopped and rose with the dry smoothness of slow worms.

The lower clergy, unnerved, barricaded the door; the monks gathered, their scapulas steaming under sun and fire, burning torches held to the sky. When smoke was seen seeping under the door, the clergy tried to dismantle the barricade, but the monks threw the clergy aside and jammed the latch, hurling their torches onto the roof. God would sort out the bones of the priests from those of the witches. Inside, the dance had halted. The women were entranced by the coils of smoke that wove above their heads; they gave a collective sigh; it sounded like resignation, as if they had expected a moment like this.

Barberae, the eldest daughter of the one-armed Loveday and the rigid Catharyne, casually opened the portal that she and few others knew was there, always there, had ever been and ever would be there. The tunnel they would talk about in the pub for centuries, yet never bother to open, too pleased with their tale to live it. Barberae split the boards apart and slipped down between the two layers of the church wall, lowering herself into the darkness, her fingers moulding to the imagined handholds, her prehensile toes reading the smooth and uneven floor like the fingers of a seer. The women followed in a flood. The vicar and the foreign clergy feared to follow into Sheol, rushing to the door where they fought with the monks to loosen the latch; their educated voices too effeminate to convince the monks that this was no female trick. The walls began to burn, the monks began to fear the consequences and planned a local massacre; they could depart the valley silently and discreetly, leaving nothing but misfortune, abandoning one more of the mysteries of God's taking. He was a shifty, tentacled beast, they knew, but never said.

The women emerged from the darkness of the tunnel into the back of the cave, just as the labourers, under the guard of the cowled monks, hiding who knew what buboes beneath their habits, arrived at the door of the chapel along the ankle-breaking incline. The sickly priest had begun to hand out drills, chisels, wedges and mallets from a pile already in place at the chapel arch. The women flooded around the painted altar and poured out into the valley, dancing and whirling. The monk-police were monetarily nonplussed; the labourers threw up their tools like weapons and the priest staggered. A shepherd from the cliff top howled derisive warnings and Barberae froze his cries with a single stony glance. The Broadhempston boy stood stock still, lost his footing and plunged into the limestone teeth below, a red star on the rock.

The monks were galvanised, the labourers confused and their tools dropped to their sides. The priest, seeing a chance, began to yell Latin exorcisms and wave his iron cross.

Urrsula, the most finely dressed of a rough crowd, commanded the youngest to follow her and they began to march, a procession of girls, backwards towards the stone chapel pillars. Did they think they could hide in the blues and greens of the altar? The working men, a moment before up in arms against the monks, now took orders from them and began to shuffle before the chapel. The priest continued to recite and wave his cross; its metal smelt of blood as it soaked in the acidy sweat of his palm. The women were soon surrounded; their pleas to fathers, brothers and sons falling on frightened minds. The labourers, commanded by the priest, closed in, holding the drills and wedges up before their faces, hiding their shameful excitement.

Then the desecration began. The men were ordered to the roof of the sacred arch and forced to beat it down with hammers, then to drive their wedges, drills and chisels into the holy orifice itself bringing down shower after shower of limestone chips as the arch to the shrine began to fill up with spill and the oak altar heaved and broke under the weight of falling stone.

The women churned; they began to dance in a tightness, curling in on themselves, as if they were dragging up a whirlpool in reverse. The priest's liturgy faltered for a moment; a mere trip upon a difficult word. The formation of women opened like a flower and Eresabet emerged like a pod, opening her serge cote-hardie to reveal a body made of pink roses, drawn by hand in the red of the fields. The village patriarchs and their sons, seeing the drawings, dropped their drills and wedges, scrambled down the cliff and fled, throwing away their hammers as they sped through an abandoned field turning to meadow. The monks gave chase, but abandoned it and instead quickly gathered what quarry tools they could for the battle ahead.

The oldest of the labourers, last in the retreating mob, cast a glance back to the old grotto and stopped mid pelt, framed by the burning village, and yelled.

"Margrete!"

His eldest daughter, stood with her back to the chapel-cave, her loose cote-hardie flapping like the wings of a strange slug from the depths, her girdle fallen away. Her face transfigured as if she saw a blue heaven in the green field.

"Margrete!"

The great neck of arms rolled out from the cave and took her. The writhe of limbs opened up in a maw and sucked her down; her eyes were last to disappear. They left a glint on the sheen of the creature's hundred tongues; its limbs blushed like flames. The women knelt before the tentacles. A few monks vomited, others fainted away. The wrung priest felt his alb rise, his excited member pushing the tunic material before him.

The thing spat. The priest shrank back. Many of the women hid their eyes. The priest, his erection withering as quickly as it had risen, expecting a jumble of limbs as oozy and inarticulate as the mound of tentacles, but it was a whole and transfigured Margrete who emerged from the thrashing and gyrating mass. Covered in mucus, she shone bright white in the mid-morning sun, the pupils of her eyes blanched colourless like their orbs, a visionary expression on her face. Her hair gone silvery blonde.

The priest, tumescent again, edged towards the thing. To him, he imagined, had been given this special moment by God the Father, for He had sent the Holy Womb to be crowned by him, Grimbaldus. Taking a fern he bent its long stem into a rough crown shape and advanced on the writhing, with his left hand stripping off his scapula and tunic and kicking off his chequered shoes. Grimbaldus, with a thin and varicose arm, raised the green crown to the thing; and with an inadvertent shudder the thorny teeth along the sucker pads of its thickest arm reduced the priest to a pile of sullen pieces; his mouth and throat and lungs too slow to cry out, his last words buried under a mound of bits. Elena, the youngest girl there, pressed forward and sifted through the parts of the priest, and finding his metal cross, she lifted it up and shook it at the sun. The thing extended a careful limb, tapped the cross, bathed it in a bluish goo, and then withdrew through the chapel arch and down the throat of the cave, chased by the yelling and singing women, who rejoiced in the cave, though their goddess was gone and they were left to celebrate with a pack of hyenas' ghosts until the sun fell and they made their way back to their homes and to their frightened men.

Overnight a second storm broke, and the loosened roof of the cave pitched into what remained of the chapel, bringing down the arch and blocking the entrance, sealing up the hyenas' ghosts until a few short hundred years later a local boy, a Lyon Widger, lowered himself, despite – or, perhaps, because of – his overwhelming fears of hobgoblins and other enemies of God, and began to, carefully, excavate. On Sundays, the boy would pray hard, straining in his pew to resist the temptation to tell his secret, the one he shared only with The Father on His Throne, fearful of the shapes that were only now re-emerging on the rood screen from under the whitewash of the puritans. Spectrally forming were Saint Catherine prone to mystical ravishment; Saint Margaret, swallowed by a dragon that choked upon her cross; Saint Ursula, a Dumnonian princess who led 11,000 of her unarmed handmaidens against the Huns; Saint Barbara carrying a tiny model of the tower from which she escaped and turned a treacherous shepherd to stone; Saint Elizabeth who opened her robe to reveal a vision of roses and Saint Helena who had found the one true cross under a Temple of Venus in Jerusalem. He particularly avoided the figure of Elizabeth for fear that lust would drag him into the arms of Teignmouth prostitutes and other such demons; but worst was Margaret and the green dragon by her side, tempting him to imagine the saintly woman inside the green and fiery throat, the green sleeve around the pink swollen limb. Passing girls on the lanes all around, in every girl in all the villages about, he felt the drawing of roses and the toothy suckers, far worse than the hairy fingers of hobgoblins or the sweet music of the doom under the fairies' hill.

Chapter 58

"Let's try it one more time."

"Please! It ain't workin', Mandi. If it ain't workin' now, it ain't gonna work, is it, loike?"

"Go on. One more?"

"Naaah!"

A dullness seemed to hang about the undergrowth. A watery sun barely bled through the shoulder-to-shoulder leaves. There was a bare tightness in the Everglades. No space for anything to get through; even the pores in the tree trunks and moss carpets were closed or jammed with filth. Nothing was emerging.

"Muddy Mary!"

Mandi tried again. The trees refused to dance. The occasional gusts that ran around the base of the trunks ignored the tops. The louder Mandi shouted the less likely it felt that she could jerk the Everglades. They were resolutely normal.

"Muddy Mary, mother of God,

Killed the Old Boy in his bath,

God went to Hell

And started to smell,

And now all the bad things are back!"

Nothing was back. She tossed a string, feather and twig fetish into the bushes. She had performed all the childish magic that Eddie had remembered, the stuff that worked back in the 1990s. She was unsure if the sickening uncertainty was down to her confusing real memories of what happened with Eddie's descriptions. Maybe she was trying too hard, trying to push it rather than believe it and let it do its thing. Eddie thought the problem was more fundamental.

"Yow can't do ritual whenever yow want! It's just for its time n' place!"

"I thought the whole point of a ritual is that you can transfer it? That's the whole history of religion and mysticism and juju everywhere!"

"Well, maybe it turns out yow can't..."

"So, what you're saying is that everyone who ever started a religion, made a Tarot pack, taught a meditation class, ordained a priest, everyone before us was wrong?"

"Yep."

"But this is the place, Eddie!"

"Yeh, but this place moved on, while we was away."

Somewhere over the railway tracks the frame of one of the rides was creaking. Plugging a gap in the soundscape of the Everglades. When the creaking stopped, it was like the place held its breath, hiding itself, stock still in fear of a passing predator. A car laboured up a hill, distantly. The air above the grove was empty, birdless, an acrid grey had crowded everything out.

"You 'ave to foind 'em in their place. When they're there."

"I saw one in a cafe."

"One what?"

"Angel."

"There was never any angels. It were much worse."

"You haven't seen these angels! Christ!"

Eddie scowled in disgust.

"At first I couldn't stop seeing them. Now, I have to chase them to see them. But I've forgotten something. Something I knew when I was a kid. Then I was certain; now I'm.... grasping, snatching at stuff. When I do see something face to face, I worry it won't show itself again. The more I try and struggle towards them, the further I'm driving them away."

"Then stop troying, matie."

"I think it might be something about... cavities."

Eddie laughed, but his yelps of hopeless joy fell dead in the Everglades.

"Listen, you fuckwit, there was a cave, then in the cafe there was a well, the chapel was like a kind of cave – the tin one with Mary in it – then the mouths with all the teeth, and the teeth being pulled out... that leaves cavities... is there a cavity here?"

"Yow won't open it until they want yow tao!"

"A single deep recess where the angels shine with darkness."

"Down't matter 'ow beautiful yow say it, yow gotta wait for them. Yow won't call 'em out!"

"Jesus. I did my best. I went to where the girls were buried at sea. I nearly drowned myself!"

Eddie took a breath...

"I know, I know!" Mandi interrupted him. "I'm trying to choose it and I shouldn't. We have to wait, but I don't think it will be long. I looked up a Nigerian Olokun ceremony. You dress in all enveloping white robes and when the angels come they're indistinguishable from the women in the robes. So no one knows which is which. They might be here already..."

Eddie put his head in his hands.

"They're not." He mimed looking about. "See anyfing supernatural?"

Mandi grabbed up the string, chalk and marbles, thrusting them deep into her pocket. She rubbed away the smeared symbols from the large oval stone and kicked over the model labyrinth of sand. What she had remembered as potent and profound was childish now, and pretentious. Her mouth felt stale from repeating the rhymes.

"You want to go and get something to drink?"

"Nah."

"Why not?"

"Tomorrow it's comin'. Yow gonna need yow sleep."

"How do you know?"

"I just dow. It all just happens and all yow have to dow is let it."

Chapter 59

That night Mandi dreamed she was out on the dunes. Some way off the shore, the white snipers were aboard 'The Loch Ness Cruiser', leaning over the sides and firing into the water. She could see four white lines of trajectory, like tracer bullets, piercing the blue water and bursting in soft phutts on the ocean floor. Four comic things, like spider crabs, but masked with the faces of C List celebrities, scuttled in confusion. After a while, a tiny plesiosaur, no bigger than a dolphin, floated to the surface, yellowy-pink blood bubbling from bullet holes in its silvery-blue back. The white snipers hauled its cadaver aboard, sat it in a folding chair and began to dress it in the messiah's clothes, erecting an easel on the deck...

The moment she woke, she knew they were there. The shapes on the curtains, the feathery silhouettes etched against a watery dawn light, confirming what the dark many-footed head had told her; that the thing deep down in the darkness of dreams had laid things out for her like a map of words, in waves of information. Each gesture of a crab leg, trickle of dolphin blood, line of a bullet's trajectory had pointed to this. They would be coming; the three, plus one. They would come to fetch her and something final would be enacted. Even in her dreams, Mandi was uneasy with commands and felt her hackles rise. She spoke back to the dark thing, but it silenced her with a twist of its beak; as if to say "even I have no control over this".

So, it was with a sense of defeat that Mandi pulled herself out of sleep and went out to meet a determined world. She guessed that the goddesses were unlikely to hang around while she enjoyed a shower; she slipped on her jeans, three tops and her padded jacket, tightened the red laces around her brown boots, swigged some cold tea, pocketed a small banana, and opened the front door.

She knew approximately what she would see; but nothing could prepare her for the electric presence of all three together. Eight feet tall, another eight feet of wingspan each, Vitruvian women, their giant and single seeing eyes circular and coloured in toy marble swirls, the others milky and tuned within to a vibration longer or shorter than light. The whole of them shone with a self-affirming force. They glowed. Even in the grey light of the dirty morning they found some orange fire; they sparked reflectors on the backs of caravans and discarded drinks cans. The deserted holiday trailers and empty gravel roads, the first measly strings of steam rising from the permanent camp, were set off more brightly by their glimmering splendour.

The three stood, the cold air shimmering around them; patiently allowing Mandi to do her thing. She was surprised when they spoke. She had expected magical communication, telepathy or something. Instead, they conversed in strong, woody voices, their lips forming the shape of words hypnotically. Mandi followed the movement of their mouths as the speaking shifted from one to another. She had an unfolding impression of the geography of what they were saying; they seemed not to use words to tell a story, but to map out a space and their motion in it. What they said was all about doing and allowing, knowing and being. As they spoke everything else – the gulls, the wind in the wires, the rumble of a bus – fell silent; the only things that mingled with their message were the waves falling against the slope of the beach. A sound that Mandi had never heard this far from the shore.

They set out, Mandi leading. Though she had no idea of how to say where they were going, she knew the way. A curtain twitched in one of the trailers on the permanent camp, a door edged open and two faces, one above the other, eased out nosily. Mandi expected there to be more impact; but when she glanced behind her the angels had folded away their wings, their light was dimmed, and rather than actual Amazons, they looked little different from three tall hikers. The curtain fell back, the door closed; perhaps they had assumed Mandi was redirecting three lost walkers or taking them to one of the camps still renting out.

Mandi was unclear how she should address the angels. In her head were the images of the three female saints; there was Mary at the chapel, Apollonia with smashed teeth (she had seen her in dreams and visions) and Sidwella from the cafe hiding undercover in April. So, they had names. They also had things; Apollonia a pair of pliers, Sidwella a scythe and Mary a silvery serpent, like a jet of water, which ran beneath her feet. Mandi dared not look back at them again, but she was certain that they would have those things now. Which gave her no comfort at all; for the things morphed into however she was trying to see them. Not that she was changing them; rather, all this morphing was keeping her from knowing who they really were. They were in a constant shuffling; Apollonia's face reminded her of Jonny; Sidwella's hand around the scythe had six fingers, then four; Mary's robe was red one moment and blue the next, her hair a mass of curls and then demure. Yet, Mandi felt no inhibition about their early morning adventure. Instead, there was a kind of pride in marching the three supernaturals along the wide service road between the camps, between their communal buildings, those in a Spanish villa style, others more like Midlands factory canteens, locked up for the winter. The plastic murals of roast dinners shrank back from the angels. Mandi had never been in a gang, not since the Everglades. She had never felt any kind of 'sisterhood' with the other women in her business; and she expected neither solidarity nor understanding from them. Even the gym she had joined briefly was too collective for her. Angels, however... with them she experienced a belonging she had not missed until right now. She was infatuated, as she had thought she could only be with April.

A sulky mist reluctantly raised itself from the surface of the stream that ran along the edge of the Everglades. This was Mucky Mary's place; and though Mandi feared to look back she could see that up ahead and to the sides something was picking out blue surfaces – a scrap of chocolate wrapper, a top from an Adidas flask, a strip of painted hull leaned against a tarp – and humming with them, jamming their wavelengths so they shimmered against the thick grey-green of the place. Then it all began to seethe; not much, but long enough for the place to show itself. The Everglades was not a simple collection of matters – stream, paths, shrubs, trees and roots, canopy and fence – but a flexing organism responding to its mistress; it was a thing with a dark throat. Mandi suspected that if she looked back now she would see an Everglades Mary, a Mucky Mary, a flurry of leaves and a mouth filled up with fluffy clouds like those puffed up from the stream's floor.

There was a steady stream of traffic along the Exeter Road. Mandi could tell from the disheartened disinterest of the early morning commuters, caged behind their wheels, even out here their futures in the hands of distant investment managers, that there was nothing they could see – if they saw anything at all but the road ahead – to distinguish the four of them from four women out for a sisterly ramble. How wrong they were. How wrong had she been, she wondered; how many times passing these sororital gangs had she sneered at a supernatural quest? Never she reckoned; if this was happening now and she was not about to wake up in bed in the camp, wonder at the dreamcatchers and put the coffee on, then it was a 'one off', a unique event, the exception that improves the rule of the norm. This was all a piece of yeast thrown into the mix to raise things up, put a little space and air into things, but leave them essentially unchanged...

A car swerved across the lanes, almost cannoning into the oncoming flow. It came to rest on the grass verge; the stream of cars paused and then gingerly began to move forward again, bending round skid marks. A hiccup in the spectacle, a tape momentarily caught in the old machine, the picture had flickered. The driver was out of his vehicle, bent over and throwing up into a ditch, his wildly disbelieving eyes were turned firmly on Mandi as she and the three angels slipped across the roundabout, over a stile and – leaving behind a tableau of sleeping motorists suddenly awakened into a dreamworld – dropped down onto the thick grass of the little used public footpath, between two banks of winter-withered nettles. Their passage singed the hairs on the nettle stems.

Mandi heard three sets of wings unfolding; they flapped against the rows of soggy grass with a squelching sound. The angels began to stride and Mandi was riding a green wave as it swept them along the path. On one side a few solitary figures were strolling tentatively across a giant lawn, hugging cigarettes to their lips, chasing clouds and blearily scouring the ground about their feet. One by one, they picked up their heads and watched the feathery procession move through the stingers, the long hair of the angels lifted in a breeze. A fox fled ahead of them. As they passed empty skeletons of redundant greenhouses, rampant with brambles, they passed out of the sight of the solitary witnesses on the shaved green. One by one these distant figures extinguished their cigarettes or clicked their vapes, turning slowly back towards the angular white buildings of the forensic mental health facility. Within the caged areas, nothing moved.

It may have been the lingering stigma around psychiatric institutions that had kept Mandi and her childhood pals away from this patch. It was only a short footpath walk and a busy road crossing from the camp, but she had no memory of ever being close to these fields. For an hour they walked, first in single file, then side by side; the paths and lanes quiet; almost deserted of humans. Disinhibited, the angels allowed more of their display; their wings spread and interleaved with each other, their useless feet dragging along the road as they slid rather than walked. Twice, at junctions, they saw the rears of disappearing lorries, but there was only one moment when a vehicle passed them on the lane; a white van driven by a woman. Mandi and the angels stepped back onto the muddy verge around a field gate, the supernaturals made little attempt to hide their selves. The driver seemed to awaken and stare, but did not stop; correcting a slight swerve the van hurried on around the next bend and out of hearing. Something to be filed under 'one of those funny things'.

The land here was of the same prehistoric shape as that around the Lovecraft villages. There were no Saxon villages with solid groundplans clustered around a green, a church, a crossroads and a square. Instead there were isolated homesteads, lodges that had become detached from their big houses, one with odd figureheads – a female accompanied by a winged sprite with its bow and arrow primed, a leaping furry thing with a beak for a muzzle – another named after a pilgrimage. On some of the houses there were plasterwork finishes like woven baskets; remnants of old patterns that elsewhere had long ago been replaced. There was also a kind of green misery; bright nitrogen fields dulled in the grey light of the morning, punctuated by redundant concrete structures overwhelmed by yellowish lichen and guarded by long abandoned caravans and railway trucks, all bathed in the same green-greyish slime.

Looking back towards the secure facility, flanked by trees at the top of a rise was an elegant water tank, its blackness standing out from the shadows, flashes of silver insulation winking from its belly. Redundant now, surely; it stood sentinel-like, gazing malevolently, exquisitely surplus. Before it the sloping and rolling fields a loaded emptiness; everything was waiting for something else. Ancient expanses that had once supported the tramp of giants; indifferent even to the passage of angels. Mandi was furious with the fields; how dare they not even notice. The only things that seemed to have any respect were the pylons, stretched out in a swinging line, from which the flat ranks of forestry had stepped back and left huge corridors. Paths criss-crossed like swollen veins. And then they found the trees.

There was no introduction, the hedges did not give way to unveil them. But for a break in the brambly weave of a badly thrashed old cut and lay to allow for a vertiginous stile she might not have noticed them at all. The angels, however, could see over the hedges. Mandi heard their sudden shaking of feathers, saw the bursts of illumination from their chests and limbs; there was an agitation in the milky maelstrom of their inner eyes.

"This is the Vale Without Depths", said Mary, "there is no way here, only a surface."

"What you see is what you get?" prompted Mandi.

"These are the old places, but there was never a cave or a well here. We left such places to the rain."

Mandi wondered whether they had kept her away, until now.

"Why here, then?"

The feathers rustled impatiently. The three were already in the field, hovering; leaving Mandi to lever herself like a clumsy crab.

"The springs come on higher ground," said Sidwella.

They were magnificent. Upwards of thirty twisted colossuses in two sets of parallel lines; a pair of illogical arboreal avenues. These ancient chestnuts were mostly dead, though; a few buds here and there and a ring of suckers around one of the giant trunks hinted at the last throes of a life almost gone for good. What must they have looked like once? Mandi thought they were still pretty sick, as big as electricity pylons, gnarly tower blocks of contorted wood, a spread of dark claws against the steely sky, serpent branches and python-boughs with leathery bark disturbed in ripples. One beast had fallen entirely, its broken boughs reaching out in smooth tentacles, the bottom of its trunk embroidered with torn roots, ripped from the field, a giant cephalopodic maw, awrithe with teeth and feelers and hunting blindly. A few cows, dwarfed, mooched about in the mud; a travesty of whatever grandness was intended once. Coach paths to a missing palace? Wooden corridors, a prelude to paradise gardens, or a manor replete with hidden rooms, priest holes, ice houses and larders hung with maggoty game? Yet there was nothing but a modest farmhouse; old, but no stately home. The landscape made no sense; it had been pulled awry.

The angels were floating back to the road. Mandi had no intention of letting them out of her sight; scampering across the slippery grass and over the stile. She snagged her jeans; turning for a moment to free them from a superfluous metal hinge, she saw the cyclopean ancients shuffle back into languor, extinguishing flashes of ire. Had she disturbed something that should be fixed? If there were no depths, how did the trees stand? By the time Mandi caught up with the angels, her questions were shrouded, there was a turning in the lane; on a corner, yet another lodge and a side road that shortly ran into multiple signs printed on newly laminated boards demanding privacy and threatening dogs running loose.

Mandi had a feeling of dreadful foreboding mixed with a want that was uncomfortably unintellectual; she had to be here, she had to do this. In real life she would have turned this down, as she had done with plenty of other poisoned chalices; indeed plenty of poisoned vessels far less glamorous than chalices. No, she felt it in her, in her liver, in her kidneys. Something was coming, as unstoppable as a storm, and she must be there to endure it, to find shelter in its eye.

"We must hurry", said Mary.

"Why don't you three fly?" Mandi suggested.

"The journey not the arriving", said Sidwella. "A pilgrim believes that at the shrine they will change, but when they get there they discover it is the road that has already changed them."

"We are spirits of place", added Apollonia, "we drag the caves, wells and springs, chapels and groves. Detach us from our grounds and you reduce us to saints."

As if to emphasise the point they paused at the gate and gazed, with glassy eyes, down the valley that stretched away from the hidden hall. Mandi only noticed now how high they had climbed on the narrow lane. At the bottom of the vale, a few scattered homes and the outline of a large walled garden marked the transition to the flatter and emptier fields, the demesne without pores. Close to the bottom, a sweeping expanse of meadow blipped; a green shape like a giant upturned soup plate, unnaturally smooth. Something dug and then rounded by the long, long years; something at odds with the formalities of the secret garden; sat side by side, a contradiction in the landscape that it was still working out. The place's delays and prevarications were finally coming to an end.

Beyond the flat grey-green fields, above the next lip of ground before the sea, a gargantuan purple cloud was reeling towards them, gathering height and darkness as it came. The lodges, lanes and avenue of trees were disappearing under a creeping shadow. The small trees to the side of the vale began to shake, and farther off the trunks of the almost dead giants howled and creaked. The angels swept urgently through the gate, Mandi in pursuit.

Mandun Hall was unveiled behind a windbreak of tall thin trees.

Mandi abruptly felt the loss of her adoptive parents; her 'Mum' and 'Dad'. At first she thought it was the sight of the Hall that had somehow frightened her; a wave of something bad sweeping up through her legs and into her chest, spreading its fingers around her heart and squeezing until she wanted to bend over in pain. But it was not fear; it was grief. A tall grey slinky grief that amazed her, a lithe and striking thing sashaying up the path, lashing out and into her.

She was not their flesh, but she felt them now as part of hers; she felt their arms picking her up after a fall, on her tongue she tasted the vegetable soup they always served, her skin goosepimpled under the rough woolly shapeless things they gave her to wear, and deepest of all she felt the shameful guilty protectiveness they had always placed around her, the brittle wall they put between her and the world, she felt its pieces buried into every part of her, the sharp pins of bitterness that poked every time she thought of them. She embraced even her resentment of them. She had had to smash through their butterscotch wall, she had had to leave them, get away from them, not just from the restrictions but from them; yet she could not help loving their memory, pulling their spectres toward and into her, embracing the essence of them and knowing that they were good people who loved her.

Then she noticed the teeth of the angels; the ruined city skylines from apocalypse movies barely standing beyond their bruised lips.

"This place incubates spectres," warned Mary.

"That is not what you think it is," said Apollonia, looking at her with a burning eye.

And the grey thing spasmed and left her, limping back along the path to the Hall. Mandi felt it leave, as if she were flushed of something alien, could see clearly now, things sharpened into focus around her. She had been living in the past, just playing tough in the present without actually being in it. No wonder she was so indestructible; she had not even been there to get hurt.

Sidwella looked hard at her, as if she knew that Mandi's revelations were bullshit.

Her sudden becoming present – to the green of the lawns, the yellow of the sandstone, the footprint of the gardens as sharp as HD – came with a flood of vulnerability. Now she was in the here, stepped through the door of now, everything would wound her now. Mandi the armoured one had fallen apart at her first brush with fake grief; it did not bode well for the battle to come. The angels' only human warrior was a born-again 'snowflake'.

The front fell off the building.

"That was quick", thought Mandi.

It was like the destruction of the Chapel of Eve and Diana... Mandi shot her angel a glance, but Sidwella's wings were pricked in concentration on the innards of the Hall. The stone hacked and the arch undermined, the mouth closed up. What invisible miners had the three angels employed; but when Mandi turned to ask the angels, they seemed perplexed and were picking their way carefully, in the clouds of dust, towards the rubble piled around the formerly grand front entrance, its ornamental pillars now fallen into a wonky 'X'.

The ripples of the monstrous "crack!" were still running down the valley sides. A great cloud of sediment was pouring from the opened rooms of the Hall and rising into the sky. It drew Mandi's eye upwards, and for the first time she could see, high up, a grid of buzzards, picking at the fringe of which was a herring gull, snapping at the tail feathers of one of the hovering raptors. The attack pulled the grid out of shape for a moment, and then, the gull repelled, it snapped back into place. Inside the Hall, white-coated figures and disoriented men in business suits staggered over upturned chairs and broken workstations; exposed to the vista they emerged from the dust and then, after a glance, withdrew, choking, back into the haze. Mandi followed the angels up the heap of broken lintels, crumbled plaster, ripped wood and torn wallpaper, trailing behind their giant bounds. By the time she had made the top of the pile, the angels were on their way down the long hall and Mandi sprinted after them. She was quickly on her own; suddenly aware that she was among enemies.

A light haze hung about the upper reaches of the tall corridors. Temporarily deserted, Mandi scoured the place for possible weapons. Possible weapons? Angels? The front of a stately home falling off? The weapon she needed most was some kind of retreat; but no, Mandi did not do rehab. Mandi won, Mandi survived, Mandi prevailed. On her own.

There was surprisingly little that she could find in the Hall. She had expected the Hexamerons' HQ to be full of antiquities, treasured objects from their long years of failure and resilient eccentricity, but there was nothing but chandeliers, arsenic-green wallpaper and long Persian carpets. No cabinets of curiosities or framed portraits of their leaders. But for the floating debris, it might have been a property prepared for sale.

"There she is!"

Mandi stepped back into a room and ran through door after door, in a movie that had run out of ideas. The deeper into the house she got, the less like a deserted mansion and more like a company the place became. Soon she was dodging workstations and water coolers; she took a chance and slipped inside a service lift, clearing the fallen hat stand jamming the doors, she pressed the button for the top floor. The lift rose swiftly. The motion of the lift stopped, but the doors stayed shut. Mandi hammered the 'open' button and the doors creaked apart.

Other than a few pillars supporting its false ceiling, this whole floor of the mansion was a single open room. Mandi felt its chill. She could still just about make out the formerly ordered ranks of servers that had stood here, but there were other things. The viewing devices like digitised camera obscura for observing the manipulated flocks of birds, and trading desks like those Mandi had seen in The City. Now, the whole place was wrecked; something had been amongst it, got into it, smashed it and soaked its electrics in a transparent ooze. The servers were fallen, their ventilators shut down; outer casings were ripped open and dripping with a membranous goo, cables were thrown into spaghetti piles and soaked in thick gobbets of muck. But there was something else there that was not the work of whatever – and Mandi had a pretty good idea what that whatever might be – had destroyed the things; for along with the recognisable machine parts and electronics, the spilled motherboards and trampled flash drives, there was an organic stratum that was different from the gelatinous residue of its nemesis.

The harder Mandi looked, the more she could see a machine that was partly made of a kind of orchid that imitated a wasp; that what had been gathered here was not simply information, but DNA. Mandi knew they had hers; stung in the shadow of the Great Hill; she had been harvested. Floral and digital technology combined; and crushed with a watery goo. Petals bent and broken, processors embedded in the carpets, a set of speakers torn, a memory stick – "BIRDSONG" in indelible marker – sat in a pool of funk. What had they been making here? Had the Hexamerons saved something from the nurseries of their old members, the Veitches and the Lucombes?

"Life", said Mary. "Of a kind. What you create, you control. That is why saints and angels suffer."

"I can't see any control here, I can't see any plan at all," Mandi complained.

"This is but the surface of the machine; it runs through all the floors and into the foundations, out along the fields; the birds and wasps are its evangelists among the lanes and hedgerows."

"But what did the Hexamerons get from it?"

"You don't get it, do you?" chastised Apollonia. "The Hexamerons do not operate the machine, they are not even the servants of the machine..."

"They have become machines!" guessed Mandi.

"No, far worse! The Hexamerons are the sexual apparatus of the machine, they are nothing more than its bio-prosthetics..."

"So," Mandi interrupted the angel, "all those ideas, evolution, race, science, spiritualism...?"

"Scripts written by a keyboard without the help of an author."

Apollonia waved a wing in a gesture figuring helplessness.

"True believers become the pattern of what they believe; what had seemed and felt to them like a leap of faith, turns out to be a murderous push from behind."

Those who had believed themselves to be the spiritual fathers of the messiah-machine had turned out to be the mechanics of their own shabby affair.

"Those of us who have taken shape in the medium of religious discourse have grown to understand that belief is a work, not an acceptance. Those who accept god have not raised themselves from human to angel, but lowered themselves from angel to human."

The room of servers – so broken now – had replaced the desks of the automatic writers and interpreters of the classical allusions of the dead who had once frequented Mandun Hall; their mummified bodies were preserved in the back rooms that Mandi had failed to reach, surrounded by a few discs to which their yellowing records had been committed. Stooping to magic in order to defy the cosmic chaos they had hated and fought for centuries, from the earliest days of their involvement in scientific palaeontology and the destruction of Christianity to their patronage of 'beyondist' eugenics in the twentieth century, the Hexamerons' machine was the ultimate expression of their plans, the kerygma of their rationalist religion. It was a mechanism to subject human peccadillo and perversity to the symmetries of Platonic plantation and information harvest; but it had fallen foul of the necessity for mimicry. Unable to siphon perfect order from the stank and funk of matter; in order to raise the material to the ideal, it had become necessary to construct a vehicle of such mimetic intervention, to give nature a nudge, so that lesser races might be raised up by invasion, lower classes elevated by correct teachers and the most distracting role models. Lost in an orchid forest, they had been stung by their own intentions. A philosophy of non-interventionist evolutionism had drawn them, absurdly, into interference at the cellular and synaptic levels, in political alliances with insects and birds. Confusion, even, had been recruited to their cause; and now they had goaded the Beast of the Deep to rise and destroy their toy. And that she had.

Mandi remembered the words of the green undertaker, about the illusory nature of belief becoming a kind of belief in itself. Trapped under a collapsed desk, one of the Hexamerons' programmers wheezed out a cry for help. Kneeling by her side, Mandi held her hand. "You invented and built and programmed it," she mused over the woman, "but you are no more than the dull impulse to survive that it needs to maintain itself."

The woman, uncomprehending, lapsed into unconsciousness.

"Have we won?" asked Mandi. "Have they all run away?"

"They have not begun to fight."

"Then what has happened here?"

"The servers? That devastation was the work of the goddess of the deep", explained Mary. "But this is not her place, she cannot have a victory here; this is their place and she has driven them from it; that is the most she can do."

"Where are they?"

The angels shrugged and flounced from the room of servers, Mandi jogging behind them, down three flights of ever widening stairs until she was picking her way around fallen plaster and moaning Hexamerons and out through the grand hallway and onto the gravel path, framed with borders of purple-blue Asters. Mary, Sidwella and Apollonia paused at the top of the stone staircase to what had been the grand entrance; they had folded their wings behind their backs and were gazing over the vista, down to the valley below. Apollonia swung her pair of pliers by her side, Sidwella shouldered the scythe and the watery snake that seemed always to play about Mary's feet had been joined by a deep pink rose and thorny stem.

Beyond the angels, where the Asters ran out, stood a small group of suited Hexamerons. Mandi recognised the Chairman from the meeting at the Bay Museum; she noticed for the first time the black disc badge that he wore on his lapel. His tweedy three piece and the staid sports jackets of his supporting tyros, inverted red triangles on their lapels, at odds with the samurai swords and machetes that dangled from their hands. They were flanked on one side by a number of 'POLITE' men and woman from the hunt, mounted on huge horses, brandishing cattle prods instead of lances. Hounds swarmed around the legs of their mounts, and around the pack clustered young execs and CEO's some on horseback and in hunting pink, others in paintball camouflage gear. On the other side, the white snipers, masked and nonchalant, toted TAC-15 crossbows. A group of Hexameron elders had fallen to one knee, raising identical handguns – Mandi doubted they had licenses for them – compact Glock 19s by the look of them. Behind the leaders stood the ranks of their forces, assembled in the estate's grounds ranged between the Capability Brown lollipop trees and atop the raised mound Mandi had noted on her way in.

They were a strange confabulation; their absurdity made them all the more scary. As if someone has assembled all Mandi's childhood fears and called them up for a reunion.

The ghoulish female mummies of the Hexamerons' automatic writers lined up alongside the turncoat Grant Kentish and his straggling band of Bank Holiday sensualists; surrounded by the rather more daunting thousand-strong ranks of Bulwer-Lytton's subterranean 'coming race' – blanched giants glowing with auras of Vril – and a sordid alliance of Necroscopes and Wamphyri Lords. Despite their obvious supernatural talents, these were all outnumbered and outbullied by a massive ghostly Saxon army of bigoted soldiers convinced of their moral superiority, stretching beyond the cluster of village hall and secret garden. Led by a cavalry of Angle nobles, Saint-King Athelstan the ethnic cleanser of Exeter rode at their head, preceded by a large detachment of junior priests and servants brandishing a thousand holy relics including a piece of the still smoking Burning Bush, enough pieces of the true cross to build a galleon, two skulls of John the Baptist (one as a young boy, the other the one presented to Salome) and Longinus's spear of destiny, with an honour guard of Bund Deutscher Mädel, still dirty with pig's blood. The nitrogen green of the fields was hidden by all the flags and uniforms. On the fringes – policed by hi viz yellow tabarded security guards – skulked denizens of the Nihils of Tarturus who had armed themselves with portable amps and speakers, while spreading across the fields, beneath the electricity pylons and to the tops of the rise that hid the view to the sea, were zombie-armies of employees, in office skirts and tops and warehouse overalls, conscripted workers of the Hexameron bosses, bewildered, cold, chattering and unbelieving of their orders; confused about their evacuation and the talk of flooding and storm and the faint unreality of what they could see in the distance around Mandun Hall.

Mandi could see the lanes were crammed with works vans and employees' vehicles and more were arriving every minute, filling up the far fields, while above, despite the breaking of the Hexameron machine, the grid of buzzards was now complemented by murmurations of starlings and a surveillance flight of parakeets, under a mountain range of barrelling purple-black clouds.

"Holy crap", breathed Mandi.

"Speaking as a martyr", laughed Sidwella and smiled at Apollonia, "it's nothing more than we have come to expect."

Under the darkening sky the phones of the employees began to flicker like an incoherent congress of fireflies; then they seemed to jolt collectively and, irrespective of pencil skirt or blue overalls, the employees began to form up in phalanxes, more orderly than the Saxon spectres. Had the pylons just moved? Mandi was unsure whether the pylons were mere bystanders or part of the troops ranged against her and her angels.

"Why me?" she whispered to herself.

It all took her aback.

"They are still communicating," she said to the angels, desperately.

"Don't make the same mistake as Her, Mandi." Sidwella looked remarkably like April now, despite the feathers and scythe. "The Hexamerons long ago transferred the software to their followers' phones."

"Mistake? I thought that She... if you mean who I think you mean... but..."

"She is a very old thing. She makes mistakes. Your Mother doesn't understand apps."

Chapter 60

At Lost Horizon, with the storm rising, the caretaker was ushering the last residents away to higher ground. Their vans, mobile caravans, kooky Beetles and antique hatchbacks were overloaded with their prized possessions. The caretaker stood sentinel as the carnival of retreat wound its way out of the camp, along the main road, past the bending trees in the Everglades and then up the hill towards higher ground. They were joined by similar, if less esoteric, processions as the local authorities moved to respond to the urgent emails from the Met Office. The less popular sites away from the coast were suddenly doing good business.

The final vehicle paused at the gate; an Iveco LWB. The passenger window wound down with an electrical whirr. Mimir tried to lean over from the driver's seat, but Cassandra pushed him back.

"You know that we know about you," she said, shouting above the howl of the wind, "and that we frittered away our chances, but..."

She shot a guilty glance at Mimir before continuing.

"He'd come with you now, if I let him. He always wanted to do what you're going to do. But I was always too close to being poor to dare to take the risk and do what I believed in. What if none of it's true? That's what I kept saying to myself. How much have we really seen? That we couldn't explain?"

The caretaker was reactionless.

"Maybe you never needed to? Being a professor... Anyway, we thought we better let you know that we know what you're up to. We can guess now who you might be! Well, good luck, may Pan and all the others be with you, Christ you're going to need them, man! Anyway, thanks for organising our safety. And whatever happens you can go knowing you did well by your girl; she's going to be wonderful, you know. You can feel proud."

"Thank you."

"Scared?"

"Happy to be going home. When you've been... down to the deep, once, it's hard to live in the shallows. I was never really happy after that. I came back here, just to be close again. Just on the off-chance, but tragedy has brought us together."

"There's no tragedy. Everything is intended."

"Not everything. Beauty just happens. Shit just happens. No god, no conspiracy has any hand in it. It just is. That's who I am going to meet now... again – a terrifying and shitty beauty that just wonderfully is."

"She loved you, you know. I saw how she looked at you."

"Amanda?"

"Yes! Who do you think I mean?"

"Sure. I wish I could have said 'goodbye' properly. Explain to her, will you?"

"She's not stupid. I think she knows that you did."

"Yes."

He looked at his feet. Cassandra's work done, she pressed the switch and the window slid back into place. Mimir saluted and gunned the big white vehicle, swinging it into the road and chasing the tail of Lost Horizon up the hill towards safety. The caretaker watched the van, increasingly startling under the darkening sky until the last of its shimmer disappeared around the brow. He looked down again. A shallow body of water had crept around the welts of his boots; its edge, pushing tiny twigs, leaves and scraps of discarded wrappers. It was coming quicker than he expected; but more importantly, it was coming.

Splashing through the flood, the caretaker ran to the far edge of the camp, to the summertime mobile homes nearest the sea, and levered himself onto the flat roof of the furthest one. From there he could see over the railway tracks, beyond the dunes to a wrestling sea that had overwhelmed the sandy spit. The gale caught in the white burst of his hair. The force that had once swept sixty houses off their blasphemous foundations was coming back for the dune; the breakers so mixed with sand they crashed into the lagoon like slithering dolphins. Tumbling in their spume were gabions of wire and rough stone. The most radical of human efforts disposed of in seconds. The rangers' hut was thrown up and smashed, a suspension of splinters hung briefly in the air before being swept away by the racing winds, thrown like darts into the rising bayou. The caretaker, his hair plastered to his skull, could barely stand. His clothes, soaked with spray, ballooned, filled with wind; he unbuttoned his jacket and overalls to stop himself from floating off like a rogue inflatable. The flapping garments whipped him mercilessly. It was not the calm demise he had hoped for.

With a bitter effort, the caretaker shook his eyes from the rising waters around him, empty mobile homes pulling free of their electrical moorings, permanent homes sparking and emitting puffs of smoke that were ripped away by the gale. Further down the coast, despite the dampening of the waters of the estuary the rising flood had already underdug the track ballast of the railway line; rails and sleepers swung above the gaping chasm like the set of a bad jungle movie. The caretaker had expected something more spectacular; less relentless; one giant wave rather than this bully's pummelling. The metal shell of an amusement parlour folded up like a crumpled paper cup and games machines were swept down the path towards the dodgems. A following swell lifted the giant concrete skull from the pirate-themed crazy golf course and buoyed it up for a few moments before it broke and sank, torn wire rigging and cracked mannequins sucked down with it.

Chapter 61

"Who are you? How are you going to save us? Are you something to do with the three statues in the graveyard?"

"Don't try to explain us," growled Mary.

The angels seemed more human, faced by swelling hordes of Hexameron allies. Even as the four gazed over the fields from the gardens of Mandun Hall, the widespread forces thickened. What Mandi had imagined were shadows thrown among the fox-hounds by the hunt's rides were also dogs, dogs the size of horses with black coats and blood-red eyes. Some of the lights that she had thought were dull glare from employees' screens, she could see now were the deprecated bodies of those the white snipers had lured over the cliff tops; their broken limbs and blanched skins drunkenly lolling. The white-coated programmers, re-grouping now from the ruins of Mandun Hall and ill at ease with their improvised weapons, were no less unreal.

"You're the saints, then? In my dream, in the paintings in the church..."

"Stop trying to rationalise," Apollonia upbraided her. "Those paintings are real enough..."

"Maybe she lined up on the wrong side?" spat Sidwella, cuttingly.

"This is what is," said Mary, and her wings fluttered over the ranks of the Hexameron forces. "There are no explanations."

The Chairman of the Hexamerons broke ranks and stepped into the empty ground between the two sides. A hush rippled back along the Hexameron troops, down the vale, up the hills and to the horizon.

"Amanda!" He pressed the palms of his hands together, as though he were about to pray; but suddenly held them up, to either side of his head in a gesture that might have been surrender or receiving adulation. "Nothing escapes death. That is the one great truth. But sometimes we Hexamerons like to give things a nudge..."

"Mandi?

"Mandi? Is that you?"

"O my... Mandi, Mandi!"

"It's us!"

A rumpus in the ranks of the white-coated programmers, beyond a riot of Wisteria still clinging to the corner of the property, resolved itself into two parts, and between them Anne and Bryan were running towards Mandi and the angels. The same Anne and Bryan; the Anne and Bryan with the irritating invisible make-up and the over-brazen bald patch and untidy jacket.

The chairman held his left palm towards them and brought them to a halt.

"Please," begged Mandi's mother. "Our little girl!"

"In a moment! You would have waited hopelessly for a lifetime without us!" The chairman turned back to Mandi. "Did you think we had killed your mother and father in order to bring you here and make all this happen? Or did you suspect your precious angels were behind it? You were always so sceptical of conspiracy theories..."

"You're fucking with my head!"

"Tut tut, my dear. Not in front of 'mother and father'. You think you are so important? The programmes produce such illusions for millions everyday! Do you think you're the only one who dreams of having better parents? Or just having any parents at all? Send your friends," and he nodded cautiously at the angels, "back to whatever chaos they came from."

"I wouldn't know how to begin to..."

The Chairman turned to the Lack of Engagement Officer who had materialised at his elbow and took from him the case filled with Widger's bone map. He held it out to Mandi.

"We know you know how this works. Go on, take it! As a gift!"

Mandi cagily took the bonelines from the Chairman.

"Now smash it. That way neither you nor anyone else will raise or find these wretched things again. Rational common-sense will prevail and family life be restored. Or keep the map and we will send your mother and father back to the digital void from which they have come."

Digital void? Anne and Bryan looked very flesh and bone to her. But if Mandi destroyed the bonelines, the Hexamerons' savage rationality would finally have won; despite all their stupidity, gracelessness and hypocrisy. Mandi would have given them victory. At least, she thought, that's how it works in the stories, but this is just a part of Devon, and she cast her eye over the strangeness all around her. Who was to say what of all this had meaning and what didn't?

"A few weeks ago," she said, looking carefully and quickly at the map, "I would have let them stay in their limbo, people are idiots after all, what difference is it to them whether they live in illusions or with real things? The difference is metaphysical. But I have learned from my three angels that the real is far more real and full and different than I could ever have possibly imagined. How can I condemn anyone, least of all the people who raised me and tried to teach me the same thing, to that lie? If I had not met you, Mary, Apollonia, Sidwella, I would have happily saved you; but what you have taught me and shown me has fucked you up totally. Real is more real."

Mandi smashed the bonelines map against a low wall. Glass splintered into a bed of Anemones; the bones bounced across the path and mixed in the blades of the lawn. The angel-priestesses faded to dark shadows of themselves, their revenant outlines barely visible under the bruised clouds.

"You're welcome to her!"

The Chairman dropped his arm and Anne and Bryan raced across to Mandi. They stopped a few short steps shy of her and of the rapidly fading revenants, momentarily daunted by Mandi's changed appearance and the fading trace of angelic shadows. She seemed so tall to them, no lesser a figure than the giant supernaturals.

"You're not dead!" Mandi blurted.

"We're part of something we don't understand."

"What happened?"

"Distraction. Deception. Dark forces..." said Bryan airily, tugging on the beginnings of a beard.

"We've been worried sick about you and the camp."

Mandi noticed that her mother's clothes were torn and grimy; she had always been an immaculate, if modest dresser; now she looked as if she had been held a prisoner, or forced to wear someone else's skirt and top. Her hair had been dragged sideways.

"I sorted it out, Mum. They're all fine..."

"O, thank you, dear."

Out of the corner of her eye, Mandi was aware of a blue car making uncertain headway up the driveway to the hall. Another no-brain employee letting their phone do their thinking for them. The grid of buzzards and starlings, almost consumed by purple-black clouds, shifted at the edges. Afar off, a pheasant clanked.

"I thought you were both dead! I dreamed of you dying!" she accused.

"We died a thousand deaths, Amanda..."

"You never called m..."

The blue car swerved out of the driveway and ploughed through a border of Asters, jumped the path and smashed into Anne and Bryan, hurling them thirty metres past the Wisteria and into the pile of rubble fallen from the facade of Mandun Hall. Anne's head was almost torn from her shoulders, Bryan's skull broke against the remains of a pillar and brain matter spilled down its polished granite. Mandi hoped, for one crazed moment, that the bodies might crumple to empty containers, like punctured balloons; but they held resolutely to the fatty, stringy mess of their ugly brokenness. Hope evaporated and she screamed a howl that chased after it.

The car had come to a halt against the steps to what had been the main entrance. The passenger door swung open, scraping along the bottom step. At the same time the driver's door was flung open, and simultaneously two figures, a middle aged man and woman, levered themselves unsteadily and manically from the car.

"O, Mandi, Mandi, Mandi!" they chorused.

The woman, dressed in denim, held the roof of the car for support and then pushed off at a run towards Mandi. Undaunted by the dark shadows of the angels, she ran up and hugged her, almost pushing her off her feet. Mandi smelt an overpowering cheap perfume. The man, in tea shirt, pool sliders and shorts, was in close pursuit and embraced them both, wrapping his long, hairy arms around the pair. His smell was male and feral. Mandi could barely shake off the shock to bring herself to struggle; after what might have seemed like her welcoming response she conjured violence from somewhere and pushed the pair savagely away.

"What the fuck?"

"Mandi, Mandi, Mandi," the woman spoke very quickly and accelerating. "We're your real parents, we're the ones who found you on the beach. Those bastards took you and kept you in the dark for thirty years, but we've been watching you all this time..."

As she spoke, she ran her hands nervously down her jeans. She bent forward and her lanky ginger hair began to hide her eyes. Beside her, the man had his fists clenched and he shook them in puzzled emotion; with the toe of one slider he was nudging one of the scattered teeth from the bonelines.

"...we fetched you from the beach. We were the two who actually found you there! We wanted to adopt you, but the bastard authorities... anyway, anyway... we waited all these years for this... to have our little girl back... and we know who your real..."

The first arrow entered one cheek and exited the other. A second struck the woman in the side of the skull and sent her whole body cartwheeling along the cinder path, while the two arrows that struck the man in the back pushed his belly forward and dragged his legs backwards, pitching his body stiffly onto its face. The white snipers reloaded as a puff of dust rose from the woman's hair. Blood sprayed from the man's lungs. A gasp, like that of a long monster, rippled back along the vale and up into the hills.

"What the Lord giveth, the Lord taketh away," quipped the Chairman; the execs at his right hand looked queasy, but ecstatic.

The angels opened their wings and they stretched further than Mandi had ever seen them go before. Whatever the magic the Hexamerons had hoped to perform, it had only worked partially. Now the angels' dark shades flexed and expanded, and as they telescoped their wings, they seemed to suck in the last silvery beams of the daylight and blast them back out. Like a giant car bumper caught in following headlights on a dark country lane. Mandi rested into their feathers as something like insanity seemed to rise up inside her, smacking her stomach aside and washing everything except itself out of her head. Mandi felt like she was levitated; that she was hovered above the old Hall, that she could see the sea and all the darkness in it. She realised that the pain in her chest was not an arrow point but she had forgotten to draw breath; and as she inhaled the chilling air she felt the darkness enter deeply with it. Thin tendrils of blood ran to the edges of her and questioned the borders, something with long arms and many mouths picked at successive images of everything she cherished. The teeth dug in, the mouths pulled apart, Mandi felt her body come apart like a wave breaking on a beach and then draw back together as the waters receded. A mermaid's purse washed up on a beach, she was dry and shiny and hard and she raised her arms to the black sky and let loose a ferocious shout.

The white snipers lowered their crossbows from the shoulder position, each arrow point was aimed to where they guessed the soft organs of Mandi and the angels might rest. The Chairman raised his arm. The horizon exploded.

Chapter 62

"Ah, theory and practice," sighed the caretaker, breathlessly, "never works out in the field the same way as at the desk", hanging on to the edge of the mobile home as it began to swing around in a vortex. Protected by the gentle rise to the disappearing railway tracks, the caretaker's chosen lookout had fared better than the other caravans and even the more permanent structures; all of them uprooted and set off towards the Vale Without Depths. It was a lonely flood the caretaker was rising on. He had expected the end to come quickly and singularly; instead the waters increased with each wave. It was the highest of spring tides and with the storm surge the winds picked up behind the waves. There was nothing apocalyptic about it; it was just happening like shit and beauty.

So, he thought.

Then She rose. A solid wall of unsolid; a melting mirror held in a frame of foam. He knew what was inside it – nothingness – but its surface was as dark as anchovy on toast. No, Marmite! He laughed like a drain. A sickening, salty sheen, rousing itself to the vertical, a horizon tipped on its end, an ocean like an erected sheet on strings of steel, the flat puppet of the deep performing, the curtain of water itself the star. There was no point in crouching, all would be done in seconds. The mobile home was dragged towards the ocean by the backdraft of the giant wave. Like the sudden in-breath before a tsunami, the trailer was drawn across what remained of the railway and above the drowned dodgems and amusement arcades, over what remained of the dunes – and that was little – and down a bubbling beach towards a hinge of land and ocean fury. He was riding that trailer like an ungainly surfer.

His legs braced to take the tipping and rising, the home still holding its shape as the season's shampooed mattresses and clean sheets played dancing games in its rooms, the caretaker stared into the mass of water for some sign of where She might be within. There was nothing. No clue, no gift, no vision, nothing. "Ah", he thought, conclusively, as the flat of the waves thudded into his face and slammed his jaw into the back of his skull, twisted his arms around his back and his legs up and above his head, and jammed his spine spherically, "that's nothing, She's..."

As the waters took him, on the other side of the estuary and braving the highest point of the sea wall, a gang of teenage boys, watching the rollers entertainingly swamp The Sett, witnessed the caretaker's elevation and transfiguration into a shoal of pieces. A promising gymnast, an impressively continent young drinker, a wise ass and a secret but unrewarded devotee of Jesus; after this, nothing quite turned out as they expected.

Chapter 63

In the chaos at the rear of the Hexameron Essay Society's forces, as the first waves of the storm topped the peak of the low coastal hills and fell into the Vale Without Depths, caravans and trailers swept along in their vanguard, Mandi and the angels made their escape. The Hexamerons did not 'do' chaos well. In panic, their elites sank back into the spectral embrace of Athelstan's Saxons while their employees ran for their motors. The hunt struggled to control its packs. The white coats of the programmers were progressively stained.

For Mandi there was already a track. The route taken by the burning wheel over the estate boundary across the field and through the trees, Mandi now took in reverse; her angels following. It was a while before the Hexamerons registered the disturbance in the avian grid. By the time they noticed the escape of their enemies, half of their forces were knee deep in sea water. Those trying to escape in vans and SUV's were digging their way deeper into submerged mud; huge blossoms of red soil opened up around their entrenched vehicles. Regrouping on the higher ranges just below Mandun Hall, their elite formations were affected for the first time by the rising winds. Isolated trees began to topple around the edges of the estate's parkland, wires between the pylons swung violently and played odd fluctuating notes as if an electric Pan were weaving mayhem. The grid of birds had been engulfed by low cloud.

"What difference does it make?" yelled the Chairman at the fringe of lieutenants and white snipers. "What did you ever really get from the birds?"

While the Saxon spectres, mindless of the waters, swept across the fields of the Vale and towards the Western slopes of Haldon Ridge, followed like hypnotised rabbits by a rag-taggle army of those office workers and maintenance staff who had escaped the surge, a tighter brigade of Hexameron leaders, CEO's, scientists, mounted huntsmen and huntswomen, packs of hounds and black dogs, and white snipers set out after Mandi and her sisters. In a second contingent, Grant Kentish and his followers, remarkably self-possessed and steely amongst all the wallowing and drowning, swept up the hill. Kentish's cloak barely rippled in the storm, his fedora majestically sealed to his scalp. His gang flowed with an unearthly blueness through the darkening, like sodium lamps obliterating the remaining colours of the flowers and hedges; Janine, scrying in her powder compact, pointed the way that Mandi had gone.

On the footpaths, the angels were even more human than before; sliding in and out of divinity. The numbers of their fingers changed; Apollonia looked gorgeously male, chin chiselled like a movie star, then with a shake of her hair she was equally gorgeously female. Mandi needed them, but she was suspicious of seduction.

"It's just what they do," she comforted herself under her breath.

And it amused her that she was leading them now. They were not far from the tree of a thousand condoms, but now, Mandi decided, it was time to take the tracks she did not know. There was something too odd and exhibitionist about hiding out at a dogging spot. They needed spaces with subtler signs and more oblique energies; perverse routes that psychologists would never guess. Being with April, Mandi had learned a super-sensitisation to the terrain. The meaning of moss, the songs of the birds or the incline in the hill were all still mysteries to her, but she was beginning to feel things about them, intuit stuff. Just as she had learned to manipulate the big shots at work, to bend their assets against them, to bring down the mighty by a strategic withdrawal of affection, so she was learning the irrational ways of her own land. To feel the give within the take of things. She had always been this person; but only now was she becoming it, far and free from exchange and management.

One other thing she knew for sure; hobgoblins were real. Once you took it for granted that what you saw in the corner of your eye had a usable meaning, then the obvious and the close to hand – the shapes and patterns and tangles – all became thicker, deeper and more responsible for themselves. The path became a partner in your escape, a co-conspirator in your strategy of avoidance; a field of awareness ran all around rather than just ahead.

Mandi was enjoying her new post as commander of angels: as she loped they loped, as she crept they crept, and as she stood and listened they did the same. Witnessing the murder of two sets of parents in a handful of minutes had barely affected her. But she had not blocked it out, she had look at it head on; and in the moment she had made herself someone else; she was a mutant, she was sure. There was something very wrong with her.

Subtle things became plain. A slight darkening in the shadows where a footpath had been allowed to grow over, a fractional contrast to an animal track that would quickly run out. When Sidwella lifted her scythe to sheer away some brambles, Mandi placed her hand on the shaft and quietly led them around the obstruction, careful to hold back the branches, picking up any shed feathers, ducking down a lane that had been walked for centuries being subtly lured recently into disuse. There were malignant forces at work.

At one point the trees to one side of the path opened up and the vista ran all the way down, over the fields and parkland of Mandun's neighbouring estate, to a small seaside town. As Mandi turned away to keep up their pace the sea swept in and only the church spire on the very inland edge of the town was left above the water. Mary remarked the loss, but made no comment to the others as they pressed on.

That was the other big thing; there was a trace in the landscape. Something in the shaping of things; transitions from one kind of green to another, curves that ran too far to be natural, a narrative in the path, the invitation remaining where a portal had been removed. Despite the gloom of the storm and the raging tree tops, the delicate overlaying of layers – historical, architectural, organic – was increasingly illuminated for Mandi. The angels cast a kind of light that illuminated different shapes of ancientness and from the shadows they helped the trace of things that were very old and huge and extensive to pick themselves out from the green and brown of the ferns. Mandi had always hated the nostalgic nationalistic bullshit that permeated her parents' milieu; of Olde England and, god help us, the 'Celts'. Picture book nursery rhyme crap. How had she become a latter-day sucker for Old Dumnonii, magic-peaceful primitives who had failed to learn any decent architecture even when the Romans were building it in their faces? Un-monumental, close to natural contours, chancels in the corners of terrain; there was something in the way the shadows bent, in the stream's bend; something that was still looking out of the cave and down from the hill.

By steep and narrow lanes and a climbing path that was old but ill-maintained, Mandi and her angels quietly put distance between themselves and Mandun Hall. Vaulting a new fence blocking the unsigned entrance to the path, they clambered up a short bank and onto a wide metalled road. It had a bad feeling, Mandi thought. All her attentiveness to the terrain and it had only brought them onto a long, wide road, stretching off in both directions, flanked by wide green verges and crowded by tall trees. It was too exposed. Why the angels were comfortable to walk it, she could not imagine. A pair of pillars, constructed of immaculate ashlars, set a few metres back on the verges, suggested that there was aristocratic appropriation from way back. The straightness felt Roman or older; the route of a trade at odds with the place. To one side of the long stretch was a villa with a tower that did nothing to ease Mandi's suspicions. On top of the tower was the dome of an observatory and Mandi had a bad feeling that the Hexamerons would have been involved here, hiding chickens in the cupboards and mixing vigils of astronomy with disrobing for some old goat.

"They did not set out to become that," said Mary. Her red hair fell across the shoulder of a wing. "They were seekers, excited when the scales fell from their eyes and they could look at things rather than old books, when they could describe to the future what it would think rather than take orders from the past. But they were not satisfied with overthrowing gods; rather than let the Old Ones have their twilight, they dreamed of making a new dawn, and when they failed, when their theory of everything turned out not to include their own immortality, they planned to neutralise the universe rather than reverence its chaos. Now, their games with magic have turned serious; they are seeking a monster to swallow all things. A total destruction to clean up what they see as their mess."

"Is that why you're here? Is that why She came to the Hall?"

Just within the first row of trees, were the outlines of a huge earthwork, running off into scrub.

"Who knows? Maybe it was the depredation of the ocean, the rising temperatures, something to do with Brexit and all the hatred that threw up, the growing tyranny of various regimes..."

"The Hexamerons have monsters too?"

"They have an idea of monsters. Hence the magicians. They want the magicians to make them a final monster to end everything. That's their idea of perfection now; a universe falling prey to itself. To pass off their psychopath-theory as an ideal."

"Only their elite know of this intention," Apollonia elaborated. "They tell the lower ranks it will be the unifying of sexual, creative and entrepreneurial energies..."

Water ran in thick streams from Apollonia's mouth and stained her chest with silt. Sidwella began to cough up sand.

"Don't think your sensitivity to the path is sufficient, you need to be worshipful," Mary wagged her wings, her face was stony and there was a lichen green and orange blemish on her cheek, "the problem for humans is that they invented gods and tainted worship. By worship, I mean extravagant love and extreme submission to the being of the world..."

"Don't waste it on gods!" Sidwella spat another mouthful of sand onto the tarmac.

"We know what they're like," bubbled Apollonia.

"Those who do not submit to being," pronounced Mary, raising her wings and pausing in the middle of the road, as if she addressed listeners skulking somewhere out beyond the earthwork, "are killers, for being is greater and more deserving to be reverenced than masters. Reverence is not reassuring, reverencing has no product, nothing is exchanged or made by reverence, reverence is wasteful, unreplaceable, unreproducible. If you can live in the poise of worship you will do well in the next few hours."

"Poise?"

"To fall before being, to bow yourself, to look at the ground of your existence, reverence the dirt and filth in which your walk, worship that... don't tell that to any gods, the fools think we are worshipping them!"

The three angels laughed and the trees shook as if a factory of gongs had fallen in a storm; even the raving treetops resonated for a while with their cheers. Mandi noted how wet and straggly the angels' long hair had become in the long climb though the trees. Then there was silence. As if a switch had been flicked. Sidwella and Apollonia shrank back. Silty water splashed to the ground. Mary sheathed her wings, her expression grew stonier, she swung around to face the direction they had just come. Just beyond the observatory tower was a phalanx of private security vehicles, blue lights flashing silently, flanked by platoons of men and women in hi-viz jackets swinging a single delivery of identical maple baseball bats.

Swinging around to face their direction of travel, the road was now occupied by the Hexameron elite; the Chairman and his acolytes, the white snipers dangling their bows over their shoulders, the pack of giant black dogs dwarfing the humans, eight ancient life-sized and featureless wooden dolls pushed on trolleys by museum staff. All around them, just within the trees, were the shades of the Saxon army holding their axes and spears, two-handed, above their heads, shields slung around them; a few wore helmets, but mostly bareheaded and roughly shaven. As Mandi and the angels turned about them, the forward ranks of Saxons were joined by row after row of soldiers, each line carrying heavier and more misshapen weapons. Until in the far distance, dark within the trees, gangs of archers appeared, feathered arrows in their quivers, and braced themselves in the firing position. All were burning with certainty.

Flanked by the modern hunt, the shade of St Athelstan rode through the Hexameron elite, who each in turn held out their fingers to touch the flesh of the King's hand. Even the giant dogs nuzzled at his long green robe, jumping up to touch the thin cream surcoat decorated with a golden cross pattée; the points of his simple crown were shining golden spheres. Across his lap he balanced a prodigiously broad, double-bladed sword. His soldiers shook their weapons and the clanking and grinding rekindled the sound of the storm so all above was roaring and wiping away. Fresh spring leaves were torn from the uppermost boughs and fell about the King.

Sidwella broke ranks.

"She's a Saxon princess," Apollonia whispered to Mandi, "it's a bullshit story, she's really a Celtic water goddess, but that's another bullshit story; so, now we find out which bullshit is strongest, or if it's all about something else!"

Blood was proudly running down Sidwella's back from a wound that had opened up across her neck. Instead of the straggly wet hair, her wild blonde locks had wrapped themselves into two long plaits. As they coiled and pointed, felt and reached, Mandi felt an odd pang of attraction and vulnerability; she wanted to be held by them, and she was unsure who her feelings were serving. When Athelstan shifted his reins and brought his cream steed alongside Sidwella, Mandi began to sweat with jealousy. She felt herself brace, ready to do something she had not yet thought of, and as she did, the forces in the forest took a step forward; their collective stride sounded like a hundred thousand drums beaten once.

Sidwella sensed Mary coming up on her and swung the scythe in a long sweeping arc, but Mary was too quick and fluid for her. Mary flowed around the arc of the blade and then moved in, holding the thorns of her rose stem to Sidwell's femoral and brachial arteries, and releasing the serpent into the weave of her plaits so that Sidwella's head was jerked backwards onto the top of her back exposing her pumping jugular.

"Some virgin," thought Mandi.

Athelstan's horse reared and backed away, scattering the Hexameron elite. Sidwella was defenceless; the plaits fell out of her hair, her scythe rattled onto the macadam, her sudden regal elegance bent in two. Mandi wanted to close her eyes, but she was frozen; she waited for more blood. But Mary withdrew the rose, and the serpent fell from Sidwella's hair onto the road alongside the scythe; Mary knelt beside them, picking up the scythe and offering it, and her neck, to Sidwella.

"There can only be three sisters," Mary pronounced, "destroy me now and you three can be powerful once more."

Controlling his horse, the Hexamerons flooding back around him, Athelstan steered his horse to Sidwella's side, then caught up his sword by the blade and held it out in invitation towards his Saxon princess. Sidwella stepped back from the sword in horror, as if waking from a nightmare. Mandi knew immediately what had happened; like her, Sidwella had been reminded by the King's gesture, turning his sword into a Christian cross, of the pub sign they had passed after being turned away from the cave, a copy of the cover art for a paedophile authoress's Arthurian romance about the overthrow of pagan goddesses. Sidwella helped Mary to her feet. The three angels clustered together, and once again their wings opened in a collective shielding of Mandi as if they expected the attack to begin. But things would get worse first.

Mandi had forgotten about Grant Kentish. Now, a fanfare of reversing vans greeted the arrival of The Old Mortality Club. The security guards cleared the road for their entrance at the head of a Roman legion, fasces flag and colours flying and tall shields giving them the appearance of a single machine. The iron points of the Roman javelins already smelt of blood. Kentish danced before the wavy sunbeam shapes on the soldiers' shields, brandishing his fedora, as if he were now the Solar God, the burning wheel turning everything.

"Think," Mandi told herself, "think!" But all she could think of was her fear, and her visions of the non-existent car crash peeling off the faces of Anne and Bryan, and how trivial that now seemed in light of what she was about to suffer. Kentish, the Chairman, Athelstan, and the Legatus Legionis of the Romans;

was there any way of setting them at each other's throats? More likely, they would each take one of the angels.

The ground shook. It was deeper than the raging of the storm. The various forces looked about them; the angels exchanged questioning glances. The shivering grew more rapid and was now accompanied by a deep booming rumble, there grew a frightened certainty that this would be the most powerful force to join the field so far. For the angels, this might mean escape, or the beginning of crushing defeat. Then a new sound, as if a giant were screwing up paper bags the size of tower blocks. Trees, already shaking in the fierce wind, began to bow and jerk, followed by the preliminary signs of the coming force.

Shadows at first, despite the general gloom, big enough to block out the miserly light. Then the things themselves, as tall as palaces, thirty twisted colossi marching in two lines; their few flowering buds worn like crowns on their vast dry trunks, spirals of lifelessness. Walking chestnut trees. Their step was a kind of drag, their roots as desiccated as their limbs, their locomotion illogical, wrong, at odds even with the forest. They kept to the design by which they had been planted; a forgotten purpose they had stuck to, even in their final shamble. They smashed down living trees and smothered shrubs as they passed, leaving a trail like that of a monstrous slug, spilling sap for slime. Here and there, their dark claws and serpent boughs pulled down the tops of the living trees and threw limbs to the ground, scattering Saxon soldiers. The Roman legionaries held their shields above their heads. The dead chestnut trees were indifferent to the battle; marching through the ranks of scattering Hexamerons and disappearing into the northern reaches of the forest. Somewhere there was a dual carriageway beyond the trees; Mandi wondered what the drivers would make of the arboreal giants. The sound of their progress intensified as the last of the two lines of arboreal cadavers disappeared into the green, dragging the uprooted woody cephalopod maw, and then was gone, swallowed in the storm.

There were more people in the trees, now, revealed by the passage of the dead trees.

Where there were traces of earthworks stood a tribe of the strangest sort. There had been a kind of unity, despite their contrasting styles of weaponry, between the white snipers, Saxon warriors, legionaries, CEO's and modern hunters. These arrivals, however, were unlike anything so far lined up around the ancient road. They wore dull diamonds and soft zigzag stripes, their wool garments made them vague and undifferentiated; and though it was mostly the men who carried the long swords and javelins, the entire tribe made up their force, sons and daughters woven into the centreless mass. Some tall men stood out for a moment and then seemed dragged back into the simple patterns on their outer coats, while the women carried sharpened spindles, some still wrapped around with whorls of wool, as if they had been surprised in the middle of an unexceptional day two thousand years ago. Even the young looked with drawn faces; pain was their daily ally against indifference. Fingers moving along the shafts of their tiny weapons. The Dumnonian children, faces red from the soil, looked with wonder at the eight huge wooden figures on the museum trolley, like kids in a store eyeing the latest toys. The museum staff backed away, hiding among the white-coated technicians. The Chairman ordered the figures taken and disposed of and the staff reappeared and began to drag these replicas along the old road, hopelessly, aware that their museum stores would have been inundated by now. Once out of sight, they threw the figures and the trolley beyond the verge and headed off towards the dual carriageway in the hope of hitching a lift to safety.

At the sight of Athelstan and his Saxon forces, their nemeses, the Dumnonii bristled. It seemed that the time of fully-fledged physical combat had come, but then the Romans did something unexpected. On seeing the materialisation of the Dumnonii, the people of their occupied territories, and on an order from their Legatus, they lowered their shields and gave an uneven salute to the folk who had become their neighbours. Hands touched brows, some flung out an arm, and then on a second command, sharper than the first, the shields were gathered up, the soldiers turned about, and, to the consternation of Kentish their Solar King, they marched away back up the road they had come, scattering the yellow jackets of the security guards into the trees.

The solemnity of the Romans' withdrawal was somewhat undermined, when, just before they passed out of sight, the phalange split and the men dived into ditches either side of the roadway. Up through their middle drove a convoy of cars; aged family saloons and the primped rides of old-boy racers. Racing up the road towards the angels, scattering security guards, the cars swerved in unison onto the verge, chewing up the turf and spilling their occupants onto the road. It was Danny, the Julie Goodyear look-alike, her muscle-bound consort and a motley crew of other doggers. To Mandi's amazement, they joined her! Incapable of explaining themselves even to each other, they had felt called, stronger even than the thrill of encounters with strangers; that was all they could say. There was no time to ask more questions as new reinforcements began to arrive and gather around Mandi and the angels; all the while the enigmatic Dumnonii, silent and watchful, held their ground under the manic trees.

Hyenas were the first, in pack after pack, loping and grinning in an unamused way; immersed in the mass of them, a tall and driven man, straggly-bearded and wild-eyed, a hair parting as thick as a classroom ruler, greasy locks in two unequal waves, his coat tightly buttoned and a crumpled black dicky-bow hunkered down at his throat. He carried the massive jawbone of a cave bear in one hand; an Old Testament warrior come to draw a flood from the sands. The snarling of the hyenas curdled with the complaints of the storm. Thunder roared around the forest. Hobgoblins with the appearance of thick and hairy children walked with their knees bent the wrong way, fitfully assembled, furious and impatient for action, pushing at each other and withering the ferns with hard looks. The Dumnonii children gazed in amazement that these familiars would display themselves so openly; their parents smiled at the confirmation of their dreams. The hobgoblins strutted about, eyeing the road for pilgrims to trip. Around their heads circled fireflies, at which they took intermittent swipes. A circle of something shy danced around the goblins and then widened their fête to surround all the assembled forces, whirling about the trees like tiny particles; while something stranger with rabbit's eyes in its breasts strode four metres tall and as thin and bending as the trees, and smaller things that switched between hare and human.

A rivulet of adders collected at Mary's feet, snapping at her own serpent. While around the horses of the local hunt, sending the hounds into frenzied howling, rode a rancid force of wild hunters, their eyes pitted and their jaws unhinged, their horns the rusted parts of old motors, holding at their head a banner with a female figure painted in the centre of it. No sooner had they appeared than they fled at the first flash of red eyes, the black dogs recognised them as charlatans; whatever portent they represented it paled before the prospects of the swelling armies. The storm swept the wild hunt away like leaves in a playground; and swept in wave after wave of compatriots for the angels: blind knockers from the silent mines tapping along the ground with broken props, the Alphington Ponies, the Bocca della Verità mask floated in like the head of 'Zardoz', North African slaves from the Venetian galley wreck off Teignmouth at last liberated from the sands, navvies, a flock of herring gulls that landed and complained, a column of narrow headed ants and lost nightingales that arrived in dribs and drabs. Then a saturated Eddie Mann with a gang of other Midlands former-kids appeared from the trees; rescued at Exeter by Eddie and guided around the edges of the flooding. And more and more were joining....

The only new figure that joined the Hexamerons was a young man with a movie camera. Mandi recognised him and nudged Sidwella. It was the meditator from the Retreat House at West Ogwell. He wore the same hoodie and his eyes were still fixed on the ground; Mandi noticed now that he wore the same badge as the Hexameron Chairman, a black disc on a white background. It was a shape Mandi had seen in other places, not just on a badge.

The storm winds in the canopy bent a branch and snapped it; it dragged other smaller boughs into a cascade of greens, striking a Saxon on the shoulder and causing him to fall.

"Is chaos on our side?"

Mandi nodded to the milling of one section around another in both armies.

"I have a feeling that once the Saxons decide to do something, they'll cut our allies to pieces."

"This is not a battle between armies," said Sidwella. "It is a war of ideas. Each player here is a part of an argument. The Dumnonii rarely ever fight; formidable when they do. They are here because they are the life this place is a trace of; they fought beside the Romans at Hadrian's Wall – that's why the legion refused to fight them. Unlike the Romans, they never invaded anyone. Why not? Isn't invasion the organising principle of civilisation? The evolutionary way? Isn't that what every cultural machine in this county, paper flag for a sand castle or literary novel, has reproduced for centuries? Yet those folk over there evolved an economy that did not excessively exploit their terrain, scorned surplus and took what they needed to live. They built no temples or theatres. Their culture was freely accessible in the natural world which they interpreted as holy, communing with the genii loci of local spaces, from the corners of springs to the depths off their beaches; priests were of no use to them. They valued the unknown over those who claimed to know it. They worshipped what is lost..."

Mandi studied the stoic faces under the trees; beneath lines of pain and smears of red there was a militant peacefulness, an armed content.

"....what had status with the Dumnonii was a reverence for the darkness and nothingness within each person."

"But they disappeared?"

"Are you sure? Their DNA is in everyone in the county outside the cities. They are not here culturally. Except perhaps in the trace they left in eroded shapes in the land. What broke them was Christianity. For a long time they kept some autonomy; even in the tenth century they were surviving in Exeter alongside Saxons, like oil and water, just as they had with the Romans. It was King Athelstan over there, his project to unite a Christian nation, that really broke them, forced them out of the city. Their descendants stayed in the villages, but they conformed eventually. Not by the sword, but routine. Even so, certain values of Domna prevail..."

Not just the blonde plaits, but the wet straggly hair had gone, the wings were folded away, her scythe leaned against a tree; she was back to the April that Mandi had felt herself falling for once before and now felt it happen again; the luring intelligence of something trying to creep beneath a gateway.

"... a tendency towards peaceful co-existence – there were no medieval pogroms here such as besmirch Norwich or York – and faint echoes of the Old Religion surviving in the veneration of certain female saints and in the eerie feel of places like the spring at Lidwell or the caves. Study the church windows, the old ones, see how many times there are three goddesses, it matters little what their names are or whether they are saints or angels. They are the three consorts of Domna; the two that remain on land to reverence her and the special one taken to the deep with Her. The one..."

She glanced at Mary and then stared hard at Mandi.

"... who by knowing knows the deep. We struggle to contact the contemporary living; most do not hear us at all, not even those who say they believe in us, too busy promoting their own magic. But in our story, our culture..."

This from an angel, who minutes before, as tribute to her Saxon King, had struggled to cut off the head of her sister, the Mother of God, the very Symbol of the Deep! Mary's robe was now as blue as clear sea water on a sunny day .

"...we are trying to make contact with people in the present county. We have always done this at times of evil – the drowning of the slaves, the Blackshirts organising in the 1930s – times when She brought the storms and swept things away, keeping at bay attempts to subject all to a prevailing idea. For at the very deepest deep of the surviving Dumnoniian spirit is the moment when the Great Squid Mother confronted the Manichaeistic God of perfection and seduced him with the power of place and thing, and thus gave birth to matter without subjection to thought. And that is why the Hexamerons and their Beyondists are so angry!"

Mandi glanced over to the restless Hexameron army. What were they waiting for? Then Mandi thought she saw a ghostly squid hovering in the trees above the Dumnonian troops, dark tendrils reaching down towards the ground, a giant head flopping about in the shaking canopy, then a lightning flash lit up an empty space of writhing leaves. Thunder exploded and branches fell all about. The clouds opened and curtains of rain fell through the leaves, lashing the assembled creeds. In the confusion, an impatient programmer seized his moment, grabbed a spear from a Saxon and launched it in a clumsy arc towards Sidwella's back. Before it could hit its mark, the white snipers had raised their crossbows and fired off four shots, two each at Mary and Apollonia. There was a series of cracks like minor lightning strikes; the Saxon spear, its shaft split down the middle, and three of the crossbow arrows skittered across the wet macadam. The fourth arrow deflected from Apollonia's cheek and took out two of the dogging males, slashing a fleshy part from one thigh and passing through a flabby upper arm, knocking them to the verge. Their fellow enthusiasts gathered them up and dragged them across the mud to one of their cars.

The lightning flashed again. It lit up a scene uncannily like that of the graveyard that Mandi and April had found at the end of their walk. The three angels were stood back to back, against attack from any side, while Mandi knelt in the rain at their feet. She looked up at them; their bodies, clothes, faces were become an unhuman white and giant, they were monumental beneath a layer of plant growth. Moss had settled on their arms, lichen in their eyes, gelatinous algae on their lips; their stone white wings were folded together, the feathers interleaved like a single shield. Upon their brows tarnished stars glowed like street lights in November mist, their hair stood up on end, their weapons were turned to hypnotic flowers and their eyes raised towards the storm as if they could see things better by not looking directly at them. Suddenly they flexed and drove a ripple of destruction through the Saxon ranks. Bodies felt apart, weapons rattled against tree trunks and embedded in them, heads were kicked in all directions by fleeing comrades. Sidwella's scythe whirled like helicopter blades, the teeth of Mary's serpent sank into the soft flesh of unshielded ears and tongues sending victims into screaming madness, Apollonia's pliers dug rib cages from chests and pulled spines out through the backs of necks; soldiers fell all around like empty costumes of skin, shopping bags robbed and dropped by deadly thieves. As the Saxons turned and ran they chose their nearest route of retreat, back down to the Vale, soon breaking from the trees and across the fields, but the waters from the coast were coming up to meet them and they were forced to tack around to the West.

The Dumnonii gave chase, followed by the doggers, their cars skidding down muddy farm tracks and careening across soggy fields, despite their wounded, the blood-spattered interiors of the cars like field hospitals. The Hexameron elite, two and three to a horse, raced away along the Port Way before tangling with astounded traffic on the B3912, cutting back down through the moor and crossing the fields above the Lovecraft villages, arcing to rejoin their panicking foot soldiers.

The angels were fixed, statuesque for a while, in the centre of their assault. A circle of evaporating spectres lay all around them. A handful of bloodied white coats were being spirited away by hobgoblins; shattered branches lay under a steaming carpet of fallen leaves, wet and shiny. Down in the Vale below, James Lyon Widger was leaping hedges again, not avoiding the goblins but leading them, his pocket bible thumping against his beating heart, a racing paradiddle, while running beside him were the horde of hyenas ready to launch horrors on any fallen Hexameron. Tiny packs would occasionally detach from the herd to despatch an unfortunate spectre.

"They who have reverence," said Apollonia.

"Will prevail," completed Sidwella.

Down in the Vale, fleeing towards the villages, the troops of the Hexameron Essay Society were struggling in the terrain. This was not their place. There were few Saxon villages, few crossroads, few greens for assembly, few manor houses around which to mount a defence. It was a place without walls or ramparts, the only earthworks were ancient gathering sites on the tops of hills, easily surrounded. How were you supposed to defend a stream or cave? For the Dumnonii, rapidly following their own faint trace in the land, the field of battle for them was the same as the space of their sacred plots; strategy was a kind of worship. A sacrifice had begun.

The strange stalking thing with rabbit eyes, the hobgoblins climbing into a mine in one field and emerging from a spring in another, the hyenas with their manipulation of the shadows, the Dumnoniian children running ahead as the fingers of a knowing hand, touching the paths for affordance or resistance; the Hexamerons had no counter troops for these lightning fast adversaries who popped up whichever way they retreated. They were helpless in the fields where they fell victim to Widger's packs. They were helpless on the paths where nothing in appearances could warn them of the strange deaths that lurked there.

Meanwhile, the angel trio intuited a map of atmospheres in their shivering feathers and spread it across the swathes of their forces; a trembling ambience by which their troops could feel their way. In a spreading act of geographical and ambient miscegenation the collective premonitions and touches of the thing with rabbit's eyes and spectres and inspired doggers fed back and became a loop between angels and soldiers, became field-like, planes without continuity, broken cosmic consistencies healed by the faintest trace of elsewhere and elsewhen, drawing the robins in.

As the angelic troupes ranged across the Vale and spilled towards the villages, surrounding and ambushing the pre-medieval hierarchies of the Hexamerons, the clouds of the storm briefly cleared and birds fell from the briefly opened skies in thousands and thousands. Mandi and her angels rushed to support them, crossing the farms of the Hoarfrost Estate and heading down the hollow ways towards the Lovecraft villages. Higher up, closer to the little moor, the Hexameron elite scanned a landscape they suddenly found they did not understand; so open and explicit, and yet every move they made drew snakes and goblins and loping things with faces in their chests from every hedge. When they took a hidden path its sides erupted with snapping badgers, catching at their feet and fastening to their heels.

Dependent on their smart phones, the Hexameron commanders struggled with the unreliable phone signal. When they were able to give orders their commitment to straight lines, targets and achievements, to the fastest route from A to B, left their troops at the mercy of everything from C to Z. Their mechanical concepts of survival, fitness, symmetry and singularity, not only did not mesh with the terrain, but were eaten up by it. Ideas learned from books about desert wars, during their contractors' urban mopping up operations or from the strategies of anxiety they sold to foreign partners did not fit here, but sent their forces in unreal formations into the jaws of reality. The programme of the Machine had been shared to the devices of their foot soldiers, but the angelic upstarts had refused to get with the rules. The Hexamerons' options were shrinking away. Their hopes for a great Idea were fading. A long battle looked to be ending prematurely.

The waters that had washed across the Vale Without Depths were spreading west, flooding caves that had once been submarine and were again. The storm surge had already broken against the base of the Great Hill and crept up towards the deconsecrated chapel on the top at West Ogwell. The salty water seeped through the cracks in the volcanic rocks and into its curling recesses, where something sealed and dry and dark had begun to regenerate, filling out and pushing itself upwards towards the surface. For the Hexameron troops, all this left only a narrow channel of land along which to retreat and regroup. As the Saxon detachments attempted to maintain their formations in retreat they became increasingly bogged down in open fields or wedged onto hollow lanes unable to raise their weapons or defend themselves against the Dumnonii and their allies who launched stinging attacks from their raised sides, the angels guiding these ambushes with the help of new allies among the recently liberated robins, who invited the angels to patch into their perceptual fields.

Observing from its vantage point, the Hexameron elite rejoiced for a while at the sight of a flock of herring gulls, taunted and tailed exactly by a flight of their rooks. The group enjoyed the extraordinary tailing capabilities of their dutiful avian collaborators, and the possibility that the birds might still hold the key, attaching themselves like warning drones to the angels' ambushers, until it dawned on one of the programmers that what they were applauding were the gulls' shadows on the hillside. Scrambled attempts to find the avian grid were unsuccessful, even in the briefly open sky; instead, the sounds of blackbirds, chaffinches, wood pigeons, green woodpeckers and goldfinches singing sunnily to the territoriality and specificity of their spaces returned combatively to the air.

"Chaos!" complained a programmer, holding up his tablet for anyone who would look. "We're losing our information!"

There came a crack. If the march-past of the dead chestnuts had rattled the ground, this din disturbed the core of the planet and the counterpane of the sky. A deep grinding sound, of two plates shifting along the Stickleback Fault; a screaming, tearing wound of rock as its subterranean layers wrenched out of alignment and fought to right their dislocation. A giant puff of dust rose in a curtain from the High Street of the Bay, throwing its manhole covers over the tops of buildings, splitting the Necroscope Hotel in two (it was consumed in fire) and ripping up the fields between West Ogwell and the Hoarfrost Estate, opening a chasm into which divisions of the Saxons, packs of black dogs and straggling security guards tumbled, cried, and fell silent. King Athelstan's horse reared on the edge of the fresh chasm, stumbled and toppled in, the King's head smacking against the side on the way down, his crown ricocheting from face to face, when abruptly the two walls of limestone slammed together again.

The filmmaker in the hoodie had early observed through his viewfinder the opening crevice as it raced through a meadow and had gone scampering up the hill towards the deconsecrated church. Far off, under the Irish Sea, parts of the sea floor fell away. Up above the surface of the sea seemed to give way, dragging a trawler under, before roaring back upwards to form a double wave that would soon inundate the coast of North Somerset and then, two hundred miles to the North-West, devastate the towns of Tramore and Dungarvan in the Republic. The tremors rattled the sea floors along the Bristol Channel and reached around Land's End to the red cliffs and limestone floors of South Devon; disturbing tiny shrimps and giant mysteries alike from their lairs of slumber.

As the dust from the earthquake began to drift across the fields, the Dumnonii women shouted and pointed, waving their spindles. A memory of beasts from the oldest days had been released and a brief translucence was modelled in falling red dust: the figures of elk, cave bear, mammoth, wolf, sabre-toothed cat and mountain lion were briefly returned. James Lyon Widger let out a violent "huzzah!" The Dumnonii hunters licked their lips, while the Saxons fled at the sight of things they thought exterminated. High up on the hill at West Ogwell, a part of the hillside slipped away; a landslide that revealed a shiny, wet, black wall of something that was moving and pulsating, its texture as strong as a hard plastic, but rippled like a puckered slug. The boy in the hoodie ran up and touched the black surface with his hand, it touched him back, and he began to shout, calling the surviving remnants of the Hexameron forces to muster to him.

Like lost children suddenly hearing a familiar voice, the remaining brigades of Saxon soldiers, a stray black dog, the whole of the local hunt and its hounds, a security van bouncing down the farm track at the bottom of the hill, a muddy and miserable group of Old Mortality sybarites with Grant Kentish at the head, his fedora squashed and cape in tatters, and then the dribs and drabs of the trailing employees of the Hexameron companies in their hundreds, a growing crowd of frightened combatants, began to gather before the boy in the hoodie. He stood authoritatively before the dark thing in the hillside, it was making the shape of a featureless eye; the touch of the thing and the surge of power from the angry planet had filled the boy in the hoodie with certainty and vision. He saw it all now, and others would see it as he saw it. His eyes shifted commandingly across his gathering detachment, while under his breath he was casting a spell to bind and destroy his enemies and secure him the leadership of the Dark Hexameron Revolution.

Chapter 64

Mandi followed the angels as if she were walking in a nightmare. She had somehow compartmentalised whatever it was she had seen slaughtered on the lawn of Mandun Hall. After all, she already thought that Anne and Bryan were dead, and the new 'parents' who had appeared, who were they? So, in the end, to her way of thinking, no one was alive who had been dead and no one was dead who had been alive. It was not so easy, however, to box up the slaughter of the Hexamerons' dupes, no matter how malign and stupid they were. It was the transience of it all. The cold trade in spectres and the fragility of limbs was getting to her. Nothing connected by nature need stay that way. All could be decapitated on the orders of mayhem. What was the point of anything? She was not a soldier. The angels had taken their opposition to the Big Idea too far; their love of things was the cause of too much dismembering.

The coldness of the quantum was worst. She felt the shivering of probability and the agitation necessary to hold the super-positions free of collapse, but there was as much a removal from the funk of things as there was immersion in its below-base matter. Wasn't it all the same inhumanity? How they would laugh at her in the office for her sentimentality, but too much that was fundamental was being rocked for Mandi. So, lamely, hating herself for it, she tagged on resentfully behind the three drowned sisters as they burned their way across the fields. She felt their disapproval; she was a chink in their armour and they let her know it. If she was honest with herself, she felt the same way. She wished she had her Remington, or her caretaker.

Skirting the Great Hill, a space too easily surrounded, the angels followed quiet lanes, their great height enabling them to see over the hedge tops; their communion with the birds providing them with coloured diagrams of their enemies' locations. Avoiding a disoriented but still dangerous gang of Saxons, they slunk into the next valley along and Mandi recognised the pub with the faux-Arthurian sign; she longed to visit the church and sit before the paintings of the female saints. She was surprised by the indifference of her angels. What she thought was important, might not be so at all. Past a tree shaped like the skeleton of a leaping horse, and then through a gate, they found a way along the bottom of the valley beside a long flat field. Mandi was anxious. She was uncertain why; then it struck her that the storm surge might find its way this far inshore where the land lay so low.

As if she made the thing appear out of her own anxiety, there in the middle of the flat field, surrounded by retreating waters was a mobile home, swept in at the head of the storm surge. It was, inevitably, her home, Anne and Bryan's extensive trailer.

She climbed the fence into the field, unpicking the point of barbed wire from her trouser leg, and ran headlong at the house. The front door seemed remarkably solid given the journey the whole structure had just taken. It opened easily; she remembered its feel. She had not locked it when the angels came to call for her. Inside, there was more than she expected, more than there had been when she had left. It was not the disappointing shell she had first returned to from London, stripped of all her things. They were all back now; her drawings, her magic objects, the shelves of favourite books read over and over, the weird charts she got from 'sending away' for stuff, her 'Misty' comics, her clothes. She tried a few, but she must have put on weight; she felt uncomfortable in them, as if they were not really hers. She was an impostor, pretending to be herself. It was usually at a time like this that she sought out the whisky bottle, but, supernaturally, the thought made her feel sick. This was an odd kind of coming home.

The curtains were drawn; that was it. Like when someone dies and before the hearse leaves the house. But she dare not pull them open, for fear that Lost Horizon would be there, and the whole thing – the thing in the sea, the saint with the smashed mouth, the walk with April, the momentous battle they were in the middle of – had never happened. It was a dream she had just woken up from. Except she had not just woken up; no one wakes up by walking through their own front door. Do they?

If all her stuff was there, so should Anne and Bryan be, but she knew they would not. Still, she checked their rooms. Pushing open their bedroom door, she thought for a moment there might be two rotted things in the bed, but it was the disturbed pillows that Mandi herself had left that way. The journey overland, at the head of the massive sea surge had disturbed nothing; such was the solidness of the life she had assumed was mostly illusions and possibly lies. There was no Anne and Bryan, of course, but there might be one thing of theirs. She dashed to the drawers. Sure enough, it was all there, just as she had found it on her return from London. Even the things that she knew were now in the possession of the solicitors' office. She pulled out the various papers, then gently eased the folder in which the manuscript should be. Yes, it was there. Maybe this time it would reveal its secret; wasn't that why she had been called back? Effectively left her job? Seen two set of parents killed? To know!

She drew the sheets of paper from the envelope. It was just as before; the same paper, the same typed script, the same words. She scrutinised every line; desperately, hurriedly. She had a sense of angels outside the door, shadows of wings that darkened the entire trailer. Vision blurred; she used her finger to run along the lines of each sentence.

"That traces of an antediluvian civilisation with its attendant flora and fauna can be so readily found in the obscure lanes, fields and woodlands of this part of Devonshire has long been known to the coarse laborers that dwell in this lugubrious place."

It was just the same as before. The words, the font, the texture of the paper, the indentations made by the keys. But as Mandi's finger brushed the word "place" she felt her nail catch on something; a small piece of the full stop had chipped off. She ran her finger over it again and a little more of the full stop stood up from the page, she flicked it away and a small line of the paper's surface concertinaed and revealed a blackness beneath.

To find some resistance against which to pull, Mandi took the page through to the living room which was unreasonably bright. She placed the page against one of the shelves of the bookcase. She struggled to find the little paper 'ring pull', distracted by the books on the shelf. She had never remembered books like these: 'Rituals of the Black Church', 'Satan's Heroes', 'Secrets of the Martyrs of Beelzebub', 'Blood Sacrifice: Liturgies'... The spines were decorated with inverted Christian crosses, blood-smeared chalices and young women tied with ropes. She drew one out from the line of titles; Bryan and Anne had never shown her these. She thought they hated this sort of thing; this was what people had said about them. It was not true. Flipping the book open, the pages were blank. She pulled down another; blank again. And another and another – all blank. Mandi hurriedly took hold of the crumbled shard of paper and pulled at it as gently as her shaking hand would allow and the page began to unpeel. The process seemed very drawn out, despite her urgency, as though her limbs were caught in treacle or packaged with cotton wool, but eventually, having reached the edge of the sheet, Mandi was able to pull the whole veneer from the page to reveal a single large black spot, slightly tilted like a disc.

She ran from the trailer and across the field which was now full of stranded jellyfish, looking like translucent cow pats. The angels were standing, statuesquely, on the path.

"What's going on?" cried Mandi. "Nothing is as I remembered it!"

"Hasn't it struck you yet," soothed Apollonia, "that we might have been on a 'different' layer of Devon for a while now?"

"What does this mean?"

She held up the page with the black disc.

"That we are going to lose," said Mary, blankly. "That we have all been fighting the wrong enemy. Even She did not see this coming. Perhaps if we had had the birds on our side from the beginning..."

"What do you mean? A trick by the Hexamerons?"

"They will be the last to know."

Chapter 65

The young man in the hoodie, his distinctive black disc badge glinting in the last rays of the sun as the purple clouds crowded in above, was addressing his troops through the medium of a hijacked and adapted HoloLens programme. Freeloading on the Hexameron's avian platform, he had patched his comrades into his website, Tony 'The Summoner' Sumner-Crabbe; from where they were downloading an AR app that allowed them to collectively and semi-virtually realise the full size and shape of the black disc he had 'discovered' – by various deductions and leaps of faith – buried beneath the West Ogwell knoll. Tony had been an unwelcome hanger-on at the fringes of local occult groups since his early teens; he had attended all the public Hexameron seminars, though none of its members would acknowledge him in public or private. The Chairman had only once responded to his many emails; he had sent an attachment of the black disc that had inspired Tony to fashion his own homemade badge. The Hexamerons never spoke about ufos at their meetings; but Tony could always hear in their talks the voices of the aliens. He understood and believed them when they spoke of evolution as a controllable thing, of the wasted potential of human mental capacities (people had sure as fuck wasted his) and its future realisation; if such things could be controlled and realised in the future then they must have been controlled in the past. Not by humans, who were too primitive then. But by visitors; visitors who – as his website proved – had never really left. They would help humans take the next step; the chasm awaited and they had nothing to fear from it.

Tony threw back his hoodie just as the clouds covered the sun, the better to review the thousands that stood before him, arms raised in a 'Roman salute', phones held up to the hill, transfixed by the shiny black disc within, part alien technology and part geological stratum, sat like an egg in the nest of a curled black shape in the rock above it. The Hexamerons – at least not the present leadership – had never fully understood the real meaning at the heart of their ideas; but then they had run away from the 'other side', turned their faces from the black sun and failed to harvest the dark spark that Tony had vacated the shell of his body to welcome inside, the sombre flame that burned away all the Demiurge's failures and transformed all flesh into the great Alien Idea.

The black eye in the hill opened and it was full of teeth.

"The stars await you. The heavens await you. The gate is open. Change defeat on Earth to victory in Paradise. Lead me and I will follow," Tony tweeted.

On the screens the teeth of the beast flashed. The first of the troops shuffled forward, still holding their phones like initiates bringing offerings or sacrifices.

"Stop this fuckery!"

Mandi stood high above Tony and the inky eye. Beside the church tower, framed in the full bulb of giant oaks, flanked by her angels in monumental splendour, their wings spread, their faces flashing bioluminescences of orange and green. Mandi cast her gaze around. Other than the crowd that the boy in the hoodie had gathered to him, the rest of the Hexameron forces lay in shattered parts, strewn in the lower branches of trees, face down in ditches, piled up in hollow ways. The weaponry they never got to fire had been trampled into mud and cow shit or tossed into ponds. A ring of Mandi's own forces, reinforced all the time by new creatures – a drenching Cutty Dyer, swan worshippers, sprites, nymphs, dryads, and water horses, things the terrified Saxons recognised from stories they had formerly frightened themselves with – had formed within the blood-drenched fields, surrounding the last remnant of the enemy army. The doggers, tending their own wounded, had made surprising alliances with those who were not really or barely there at all; their familiarity with scrubland and improvised cover, their aptitude for arriving discreetly and leaving suddenly had served them well in the fighting.

"Who the fuck are you?"

The boy in the hoodie turned and looked up to the church. It was the boy that April and Mandi had seen right there, the 'meditator' with down-turned eyes. Only now that he looked up did Mandi recognise him as the round-faced conspiracy nut on the dunes, who had dropped the article on birds, a theory that turned out to be something like true. He was no longer in fatigues, but his blond hair and featureless face were enough. He stood out by his vacuity. He was the malevolent vacuum that had replaced the Hexameron leadership.

"And who the fuck are you?" Mandi responded.

The boy replied, "My name is Tony Sumner-Crabbe! People online call me 'The Summoner'! Ufologist, chaos magician, researcher! These are my flock!"

He prodded a finger towards the figures forlornly tramping up the side of the hill to the shadowy mouth in its exposed side.

"C – R – A – B – B – E. Yes, I'm the son of that bastard!"

Mandi knew who he meant.

"He abandoned me, like he abandons all his children. He was a fucking coward, Amanda! Forget him! He did stuff, but he couldn't be arsed to face up to his responsibility! He left me and my mum to get by on our own; she was his student!!! He should have been prosecuted! If they were in love, why did he leave her, eh? He was on good money! Why did he leave you?"

Tony pointed his finger at Mandi and some of the climbers looked briefly up towards the four figures beside the church.

"Going on pilgrimage, was he? Where to? Up his own arsehole? Don't look so fucking surprised, you know who you are! Sister!"

"Half-sister!"

"Same thing!"

"No! My Mother is no fucking student of anything or anyone!" And with that fury, Mandi threw out her arms and the air around her seemed to ripple.

"Be careful," counselled Mary, "his is a magic that eats the soul. See his followers, see how they are lost? His disc beneath the hill, his mirage of your home washed up in the field..."

"That was him?"

"Don't be fooled by appearances," Apollonia chipped in, unnecessarily.

"Those are the transferable rituals that destroy all places."

The first of the Hexameron foot soldiers entered the toothy eye in the hill. Mandi expected a spurt of blood, the sound of tearing flesh, but they walked quietly into the orifice and disappeared from sight. Tony 'The Summoner' was wide-eyed in gratified astonishment. Nothing else he had ever done had worked; the universe had been saving him up for its final moment.

"He's murdering people down there... with his Pokemon Go shit..."

"They seem very happy," said Sidwella, drily. Those forces yet to join the queue into the hill were waving their phones and cheering. As the light once more failed, their screens shone brighter. The crowd milled and seethed and then drew back to reveal the four white snipers, their bows slung over their shoulders, their masks pushed up to the crowns of their heads, their white jumpsuits splashed with gore, and bearing in each hand the heads of the Chairman and his CEO's. They laid the heads at the feet of 'The Summoner'.

"Can't you stop this?" Mandi whispered to Mary. "We've got them completely surrounded and we're letting them carry on like this!"

"There is something else here. Something that is guarding their greed for death... do you dare to call it out, because we do not..."

"But we can't just stand here and watch them!"

"We are statues. Just standing and watching is what we do."

"I thought you were saints!"

Mandi turned on her heels and began to run down the hill.

"Stop, you fuckers!"

The white snipers had time neither to raise their eyes or unsling their bows, Tony was mid-swivel and Mandi was within the arc of a leap, when the hill broke. Sheets of turf shot into the air and fell among the Hexameron revenant. Cows panicked, broke down a stile and threw themselves against the wall of the church, rebounding and scattering gravestones. A grinding sound went up, like the groan of a long-tortured prisoner; a curtain was drawn in heaven and a deeper purple gloom fell across the hill. Tony fell to his knees; the lithesome snipers joined him more coherently. The white of their costumes stood out from everything else, which had taken on the glamour of spilled blood.

Tony screamed above the industrial clamour.

"The second seeding of England!!"

Like a thick stream of volcanic ooze, squeezing itself through the toothy eye in the side of the hill, a cyclopean turd, a slug-like sliding thing heaved itself from the darkness into the gloom, its fanged fringes fastening upon the turf and dragging its mucus-spilling sides down the hill, huge bulges like fat seals fighting inside a black sack struggling beneath the surface and a giant and obscure limb flopping about and pulled along behind, while the eyeless prow ploughed through the topsoil, swallowing the Hexameron pilgrims and their screens beneath its oily bulk. Not quite enthusiastic enough to have been consumed, Grant Kentish danced around the skirt of the dusky beast, waving his fedora around his head in salute to the featureless thing, as bland in its dark way as Tony was in his fair looks. The Slug-Protector of the black sun disc shook itself three times, each time pulling another misshapen lump of lolloping worm-body from its orifice, each time the elongated organism shuddering before settling its skin into a rounded, bulging and embrocated smoothness, before drawing itself up for a fourth and final contraction. With a filthy sloshing sound the Thing spilled from the hill, folding the eye-mouth inside itself as it fully emerged. The pilgrims had been processing into its arse. To be born, the lubricious monster had turned itself inside out.

The Slug tipped the undigested organs of pilgrims onto the ground, which shook again. The three angels pulled Mandi away, racing in their floating-dragging way down the Retreat side of the hill and back along the valley bottom by which they had come. The church tower on the top of West Ogwell Hill shivered and fell with a crash into a chasm that opened up below, followed by the nave and the giant oaks; the hill belched a grey mushroom cloud of dust. The disturbance in the volcanic rocks had triggered the general plates once more and the crevices that had closed after the earthquake now opened up again. From their slits issued the Hexameron forces in lava-like forms, bodies crusted black, features charcoal and eyes jet. In the gloom they barely registered, but their heat seared the hedges; some low branches burst into flames, the fires driving the angelic forces surrounding the hill and its blasphemous worshippers towards the West, while the great form of the slithering beast, almost a mile long, further cut the angels and Mandi from their supporters.

Racing Northwards, egged on digitally by 'The Summoner', the revived remnant of the late Chairman's troops, reinforced by obsidian forces with a charcoal Athelstan at their head, strained to isolate and interdict the angels' retreat. As they ran, the remnant held their phones above their heads where Tony had replaced the grid of birds with one of back-engineered alien saucers, in swastika and Balkenkreuz livery. There was nothing there, of course; but then, by the time Tony had realised his dreams and brought the Hexamerons' war with being to a close, there would be nothing anywhere.

Chapter 66

Explosions bloomed across the fields, accentuated by the imperial gloom. Plumes blossomed subtly. Flashes in the paths and green lanes, among the trees and in the centre of expanses of common, marking the ubiquity of the infiltration. The angels drew back into the shadows of the trees, followed the streams and hid as long as they dared in caves and within the lips of wells. Each time they switched direction or terrain, the explosions would still come closer; until they found they were not choosing their route but had it chosen for them by the ordnance. Driven upwards, they re-crossed the Hoarfrost Estate, forced towards the moor and the beginning of Haldon Ridge. There, in a field below a ruined chapel, far from homes or farms, the full horror of the blasts became evident; they were caused by small birds, sparrow and starling mostly, devices strapped to their legs, detonated remotely. The birds themselves were no longer under the control of the Hexamerons, but while they were they had been weaponised, and when now by random they landed near a target identified by a drone they were triggered.

Mandi was unsurprised by the brutality, what mystified her was the crudeness; the ham-fisted nineteenth century industrial stupidity of it. When she saw the Queen Bee being helped across the ruts of the steep field by one of her toy boys, while another detonated the tiny birds from a tablet, she understood the irony with which everything over the last few hours would have to be re-read.

'After them, our turn.' That was her plan. The Queen Bee had digitised the violent fantasies of Edward Hyams, sitting in his wooden neo-classical temple at Hill House, chatting to the Blackshirt Soil-Associates and daughters of the esoteric elite; what a buzz it must have been for a former factory worker to say the dirty things that his precious betters feared to!

"Fucking moron," thought Mandi, "there would be no 'after'."

Mandi had no wish to confront, strangle, converse with or even see the Queen Bee. Mandi led the angels through a rickety cast-iron gate and into the railed compound of the ruins; surprised that the angels would let her take them into such an obvious trap. Instead of getting away, they seemed content to wait. Mandi dare not speak, hoping that by some miracle the Hexamerons would pick up a false trail and pass them by. But slowly, stone by stone, branch by branch, railing by railing, the surrounds of the chapel were occupied by the faces of insane personal assistants, blood-soaked huntswomen, Tony 'The Summoner', the sniper quartet, the Queen Bee and her toy boys with Professor Marley of the Erithacus group of 'ornithologists', a lone and gibbering security guard with a hi-viz tabard thick with his own vomit, the charred visages of senseless Saxon zombies, and a host of others whose exact identities had been torn up or melted in the passage of the previous few hours. Many of these were illuminated by the lights of their own screens; making the whole scene a gothic joke, with the glowering gloom wall and the barbed railings, the jumbled and chaotic masonry and the thick bush of ferns and brambles clogging the body of what had been the chapel nave, a thick web of green folded over the mouth of the former holy well.

"Very appropriate," said Tony, "the chapel of the Mad Murdering Monk; nice lonely place to die. And who do you think you are, thinking you can lead anything?" And with that he took a piece of the masonry and with a backhand swing smashed it into the face of King Athelstan, which, along with his royal body, crumbled into cinders. The Slug-Thing, catching up with its followers, rose above the chapel, arching high over the tallest trees and blotting out even more of the strangled light. "Your turn now," said Tony to Mandi, "sister."

Mandi spoke under her breath to the angels.

"Do the helicopter blade thing!"

"No use against Him," rasped Sidwella, nodding up at the Slug-Thing.

"You must have something more powerful. The darkness! The nothingness at the heart of everything, everyone, Her darkness! Use that!"

"It would be irreverent," explained Mary. "Only the three can use the nothingness, and we are... crowded."

"They'll win!"

The angels had never looked this human. Even Sidwella in her April form. Their wings were sheathed, their faces pink with the exertion of retreat, their cheeks soft and their lips bruised, their hair hung sweatily over their shoulders; red, blonde and black.

"Not every battle is fought to be won, our enemies are only fighting so that one day they will drive us to such desperation that we will bring our darkness onto the battlefield and then they will have everything, for even though we might win, they will have access to what is holy. The darkness is only the darkness so long as it refuses to step into the light, the nothingness is only nothingness for as long as it can resist manifesting itself, the unknown for as long as it refuses to explain itself. We only have reverence for being as long as we refuse to give up our inner lives. That is why we always fight by proxies..."

"You are the darkness! You are the darkness hiding inside light!"

Mandi had given up caring whether the Hexamerons heard her or not. They were arguing over being. Not her own being; all being. The peering faces were fascinated by the defeatism of their enemies. It was with some disappointment that Tony turned to his snipers, nodding for them to arm their bows.

Sidwella held out the scythe inviting Mandi to take it. Mary walked to stand before the centre of the gloom wall, where the altar had once stood, where now a pile of rubble was topped by mountains of moss and a bundle of thick brambles.

"This is dark magic?" whispered Mandi to Sidwella. The Slug beast up above chuckled as if a swimming bath of water went gurgling down a drain. His followers joined in with chirruping hiccups and jiggling heads.

"There can only be three of us, we must not squander our power."

"But why not me, why not you?"

Sidwella shook her head and lifted up her robe, beneath which another head, the same as the one upon her neck, and sentient, was fused to her belly, its eyes open, its lips smiling just as the other one was. The fused head spoke; its tongue splitting into many tentacles:

"I am already dead."

"Christ on a stick, you're a dark horse! Why Mary? She's not a martyr..."

"But she's not Mary, not really," said the fused head, "you are."

Somehow Mandi knew what it meant. Somehow she had always known what that meant. That she was neither Mandi, nor Amanda, nor anything else identifiable. She seized the scythe handle and, screaming "Muddy Mary, Mucky Mary, Murdering Mary, Hail Mary full of dirt and scum!" and with all the force she could muster from her battle-weary body, she swung the blade down on Mary and Mary was slain. A head useless in the moss. A body toppled into brambles and pricked.

Blood was splashed across Mandi's face. She could taste it on her lips, and suddenly she could hear and understand the many songs of the birds, even above the rumble of the Slug and the crying and howling of the wind in the apple trees above the chapel; they sang in confusion and horror at the ferocity and unnaturalness of the storm, while the herring gulls poured streams of untranslatable invective at the complacency of all other birds.

Sidwella's fused head spoke. "Now, you must join us in our world." Tentacles began to reach for her, curling around Mandi's chastened and apprehensive form, tickling feathers out from beneath her shoulders.

Before the two angels could complete their transformation of Mandi, one of the Hexameron personal assistants, her eyes burning with a fierce self-immolating passion, seized a mace from a Saxon noble's burned hand and flung it. Mandi, her nascent tentacles waving around her, teetered and the walls of the ruined chapel were instantly overwhelmed as the troops of the Slug poured into the nave, flattening what grew there, and engaging with the two angels. There was hardly much intention in the act, but hundreds of hands reached for her, the budding Mary-Mandi was pushed backwards over the well and with only a moment's resistance, the ferns and long grasses that grew over the deep funnel gave way, and she plunged in.

As she fell back, Mary-Mandi felt for a moment the release from the squeezing bony fingers of the Saxon troops, with a second's relief and then the thwack thwack thwack as the back of her skull struck stony outcrops from the sides of the well, driving sharp flints and pieces of skull into her brain, effecting the painless severing of the corridors between the various chapels of her abbey mind. She saw nothing, but felt the separating of the parts of her consciousness; memory running off in one direction, critical thought in another, desire yet another – mice scampering back to their cosy little nests. In the dank bottom of the well, barely damp now, her body landed, limp and uncoordinated; one arm trapped beneath her body, the other swept out in a gesture, tentacles in a knotted sprawl, one leg in a high kick and the other folded over and snapped.

Black soil settled over her eyelids. Her mouth was filled with a wet compost that she was beyond tasting. A puff of breath crept from the edges of her whitening lips and rose like a smoke ring up the chamber of the well. An indifferent puppet, tossed in a waste bin. Her eyes turned inwards; her soul guttered and was gone.

All was hidden. All was discreet. All was precious. All was protected.

The cosmos clicked; the turning of a page, the fall of a domino, the snap of a mousetrap. A deep yet barely discernible rumble spread through the loam and grit, the limestone ground its teeth and the shiver ran through the county. The Sticklepath Fault moved for the third time in a few hours. The low grumble disturbed folk in villages far to the North, sands tumbled on the county's Northern shore and its two parts moved a little further apart. Through cells and tissues came rumbles of realignments, switching of allegiances, revealing of motives, casting of lots, settling of scores and plumping of choices. It was the sound of metamorphosis.

Mandi had heard of near-death experiences – she could not get any closer – she waited for the tunnel of white light, for feelings of relief or euphoria. Instead she sat in what might have been a modern chapel or a doctor's waiting room and she thought. She thought about the life she had led for the last few years. The woman she had become. The battles she had won for herself, the crusades and pilgrimages she had forged through a male-dominated and self-satisfied world, hooked on its own complacency; how she had remained true to principles she was fabricating every day, how she had never been bettered in private interview or public debate, how she had been a modern warrior for unfashionable and traditional causes, a conservative who never gave an inch to prejudice or vested interest or narrowness of mind, never stayed silent when others were wronged, never paused before running to the side of those who needed finishing off with a merciful slash to the proverbial throat, first metaphorically speaking, and now for real. How she had been a scourge to the semi-intellectual and the radical hypocrite; an autodidact brought up in a trailer park she deferred to no one on class. She had empowered women and the best men – but never above herself – she had pulled up the weak with good ideas and she had brought down the powerful with bad ones.

And all of that, now or henceforth, meant absolutely fuck all.

The black walls of the antechamber spasmed. She heard the slosh of a distant grue. Everything moved in on her; both her names were gone now. The past squeezed out. Thick rivulets of a black fatty loam entered every orifice, gland and pore and convened; the shallow shell that had once constituted Mandi Lyon and then Aspirant Mary slipped easily into the dark maw of Muddy Mary and the long tendrils covered with toothy suckers pulled her deeper down to a single spark of consciousness that then fell upon the giant golden disc of Her One Eye. In a moment the lifetime of the cosmos flashed before her; from the breath of inspiration to a light that flared blackly, furious and cold, closing fold upon fold around itself, until it built from the grasping tentacles upwards to a chequerboard wing, a tree rooted in the oily ocean sprouting feathers from its bark, lifted on a rising flush.

Great Mary, muddy and squirty, mucky and murdering, flexed, as the universe retched.

The well of the lonely chapel spat the transformed Mandi out, in a spout of black bile, squid ink and afterbirth.

The troops of the Hexamerons stepped backwards from the mess. Saxon swords fell to the sides of disconsolate charcoal warriors when they saw that the well had given them back the woman; this was not how their stories went. Warrior-scientists glanced back and forth to each other and smeared their hands on their filthy coats; who would clear up this mess?

The eyes of the angels fell on the broken and bedraggled form that had once been the fearless Mandi Lyon; capable of slaughtering the Mother of God. Strips of her shirt hung down in shreds, her hair, matted in gunk and beetles stuck to the remnants of tiling that poked through the scrappy turf and moss; she was fused to the chapel. A black hinterland of scum spread from her carcass. Angelic heads fell and wings drooped.

It was as though the planet were confounded by the fate of Mandi Lyon; that no one could claim victory. That all were set back, everything was routed. Tony 'The Summoner' glowed with jubilant schadenfreude. There was still envy with some life in it; and up stepped the guru of The Old Mortality Club, Grant Kentish, his fedora finally lost and his hair scraped forward, picking the Saxon mace from the ground and raising it ceremoniously like a giant brass phallus above his head, placing his left foot carefully ahead of him and swinging the brazen instrument, he revolved it once around his shoulders and then swung it down towards Mandi's skull.

The phallus struck a piece of tiling beside Mandi's head and bounced back on the guru, catching him where a grin had just escaped his enhanced lips and sent him toppling backwards like sawn timber. The Slug-Thing gurgled, the angels did not react. The magic battle was ending in farce and stupidity. That was that. So much for magic.

The wounded guru pushed himself up to his knees and then, though he wished only to lie down and rest his pounding face, he grimaced in defiance and with a sound like glass trodden underfoot, his teeth began to fall, one by one, upon the chequered tiles. The sound expanded, a booming crunch, another, another, then a crack like bone breaking; out of all proportion to the guru's injuries. He turned and reached his hand up to and inside his mouth, checked the flecks of blood and white splinters on his fingers, as behind him something black and magnificent arose.

Looking up, the Old Mortality man saw horror drop from the eyes of warehouse operatives and reception clerks. He turned, took one glance at what had begun behind his back, and ran from the chapel, swinging on the iron gate and fleeing across the fields, drops of his blood and enamel falling in between the furrows, fertilising next year's harvest.

The snapping, cracking and crunching grew, then they were subsumed by an angry squelching as what had been Mandi was borne up on struts of thick red tentacle and a wide scarlet skirt held open by spokes of cartilage armed with needle-like spines. Sitting on all this pulsating structure, Mandi's torso bobbed, raised almost to the height of the chapel roof, torn from side to side by the storm; and from her back, with a great tearing roar, two huge wings of black and white feathers broke free and reached up, brushing aside the upper branches of the trees, sending the Slug-Thing slithering away and across the fields of the Hoarfrost Estate. Mandi's thick, black hair fell back, and though the face they all looked on now was transfigured by its setting in a biological tiara of monstrous magic, it was still that of the woman who had returned from a successful media career to sort out funeral arrangements a few weeks before.

Like two accompanists taking their lead from a soloist, first Sidwella and then Apollonia transformed. Above them a murmuration of starlings fanned out and fell inwards, shuffling like cards, and suddenly it fell apart. Individual birds started out in all directions, unaware of each other; gradually re-gathering in twos and threes, then in gangs of twenty or thirty, finally regrouping in a familiar folding and unfolding, they haloed the three angel-squids. As they did so a dazzling map spread from them and a revived Mandi-Mary looked up to its crackling expansion and in its bursts of energy, digital synapses firing in horizon snaps, she saw that the Hexamerons and their machine were not alone, but one part of any number of similar conspiracies, some open, some hidden, others simply obscure and that their information was not only shared, but looped and incremental, in rushes and assemblages like agentive conspiracies in themselves, invasive and interventional and all fired by the big idea of two digits at odds with each other, of conflict and supremacy, of the spread and distribution of things on the basis of domination and piracy, that nothing was sacred and nowhere was safe. Even transformed Mandi-Mary felt the digital antennae, virtual feelers approaching her, lighting up insecurities, secrets, a mad desire to tell all and confess to anything, begging her to share her deepest fears and profoundest thoughts. But instead, defiant, she folded dark and powerful tentacles within herself, set them as monstrous guards at the caves of her darkness and shook her giant wings to bat away the offers and invitations.

As if they took their lead from her, sprites and hyenas, archaeologists, doggers and Dumnonii appeared to chase the seductions and enticements away across the tree tops, re-gathering to swoop in waves upon the fleeing Hexameron ranks, chasing Tony the Summoner into the opening of an old mine, a goblin holding him up against its iron door, while the white snipers for once made a bad call, leaping from the broken wall of the Lady's Chapel, escaping along a stream bed that quickly led them into a darker and deeper chasm, turning around in confusion, trapped by the ghosts of suicides.

"You thought you were destroying Mary but you were destroying yourself," said Apollonia. "You have always been Mary. She was only ever, these thousands of years, a shell of you. You were reborn when you died, taken by our Mother into the deep, where you drowned and were re-made as a part of Her. And there you have been waiting, sleeping, while your story has been told again and again. Stolen again and again. But there was always, behind the lies and re-namings, a real child, taken on a beach, and now you are finally and truly here again through the love of a man and a beast."

Mandi-Mary, mucky and murdering, placed her hand, lovingly, upon the soft gelatinous skin of their towering Old Mother rising from their belief.

"The blank space on the bonelines map," Mary said to Sidwella. "That was here. I found the others – the tin chapel, the cafe, the cave – never by myself, I was always led, and the same here."

"Yes, but you knew you were being led; and you came. Others are just led and find nothing."

The spring in the floor of the ruined chapel had begun to run again. Mandi-Mary knelt beside its streaming water; her wings folded back into her shoulders, her tentacles tucked themselves in under her breasts and she was fully back to Mandi once more, ready to empty the water from her walking boots, pour herself a large glass of Scotch and run a bath.

Chapter 67

The Vale Without Depths was the place. There was something about the caravan in the patch of ground with concrete platforms, the tint of green that hung over it all, the baroque decorations and hints of hermitage, sea voyage and arts and crafts. Details floated free from the self-possession of the Vale. It was that autonomy that Mandi loved, the resistance to influence. It was itself. Visible from the train – when the line was up and running and not, as now, fallen in the sand – the Vale went almost entirely unremarked, a barely visited zone, only ever on the way to somewhere else. It was the disconnection from the throb of commercial life that set it free, glorying in its unproductiveness, unremarkably.

Mandi had never had any illusions about the nature of her work. She was a parasite, living off the fat of a market while telling everyone else not to do so. She was not an entrepreneur, wealth-creator, businesswoman or producer. Only in the Vale did she feel the need to apologise to herself. Otherwise, she apologised to no one and about nothing. Just as the glasshouse full of brambles, the algae-tinted unoccupied caravan and the redundant platforms felt no need to apologise. They were and that was enough. Enough, she would be enough. Since her return from London, Mandi had developed a violent prejudice against existences predicated on destroying other existences.

She wanted Eddie to share in her experiences. She felt sorry for him. Despite the inundation of Lost Horizon the mobility of the trailers had been their salvation. A few were ripped up and scattered in bits, two or three floated out to sea, but a number had got trapped at the gates of the camp. There was water damage, but they had floated and were drier than their owners could ever have hoped. Almost immediately the waters had receded, residents returned and began to drag the surviving homes back to their lots. Not everywhere were folk as organised as the pagans of Lost Horizon. Society might scorn their eccentricity, but now there was general admiration for their communal coherence.

Mandi had found Eddie, alone, in the trailer she had allotted him, washed up against the inland fence. He seemed hungry and exhausted, he had observably lost weight in just a few days. Even when she brought him food, he seemed to have difficulty eating it. He became increasing listless, complained about "not feeling myself" and was unnerved at the prospect of returning to Birmingham. Mandi had her own bad memories to deal with; she could not be bothered to imagine what Eddie had been through.

She took a chance. As they wandered on the lanes between fields struggling to recover from their recent salty inundation, past the deep scores where ancient trunks had been dragged away, and shards of silvery wood were scattered like flying saucer crash sites, Mandi offered Eddie the vacant post of caretaker at Lost Horizon. Once the repairs and reassembling of the camp were in full swing, Mandi would appoint a new manager and Eddie, if he accepted, would work under their instruction. She wanted to make that offer out there, in 'The Vale', to help him understand her values now. Since her adventures on foot around the Lovecraft villages, Mandi felt comfortable holding a meeting in the open air. Efficient and informal; it was something she might sell on later.

Eddie seemed to enjoy the novelty of the walk. He was more 'himself'. As they strolled gently along the lanes, he began to chatter excitedly about the future, staring at the ground in front of him, trying to recall the hours of the battle, of which he had almost no memory. He told of how he remembered meeting the reunionists off the Birmingham train, and guiding them around the danger zone, but about what happened after meeting up on the Port Way, where Mandi had seen his party arrive, Eddie became hazy and then disturbed and then changed the subject. Mandi had no memory of him after that, either. Perhaps he had run away in fear and was hiding that from himself, or perhaps his memory was protecting him from what had happened to him or what he had seen happen to others. Or there was something he did.

There were many victims. The media reported it as the worst climate related catastrophe since the flooding of East Anglia by the North Sea in 1953. Many of the fatalities from the fighting had been spectral; of those there was no corpse-residue. Otherwise, the authorities were overwhelmed. The living were bumped to the front of every queue; cadavers were processed rapidly and superficially. There were thousands of serious injuries to contend with, partly as a result of the waters, partly the numerous accidents as people fled in panic. As a result, those fatalities from the battle that were extant were mostly put down to the high winds and severe earth tremors. The few blunt force trauma injuries that were examined by pathologists were not ones they could easily attribute to modern weapons, and were mostly assigned to blows from falling boughs, dislodged boulders or car accidents.

The evidence of discharged weapons meant that an official police investigation was opened. It would be closed a year later, with no decisive conclusions presented. The media rehearsed a theory – clearly encouraged by the authorities – that some private local grudges had been paid off under cover of the storm. There was even a BBC drama. Some deaths were recorded without bodies; the flooding and destruction of morgues and funeral directors' properties had led to a number of disappearances. Some bodies were found with serious wounds in submerged car wrecks. Others had been burned out. A few tight-lipped survivors suffering serious injuries presented themselves at A&E, but there were many reports of others who chose to nurse themselves.

The effects on private property were uneven; residents returning from evacuation to their homes on the edge of the Hoarfrost Estate were surprised by the violence of the devastation. The seaside town was almost finished; it would be years under repair. Indeed, there were calls to abandon the town as too vulnerable to future storms and too expensive to protect. It was here, rather than in the villages, that the media congregated. The deserted streets, the ruined amusement parlours, the household furniture and other domestic items damming the town's stream, and the strange sculpture the waves had made of a church's pews were gifts to reporters and photographers. The railway, the only line that crossed the county, was to be rebuilt, but this time on a causeway over the sea. In pubs and cafes and homes along the stretch of affected coast, discussions were oddly discreet and muted; as if no one had quite noticed what they had experienced, as if they had all lived a much reduced and trivial version of their lives. It had been an anomaly; normal service would be resumed shortly, surely.

Lost Horizon had suffered badly, but because it was already a mobile community, and much of the site had been cleared by the waters, insurance claims were already being settled. There was not much debate about properties found up trees or scattered across hillsides. The government had stepped in with a mixture of instant grants and loans. Mandi had been helping residents with the online applications. New homes were already rolling up the potholed access road. Electricity was reconnected, sewage pipes cleared, broadband restored. Most of the residents wanted to return.

Once there were sufficient people back in their homes, Mandi intended to organise a memorial service for their former caretaker. She was relieved that, of the residents, only Cassandra and Mimir seemed to suspect the true nature of their relationship. Ten days after the storm, Mandi's father's body was found washed up on the Sett, tangled in driftwood, fishing line and rope. Whether a gift from her Mother, or Her rejection of him, Mandi would never know. Once more she found herself organising a funeral and visiting solicitors and the Green funeral director.

Professor Crabbe's son, Tony, Mandi's brother, had been found in the tunnels of an old slate mine. The authorities were at a loss to explain how the iron door sealing the tunnel had been closed behind him, but some suggested that Tony had been sheltering from the flood and the surge had shut the door on him. The rescue services told Mandi that they had found Tony with a peaceful look on his face; what they didn't tell her was that, after death, his mouth had been wedged with a large piece of slate. Of course, there was no explanation for the bodies of the hobgoblins, sprites and dogs the size of horses that turned up intermittently; despite their random scattering their treatment was remarkably consistent. Storms often washed up odd things – rotting basking sharks that looked like plesiosaurs – and, now, these mangled folkloric mutations were assigned to the same fate as the sea monsters; buried quickly and anonymously in landfill. Those who participated in the burials saw their mobiles thrown into the sea and replaced with Samsung Galaxy Note 10s. Odd stories about tiny people and giant hounds with red coals for eyes, shared selectively in canteens and the cabs of service vehicles, were all that marked the supernaturals' demise.

Eddie said "yes". He cried a little with excitement. Purpose seemed to flood back into his cheeks. Mandi felt disproportionately gratified. He did not seem capable of understanding what she felt about the Vale, fixated by his own stupidity, slow to grasp the feelings she tried to share with him; but, hell, he didn't need to be a professor to be a caretaker. He would be fine. He had been in on the whole thing from the start and it seemed appropriate that he might help to tie up the loose ends. OK, if he wasn't the sharpest knife in the drawer, he had been the one who knew all along what had been going down, who held onto that truth while the rest of them had built their own fantasies. He could see what was what, he would not let things drift.

"I hope yow know what yow is doin'!" he said, thanking her, oddly.

"I think so."

They had not long left the few houses and community hall that passed for a village in the Vale, stepped off the lane, a small bonfire smoking unattended, and ducked through a grove of thorns trees and had come out into open fields. Woods fringed low hills around the horizon, the sea was hidden by the gentle incline, and the path bent violently around bright green empty fields. At the top of the rise, where the path disappeared between thick and disorderly hedges, with that rich but disconcerting promise of all the things that it might lead an inquirer to, a giant electricity pylon was waiting. Not just standing there, as far as Mandi was concerned, but waiting. It was evil; its shape, its malevolent hum, its ordering everything, the way the trees cowered back from it, its skipping rope wires impossibly taut. A flensed megalith, only skeleton remaining; it distilled the malignancy of the old stone circles and trapped souls in its wires. The wind, rising as a warning, began to protest in its struts.

"Eddie, do you think there's anything odd about that pylon? That one, up ahead?"

Eddie looked up, as if he were seeing the fields and woods for the first time.

"Which one?"

"That one!"

"What's up wi' it?"

"Yeh, you're right. We can walk that way, right?"

"Roight..."

As they approached, the pylon leaned over them, falling back into the sky. It swayed. Its empty heart and echoing brain vault whirring, its dead structure implausibly motivated, shaking, barely. The path veered away as if repulsed by it. Mandi paused involuntarily. Eddie took her arm by the elbow.

"There's nought to fear 'ere, silly booger."

He pulled her gently, like persuading a frightened horse. She stumbled, then fixed her eyes to the ground and walked quickly on. She did not look back; for fear of what? That it was chasing them? No. For fear that it was witnessing them, blindly sensing them, its empty feelings reaching out and intuiting them? Trying to distract herself, Mandi looked about the vacant fields, finely balanced between being and abjection. There was nothing easy.

Eddie dropped her elbow. They did not speak until they were in sight of the gates of Lost Horizon.

"Have you been to the Everglades since the storm?"

"Why should I?"

"No reason, but I think we should check on it."

"OK. If yow want..."

The Everglades were in a bad way. The storm had lifted tons of sand from The Sett over the railway lines and tipped them into the back of the Everglades. Mature trees were buried halfway up their trunks. There was almost an alternative beach there, a vertiginous cliff of sand that looked unstable to Mandi; the sort of hazard that they should get cleared up. The last thing she wanted was some kid wandering in there and getting buried and kick the whole thing off again. The perfect project to get Eddie started on; but he had wandered off towards the junkyards further inland, where he was picking up carpet squares and strips of corrugated iron, blown in by the gale. Looking for something.

Where the storm waters had lifted the rail embankment clean away, it had also ripped into the loamy surface of the Everglades, tearing out the roots of ferns and spilling a darker, drier soil into the widened stream. The waters had been cloudy with the disruption, but they were almost clear again now. Staring down at the bottom, like a picture coming into focus, Mandi could see that the silt had been deeply disturbed; long lost toys and tinsel and animal bones had been exposed.

"What are you looking for?" Mandi yelled.

"Nothing. Slow worms!"

"Won't they all have drowned?"

"Ain' they trans?"

"What?"

"Live in water too?"

"For fuck's sake..." Mandi turned away. Maybe she had made a mistake about Eddie. "All sorts of crap has got dug up! We've got to clear it up. We don't know what was on here before it was a holiday camp."

Mandi felt a chill. There might be chemicals or something. Maybe dumped during the time they made the railways. Did they use chemicals? Maybe to help season the sleepers? Three little kids had died here. What if it had been something contaminating in the ground, like the authorities said? Everybody had come back the next year, but not to Lost Horizon, all the other camps were full; then every year afterwards, less and less people remembered. Even Mandi had forgotten eventually. Chemicals? O Jesus Christ, please don't let it be starting again...

"Did you find any?"

"What?"

"Slow worms!"

"O... sure. Loads."

"No? really?"

Mandi skipped the stream and vaulted a fallen trunk. Before Eddie could react, she had pulled up the first carpet square.

The bones, like the remains of a beef rib starter, were neatly lain in a row, just above the surface of veined loam. Webs of tiny roots were broken around them, where some force had pushed the bones up. They had the same curve about them, the same size, as the ones in the bottom of the stream. Mandi's mind was racing.

"It wasn't dogshit, Eddie, it was us!" She blurted. "It wasn't Satanic Abuse or whatever, ritual abuse fucking nonsense, I know that! But it was not the dogshit either. Was it? Was it!!! For Christ sake, Eddie, please! Was it??? We killed those kids. We opened up a space, a hole, a way through, I don't know what, and we couldn't handle it... we were kids too, remember... we didn't protect ourselves... from what we were bringing through... and maybe that thing itself didn't know what it could do... She's a wonderful.... maybe it wasn't that thing's fault either, it was just so powerful... inappropriately powerful..."

"Yow think you opened up evil, Mans?"

"It isn't evil!!! You know She isn't that!! It's just different... more different than little kids can cope with. We were kids like them; and we had a whole underworld coursing through our little bodies. Children are not... they are not... what's the word... there isn't something essentially strong in a child that makes it able to contain the natural... do you understand what I'm trying to say? We were plugging directly into life, without any... life training... did you ever learn any magic?"

Eddie shook his head, vigorously.

"No, me neither! I don't know why it chose me; that isn't clear..."

"I don't think it was us, Mans. Look at us! Look-at-us!"

Mandi looked very, very, very hard at Eddie. He looked every bit the same as he had all day. But in the last few moments his voice had changed completely. The Brummie accent had dropped away and he had spoken like an actor, the kind who come from a family of shopkeepers but play public schoolboys in movies. When he spoke again, she listened very carefully.

"We were never anything special, were we? Children on holiday. At The Sett? Known for it. You, a camp owners' daughter... no offence intended..."

"None taken..."

Fuck. Where had his voice gone? Where had Eddie gone?

"It was the place. The place chose you, Amanda."

Mandi blew out a mouthful of air.

"You happened to be in the wrong place at the wrong time."

"Or the right one."

"Or the right. 'Not special', not our 'special Amanda'? You were very special, you were incredible! We were all in love with Mandi, girls and boys. But I was the chosen one. You see, it wasn't you and it wasn't us. It wasn't dogshit and it wasn't Satan. It wasn't chemicals either, Amanda..."

"The authorities said..."

"The authorities! You think they were ever going to tell anyone what really happens here?"

"What's going on with you, Ed?"

He ignored her.

"They did it perfectly; firstly the abuse scare that as near as dammit finished your fake Mum and Dad, and then they uncover the real truth! Badah! Dogshit and e-coli! And that was a stroke of genius because it looked like a cover-up of bad drains in a holiday camp full of people that no one gives a shit about. People like me. People they underestimate, people they don't even see as people. So everyone was happy. The stupid conservative ones believed that the truth had come out and could not care less, and the paranoid ones thought they knew what the real cover-up was and could keep on bleating about it without doing anything to solve it. But the only really powerful people in the situation, the only two magicians involved, were us. And I was the stronger; I was the one strong enough to kill, and you were the one weak enough to forget."

"Why? Why would you do that? We were only kids? Stop it. You didn't kill anyone!"

"Why did I do it? Fuck knows. I was born to it, probably. Many are called, but few are chosen. It was a natural talent, with me. Nothing calculated. It just happened. And when others mistook my eccentric little talent for retardedness, I found a way to protect my genius, by cultivating ways of destroying. You know, I can't even remember their names. Their ribs are in that stream, under those carpet tiles, but I don't know who they were, the ones no one found. Additional to the 'Dogshit Three'. And all that time, while I was having a whale of a time, you 'mazed' yourself... that's what they say down here, isn't it? – mazed yourself with your Mucky Mary Old Ma Squid crap. Juju and black magic with girls starkers, it's a great way of pulling the wool over folk's eyes."

"Christ."

Mandi was shaking so hard it was hurting her teeth.

"Why would you want to hurt people? I mean, get one over on people, show them who's boss, but to erase their lives? What's that about, you fucking cunt?"

"O, dear. It was nothing so vulgar as competitiveness, my lovely Amanda. The girl I longed for. But when I couldn't have you, I wanted the emptiness that you left behind..."

"O fuck you!"

"When I felt the life go out of them, I felt the life go out of me, and I loved that. To be so calm, so empty, so controlled; joy and pain could not touch me. Only smack comes close. Feeling like that, I discovered I could do anything. I realised that people who think they are clever think stupid people can't do anything; so I acted stupid. Dumbest of the dumb; I got to do anything I wanted. No one ever suspected me. They think if they can laugh at you, they control you. I let them laugh, then I killed them. Those so-called friends I had in Birmingham, the kids who holidayed here, the ones who survived, they laughed at me, even when I was helping them around the storm, they thought they were so clever having fun at my expense; but they paid me back. As I watched the light fade in their eyes, I felt the darkness grow in mine, the pure dark roundedness of it; that beautiful strong calm, that empty landscape that reached right down inside, lit by a black sun. The dark side of your depths. There's no difference between you and me. And now there are no witnesses left to what we did."

He gestured to her as if to say "over to you."

"I don't know what to say."

In the long silence, one of the faces of the dune that had invaded the Everglades began to crumble, handfuls of sand breaking off and piling up in a smooth heap.

"Are you going to hurt me, Eddie?"

"Not in the way you think. Not if you give me your nothingness."

"You fuckwit! You fucking fuckwit!"

Mandi pirouetted and swept her hand along the bruised ground, her fingers settling around a metal stave discarded who knows when and yanked it out of the earth. She brandished it at Eddie.

"Amanda..."

"Don't fucking 'Amanda' me..."

She rose up on tentacular legs, shimmering in the canopy, spreading out her wings as hot tears fell from her eyes and dropped on Eddie far below; then she slumped down to his level, and touched the grey-brown earth with her finger tips.

"Poor kids."

Eddie shook his head.

"I went back to Birmingham with the same sort of kids – they turned into drunks, smackheads, benefit cheats, wankers, lazy scum, diseased. The kids I left in the ground here were the lucky ones."

He stamped on the loamy soil. A chunk more of the sand felt from the face of the dune.

Mandi snorted in disgust, holding the point of the metal stave closer to Eddie's throat.

"I suppose that caretaker's job is out of the question now?" he chivvied. "Thought I could replace your Dad, did you?"

"Your knew about that?"

"I don't forget anything, Amanda. I knew about your Mum and Dad, the real ones... you inherited his brains, but from Her you got your depth. Haha. I loved you, really really really fancied you, but I always knew I would never have you, so I took the next best thing, in a darker way of course, but just as empty, just as dark..."

"No, no. You tried that on before. You are not the dark side of me, you bastard. I already have the dark side. There's no job vacancy for my dark side. Your emptiness is inadequacy, substitution, and transference."

"Wow. And you... what do your kind call it? O yes, 'nothingness'? That's kind of obfuscation for emptiness, right?"

"And that is the difference between you and me. The emptiness inside you is yours, you possess it, it's your own little empire. The nothingness inside me, is not mine, I do not own it, I worship it. IT IS HER INSIDE ME!"

And with that Mandi's tongue split into scores of wriggling tendrils, spilling over her chin, before pulling themselves back through her lips.

"Impressive! Would make a nice sideshow." He made jazz hands. "But I did not despatch the little kiddies and the big Brummie smackheads for a circus freakshow!"

"Why were you even on our side?"

Eddie laughed.

"You really don't get it do you? All the way back to when we were children here, you never got it. I was never on your side, Mandi. I knew I could never be on your side, because I could never be at your side..."

"What did you do? What happened up there, in the fields?"

"O, something like this."

Nothing happened that Mandi could see.

"Like what?"

The seat of Eddie trousers began to bulge architecturally, as if he were having a giant reverse erection, or had inflated his pants with a cyclopean fart. A balloon of denim expanded around Eddie's thighs; then with a wet-sounding 'Pflap!" his trousers burst apart and hung in twin curtains from his belt. He began to fold forward from the middle of his chest, his ribs turning to marrow, his vertebrae crunching and detaching, a thick grey gooey flap issuing from beneath what had been his crotch and soaking up his front, swamping his collapsing legs, while another fat grey lip began to swallow his crumbling back, neck and head, pulling what had been Eddie down inside itself growing upwards as it enveloped him, pulling itself up on the last splinters of rib cage, femur and thigh bone, lifting the final fragment of Eddie high above Mandi's head, its arsehole closing over Eddie's bald patch and snapping together with a clap.

"You fucking maggot!" screamed Mandi and hurled the metal stave into the slug's seething mass of grey ooziness. It slithered, a gob of goo flobbed out, and the stave wedged, appropriated in the gelatinous mass. Mandi's wings drooped. Her head dropped. She knew, somehow, that it would not strike until she looked directly at it. She should keep her eyes down; but since when had Mandi ever done what she should do? Crap, did she really believe herself? That she had no responsibility for this abomination? That there wasn't something in her magic that was this dark? That Dumna's nothingness: was not the other side of Eddie's? Only one way to find out. To let the slug have her. If there was love, if there was ever any real love, she would be lost in its stinking shit and digested down to emptiness. If the love was not between them, but was her love for her Mother and her Mother's love for her, then maybe she would stick in its throat, spoil its emptiness, irritate the fuck out of its sad little world of control and death. Muttering to herself "angel outside, dark squid within, demon will die, Domna will swim", she raised her eyes to the slug.

It had a peculiar tentacle in its brain.

Mandi, surprised at her own composure, heard herself think: "do slugs have tentacles?"

As if in answer, the tentacle withdrew through the slug-thing's prow and the towering demon eroded, bubbling and heaving, its sheets of membrane, spew, shit and intestine dropping to the floor of the Everglades and spilling to the bank of the stream, the running waters dragging on the first gobbets of gunk and slowly dragging larger and larger portions into the current, pulling the lifeless slug away. In the gush of evil-smelling slime, there was nothing of Eddie, not a cheap shirt nor a chunk of fat or a finger bone. For the second time in a few minutes, Mandi had lost the last person alive she had shared this whole thing with.

Abruptly, with no crescendo, but starting at a roar the lid flew off the underworld. The already shattered trees were shredded in a moment. Pieces of leaf fluttered down like confetti bleeding green. Trunks split and fell in slivers, opening like chocolate oranges. The shadowy Everglades opened to the angry sky. The gale of sound died as quickly as it rose and was replaced by a deep creaking, as if a subterranean shelter were digging its way up to the surface, bending steel and grinding sand and gravel. The soil grew uncomfortably warm, the remnants of grass wilted.

"She's coming," Mandi said to herself.

Her frame was dwarfed by the Squid that raised her up and the life ran out of Dumna into her; raised up on Her tentacles, above where the tree canopy had been. She felt her wings like cliffs unpeeling and sliding into place, like the hangar doors of heaven, a wild clanging ran along the coastline.

The sky began to fall in thick sheets of rain, slapping down on the dome of the cyclopean Mother, a stream waterfalling off her beak. Mandi looked down on her Mother; she ran from horizon to shore, from one arm of the bay to the other. She wore the thunderburst like a magnificent cloak encrusted with sparkling gems. In the face of vulnerable truth and unhuman power there was no emptiness.

The Squid-Mother placed Mandi down, carefully, as if within Her gelatine swathes a muscle-memory had kicked in, of laying her daughter down on the shoreline so many years before, so gently that Mandi wanted to scream "I'm not a child anymore!" The monster paused, as if equally taken about by the curl in time, then in an explosion of sand She disappeared under the remains of the railway line and was dragging Herself towards Her sea. Mandi could not follow that way, but screaming "Mother! Mother!" she sprinted through the camp, out of the gates, cut under The Creep, its tunnel half-filled with sand by the storm, and raced past the twisted rides towards the shifted shoreline.

There was no sign of her Mother, but the surface of the sea was boiling as if a bob of seals were dancing.

Mandi pulled up at the edge of the water, gentle waves breaking over the stones and tumbling hermit crabs, easy after all the epic violence of the storms. She shook her head.

"What had I expected," she said to herself, breathlessly. "Mother is not that clever, not that intellectual. She just is, and she just is..."

She yelled at the ocean: "I love you! I fucking love you, Mum!!! Why can't I be with you!!"

And in response there was no response. The sea went on wriggling and bubbling just the same. There was no accommodation to the human; her Mum was chaos, that was it, she was not smart or an idea, she was something else.

In the Bible, her Mother had been reduced to just one of the seven days of creation; the Hexamerons excluded her entirely. But the essential component of being is its opposite, there's no meaningful creation without leisure and no being without nothingness. Her Mother had challenged the God-That-Was-All-Being. As nothingness, She was the only thing the Clumsy Old Bastard was not, the one thing He had forgotten to create. He bungled the one job he had, made the cosmos too full, too bright, too unforgiving until she swam into it and brought forth tension, drama, love and stuff. She came from the Abyss and She left a part of Herself in everything, except in those who would be God, those who, despite knowing Her, chose to struggle for oneness or wholeness or transcendence and obliteration, condemning others to suffer in their ashrams and laboratories. But She was a darkness where anyone could hide from crazy Perfectionists and cold Nihilists, in nothingness; without Her there was no good being.

Mandi knelt in the sand and wept extravagant tears, her wings reached out hopelessly; but as she watched the seething ocean subside and the dark shadow move away towards deeper waters, she was already wondering about whether Mimir might be interested in earning some extra cash as a caretaker, and whether Cassandra was up to being manager.

Chapter 68

Next season there were no temporary guests at Lost Horizon. Forensic teams were at work in the Everglades, DNA samples were recovered and compared, Mandi gave numerous interviews to detectives.

The torn remains of Eddie Mann had turned up in an Exmouth trawler's nets and were the subject of an autopsy report. No signs of foul play. No signs of very much at all. Mandi's blog posts were as acerbic as ever, but her London friends chivvied her about a new metaphysical tone.

"What else are you left with, without metaphysics? Power?"

That usually shut them up.

Mimir and Cassandra did not accept their job offers, but they knew a couple who might and, after interviews, Mandi, with the distinct feeling that she now had a perpetual bit part in 'The Shining', appointed Loki and Sarah. For a Norse god and an empathic medium, they were remarkably efficient managers; within eighteen months Lost Horizon was restored, cleaned up, re-enthused, renamed and open for summer bookings.

As the hot August weeks melted into September, Mandi took a few days out from the London swelter and fighting white supremacist shug monkeys, and booked in for a couple of days at Devon Deep Holiday Park, for families and everyone, dogs welcome.

After stowing away the contents of her suitcase, Mandi joined Loki and Sarah on the veranda of their giant trailer for pagan cocktails.

"Mmm, angelic! Haha!"

Mandi never ceased to enjoy the first salty sip of a Margarita. Loki spoke of a little shrine he wanted to build to Mandi's Dad. Football commentary and burnt sausage embroidered his thoughtfulness. Sarah was crocheting a cap for an expected grandchild, their first.

Across the ranks of caravans and trailers, interwoven with the metallic creak of the rides beyond the Creep and above the cry of the herring gulls, the thuds of keepy-uppy and the scrunch of finished cans of cheap Polish Karpackie, Mandi could hear the voices of children, singing in Midlands drawl, floating in from the Everglades:

"Muddy Mary, mother of God,
Killed the Old Boy in his bath,
God went to Hell
And started to smell,
And now all the bad things are back!"

About the Authors

Tony Whitehead is a Devon based artist with a deep interest in the landscape, its natural and human histories, the interactions between people and place, and the stories that emerge from walking and listening deeply to the land. He has been involved in numerous sound art projects, from Sonic Arts Network's Sonic Postcards in the early 2000s to long term involvement with Soundart Radio in Totnes. He is a co-curator of the Quiet Night In concert series.

Recently he has become a director of Skylark FM, a community based experimental radio station for Dartmoor. Tony is also a sound recordist and runs the Very Quiet Records Netlabel. He has a love of walking, myth, psychogeography, and landscape and has walked many miles with Phil Smith, co-author of *Bonelines*. For over thirty years Tony has also worked for the RSPB, and with a love of birds, runs regular workshops to help people identify birdsong.

Phil Smith is a writer, performer and researcher, specialising in walking, site-specificity and mythogeographies. With Helen Billinghurst he is one half of Crab & Bee, who created the art project 'Plymouth Labyrinth': (plymouthlabyrinth.wordpress.com).

Phil's publications include *Guidebook for an Armchair Pilgrimage* (2019) with Tony Whitehead and John Schott; *Making Site-Specific Theatre and Performance* (2018); *Walking's New Movement* (2015); and *Mythogeography* (2010). He is the company dramaturg

Photo: Rachel Sved

of TNT Theatre (Munich) and Associate Professor (Reader) at the University of Plymouth. More information at: www.triarchypress.net/smithereens

Also from Triarchy Press

Bonelines is a story created by the authors as they walked the *Guidebook for an Armchair Pilgrimage* into existence. The *Guidebook* is beautifully photographed by John Schott and is available from Triarchy Press along with many other books about walking arts, radical walking, hypersensitised walking, misguided walking, and walk-performances:

Anywhere
Counter-Tourism: The Handbook
Desire Paths
Enchanted Things (A Photo Essay)
Guidebook for an Armchair Pilgrimage
Mythogeography
On Walking …and Stalking Sebald
Rethinking Mythogeography
The Architect-Walker
The Footbook of Zombie Walking
The MK Myth
The Pilgrimage of Piltdown Man
Walking Art Practice
Walking Bodies
Walking Stumbling Limping Falling
Walking's New Movement
Ways to Wander

www.triarchypress.net/walking